Ambiguity Machines

Ambiguity
Machines
&
Other
Stories

Vandana Singh

Small Beer Press
Easthampton, MA

Small Beer Press
150 Pleasant Street #306
Easthampton, MA 01027
smallbeerpress.com
weightlessbooks.com
info@smallbeerpress.com

Distributed to the trade by Consortium.

Library of Congress Cataloging-in-Publication Data

Names: Singh, Vandana, author.
Title: Ambiguity machines : and other stories / Vandana Singh.
Description: Easthampton, MA : Small Beer Press, 2018.
Identifiers: LCCN 2017024759 (print) | LCCN 2017027227 (ebook) | ISBN
  9781618731425 | ISBN 9781618731432 (softcover : acid-free paper)
Subjects: | BISAC: FICTION / Science Fiction / Short Stories.
Classification: LCC PR9499.4.S556 (ebook) | LCC PR9499.4.S556 A6 2018 (print)
  | DDC 823/.92--dc23
LC record available at https://lccn.loc.gov/2017024759

First edition 1 2 3 4 5 6 7 8 9

Text set in Centaur 12pt.

Printed on 50# Natures 30% recycled paper by the Maple Press in York, PA.

For S.
je t'aime pour toujours

Contents

With Fate Conspire

I saw him in a dream, the dead man. He was dreaming too, and I couldn't tell if I was in his dream or he in mine. He was floating over a delta, watching a web of rivulets running this way and that, the whole stream rushing to a destination I couldn't see.

I woke up with the haunted feeling that I had been used to in my youth. I haven't felt like that in a long time. The feeling of being possessed, inhabited, although lightly, as though a homeless person was sleeping in the courtyard of my consciousness. The dead man wasn't any trouble; he was just sharing the space in my mind, not really caring who I was. But this returning of my old ability, as unexpected as it was, startled me out of the apathy in which I had been living my life. I wanted to find him, this dead man.

I think it is because of the Machine that these old feelings are being resurrected. It takes up an entire room, although the only part of it I see is the thing that looks like a durbeen, a telescope. The Machine looks into the past, which is why I've been thinking about my own girlhood. If I could spy on myself as I ran up and down the crowded streets and alleys of Park Circus! But the scientists who work the Machine tell me that the scope can't look into the recent past. They never tell me the *why* of anything, even when I ask—they smile and say, "Don't bother about things like that, Gargi-di! What you are doing is great, a great contribution." To my captors—they think they are my benefactors but truly, they are my captors—to them, I am something very special, because of my ability with the scope; but because I am

1

not like them, they don't really see me as I am. An illiterate woman, bred in the back streets and alleyways of Old Kolkata, of no more importance than a cockroach—what saved me from being stamped out by the great, indifferent foot of the mighty is this . . . ability. The Machine gives sight to a select few, and it doesn't care if you are rich or poor, man or woman.

I wonder if they guess I'm lying to them?

They've set the scope at a particular moment of history: the spring of 1856, and a particular place: Metiabruz in Kolkata. I am supposed to spy on an exiled ruler of that time, to see what he does every morning, out on the terrace, and to record what he says. He is a large, sad, weepy man. He is the Nawab of Awadh, ousted from his beloved home by the conquering British. He is a poet.

They tell me he wrote the song "Babul Mora," which to me is the most interesting and important thing about him, because I learned that song as a girl. The song is about a woman leaving, looking back at her childhood home, and it makes me cry sometimes—even though my childhood wasn't idyllic. And yet there are things I remember, incongruous things like a great field of rice, and water gleaming between the new shoots, and a bagula, hunched and dignified like an old priest, standing knee-deep in water, waiting for fish. I remember the smell of the sea, many miles away, borne on the wind. My mother's village, Siridanga.

How I began to lie to my captors was sheer chance. There was something wrong with the Machine. I don't understand how it works, of course, but the scientists were having trouble setting the date. The girl called Nondini kept cursing and muttering about spacetime fuzziness. The fact that they could not look through the scope to verify what they were doing, not having the kind of brain suitable for it, meant that I had to keep looking to check whether they had got back to Wajid Ali Shah in the Kolkata of 1856.

I'll never forget when I first saw the woman. I knew it was the wrong place and time, but, instead of telling my captors, I kept quiet. She was looking up toward me (my viewpoint must have been near the ceiling). She was not young, but she was respectable, you could see that. A housewife squatting on her haunches in a big, old-fashioned kitchen, stacking dirty dishes. I don't know why she looked up for that moment but it struck me at once: the furtive expression on her face. A sensitive face, with beautiful eyes, a woman who, I could tell, was a warm-hearted motherly type—so why did she look like that, as though she had a dirty secret? The scope doesn't stay connected to the past for more than a few blinks of the eye, so that was all I had: a glimpse.

Nondini nudged me, asking, "Gargi-di, is that the right place and time?" Without thinking, I said yes.

That is how it begins: the story of my deception. That simple "yes" began the unraveling of everything.

The institute is a great glass monstrosity that towers above the ground somewhere in New Parktown, which I am told is many miles south of Kolkata. Only the part we're on is not flooded. All around my building are other such buildings, so that when I look out of the window I see only reflections—of my building, and the others, and my own face, a small, dark oval. At first it drove me crazy, being trapped not only by the building but also by these tricks of light. And my captors were trapped too, but they seemed unmindful of the fact. They had grown accustomed. I resolved in my first week that I would not become accustomed. No, I didn't regret leaving behind my mean little life, with all its difficulties and constraints, but I was under no illusions. I had exchanged one prison for another.

In any life, I think, there are apparently unimportant moments that turn out to matter the most. For me as a girl it was those glimpses of my mother's village, poor as it was. I don't remember the bad things. I remember the sky, the view of paddy fields from my grandfather's hut on a hillock, and the tame pigeon who cooed and postured on a wooden post in the muddy little courtyard. I think it was here that I must have drawn my first real breath. There was an older cousin I don't recall very well, except as a voice, a guide through this exhilarating new world, where I realized that food grew on trees, that birds and animals had their own tongues, their languages, their stories. The world exploded into wonders during those brief visits. But always they were just small breaks in my life as one more poor child in the great city. Or so I thought. What I now think is that those moments gave me a taste for something I've never had—a kind of freedom, a soaring.

I want to be able to share this with the dead man who haunts my dreams. I want him, whoever he is, wherever he is, to have what I had so briefly. The great open spaces, the chance to run through the fields and listen to the birds tell their stories. He might wake up from being dead then, might think of other things besides deltas. He sits in my consciousness so lightly, I wonder if he even exists, whether he is an imagining rather than a haunting. But I recognize the feeling of a haunting like that, even though it has been years since I experienced the last one.

The most important haunting of my life was when I was, maybe, fourteen. We didn't know our birthdays, so I can't be sure. But I remember that an old man crept into my mind, a tired old man. Like Wajid Ali Shah more than a hundred years ago, this man was a poet. But there the similarity ended, because he had been ground down by poverty; his respectability was all he had left. When I saw him in my mind he was sitting under an awning. There was a lot of noise nearby, the kind of hullabaloo that a vegetable market generates. I sensed immediately that he was miserable, and this was confirmed later when I met him. All my hauntings have been of people who are hurt, or grieving, or otherwise in distress.

He wasn't a mullah, Rahman Khan, but the street kids all called him Maula, so I did too. I think he accepted it with deprecation. He was a kind man. He would sit under a tree at the edge of the road with an old typewriter, waiting for people to come to him for typing letters and important documents and so on. He only had a few customers. Most of the time he would stare into the distance with rheumy eyes, seeing not the noisy market but some other vista, and he would recite poetry. I found time from my little jobs in the fruit market to sit by him and sometimes I would bring him a stolen pear or mango. He was the one who taught me to appreciate language, the meanings of words. He told me about poets he loved, Wajid Ali Shah and Khayyam and Rumi, and our own Rabindranath and Nazrul, and the poets of the humbler folk, the baul and the maajhis. Once I asked him to teach me how to read and write. He had me practice letters in Hindi and Bengali on discarded sheets of typing paper, but the need to fill our stomachs prevented me from giving time to the task, and I soon forgot what I'd learned. In any case at that age I didn't realize its importance—it was no more than a passing fancy. But he did improve my Hindi, which I had picked up from my father, and taught me some Urdu, and a handful of songs, including "Babul Mora."

Babul Mora, he would sing in his thin, cracked voice. *Naihar chuuto hi jaaye.*

It is a woman's song, a woman leaving her childhood home with her newlywed husband, looking back from the cart for the last time. Father mine, my home slips away from me. Although my father died before I was grown, the song still brings tears to my eyes.

The old man gave me my fancy way of speaking. People laugh at me sometimes when I use nice words, nicely, when a few plain ones would do. What good is fancy speech to a woman who grew up poor and illiterate? But I don't care. When I talk in that way I feel as though I am touching the essence of the world. I got that from Maula. All my life I have tried to give away what I received but my one child died soon after birth and nobody else wanted what I had. Poetry. A vision of freedom. Rice fields, birds, the distant blue line of the sea. Siridanga.

Later, after my father died, I started to work in people's houses with my mother. Clean and cook, and go to another house, clean and cook. Some of the people were nice but others yelled at us and were suspicious of us. I remember one fat lady who smelled strongly of flowers and sweat, who got angry because I touched the curtains. The curtains were blue and white and had lace on them, and I had never seen anything as delicate and beautiful. I reached my hand out and touched them and she yelled at me. I was just a child, and whatever she said, my hands weren't dirty. I tried to defend myself but my mother herself shut me up. She didn't want to lose her job. I remember being so angry I thought I would catch fire from inside. I think all those houses must be underwater now. There will be fish nibbling at the fine lace drawing-room curtains. Slime on the walls, the carpets rotted. All our cleaning for nothing!

I have to find the dead man. I have to get out of here somehow.

The scientist called Nondini sees me as a real person, I think, not just as someone with a special ability who is otherwise nothing special. She has sympathy for me partly because there is a relative of hers who might still be in a refugee camp, and she has been going from one to the other to try to find her. The camps are mostly full of slum-dwellers because when the river overflowed and the sea came over the land, it drowned everything except for the skyscrapers. All the people who lived in slums or low buildings, who didn't have relatives with intact homes, had to go to the camps. I was in the big one, Sahapur, where they actually tried to help people find jobs, and tested them for all kinds of practical skills, because we were most of us laborers, domestic help, that sort of thing. And they gave us medical tests also. That's how I got my job, my large, clean room with a big-screen TV and all the food I want—after they found out I had the kind of brain the Machine can use.

But I can't go back to the camp to see my friends. Many of them had left before me anyway, farmed out to corporations where they could be useful with medical tests and get free medicines also. Ashima had cancer and she got to go to one of those places, but there is no way I can find out what happened to her. I imagine her somewhere like this place, with everything free and all the mishti doi she can eat. I hope she's all right. Kabir had a limp from birth but he's only eighteen so maybe they can fix it. When she has time, Nondini lets me talk about them. Otherwise I feel as though nothing from that time was real, that I never had a mother and father, or a husband who left me after our son died. As if my friends never existed. It drives me crazy sometimes to return to my room after working in the same building, and to find nothing but the same programs on the TV. At first I was so excited about all the luxury but now I get bored and fretful to the point where I am scared of my impulses. Especially when the night market comes and sets up on the streets below, every week. I can't see the market from my high window, but I can see the lights dancing on the windows of the building on the other side of the square. I can smell fish frying, and hear people talking, yelling out prices, and I hear singing. It is the singing that makes my blood wild. The first time they had a group of maajhis come, I nearly broke the window glass, I so wanted to jump out. They know how to sing to the soul.

> *Maajhi, O Maajhi*
> *My beloved waits*
> *On the other shore . . .*

I think the scientists are out at the market all night, because when they come in the next day, on Monday, their eyes are red, and they are bad-tempered, and there is something far away about them, as though they've been in another world. It could just be the rice beer, of course.

My captors won't let me out for some months, until they are sure I've "settled down." I can't even go to another floor of this building. There have been cases of people from the refugee camps escaping from their jobs, trying to go back to their old lives, their old friends, as though those things existed anymore. So there are rules that you have to be on probation before you are granted citizenship of the city, which then allows you to go freely everywhere. Of course "everywhere" is mostly under water, for what it's worth. Meanwhile Nondini lets me have this recorder that I'm speaking into, so I won't get too lonely. So I can hear my own voice played back. What a strange one she is!

Nondini is small and slight, with eyes that slant up just a little at the corners. She has worked hard all her life to study history. I never knew there was so much history in the world until my job began! She keeps giving me videos about the past—not just Wajid Ali Shah but also further back, to the time when the British were here, and before that when Kolkata was just a little village on the Hugli river. It is nearly impossible to believe that there was a time when the alleyways and marketplaces and shantytowns and skyscrapers didn't exist—there were forests and fields, and the slow windings of the river, and wild animals. I wish I could see that. But they—the scientists—aren't interested in that period.

What they *do* want to know is whether there were poems or songs of Wajid Ali Shah that were unrecorded. They want me to catch him at a moment when he would recite something new that had been forgotten over the centuries. What I don't understand is, why all this fuss about old poetry? I like poetry more than most people, but it isn't what you'd do in the middle of a great flood. When I challenge the scientists some of them look embarrassed, like Brijesh, and Unnikrishnan shakes his head. Their leader, Dr. Mitra, she just looks impatient, and Nondini says, "Poetry can save the world."

I may be uneducated but I am not stupid. They're hiding something from me.

The housewife—the woman for whom I have abandoned Wajid Ali Shah—interests me. Her name is Rassundari—I know, because someone in her household called her name. Most of the time they call her Rasu or Sundari, or daughter-in-law, or sister-in-law, etc., but this time some visitor called out her full name, carefully and formally. I wish I could talk to her. It would be nice to talk to someone who is like me. How stupid that sounds! This woman clearly comes from a rich rural family—a big joint family it is, all under the same roof. She is nothing like me. But I feel she could talk to me as an ordinary woman, which is what I am.

I wish I could see the outside of her house. They are rich landowners, so it must be beautiful outside. I wonder if it is like my mother's village. Odd that although I have hardly spent any time in Siridanga, I long for it now as though I had been born there.

The first time after I found Rassundari, Nondini asked me if I'd discovered anything new about Wajid Ali Shah. I felt a bit sorry for her because I was deceiving her, so I said, out of my head, without thinking:

"I think he's writing a new song."

The scope doesn't give you a clear enough view to read writing in a book, even if I could read. But Wajid Ali Shah loves gatherings of poets and musicians, where he sings or recites his own works. So Nondini asked me:

"Did he say anything out loud?"

Again without thinking I said, maybe because I was tired, and lonely, and missing my friends:

"Yes, but only one line: '*If there was someone for such as me . . .*'"

I had spoken out of the isolation I had been feeling, and out of irritation, because I wanted to get back to my housewife. I would have taken my lie back at once if I could. Nondini's eyes lit up.

"That is new! I must record that!" And in the next room there was a flurry of activity.

So began my secret career as a poet.

Rassundari works really hard. One day I watched her nearly all day, and she was in the kitchen almost the whole time. Cooking, cleaning, supervising a boy who comes to clean the dishes. The people of the house seem to eat all the time. She always waits for them to finish before she eats, but that day she didn't get a chance at all. A guest came at the last minute after everyone had eaten lunch, so she cooked for him, and after that one of the small children was fussing so she took him on her lap and tried to eat her rice, which was on a plate on the floor in front of her, but she had taken just one mouthful when he urinated all over her and her food. The look on her face! There was such anguish, but after a moment she began to laugh. She comforted the child and took him away to clean up, and came back and cleaned the kitchen, and by that time it was evening and time to cook the evening meal. I felt so bad for her! I have known hunger sometimes as a girl, and I could not have imagined that a person who was the daughter-in-law of such a big house could go hungry too. She never seems to get angry about it—I don't understand that, because I can be quick to anger myself. But maybe it is because everyone in the house is nice to her. I can only see the kitchen of course, but whenever people come in to eat or just to talk with her, they treat her well—even her mother-in-law speaks kindly to her.

Her older son is a charming little boy, who comes and sits near her when he is practicing his lessons. He is learning the alphabet. She makes him repeat everything to her several times. Seeing him revives the dull pain in my heart that never goes away. I wonder what my child would have looked like, had he survived. He only lived two days. But those are old sorrows.

I want to know why Rassundari looks, sometimes, like she has a guilty secret.

The dead man has started talking to me in my dreams. He thinks I am someone called Kajori, who must have been a lover. He cries for me, thinking I'm her. He weeps with agony, calls to me to come to his arms, sleep in his bed. I have to say that while I am not the kind of woman who would jump into the arms of just any man, let alone one who is dead, his longing awakes the loneliness in me. I remember what it was like to love a man, even though my husband turned out to be a cowardly bastard. In between his sobs the dead man mutters things that perhaps only this Kajori understands. Floating over the silver webbing of the delta, he babbles about space and time.

"Time!" he tells me. "Look, look at that rivulet. Look at this one."

It seems to me that he thinks the delta is made by a river of time, not water. He says time has thickness—and it doesn't flow in one straight line—it meanders. It splits up into little branches, some of which join up again. He calls this *fine structure*. I have never thought about this before, but the idea makes sense. The dead man shows me history, the sweep of it, the rise and fall of kings and dynasties, how the branches intersect and move on, and how some of the rivulets dry up and die. He tells me how the weight of events and possibilities determines how the rivulets of time flow.

"I must save the world," he says at the end, just before he starts to cry.

I know Rassundari's secret now.

She was sitting in the kitchen alone, after everyone had eaten. She squatted among the pots and pans, scouring them, looking around her warily like a thief in her own house. She dipped a wet finger into the ash pile and wrote on the thali the letter her son had been practicing in the afternoon: *kah*. She wrote it big, which is how I could see it. She said it aloud: that's how I know what letter it was. She erased it, wrote it again. The triangular shape of the first loop, the down-curve of the next stroke, like a bird bending to drink. Yes, and the line of the roof from which the character was suspended, like wet socks on a clothes-line. She shivered with pleasure. Then someone called her name, and she hastily scrubbed the letter away.

How strange this is! There she is, in an age when a woman, a respectable upper-caste woman, isn't supposed to be able to read, so she has to learn on the sly, like a criminal. Here I am, in an age when women can be scientists like Nondini, yet I can't read. What I learned from the Maula, I forgot. I can recognize familiar shop signs and so on from their shapes, not the sounds the shapes are supposed to represent, and anyway machines tell you everything. Nondini tells me that now very few people need to read because of mobiles, and because information can be shown and spoken by machines.

After watching Rassundari write for the first time, that desire woke in me, to learn how to read. My captors would not have denied me materials if I'd asked them, but I thought it would be much more interesting to learn from a woman dead for maybe hundreds of years. This is possible because the Machine now stays stuck in the set time and place for hours instead of minutes. Earlier it would keep disconnecting after five or ten minutes and you would have to wait until it came back. Its new steadiness makes the scientists very happy.

So now when I am at the scope, my captors leave me to myself. As Rassundari writes, I copy the letters on a sheet of paper and whisper the sounds under my breath.

The scientists annoy me after each session with their questions, and sometimes when I feel wicked I tell them that Wajid Ali Shah is going through a dry spell. Other times I make up lines that he supposedly spoke to his gathering of fellow poets. I tell them these are bits and fragments and pieces of longer works.

> *If there was someone for such as me*
> *Would that cause great inconvenience for you, O universe?*
> *Would the stars go out and fall from the sky?*

I am enjoying this, even though my poetry is that of a beginner, crude and direct. Wajid Ali Shah also wrote in the commoner's tongue, which makes my deception possible. I also suspect that these scientists don't know enough about poetry to tell the difference. My dear teacher, the Maula, would talk for hours about rhyme and lilt, and the difference between a ghazal and a rubayi. I didn't understand half of what he said but I learned enough to know that there is a way of talking about poetry if you are learned in the subject. And the scientists don't seem to react like that. They just exclaim and repeat my lines and wonder whether this is a fragment or a complete poem.

One day I want to write my poetry in my own hand.

Imagine me, Gargi, doing all this! A person of no importance— and look where life has got me!

I now know who Kajori is.

I didn't know that was her first name. Even the older scientists call her Dr. Mitra. She's a tall, thin woman, the boss of the others, and she always looks busy and harassed. Sometimes she smiles, and her smile is twisted. I took a dislike to her at first because she always looked through me, as though I wasn't there. Now I still dislike her but I'm sorry for her. And angry with her. The dead man, her lover, she must have sent him away, trapped him in that place where he floats above the delta of the river of time. It's my dreams he comes into, not hers. I can hardly bear his agony, his weeping, the way he calls out for her. I wonder why she has abandoned him.

I think he's in this building. The first time this thought occurred to me I couldn't stop shaking. It made sense. All my hauntings have been people physically close to me.

They won't let me leave this floor. I can leave my room now, but the doors to the stairs are locked, and the lifts don't work after everyone leaves. But I will find a way. I'm tired of being confined like this.

I realize now that although I was raised poor and illiterate, I was then at least free to move about, to breathe the air, to dream of my mother's home. Siridanga! I want to go back there and see it before I die. I know that the sea has entered the cities and drowned the land, but Siridanga was on a rise overlooking the paddy fields. My grandparents' hut was on the hillock. Could it still be there?

The night market makes me feel restless. The reflections of the lights dance on the windowpanes of the opposite building, as though they are writing something. All this learning to read is making me crazy, because I see letters where they don't exist. In the reflections. In people's hand gestures. And even more strangely, I see some kind of writing in the flow of time, in the dreams the dead man brings me. Those are written in a script I cannot read.

I "discovered" a whole verse of Wajid Ali Shah's poem today, after hours at the scope. There was so much excitement in the analysis room that the scientists let me go to my quarters early. I pleaded a headache but they hardly noticed. So I slipped out, into the elevator, and went up, and down, and got off on floors and walked around. I felt like a mad person, a thief, a free bird. It was ridiculous what an effect this small freedom had!

But after a while I began to get frightened. There was nobody else on the other floors as far as I could tell. The rooms were silent, dark behind doors with glass slits. I know that the scientists live somewhere here, maybe in the other buildings. Nondini tells me we are in a cluster of buildings near the sea that was built to withstand the flood. From her hints and from the TV I know that the world is ending. It's not just here. Everywhere cities are flooded or consumed by fire. Everything is dying. I have never been able to quite believe this before, perhaps because of my peculiar situation, which prevents me from seeing things for myself. But ultimately the silence and darkness of the rest of the building brought it home to me, and I felt as if I were drowning in sadness.

Then I sensed a pull, a current—a shout in my mind. It was him, the dead man. *Kajori!* he called again and again, and I found myself climbing to the floor above, to a closed door in the dark corridor.

I tried the handle, felt the smooth, paneled wood, but of course it was locked. With my ear against the door I could feel the hum of machinery, and there was a soft flow of air from beneath the door. I called back to him in my mind.

I can't get in, I said. *Talk to me!*

His voice in my mind was full of static, so I couldn't understand everything. Even when I heard the words, they didn't make sense. I think he was muttering to himself, or to Kajori.

". . . rivulets of time . . . two time-streams come together . . . ah . . . in a loop . . . if only . . . shift the flow, shift the flow . . . another future . . . must lock to past coordinate, establish resonance . . . new tomorrow . . ."

The chowkidar who is supposed to guard the elevator caught me on my way downstairs. He is a lazy, sullen fellow who never misses an opportunity to throw his weight around. I am more than a match for him though. He reported me, of course, to Nondini and Unnikrish-nan, but I argued my case well. I simply said I was restless and wanted to see if there was a nice view from the other floors. What could they say to that?

I tried to make sense of the dead man's gibberish all day. At night he came into my dreams as usual. I let him talk, prompting him with questions when something didn't make sense. I had to be clever to conceal my ignorance, since he thought I was Kajori, but the poor fellow is so emotionally overwrought that he is unlikely to be suspicious. But when he started weeping in his loneliness, I couldn't bear it. I thought: I will distract him with poetry.

I told him about the poem I am writing. It turns out he likes poetry. The poem he and Kajori love the best is an English translation of something by Omar Khayyam.

"Remember it, Kajori?" he said to me. He recited it in English, which I don't understand, and then in Bangla: "Oh love, if you and I could, with fate conspire," he said, taking me with a jolt back to my girlhood: me sitting by the Maula in the mad confusion of the market, the two of us seeing nothing but poetry, mango juice running down our chins. Oh yes, I remember, I said to my dead man. Then it was my turn. I told him about what I was writing and he got really interested. Suggested words, gave me ideas. So two lines of "Wajid Ali Shah's poem" came to me.

Clouds are borne on the wind
The river winds toward home

It was only the next day that I started to connect things in my mind. I think I know what the project is really about.

These people are not scientists, they are jadugars. Or maybe that's what scientists are, magicians who try to pass themselves off as ordinary people.

See, the dead man's idea is that time is like a river delta, lots of thin streams and fat streams, flowing from past to present, but fanning out. History and time control each other, so that if some future place is deeply affected by some past history, those two time-streams will connect. When that happens it diverts time from the future place and shifts the flow in each channel so that the river as a whole might change its course.

They're trying to change the future.

I am stunned. If this is true, why didn't they tell me? Don't I also want the world to survive? It's my world too. This also means that I am more important to them than they ever let me know. I didn't realize all this at once; it is just now beginning to connect in my mind.

I burn inside with anger. At the same time, I am undone with wonder.

I think the dead man is trying to save the world. I think the scope and the dead man are part of the same Machine.

I wonder how much of their schemes I have messed up by locking the Machine into a different time and place than their calculations required.

What shall I do?

———

For now I have done nothing.

I need to find out more. How terrible it is to be ignorant! One doesn't even know where to start.

I looked at the history books Nondini had let me have—talking books—but they told me nothing about Rassundari. Then I remembered that one of the rooms on my floor housed a library—from the days before the scientists had taken over the building.

I think Nondini sensed how restless I was feeling, and she must have talked to Kajori (I can't think of her as Dr. Mitra now), so I have permission to spend some of my spare time in the library. They might let me go to the night market tomorrow too, with an escort. I went and thanked Kajori. I said that I was homesick for my mother's village home, Siridanga, and it made me feel crazy sometimes not to be able to walk around. At that she really looked at me, a surprised look, and smiled. I don't think it was a nice smile, but I couldn't be certain.

So, the library. It is a whole apartment full of books of the old kind. But the best thing about it is that there is a corner window from which I can see between two tall buildings. I can see the ocean! These windows don't open but when I saw the ocean I wept. I was in such a state of sadness and joy all at once, I forgot what I was there for.

The books were divided according to subject, so I practiced reading the subject labels first. It took me two days and some help from Nondini (I had to disguise the intent of my search) before I learned how to use the computer to search for information. I was astonished to find out that my housewife had written a book! So all that painful learning on the sly had come to something! I felt proud of her. There was the book in the autobiography section: *Amar Jiban*, written by a woman called Rassundari more than two hundred and fifty years ago. I clutched the book to me and took it with me to read.

It is very hard reading a real book. I have to keep looking at my notes from my lessons with Rassundari. It helps that Nondini got me some alphabet books. She finds my interest in reading rather touching, I think.

But I am getting through Rassundari's work. Her writing is simple and so moving. What I can't understand is why she is so calm about the injustices in her life. Where is her anger? I would have gotten angry. I feel for her as I read.

I wish I could tell Rassundari that her efforts will not be in vain—that she will write her autobiography and publish it at the age of sixty, and that the future will honor her. But how can I tell her that, even if there was a way she could hear me? What can I tell her about this world? My wanderings through the building have made me realize that the world I've known is going away, as inevitably as the tide, with no hope of return.

Unless the dead man and I save it.

I have been talking to Rassundari. Of course she can't hear me, but it comforts me to be able to talk to someone, really talk to them. Sometimes Rassundari looks up toward the point near the ceiling from which I am observing her. At those moments it seems to me that she senses my presence. Once she seemed about to say something, then shook her head and went back to the cooking.

I still haven't told anybody about my deceit. I have found out that Wajid Ali Shah and Rassundari lived at around the same time, although he was in Kolkata and she in a village that is now in Bangladesh. From what the dead man tells me, it is time that is important, not space. At least that is what I can gather from his babblings, although spacetime fuzziness or resolution is also important. So maybe my deception hasn't caused any harm. I hope not. I am an uneducated woman, and when I sit in that library I feel as though there is so much to know. If someone had told me that, encouraged me as a child, where might I have been today?

And yet think about the dead man, with all his education. There he is, a hundred times more trapped than me, a thousand times lonelier. Still, he must be a good man, to give himself for the world. He's been asking me anxiously: *Kajori, can you feel the shift in the timeflow? Have we locked into the pastpoint?* I always tell him I feel it just a little, which reassures him that his sacrifice is not for nothing. I wish I could tell him: I am Gargi, not Kajori. Instead I tell him I love him, I miss him. Sometimes I really feel that I do.

I have been speaking to Rassundari for nearly a week.

One of the scientists, Brijesh, caught me talking into the scope. He came into the room to get some papers he'd left behind. I jumped guiltily.

"Gargi-di? What are you doing . . . ?" he says with eyebrows raised.

"I just like to talk to myself. Repeat things Wajid Ali Shah is saying."

He looks interested. "A new poem?"

"Bah!" I say. "You people think he says nothing but poetry all the time? Right now he's trying to woo his mistress."

This embarrasses Brijesh, as I know it would. I smile at him and go back to the scope.

But yes, I was talking about Rassundari.

Now I know that she senses something. She always looks up at me, puzzled as to how a corner of the ceiling appears to call to her. Does she hear me, or see some kind of image? I don't know. I keep telling her not to be afraid, that I am from the future, and that she is famous for her writing. Whether she can tell what I am saying I don't know. She does look around from time to time, afraid as though others might be there, so I think maybe she hears me, faintly, like an echo.

Does this mean that our rivulet of time is beginning to connect with her time-stream?

I think my mind must be like an old-fashioned radio. It picks up things: the dead man's ramblings, the sounds and sights of the past. Now it seems to be picking up the voices from the books in this room. I was deaf once, but now I can hear them as I read, slowly and painfully. All those stories, all those wonders. If I'd only known!

I talk to the dead. I talk to the dead of my time, and the woman Rassundari of the past, who is dead now. My closest confidants are the dead.

The dead man—I wish I knew his name—tells me that we have made a loop in time. He is not sure how the great delta's direction will change—whether it will be enough, or too little, or too much. He has not quite understood the calculations that the Machine is doing. He is preoccupied. But when I call to him, he is tender, grateful. "Kajori," he says, "I have no regrets. Just this one thing, please do it for me. What you promised. Let me die once the loop has fully stabilized." In one dream I saw through his eyes. He was in a tank, wires coming out of his body, floating. In that scene there was no river of time, just the luminous water below him, and the glass casing around. What a terrible prison! If he really does live like that, I think he can no longer survive outside the tank, which is why he wants to die.

It is so painful to think about this that I must distract us both. We talk about poetry, and later the next few lines of the poem come to me.

> *Clouds are borne on the wind*
> *The river winds toward home*
> *From my prison window I see the way to my village*
> *In its cage of bone my heart weeps*
> *When I was the river, you were the shore*
> *Why have you forsaken me?*

I am getting confused. It is Kajori who is supposed to be in love with the dead man, not me.

———

So many things happened these last two days.

The night before last, the maajhis sang in the night market. I heard their voices ululating, the dotaras throbbing in time with the flute's sadness. A man's voice, and then a woman's, weaving in and out. I imagined them on their boats, plying the waters all over the drowned city as they had once sailed the rivers of my drowned land. I was filled with a painful ecstasy that made me want to run, or fly. I wanted to break the windows.

The next morning I spent some hours at the scope. I told Rassundari my whole story. I still can't be sure she hears me, but her upturned, attentive face gives me hope. She senses something, for certain, because she put her hand to her ear as though straining to hear. Another new thing is that she is sometimes snappy. This has never happened before. She snapped at her nephew the other day, and later spoke sharply to her husband. After both those instances she felt so bad! She begged forgiveness about twelve times. Both her nephew and her husband seemed confused, but accepted her apology. I wonder if the distraction I am bringing into her life is having an effect on her mind. It occurs to me that perhaps, like the dead man, she can sense my thoughts, or at least feel the currents of my mind.

The loop in the time-stream has stabilized. Unnikrishnan told me I need not be at the scope all the time, because the connection is always there, instead of timing out. The scientists were nervous and irritable; Kajori had shut herself up in her office. Were they waiting for the change? How will they tell that the change has come? Have we saved the world? Or did my duplicity ruin it?

I was in the library in the afternoon, a book on my lap, watching the grey waves far over the sea, when the dead man shouted in my mind. At this I peered out—the hall was empty. The scientists have been getting increasingly careless. The lift was unguarded.

So up I went to the floor above. The great wood-paneled door was open. Inside the long, dimly lit room stood Kajori, her face wet with tears, calling his name.

"Subir! Subir!"

She didn't notice me.

He lay naked in the enormous tank like a child sleeping on its belly. He was neither young nor old; his long hair, afloat in the water like seaweed, was sprinkled with grey, his dangling arms thin as sticks. Wires came out of him at dozens of places, and there were large banks of machinery all around the tank. His skin gleamed as though encased in some kind of oil.

He didn't know she was there, I think. His mind was seething with confusion. He wanted to die, and his death hadn't happened on schedule. A terror was growing in him.

"You promised, Kajori!"

She just wept with her face against the tank. She didn't turn off any switches. She didn't hear him, but I felt his cry in every fiber of my being.

"He wants to die," I said.

She turned, her face twisted with hatred.

"What are you doing here? Get out!"

"Go free, Subir!" said I. I ran in and began pulling out plugs, turning off switches in the banks of machines around the tank. Kajori tried to stop me but I pushed her away. The lights in the tank dimmed. His arms flailed for a while, then grew still. Over Kajori's scream I heard his mind going out like the tide goes out, wafting toward me a whisper: thank you, thank you, thank you.

I became aware of the others around me, and Kajori shouting and sobbing.

"She went mad! She killed him!"

"You know he had to die," I said to her. I swallowed. "I could hear his thoughts. He . . . he loved you very much."

She shouted something incomprehensible at me. Her sobbing subsided. Even though she hated me, I could tell that she was beginning to accept what had happened. I'd done her a favor, after all, done the thing she had feared to do. I stared at her sadly and she looked away.

"Take her back to her room," she said. I drew myself up.

"I am leaving here," I said, "to go home to Siridanga. To find my family."

"You fool," Kajori said. "Don't you know, *this* place used to be Siridanga. You are standing on it."

They took me to my room and locked me in.

After a long time of lying in my bed, watching the shadows grow as the light faded, I made myself get up. I washed my face. I felt so empty, so faint. I had lost my family and my friends, and the dead man, Subir. I hadn't even been able to say good-bye to Rassundari. And Siridanga, where was Siridanga? The city had taken it from me. And eventually the sea would take it from the city. Where were my people? Where was home?

That night the maajhis sang. They sang of the water that had overflowed the rivers. They sang of the rivers that the city streets had become. They sang of the boats they had plied over river after river, time after time. They sang, at last, of the sea.

The fires from the night market lit up the windows of the opposite building. The reflections went from windowpane to windowpane, with the same deliberate care that Rassundari took with her writing. I felt that at last she was reaching through time to me, to our dying world, writing her messages on the walls of our building in letters of fire. She was writing my song.

Nondini came and unlocked my door sometime before dawn. Her face was filled with something that had not been there before, a defiance. I pulled her into my room.

"I have to tell you something," I said. I sat her down in a chair and told her the whole story of how I'd deceived them.

"Did I ruin everything?" I said at the end, fearful at her silence.

"I don't know, Gargi-di," she said at last. She sounded very young, and tired. "We don't know what happens when a time-loop is formed artificially. It may bring in a world that is much worse than this one. Or not. There's always a risk. We argued about it a lot and finally we thought it was worth doing. As a last-ditch effort."

"If you'd told me all this, I wouldn't have done any of it," I said, astounded. Who were they to act as Kalki? How could they have done something of this magnitude, not even knowing whether it would make for a better world?

"That's why we didn't tell you," she said. "You don't understand, we—scientists, governments, people like us around the world—tried everything to avert catastrophe. But it was too late. Nothing worked. And now we are past the point where any change can make a difference."

"'People like us,' you say," I said. "What about people like me? We don't count, do we?"

She shook her head at that, but she had no answer.

It was time to go. I said good-bye, leaving her sitting in the darkness of my room, and ran down the stairs. All the way to the front steps, out of the building, out of my old life, the tired old timestream. The square was full of the night-market people packing up—fish vendors, and entertainers, getting ready to return another day. I looked around at the tall buildings, the long shafts of paling sky between them, water at the edge of the island lapping ever higher. The long boats were tethered there, weather-beaten and much-mended. The maajhis were leaving, but not to return. I talked to an old man by one of their boats. He said they were going to sea.

"There's nothing left for us here," he said. "Ever since last night the wind has been blowing us seaward, telling us to hasten, so we will follow it. Come with us if you wish."

So in that grey dawn, with the wind whipping at the tattered sails and the water making its music against the boats, we took off for the open sea. Looking back, I saw Rassundari writing with dawn's pale fingers on the windows of the skyscrapers, the start of the letter *kah*, conjugated with *r. Kra* . . . But the boat and the wind took us away before I could finish reading the word. I thought the word reached all the way into the ocean with the paling moonlight still reflected in the surging water.

Naihar chhuto hi jaaye, I thought, and wept.

Now the wind writes on my forehead with invisible tendrils of air, a language I must practice to read. I have left my life and loves behind me, and wish only to be blown about as the sea desires, to have the freedom of the open air, and be witness to the remaking of the world.

A Handful of Rice

At last Vishnumitra saw the king.

The city was alive with beasts, mechanical and organic; there were elephants in the procession, stately and benign, draped with silk and brocade, bearing jeweled howdahs on their backs; then the the metal men, marching in formation, sun glinting off their armor; the king's black horse, riderless and unsaddled, hooves ringing, leading the king's glory, the tallest howdah on the tallest elephant. Crowds leaned out of balconies, lined the roads, throwing rose petals into the parade. Horseless carriages of the latest fashion, just out from the king's own factories, led the procession, but it would not do for the king to sit in one of those. There were few things, said the traitor to Vishnumitra, as royal as elephants.

To Vishnumitra the elephants looked out of place. He was an outsider from a village in the far reaches of the kingdom, and the bright, ringing clamor of the streets, the heavy scent of roses and sweat, were all too much for him. His opinion was of no account, so he said nothing. But he thought with some nostalgia about the home he had left behind these many, weary months, although the picture that came into his mind was one from his boyhood. Kind-eyed elephants bathing on the shore of the Ganga with the village boys, the water a grey sheet under a cloudy sky. Ahead were the steps of the ghat going down to the water and on the steps his mother and sisters, saris billowing red and orange. It was early morning; it was going to rain. On the rise along the shore the shisham trees spoke sibilantly in the breeze, their leaves a tender green. He saw his mother bend down and release the little earthen diya in the water, in its garland-boat of woven leaves and marigolds. Her hands cupped the small flame to make certain it did not go out in the wind, but the currents pulled the diya away from her, and she straightened and looked at the little boat—fire on water—sail off mid-stream. Fire on water, a prayer released into the world.

He shook his head to clear it of old memories and immediately the noise and pomp of the procession assaulted his senses again. Annoyed with himself for dwelling so much on the past lately, he tried to turn his attention to the task at hand: to get a good look at that elusive, all-powerful monarch, the great man who ruled Hindustan, the man who, it was said, would live for ever. Harbinger of Peace and Prosperity, they called him, this mysterious man who would not let anybody draw his portrait or take his picture. He was not quite mortal, it was said. He had held off Sher Shah's kingdom in the North-West, the Portuguese colony in the East, and the British territories to the South, and only magic of some kind could have accomplished that, said the sycophants and admirers of the king.

Vishnumitra did not believe in magic; instead he believed in rigorous observation and systematic study. The glimpse was the first step; after that he didn't know whether he was going to do it, or how he was going to do it. He was not an assassin, he had told the traitor. The traitor nodded as though to imply that all the assassins said that anyway, and Vishnumitra had felt soiled by the man's polite disbelief. Somehow these days of waiting and plotting in the great nation's capital had been the hardest period since he had left home two years ago. Perhaps it was no wonder that he was tired; that his resolve was shaken by that deep, inexpressible desire to go home. Looking at the King's portrait on the coinage of the country, the abstract, fluid lines suggesting a face beautiful in repose, he had thought about his mother making kheer in the kitchen. A portrait of the king, made illegally and paid for in blood, showed the lean, aristocratic face, the eyes large, clear, cold. "This is not very accurate, but maybe it is good enough?" the traitor had said. Vishnumitra had a sudden clear vision of the schoolroom in his village, the foot-thick mud walls, the golden thatch overhead, the view of the distant river. It took him some time to frown and say that he really needed to be able to recognize the king clearly before he could be certain he had killed the right man. It was known that the king had proxies who sometimes spoke for him on lesser public occasions. At least once, such a proxy had been killed. No, Vishnumitra needed to see the king face-to-face.

"How can I be certain," he asked the traitor, "that the man in the procession is indeed the king?"

"For the anniversary of his coronation? Only the real king rides the royal elephant, my friend."

The broad way was divided in the middle by a long water channel that had been sprinkled with rose petals. Along each side of the road was a five-foot-high divan, a raised platform bristling with tall, plumed soldiers. The noise was tremendous, with shouts and the baying of horns.

And Vishnumitra saw the king.

The room he was in was level with the howdah in which the king rode. The building was too far from the street for clear viewing with the naked eye; they had already been searched for weapons by guards. So Vishnumitra put the telescope in position and squinted through it, waiting for the attendant inside the howdah to do his job.

The attendant, in the pay of the traitor, did his job. He had an embroidered palm-leaf punkha in his hand and while fanning the king he let it catch in one of the king's long braids. The king wore his ceremonial turban above his coiffure; the crown shifted, the black braids parted. The king turned instinctively toward the punkha, his hand already up to adjust the braid, his mouth an O of surprise and irritation, and in that moment Vishnumitra saw him.

The procession continued. Vishnumitra lowered the telescope, stood staring out through the latticed window, his mind a maelstrom.

No wonder he had been thinking so much about his youth.

The king—surely there could be no mistaking it—the king was no other than Upamanyu, the young man he had befriended in his boyhood, the wanderer who had made a home with them for four unforgettable years, closer than a brother. But no, it could not be. In the interim Vishnumitra had aged; despite his practice of the forbidden sciences, he had a few gray hairs. He looked younger than his fifty-seven years, but the king looked twenty-five.

Upamanyu . . . the face burned into his mind, thirty-eight years ago, never forgotten. Remembered always, with yearning.

If the king was, indeed, Upamanyu, that could only mean one thing.

"Well?" said the traitor. "Can you . . . will you do it?"

Vishnumitra took a deep breath. He controlled the needless dissipation of his body's prana with an effort, a skill learned over years, and felt his mind and body getting back to equilibrium. He now understood that his wanderings in search of the hidden sciences and their practitioners, his investigations into the murder of the girl Shankara, whose name he still could not say without pain—were all intended to bring him to this place at this point. He was the only man in the four kingdoms who knew who the king was.

"This is where our association ends," Vishnumitra said to the traitor. "You have been paid. If I do it, I will do it alone."

That night, Vishnumitra went walking through the long, lamp-lit streets of Dilli.

The city rose over the banks of the Yamuna like a poet's dream. Here was the delicate arch of a doorway, the doors carved with scenes from a fairy tale; there was a temple spire, beside the dark crown of a mango tree. The dome of a mosque, silver in the twilight, and above it the fort itself, red sandstone, turrets, and tessellations. Closer at hand: a man selling roasted shakarkand under a tree by the road-side: the smell of coal and sweetness and spices, the flare of the fire. Voices from within a walled garden where somebody was watering rosebushes. He could smell wet earth and the inescapable fragrance of roses. The horseless carriages still startled him as they went by, leaving behind a wet smell, coal and steam, and the image of a face or faces at a window. Here and there were patrols of the king, guards in red and brown, with green turbans, riding horses. And the ornate carriages filled with nobility, pulled by the great, white, humped oxen that stood six feet high at the shoulder. One time he saw a patrol accompanying those curious artifacts, the metal men (borrowed for the parade), back to the factories where they worked. The metal men walked stiffly; with each step the joints clanged faintly, metal on metal, and there was a sigh of steam. Vishnumitra could not get used to their swiveling heads, their eyeless gaze.

He walked swiftly, like a man with a purpose, so as not to draw attention to himself. But his back was against the wall. There really was no place to go anymore. This place, this moment, was where the last two decades had brought him. He could give himself the illusion of being free, the stranger in the city who must be on his way soon, but he was chained by his promise to the dead. He had to kill the king.

But Upamanyu . . .

If even that is his real name, Vishnumitra thought, with bitter humor. The king called himself Akbar Khan. Every child in the kingdom knew how he had come to occupy the throne of the Mughals; in towns all over, people still enacted the story. The British forces fighting their way all the way to Dilli from the South, burning and looting, setting the bazaar on fire. The valiant Mughal army, with the king, Mirza Mughal, in the lead. All the king's sons fall in battle that black day, until there is only Mirza Mughal chasing a knot of enemy soldiers into an alleyway and out in the open by the river. He is known for his swordsmanship; he dispatches three of them quickly, a few of the others flee, but there is one left. Mirza Mughal leaps from his great black horse, fighting hard, blood on his sword, his armour broken across the chest. Last of the Mughals, he is holding back a pale, yellow-haired youth with a bayonet. There's the Yamuna before him, and in the black water he can see his city burning. At the last minute, when Mirza Mughal is so tired he almost wants to die, there comes a madman leaping into the fray, challenging the British soldier, wielding a sword but in a style Mirza Mughal has never seen. Then a strange thing happens: the bayonet falls from the British soldier's hand as if of its own accord; the boy seems surprised, horrified, and the madman's sword makes short work of him. The stranger bows, introduces himself to his king. His name is Akbar Khan. The king and his subject return to the fray, fighting side by side until a stray bullet hits the king. In the last scene of the tragedy, Mirza Mughal is dying in Akbar Khan's arms while Dilli burns. The river is burning too: boats succumb first to fire, then water. In the presence of what is left of his army, Mirza Mughal tells Akbar Khan: my sons are dead. I give you my kingdom. Drive out the enemy and rule!

Over the body of the dead king, Akbar Khan rouses the soldiers and the common people of the city with a speech that is still recited today in the dramas. Men leap over courtyard walls, where they have been cowering, and throng the streets; mothers lock the children in their homes and take up kitchen knives and burning brands, and leap into the fray. It is as though a tsunami has suddenly hit the invaders. In the narrow alleyways, the once-gracious city squares, in courtyards and on the riverbank the British are cut to bits. The invading armies flee.

In the dark and smoke, the smell of blood and burning flesh, the wails of the bereaved, Akbar Khan stands still for a moment, outlined in the archway of a garden that has become a charnel house. Watchers see him limned in the light from the fires behind him, his bloody, smoking sword by his side.

Then, in a moment immortalized by innumerable dramas, Mirza Mughal's great black horse comes up to Akbar Khan. He has lost his saddle, and there is a gash on his side, but the great beast simply bows his head, stands and waits. Akbar Khan pauses for a moment, strokes the horse's head, and with a lithe movement that no theater performer can quite emulate, leaps upon the horse. The horse bears the new king to the fort.

Vishnumitra had to concede that it was quite a story: how the nobody, Akbar Khan, ascended the throne of Dilli. But holding on to that throne for so many years was an even greater achievement. What Akbar Khan did, the stories went, was to first consolidate that nexus of power, the harem. Mirza Mughal's harem was fairly modest, with two chief queens, seventy-five lesser wives and about five hundred concubines, along with hundreds of female administrators, a corps of eunuchs and female guards. This was where the king had lived, where the affairs of state were decided, and where he opened reports from his spies. It was said that Akbar Khan won over the queen mother first. The dead princes were given elaborate funerals and the queens shown the utmost respect. So when the intrigues and assassination attempts began, Akbar Khan was not without friends. His pleasing mien and obvious wizardry with the sword were rivaled only by his political acumen. When Mirza Mughal's relatives challenged him he played one faction against the other until most of his rivals were eliminated. As for the rest, he invited them to challenge him in a duel unto death.

Those were the early years. The challenges were issued mostly by nobles outraged that a man without a lineage, let alone a proper Persian lineage, could sit upon the throne of Hindustan with such insouciant ease. Such challenges were the talk of the citizenry, because Akbar Khan received and accepted them in the public durbar. Sometimes the challenger wanted a game of chess; sometimes it was a duel by arms, but always it was the throne at stake, and always, failure meant death. The challenge itself was held in a private room off the durbar, with only the king and the challenger present. And always, the challenger would be found dead the next morning, in the trash heap outside the city walls. There was no evidence of poison or other underhand means, only a bruising about the skin, and a neat sword-cut to the throat. The victim didn't bleed much, it was said. There were rumors of magic and other skullduggery, but the king, while contradicting these, did not work too hard to suppress the imaginations of the credulous. Always, he generously compensated the families of the victims.

After his first two years in office, Akbar Khan stopped accepting challenges. The occasional madman would still issue a challenge but Akbar Khan showed great compassion in turning such fools away. Enough blood had been shed. His kingdom was established.

Having silenced his critics, Akbar Khan had set his skill and charisma to work on the rest of the country, bringing to it a relatively stable economy and a robust peace. He befriended Sher Shah of the North-West Kingdom and played the Portuguese and the British against each other while making neighborly noises to both. It was rumored that he gave covert support to the revolutionaries in the South so the British had their hands full. This was the king who embraced the modern science of Europe's industrial revolution, and in doing so revived the metallurgical genius of the ancient Indians by searching for and bringing to his capital all indigenous talent; he brought over some of Europe's finest engineers to work with them. The manufactories of Dilli rolled out horseless carriages of gleaming steel that moved on the new-paved roads like boats on still water. They were becoming popular in Britain; the manufactories were having a difficult time keeping up with the frenzied demands from abroad.

At the same time, Akbar Khan had been careful not to create a culture of demand in his own land. Very few Indians owned their own cars; for long-distance travel there were the railways, laid across the land like lines on a palm. Vishnumitra had, during his wanderings, acquired a reluctant fascination for this mode of transport; there was something about the sway and rhythm of these sleek, serpentine monsters that brought to his heart an inexplicable joy. It was also easy to think while traveling like this, and he had spent some of his most contemplative moments in the last two years on a train, watching the countryside flash by.

It was said that while the South-West reeled under the despotism of the Portuguese king, and the South itself knew mass poverty and economic collapse for the first time under the rule of the British general, Hindustan was free. And prosperous. Glory be to the king, Akbar Khan the First. So what if he used magic and was rumored to be unconventional, even heretical? So what if he defied the kazis and brought back the syncretic, hybrid Hindu-Muslim culture of his namesake, Akbar the Great? So what if he kept his hair in long braids, had private quarters outside the harem atop a small tower, where only he and invited guests could go?

So what if his eccentricities included banning of the ancient science of healing?

Vishnumitra had, from afar, supported the rise of Akbar Khan until then. For him Akbar Khan had been a person of legend in distant Dilli, a man of whom absurdly tall tales were told, who had somehow been able to consolidate the kingdom and keep its enemies at bay. Then the news came, slowly at first, trickling into the outer reaches of the kingdom from wanderers and tradespeople, and finally from local officials: the practice of the ancient arts was banned. Some of the herbal lore was all right to practice, but the rest of it, referred to by the king as quackery, was no longer allowed. Significant parts of the ancient medical system of Ayurveda, particularly those concerned with the prana vidya, as well as the various methods of acupuncture brought by Chinese scholars, were now forbidden. A system of national medical care had been set up by the king, employing a mishmash of traditions, from the European to the Yunnani, and the textbooks had been standardized and rewritten. So while a practitioner of Ayurveda would have studied the works of, say, Charaka, or Patanjali, now only "relevant" extracts were read, the implication being that the rest was not worth learning. The king claimed he wanted to modernize the country. Yet he did nothing to stop other kinds of quackery; charlatan astrologers could wander the land at will, but a traditional healer could find himself thrown in jail. Yoga as exercise was all right, but healing through the control and manipulation of prana was quackery, and its practice punishable by imprisonment. Vishnumitra had been angry and bewildered, but there was nothing to be done. He had to keep his true vocation a secret and lie about his age.

But now, walking through the city like a man possessed, Vishnumitra thought he knew why the king had banned the ancient sciences of healing, while reserving them for himself under the guise of magic. Still, it made no sense that a man who was sixty-two years old should look twenty-five, even with the practice of the prana vidya. They gave good health, not immortality. Something was very wrong.

He thought of the girl Shankara, whom he himself had trained in the forbidden sciences. For his first year of wandering she and a handful of others had been his dear companions. She had cut off her hair and disguised herself as a man so as to be able to travel with less trouble. With their help Vishnumitra had established over much of Hindustan a secret network of the practitioners of prana vidya, all of whom had once operated alone, and in fear. The fear was still there, but with it now there was comradeship, the exchange and enhancement of knowledge. No longer did one healer or scholar of such arts fear that the knowledge would die with him or her.

And the best of them had been Shankara.

She had gone to Dilli against his advice, to challenge the king.

Since the months after a friend discovered her body on the refuse pile outside the city, Vishnumitra had wondered how it had happened. Why had the king, who no longer accepted challenges, accepted one from Shankara? And how had someone of Shankara's skill been outmaneuvered?

Oh, those months of grief and rage . . .

Vishnumitra paused by a shop selling sugarcane juice. He had a cupful so he could sit down for a moment, away from the crowd around the stall. There was a cracked marble platform around the roots of a pipal tree; he sat himself down on it. Behind him, under the tree's great canopy, was the mausoleum of a minor Sufi poet. He could smell incense and flowers.

Upamanyu . . .

He could not let himself feel what he had once felt, but even now, thinking of the name was enough to quicken his pulse. Once dearest friend, dearer than a brother! How lonely the years had been without him. He could never have imagined that he, Vishnumitra, who would once have defended Upamanyu with his life, would one day be plotting his death. He took a deep, shaky breath. A great wave of resistance to the notion rose in him, and along with it a desire to see Upamanyu again, and to leave this matter of revenge and murder to someone else. After all, there was all of Hindustan at stake. What would happen to its freedom and prosperity when Upamanyu was gone? He had thought through it all before, before he knew who the king was, and settled on the idea that what is right is right, and if a right act leads to great evil, then that evil must be thought of as independent of the act that preceded it, and fought on its own terms. But here, in the great city, with its show of might, power and glory, and the terrible news streaming in from the South as though to say: this is what will happen to Hindustan if you kill the king, it was difficult enough to justify this reasoning. And now that he knew who the king was, could he lift a hand against him?

And yet, and yet . . .

Shankara.

And the rest of the practitioners, who now worked in fear and secrecy, and the ones who had been found and killed. He had to do what he had set out to do.

He thought: after this I will go back home to my village, to what is left of my father's ashram by the Ganga. He did not tell himself that the very air, there, would remind him of Upamanyu. That after this Upamanyu's name might well be written on the paths they had once walked in the forests, together, or on the mud walls of the now-abandoned ashram.

The ashram was the place of his earliest memory. The walls were nearly a foot thick, made from a mixture of mud and straw; in the sun they glowed as though they were made of gold. Some of the walls were carved with images such as a god on a chariot or a hero atop an elephant. To the small boy he had been, the walls of the ashram told stories without saying a word. Inside, under the thatch roof, it was always cool in summer and warm in winter; even now he remembered leaning his head against the textured surface, feeling safe, feeling he was home.

The first time he saw Upamanyu . . . Nearly forty years ago. That face, in its youthful, unchanged beauty, had burned in his memory for all these years.

He remembered. How could he not? It was the first time that the world had come to his doorstep, after all, in the form of a young man, wanderer and eternal traveler. On his clothes was the dust of Baluchistan, Mysore, and Assam. He had stories to tell about the fall of Travancore in the South, the winds of the Western Desert, the arid cliffs of the North-West where Sher Shah had his citadel.

That morning Vishnumitra had been reading a copy of the Charaka Samhita on the verandah, practicing his Sanskrit while trying to learn something about healing. He was fifteen, a tall, quiet boy grown golden in the sun like the walls, and had acquired some of their contemplative silence. He wanted to be a healer, to use the knowledge of the ancients to heal the sick. His world had been whole, complete, until Upamanyu walked into it.

The children had been singing multiplication tables out in the courtyard, swaying with the music of it, making Vishnumitra feel pleasantly sleepy, so that he couldn't go beyond stanza one of the first verse of the *Charaka Samhita* (that great medical treatise being written in poetry, as was once the norm). The other children were bringing in mustard leaves from the garden they had been tending, the leaves scenting the air with their delicate pungency. And there was the stranger at the gate, as though the air had conjured him up: a tall, long-limbed fellow in the outlandish loose pants and long shirt of the North-West, with a mane of unruly black hair. He stood there unhurried and smiling, hefting his cloth bag on his shoulder, rubbing the stubble on his chin with his other hand.

Vishnumitra rose to greet the stranger but his father had already waved the children to silence. His father loved wanderers and outcasts, having been one himself for so long. In a few minutes the stranger was seated on a low wooden seat under the pipal tree. Water was brought for his hands and feet, and to drink. That was what he had stopped for: water, and five minutes of rest before wandering on to the town twelve miles away. Later Upamanyu would tell Vishnumitra: I stopped for five minutes and stayed five years—I, who have never stayed in a place longer than a month!

All these years later Vishnumitra wondered why Upamanyu had stayed so long. He had always thought it was because of the love that had arisen between them, the love of brother for brother and friend for friend; but now he was not so sure. Perhaps all that had been an illusion. His mentor and dear friend, who had taught him sword-fighting and filled his ears with the knowledge of a world far greater than the little ashram, may have had other reasons to linger. Who knew if even Upamanyu were his real name?

Every morning Vishnumitra would recite verses from the *Charaka Samhita* for his father. Upamanyu would be leaning against the wall, his mane of hair tied casually into a knot, his eyes bright with curiosity. Maitreya would explain each concept.

"Prana is the life force. Some people call it breath but it is that which comes before breath. In every healthy living being prana flows unimpeded through its designated channels. Sickness is when there is a blockage or abnormality in the prana flow, and then the healer must restore its pathways in order to restore health . . ."

"But is prana not the same as blood?" This from Upamanyu.

"No, indeed. Prana cannot be seen, heard, or felt, except by the one trained in the ancient art of healing. Such a practitioner can tell the state of the prana flow when he feels the patient's pulse, for the quality of the flow is reflected in the characteristics of the pulse. But the true sage can induce in himself a state of direct prana perception, in which the flow of prana appears manifest to the inner eye as the flow of the Ganga is manifest to the outer."

"Can you do this, Guruji? Will you teach me?"

Maitreya laughed.

"It is not so easily done. It takes the discipline of years. You will have to set down your traveling staff, my son, and study like Vishnu-mitra here. I myself have only touched the edge of that perceptive state. This knowledge is very arcane; I have found one version of it in a Tibetan text that I found by chance. But here too the greater truth is hinted at and concealed in a morass of lesser truths. This is the language of the twilight, as they say. It takes a lifetime to interpret these hints and intimations."

"Teach me, then, Guruji! For you I lay down my staff. You will find your pupil unused to instruction and too full of questions and impatience, but he will be grateful to be schooled . . ."

What Vishnumitra realized was that his father was in fact pleased. Later he wondered if Upamanyu had reminded his father of his own youth. Upamanyu's habit of asking questions as though he were issuing a challenge in a duel instigated in Maitreya delight instead of anger, and in fact Vishnumitra spent the next few days hating their guest, thinking himself less loved, a boring, overly obedient, dull sluggard of a student. But it all changed when Upamanyu asked Vishnumitra if he would help him achieve a better hand—his writing was atrocious. After that they went for walks in the forest, swam in the river, and engaged the village youth in games like kho and stick-fighting. Upamanyu revealed himself to be skilled with stick and sword, prideful and quick to temper, but just as easily recovering his good nature. In the forest one day Upamanyu brushed his hand across a chameli bush. Its white, scented flowers were like stars.

"Do you think plants have prana too, Vishnu?"

Vishnumitra thought, with a little surge of triumph: so you don't know everything, my friend!

Aloud he said:

"They do. My father has not yet taught you about cosmic prana. The prana that is in us flows into us and out again, and into and out of other things also. I don't quite understand it myself. But once, during meditation, he achieved the deepest state of prana perception—just for a few seconds—and he told me later it was like rivers of light falling out of the sky, flowing in and out of everything. Like the delta of a river, small streams coming together and then flowing apart . . ."

"That's what I want to see," Upamanyu said enthusiastically. Ahead of them the Ganga lay silver in the semi-darkness. They sat on the bank in companionable silence.

So long ago, it had been. It amazed Vishnumitra to think that the ashram had so long withstood the depredation of time and prejudice. His father had been a maverick, a madman. An outcast who had given up the Brahmin's sacred thread to marry a Muslim woman and not even insist on her conversion, let alone the various purification rituals! It was said that while she performed Hindu rituals such as the chhat fast, she also kept to her daily Islamic prayers! So Maitreya had lost caste and status, been turned out with his wife to roam the world. In his late youth he had finally found this place by the great, slow river, where among the trees a new kind of ashram had been founded. Eklavya, where any child could come to learn, irrespective of caste or creed or religion. The Brahmins kept their sons at home but in time the other castes sent their children, afraid to miss out on such an education. Apart from learning the duties of a householder, they would learn mathematics, music, astronomy, Ayurveda, yoga, tending a garden, cooking, sword-fighting and wrestling. Maitreya found teachers from the ranks of swordsmen and wandering dervishes, Sufi healers and itinerant craftsmen. So in time the children of petty tradesmen, Hindu or Muslim, sat with those of cowherds, rich landowners, and the occasional defiant Brahmin and sang their multiplication tables, or learned to cook and eat together and thus destroy both caste and religion. But what they created, Maitreya would say, was more important: a hybrid culture, a *din-i-illahi* made real, imbued with the best of both traditions. Friendship, community, a temple of knowledge.

And it was that. In the kitchen Vishnumitra's mother, Tasleem, took the clay pot of rice off the earthen stove and carried it out to the courtyard, swept clean by the children. There was a daal and some vegetables, and berries the children had picked in the forest. Everyone was sitting cross-legged on the ground, in a row, waiting to be served. The platters were made of dried, woven leaves, and soon each held a mound of rice, the famous red-tinged rice of that region. Many years after he had left home, Vishnumitra remembered the aroma of that rice: rich, earthy, with a touch of walnut. Whenever he met a trader from those parts he was sure to buy enough red rice to last him some time.

And in the night-time, sleeping in the open under the stars, with the crickets singing in the undergrowth, and from the forest the low, sweet call of a koel. His father would tell the small ones stories of pirs, or gods, or kings.

"And so Krishna became the king of Dwarka, but his friend of childhood, Sudama, remained poor even as a grown man. He lived in a hut with his wife and children, and they were hungry many times. One day he decided he would go to Dwarka to see his old friend. All he had that he could bring as a gift was a bag of rice, just the kind you ate today. So he walked all the way to Dwarka . . ."

It was an old, comforting story: the friend, Sudama, in his rags, with his lowly gift, being laughed at by the courtiers until the king saw him and came to him and embraced him, and expressed inordinate delight at the gift of rice. And Sudama spent a few days with Krishna, and when he returned home he found that his fortunes had changed. Where his rude hut had been, there stood a mansion, and his wife and children were well-fed and well-clothed.

"So, children, wherever you go when you are grown, may you remember your days together and be friends to each other as Krishna and Sudama were . . ."

Somewhere a queen-of-the-night bush was in bloom; its heavy scent was wafted by the breeze from the river. In the quiet after the story, Vishnumitra stole a glance at his friend, who was stretched out in the next pallet. He wanted to touch Upamanyu's hand, to make real his feeling that they were and always would be as Krishna and Sudama had been to each other, but shyness held him back. Upamanyu's fine, clever face was soft with moonlight, and listening.

And after all, Upamanyu had been the first to leave. He wanted to go to Tibet, he said, to look for the lost books on prana lore. But even before that Vishnumitra had sensed a restlessness in him, a preoccupation. He had known, but not admitted to himself until years later, that what called to Upamanyu was not just old palm-leaf manuscripts on prana lore but the long journey, the new sights along the way, and new adventures. He was tired of staying in one place. It was time to move on.

He had gone away one day with promises to be back in a year or two. There were disturbances from the South: the British invaders were marching north. Nothing was certain.

Maitreya knew he wouldn't be back, and he kept his disappointment and sorrow to himself. Vishnumitra's heart broke. The world became empty to him, and every familiar place reminded him of Upamanyu's absence. Only a few years later his father died in a skirmish during the confusion of the first British incursion north. Vishnumitra ran the ashram as best he could until his mother died. Some years after that the news came that the new king had banned the practice of the ancient arts. Vishnumitra could have kept the ashram going with all the remaining disciplines, but its existence was already a thorn in the side of the new provincial governor, who frowned upon such sacrilegious intermingling of caste and religion. Vishnumitra had no heart left for trouble. When the ashram closed he found that the wanderlust had come to him after all.

He set off into the world, not knowing what it held in store for him. He hid his true occupation, calling himself a scribe or a scholar, practicing his healing arts when they were truly needed. He found that if he stayed in a place more than a few days after a healing, others would come to him in the dark of night, begging for help to save a life or work a miracle. Sometimes he could do something; at other times he found himself on the run like a criminal.

But what he valued most was the discovery of those already versed in the arts; although few were superior to him, it was a delight to be able to discuss the finer points of prana control and manipulation, and the techniques to restore harmony for different conditions. When he met such people he taught them what he knew and learned from them as well. He found that his travels could help connect one practitioner with another, across cities and villages. And as he wandered, he picked up companions who wanted to be trained in the art. Mostly young people who became his family.

Now they were all scattered, doing the same work he had set out to do. Except for Shankara, who was dead.

After all, it was the bag of rice that did it.

The clerk in the royal court had shaken his old head as he watched Vishnumitra sign the document of challenge. He had reluctantly agreed to submit the bag of rice that Vishnumitra handed him with the scroll. "He will not see you," he had said, darkly. "He turns away all . . . nearly all who challenge him."

But the summons came two days later. The king would receive Vishnumitra—not in the Diwan-i-Khas but in his private room atop the tower. In the hour of twilight.

In the late afternoon Vishnumitra hired a boatman to take him to the opposite bank of the Yamuna. He chose a small pipal tree on the bank and sat down in the lotus position. Slowly he steadied his wildly beating heart. In the golden light the fort was a vision in red sandstone and marble.

Breathing slowly, Vishnumitra calmed his body, balancing out the prana flow in the two main channels on either side of his spine. He felt the slow shock of kundalini energy flowing up the sushumna channel toward the crown of his head, a wave of exhilaration, of limitless strength flooding him. He let his consciousness flow and become one with the prana, softening the flow in the seventy-two thousand distributories of the subtle body. In this deep, receptive state he opened his inner eye. With years of discipline he had come close to mastering what his father had taught him: the perception of the mahaprana, the cosmic channels of the life force. He saw the mahaprana as a faint skein of unearthly light, limning every living thing: tree or grazing cow or the waiting boatman. Raining down from the vastness of the sky were the greater channels, joining and connecting one life to another, from the smallest beetle now crawling along his arm to the King himself, awaiting him at the palace. When Vishnumitra had first glimpsed this cosmic marvel, two years after Upamanyu's own initiation, he had asked his father the same question Upamanyu had: From whence did the mahaprana flow? What was the source of it, beyond the sky? His father did not know.

Slowly Vishnumitra drew himself out of the meditation. He brushed the beetle from his arm with infinite tenderness and watched it scuttle away over the rock on which he was sitting. He waved to the silent boatman. It was time to go.

Between the fort walls are wonders: gracious gardens abloom with flowers, fountains that sing as water soars up into the air, a metal woman dancing in the center of a stone circle. Officials in small groups leave lighted rooms and confer in the scented gloom, as lamps flicker on, creating moving shadows. Vishnumitra is deep in the centered peacefulness that any glimpse of the mahaprana affords him—he has accepted what he must do, with all its moral ambiguity. Dharma is dharma, and if it is his fate to commit murder of one dearer to him than a brother, he will meet it like a scholar and a man.

To his surprise the king meets him at the base of the tower. His face is luminous in the light of the lamps, he makes an impatient gesture and his guards leave his side, watching from several paces away, out of earshot. Vishnumitra hesitates, but the king is holding out his arms.

The braids are held back, the face open, young as when Vishnumitra last saw him, filled with humor and intelligence, and at this moment—yes, this is so—the king's eyes are moist with tears.

"Dear brother! Vishnumitra!"

Vishnumitra cannot but accept the embrace, feeling tears pricking his own eyelids while simultaneously his mind warns him not to deviate from his purpose.

"Upamanyu!"

"Hush! Only to you, my friend!"

They stand apart, looking at each other. Vishnumitra feels his purpose like a burden whose weight he can hardly bear. Under other circumstances this would be a joyous reunion. He breathes deep.

"You know why I am here."

"We will talk of that in a few moments. As a condemned man, surely I have a right to ask for one last wish: a walk with my brother in the gardens? Come now, do not deny me!"

The old, affectionate, mocking tone. Vishnumitra's composure is shaken; he finds himself being led through the magical garden, with one wonder after another being pointed out. His heart is a traitor—this is what he has yearned for since Upamanyu left: this reunion, where he is Sudama to Upamanyu's Krishna, treated like an honored guest. Now the king's guards fling open the great doors of a large, circular building surrounded by ashoka trees. Within are bright lights, the hiss of steam and the noise of metal upon metal. Mechanical men are working in clusters, monitoring pulleys and wheels, fitting together beautifully wrought pieces of metal with exquisite precision. Vishnumitra, his mouth agape in wonder, understands nothing, recognizes nothing. What are they building? This is no manufactory of horseless carriages.

"This is my personal laboratory," the king says with pride. "For these many years I have become interested in the forces of nature apart from . . . from the life force itself. I have read the ancient Yunnanis Aristut, and Sukrat, and our own atomist schools. I have perused the barbarian vilayati scholar Niyuton. You have seen for yourself what wonders their discoveries have brought to us! Yet what I seek is to understand how these different imperatives, these forces, are related. Observe, my friend!"

He hands Vishnumitra a wooden tray upon which silver wires have been arranged in a rectangular array. Within this lattice are small canisters of metal. The king asks Vishnumitra to place his finger in such a way as to bridge a gap between the wires. Vishnumitra does so and feels the faintest shock, a jolt not unlike the sting one feels touching a metal gate before a thunderstorm. Not unlike the first experience of kundalini energy for a beginner. He jerks his finger away, raises startled eyes to Upamanyu.

"Ah, I see you are wondering if I have captured a storm in a few pieces of wire! Or is it a jolt of prana? So similar, yet the two forces are different—this one arises from inanimate matter, and the other from life itself! A mystery, is it not?"

They emerge from the chamber; the doors clang behind them, and a sweet silence descends. In the lamp-lit dark the king is leading him to the tower. Courtiers and guards watch curiously from afar.

The stairs spiral upwards and at the top there is a door, and a room furnished relatively simply—a small Persian rug over the marble floor, a low divan, a few chairs. A table with neat stacks of paperwork. Shelves filled with books—forbidden books! The *Charaka Samhita*, the works of the great physician Sushruta, Patanjali's Yoga *Sutra*, works on the tantric mysteries, tomes in Tibetan, Pali, and Sanskrit, and in languages he does not know. Vishnumitra stares at the books and then at Upamanyu, who is smiling indulgently, as an older brother might.

"You've seen what I've wrought in this kingdom, dear brother. And yet through all these years I have been alone. A decade ago I sent my spies to find you, but all they found was the ashram, abandoned, and you flown. And now you stand before me, bent upon revenge. And yet when we embraced there were tears in your eyes in answer to my own. Dear friend! Let us forget about this challenge! I have needed you for a long time, and you are here at last."

Vishnumitra feels his purpose weakening. The promise he has made to his art, to his dead, feels now like a burden whose weight he can hardly bear. Bitterness and sorrow rise in his throat like bile. He wants to say: Why didn't you come back and keep your promise? Why did you abandon me? Why did you betray us all, betray the prana vidya itself?

Vishnumitra draws himself up, remembers his dharma. He brings deliberately to memory the imprisonments and murders that have befallen his dear companions, the practitioners of the art. He remains standing, ignoring Upamanyu's invitation to sit down.

"I need answers, Upamanyu, not pretty speeches. Tell me, why did you ban the prana vidya? Why have your spies pursued and killed the practitioners these many years?"

"Come, my friend, can I afford to have every fool in the empire learn and use what is the most arcane of arts? Why do you think I look so young, although I am older than you in years? Ah, I can see from your face that you know, or suspect. I am the best practitioner of the art in the empire, and it is that which has kept me young. It is that which allows me to defend myself from my enemies. Do you blame me for making sure that nobody else can be an adept in the art?"

"I am also an adept," Vishnumitra says softly. "And I might look twenty years younger, but I have aged, Upamanyu. What you are doing is against cosmic order. The prana vidya is not to be misused to confer immortality."

"Cosmic order will survive, my friend! Do you not recall the old stories about the sages who lived for thousands of years? Here I thought you'd congratulate me upon my great discovery! I have wandered far, from mountain to desert, read countless ancient tomes, studied under the most learned of teachers to teach myself what nobody else would, or could. The manipulation of the mahaprana itself!"

Looking at him, Vishnumitra is struck by how young Upamanyu is, not only in appearance but in mind. It is as though the companion of his boyhood is back, with his lively intelligence, his curiosity, his unending propensity for play. The playful look is in those bright eyes.

"I wish to choose my weapon."

"What if I refuse your challenge?"

"You will not refuse, Upamanyu."

An unreadable expression in Upamanyu's eyes. The shoulders drop, and when he speaks it is the same light tone, but resigned. Regretful.

"Choose, then."

"I choose combat by prana vidya."

Vishnumitra has done this before, used manipulation of prana to kill. When someone is dying in great pain, it is a mercy to let the individual prana flow cease, to draw life out gently, as one draws the last of thread from a spindle. He has never used this skill to murder. But his way is clear.

Upamanyu is shaking his head as though Vishnumitra has just proposed something quite absurd, but he comes up to Vishnumitra, and their hands meet. Fingertip to fingertip, then clasping lightly, as though they might be about to draw each other into an embrace. Vishnumitra can sense the prana flow in the other's body—thick and strong. He senses the other finding his own prana flow as a bird on the wing might sense the landscape below. The duel begins.

Vishnumitra attempts to still the flow, to draw life and breath and consciousness from Upamanyu, and in the beginning Upamanyu simply resists. He is smiling a little, but Vishnumitra hardly notices. He is intent upon the task, looking for weaknesses in the chakras, turbulence in the nadis. The thing is to take Upamanyu by surprise, to strike without warning, as he scans his friend's subtle body with that gentle inner gaze. Then he's hit.

It feels as though the world has suddenly grown dark. Controlling his breath, Vishnumitra finds his balance; the light returns. He fights back. They are going back and forth, sending great waves of weakness, invisible sword-cuts that might stop the heart or constrict a blood vessel. Every few minutes Vishnumitra is aware of that gaze, so light, contemplative even. He is aware that deep within him there is a great resistance to kill the man he loves. Surely there is another way! In his pain and love he cries out:

"In the name of the art, which you betrayed, in the names of those whom you had imprisoned and killed, for Shankara, who was innocent in her fierceness and courage, I beg you, Upamanyu, to repent by choosing death! Do not make me kill you!"

Upamanyu's face is intent, sweat has broken out over his brow.

"*Nobody* can kill me . . ."

And Vishnumitra sees with his inner eye what Upamanyu has done, how he can kill an adept in the art, how he must have killed

Shankara. The columns of mahaprana that rain down from the sky are joining and coalescing, coming down at him, filling every part of his being with the life force, a fullness that his body cannot take. For a moment Upamanyu is Indra himself, wielding the thunderbolt. Vishnumitra knows for a split second the beauty of the cosmic prana, the vastness of the mystery that they have barely begun to comprehend, and he knows that he has done wrong, just as Upamanyu has, to use the prana vidya for murder. As he accepts his death, welcomes it as a man guided by dharma must, he senses the capillaries on his skin bursting. A pain in his chest, his lungs, and he is losing consciousness, falling to the floor. Then blessed darkness and he knows nothing at all.

When Vishnumitra came to, the first thing he noticed was the smell. It was a rotten odor, sickly sweet, like spoiled fruit. He hurt all over. Gradually, through the pain, he realized he was alive. He was lying on a great pile of refuse, above which he could see the silhouette of the fort wall, a dark wave against the starlit sky. He tried to sit up and groaned as the pain hit him anew. Lying back in the filth, he tasted his defeat, and the struggles that still lay ahead, and the bitterness of knowing that he—greatest of the practitioners of the art (or so he'd thought), defender of the prana vidya, had ultimately betrayed it and failed all the ones he loved. He shuddered in the cold air.

Why had Upamanyu left him alive?

He should be dead!

He must have lain there for many hours before he noticed the horse. There was a faint radiance in the eastern sky, although the darkness was still profound. Against that sky stood the king's stallion, black, strong, unmistakable. There was no rider.

Vishnumitra dragged his broken body off the pile of trash and crawled to where the stallion stood. The horse bent its great head, snorting softly, blowing twin puffs of breath from the enormous nostrils. Vishnumitra saw the pale shape of a rolled scroll hanging from the saddle and reached for it. He lay gasping on the hard ground, waiting for the light. The horse waited too.

Dear brother, [Upamanyu wrote]

I regret the pain I have caused you, but perhaps it is better this way. As I said I have awaited your coming these many years. Kingship has been very interesting but I grow weary of it. You recall that your father's explanation of the mahaprana when I was just a boy launched me on a journey of discovery. My kingdom was but a stop on the way to greater adventures, one that enabled me to consolidate my knowledge and distracted me pleasantly with interesting dilemmas. I have as yet no answer to the question I once posed your father: From whence does the cosmic prana arise? What is the origin of the life force beyond this earth? Some invoke gods but I seek no such convenient answers. My dabbling with the knowledge of the mechanical forces convinces me that one will lead me to the other. The Chinese have been experimenting with propulsion power for eons, and in my own small laboratory I have found enough evidence that a carefully designed craft might bear the weight of a man to the endless skies. There I will fly as the Vidyadharas are said to do, and seek the adventures that have constantly beckoned my soul.

Meanwhile, I leave you my horse (with great regret as he, strengthened by my knowledge of prana vidya, has been my dear companion these many years). And I leave you my kingdom. I have talked all night with my chief queen, the peerless Jahanara, who has known for some time that I have a brother in spirit. She is to be trusted, as is Noori, her slave and my best spy, who is an expert archer and fighter. My minister, Sukhwant Singh, will guide you as well. Your name, my friend, is Ambar Khan, and you are born of a Muslim father and a Hindu mother (this small reversal of the truth I deemed necessary in order to explain away any Hindu traits that you, the next Mughal king, might display). Do not fear that such a thing would betray you, for I have attempted to re-create as much as possible the vibrant hybrid culture that I so enjoyed in your father's ashram. I have prepared the ground, you see, for the past few years, in the hope that you might come, although what it took to draw you out was the girl Shankara's death. It might comfort you to know that she fought bravely to the end, and that I spared her pain at the passing. So I bid you, dear brother, to save and keep what I have built—the most prosperous kingdom in the hemisphere, if not the world. This morning at dawn one of my proxies will appear at the jharokha as usual, for the people of the city must see their king daily. I will be well on my way by then, on the north road out of Dilli, once more a traveler on a quest, unhampered by the burdens of the settled life. My heart will be as light as my pack, which contains little besides a device or two of my invention, a few books—and a bagful of rice from the one place that felt like home to me.

Now you must take my horse to the inn an hour's journey from the gate, and rest and recover a while. Just before sunset I bid you ride into the city from the Eastern gate on my horse. The smallest child in the city knows that the new king will, like Akbar Khan, take the kingdom without a single weapon, riding in on this very horse, the noble Vikram. I have signed documents stating that none of my offspring will inherit the throne, which is perhaps the main reason they have not killed each other. Apparently the latter is a tradition among the Mughals.

If you do not wish to be king, simply let my horse return to the city. Sukhwant Singh will know what to do. But I am confident that you, who have always been led by your dharma, will not betray the people who await you.

Through all my life I have resisted giving my heart to another. It would only be a distraction from my quest, which is to comprehend the mysteries that surround me, and thus to comprehend myself. I have never even told anyone the name I was born with—I have worn names as another man might wear clothes. Yet you, Vishnumitra, took my heart from me without my knowledge or permission. I knew this as I stood over your body. My anger—unused to defiance all these years, and honed by the sutras of the ancient, rageful sage Durvasa, who lived five thousand years—flared up as we dueled. In that moment I would have given up my careful plans to install you in my place (a wise ruler always has other options prepared)—*I would have killed you, my friend, but when I held the hand that had brought me the rice from his mother's kitchen, I could not do it. So have I learned that my knowledge of myself is far from complete, and this humbles me.*

I do not know if you will forgive me. I will not insult you or those dear to you I killed by asking it of you. But consider this: you have a vast network of practitioners of the prana vidya spread all over the country. This great instrument I have forged as much as you have, by pruning the incompetent or the rash. Use it as you will, for in the days ahead there will be much turmoil. Sher Shah in the North-West shows signs of impatience, there are rumors the Portuguese king is mad, and as the British lose their hold over the South, their envious gaze turns northwards.

So, dear brother, farewell! I go north to China now, to the next adventure. Only the sky—Ambar!—is my limit! May you and yours find peace.

Your brother in spirit,
Upamanyu

Vishnumitra read this missive three times. The horse whinnied softly, and at last he put the scroll away in his shirt and staggered shakily to his feet. He leaned against the horse's side and wept for all he had lost, and for all the losses still to come. He thought of the curve of the great river of his home, and the steps of the ghat leading down to the grey water, and the kind-eyed elephants sporting by the shore. He saw in memory the bright saris of his mother and sisters, and the golden walls of the ashram. Then, with great difficulty, he hoisted himself upon the horse, and lay for a moment against his neck, panting. He wiped his tears with his tattered sleeve and turned the horse away from the city toward the inn, to await the sunset of all he had known. Above him the last stars went out in the vast bowl of the sky.

Peripeteia

I T OCCURRED TO Sujata that what she was experiencing was a kind of life-after-living. Veenu's abrupt and unexplained departure three days ago was a clean dividing line between what she had thought of as her life and the inexplicable state of being that came after. A phase transition as fundamental as that of water boiling in the saucepan, turning to steam, she thought, stirring in the tea leaves. The brown ink spread through the water the way pain seeped through every part of her being. She'd become, in her post-life, a sponge for metaphors, a hammer to which everything was yet another nail in the coffin of that earlier existence. The other day she had found herself wandering disconsolately through the park between frolicking, screaming children, staring at Lost Cat notices on the utility poles, and she'd thought of posting a notice—Lost: The Ground Under My Feet.

It was getting dark; she left the tea steeping in the pan and turned on the kitchen light. The brightness hurt her eyes. White walls, white counters, the potted coriander on the windowsill, the small dining table piled with sympathy cards. The fridge snored like a polar bear. On a shelf to its left was a little altar from the time Sujata's mother had visited last year; it held a smiling Buddha and a Nataraja, a somewhat garish print of Lakshmi, and a Jehovah's Witness pamphlet showing an equally garish Christ. Sujata's mother didn't really have any basis for believing in God, a fact she would readily admit, but she liked to plan for contingencies. She'd put Jesus up there with the others, as she said, "just in case." The wall across from the window bore witness to Sujata's own probabilistic approach to the universe: it was covered almost entirely with sticky notes in yellow, green, and pink, fluttering in the breeze from the window like so many prayer flags. Here, in Sujata's tiny, neat hand, were maps of possibility, random thoughts, and notes on a variety of subjects that had caught her interest. In the middle there was a large sheet of paper with a graph showing two world-lines, hers in purple, Veenu's in green, two lines crawling across the white space, more or less parallel, until three days ago when Veenu packed up and left. Since that time the purple line had crawled forward, tentative and alone.

The latest series of sticky notes was an exercise in possibility. Imagine a phenomenon, and write down all possible explanations and descriptions. Then some time-dependent weighted combination of these was (maybe) an approximation to the ever-changing truth.

Who or What is Veenu?

An idea. A beginning and end in one, a snake chasing its tail.

A lover, a partner, a friend.

An offspring of the mind's deepest sigh.

A neural implant, an AI that enables us to network with others at a thought.

Defined by my existence, the way Veenu's existence defines mine.

A traveler through the whorls and eddies of space and time, whose world-line sometimes intercepts with mine.

An imaginary friend who didn't go away when I grew up.

She picked up the last one, which had fallen off the wall, and stuck it back next to the others.

"You're so *weird*," Veenu used to say, in an indulgent tone. She approved of eccentricity as a matter of principle, but was the more practical of the two of them. "Why don't you go back to your paper on the Higgs field?"

The paper on the Higgs field had been sitting in Sujata's laptop for three months. The trouble, she had said to Veenu—goodness, was that just a few days ago?—the trouble was that the paper was straightforward and eminently publishable, and therefore not very interesting. She'd rather write a paper entitled "The Higgs Field Considered as a Metaphor for the Entanglement of Matter in Time," or "Alien Manipulations and the Unfinished Universe."

She was sipping the too-bitter tea when the road appeared. As always the apparition came without warning; the only hint of its impending arrival was a dull headache and a slight visual aura. Then the wall, the one with the sticky notes and the graph, began to shimmer and crackle like an old television set between channels. After which there was no wall at all, just the white and dusty road.

She dropped the cup. Bits of china crunched under her shoes as she walked through where the wall had been, and stood on the road. It smelled vaguely of burning insulation, with a hint of cinnamon.

She had developed a ritual by now: look to the left, into the past first, a check for accuracy. Yes, there was the misty bulk of the university building where she worked, and the coffee shop where she and Veenu used to hang out most evenings until the impossible happened—and beyond that, a sloping green hill from her undergraduate days, and then the trees she climbed as a child, and the chai shop she frequented in high school. The order was a little muddled, and the images vague and shifting in the mist, but she could recognize each thing.

She steeled herself to look to the right, toward the future. There was a deafening beat in her ears. Would there be any indication of Veenu's return?

On every previous sighting the future had appeared as a turbulent dust haze, a shifting cloud bank, through which vague images were sometimes discernible. On occasion these were visions of the road itself, flowing like a dark river through an unfamiliar green land, branching and bifurcating into the horizon. This she had interpreted as some kind of probability graph, a reassurance that the future was not determined, that she could choose her path. Sometimes other, more mysterious or terrifying silhouettes emerged from the cloud bank—a decrepit house by a river, a figure on a sloping roof, a sadness that was without shape or form, but recognizable as a sharp jab in the ribs, a sudden breathlessness. Once there had been an incongruous white tower like one of the minarets of the Taj, but she had never encountered it in real life, and it had not been there in subsequent sightings of the road. Her hypothesis was that some futures were more likely than others, and that the future with the white minaret had simply been eliminated through the games of chance.

She closed her eyes before looking. When she opened them, she saw, to her complete astonishment, that the road ended to her right. No mist, no vague shapes, no branching paths into a semi-determined future, but just a clean line where the road abruptly stopped. There was nothing beyond it but a blank wall. She was so astounded by this that she staggered toward the demarcation before remembering that it was never any use walking on the road, left or right. It was the sort of road where the destination maintained a constant distance from the traveler, no matter how fast or far she walked. She rubbed her eyes and looked again, but nothing had changed. She thought: this means I'm going to die.

Abruptly she was back in the kitchen. The lower part of her left trouser-leg was cold and wet with tea, and there were bits of china on the floor everywhere. The air was still. The familiarity and emptiness filled her with foreboding. She looked at the wall she had walked through—it was solid again, and a few more of the sticky notes had fallen off.

There was no sign of impending death. Perhaps it would come tomorrow, or the day after. Or maybe there was another interpretation for that clearly demarcated finish line. *Something* had ended. But what, exactly?

She stayed up half the night, sipping tea and munching on dry crackers, thinking about Veenu and waiting for death. When death refused to oblige, she went to bed.

Next evening, after a day at work in which she felt as though she were swimming upstream through a bewilderingly swift river, Sujata returned to the house, exhausted.

There were more cards in the mailbox. She picked them up and threw them on the dining table in the kitchen. The house was silent as a tomb, except for the refrigerator's constant purr. She stood in the dark by the window. The neighborhood was quiet, lights on behind curtained windows. There wasn't a soul in sight. The neat lawns and fenced back-yards of suburban America—every house a prison unto itself. Her rev-erie was disturbed by the cards falling off the table. A fury took hold of her then—she picked up a mass of cards in her hands and threw them up into the air. They were all around her like a pack of predatory birds. She was finally going insane, or so it seemed; the cards flapped away at her, calling out what was written in them in high-pitched voices. *Thinking of you, wishing you strength for this difficult time.* Theater tickets. People trying to be kind, without actually getting involved, people trying to mask their shock at the unthinkable: Veenu leaving, without warning, without a word! As though what had happened to Sujata was something shame-ful, something that might infect their own blessedly ordinary lives or threaten the security of their relationships. She batted at the cards, tear-ing them from the air, tearing them into little bits. At last the cards fell silent, lying torn and tattered on the floor, and she knelt down, sobbing like a child, pleading with the universe for some kind of explanation. The universe, not being obliged to reply, remained silent.

At last she gathered the torn cards and put them in the recycling, and washed her face. Three of her sticky notes had fallen off the white wall. She picked them up and stuck them back on.

Alien Manipulations in an Unfinished Universe: an Anti-Occam's Razor Hypothesis

The neutrino was predicted by Wolfgang Pauli in 1930. It took until 1956 to discover that it actually existed.

One of the great predictions of particle physics, from considerations of symmetry, was the Omega particle. Predicted in 1962, discovered in 1964.

In an effort to distract herself, Sujata made some tea, set out a plate of cookies, and began to complete the list. Pink sticky notes on the prediction and discovery of the tau neutrino, the top and bottom quarks, dark matter, the Higgs boson.

When Sujata was in graduate school, she had founded the Anti-Occam's Razor Society. Membership varied between one and four.

Occam's Razor, a guiding principle of science, posited that the simplest idea that explained a phenomenon was most likely to be correct. She had always found this a dull notion, a surrendering of the imagination to the tyranny of the mundane. She liked to invent complicated explanations for straightforward phenomena, a kind of intellectual Rube-Goldbergism, just to thumb her nose at William of Occam. It was a joke, of course.

Over the years, as an extension of the long joke of ideas, she'd come up with the Alien Manipulation hypothesis. This is how she had first explained it to Veenu:

The universe is a massive quantum-mechanical relativistic Rube Goldberg machine in continual need of adjustment by a bunch of super-intelligent aliens. Suppose an intelligent species comes up with a theory, and a prediction. The aliens then adjust the machine in order to make the prediction come true. One reason why interstellar civilizations cannot meet is because contradictory predictions must be avoided. There is bedrock reality—you know, Pythagoras' theorem, gravity, not falling through floors. But beyond bedrock reality there are multiple ways to explain the universe, and the duplicitous alien manipulators ensure that we are taken in by our own illusions. But—if everything we predicted was exactly right, we would become suspicious, or worse, even more arrogant than we are now. So they throw in the occasional surprise result—accelerating expansion of the universe, stars at the edges of galaxies moving faster than visible matter would entail.

They had laughed about it, she and Veenu. That the universe is an illusion had been suspected by many a mystic in many a tradition, but to construct an argument based on logic and physics was truly fun. Every once in a while Sujata would get a feeling of a feather (or antenna) being drawn slowly down her spine, and she would shiver. It was as though the alien overlords of the universe were warning her not to think (outside the box) too much. Because however indulgent these entities might be toward the intellectual inventions of human beings, the one idea they would not want people to take too seriously was this: that the whole thing was a goddamned magic show; that all laws were ad hoc, imperfect, made-up, inelegant. If the Standard Model was so messy that even particle physicists called it the sub-standard model, then better to let people believe that it was only a part of a greater, more elegant truth, instead of accepting that reality itself was a mess.

Veenu: How would you know that the universe is one giant theater performance, with your hypothetical aliens running the show? I mean, if it is all show, how would you get to go backstage?

Sujata (after a week): I think you'd have to bump up against something that was irrefutably there—a phenomenon or an artifact or a prop—that didn't fit anywhere on stage. Something that couldn't be explained in any schema.

Veenu: So you mean you'd have to catch the aliens napping?

Sujata: Yes. Yes, I know. Sounds unlikely.

Veenu (accusingly): And you wouldn't know whether your unexplained phenomenon was just a really hard problem you were up against, or whether it was something that violated all explanations of reality . . . I think your idea is full of shit.

Sujata (unreasonably annoyed): Well, of course! Can't you take a joke? Of course it's full of shit!

It was at that moment she realized she sort-of believed the shit. Despite all reason, all sensible feeling, it rang true, at least in a coarse-grained way. There were details to work out . . . So far, for each phenomenon in her life she had found a schema, a scaffolding in which things fit, made sense. When they didn't, it usually meant that there were other schemas to be invented and elaborated. An essential element of science was the faith, after all, that the universe was comprehensible.

Until the day Veenu walked away.

Furiously she began to scribble a new series of sticky notes, in green:

Hypotheses for Veenu's Departure

Schema One: I am a terrible person who did something wrong. I am so stupid that I don't even know what it is I did wrong. Stupid, naïve, what's the difference? (Unless she has amnesia, she can't recall anything that could cause Veenu to leave.)

Schema Two: There's been some misunderstanding. (There've been misunderstandings before and they've always managed to work through them.)

Schema Three: Veenu left because there was something urgent that needed doing, nothing to do with me. (An attractive idea: Veenu as a secret agent with some kind of covert agenda, but there are no supporting pieces of evidence—although if the agent was really secret, would there be?)

Schema Four: Veenu is insane and irrational. (Veenu is one of the most clear-headed and rational people she knows.)

Schema Five: Veenu is not what I thought she was; despite these years of knowing Veenu, I really don't know Veenu. So I am blind as well as naïve and stupid.

She stayed up that night coming up with seventeen more schemas, researching each, and coming up empty. The facts didn't fit the hypotheses, although there were some facts that fit some, if only slightly. Of all of them, only Schema Five had a somewhat higher probability than the others.

To know something, or someone, is to be able to see them without the cloud of preconceived notions, prejudices, and paradigms that we carry around with us. But is it even possible to lose that cloud? Everyone goes about with such a cloud, and inevitably their world-view is distorted, refracted, diffracted. It's as inevitable as an electron carrying around with it its cloak of virtual particles. Nothing in the frigging universe is naked.

The interesting thing was this: Schema Five was consistent with her half-in-jest notion that the universe was a sham controlled by crazed aliens. As the dawn light poured in through the kitchen window, she remembered another conversation she had once had with Veenu.

Veenu: So tell me more about your idea.

Sujata: Well, there are the deadjims.

Veenu: The what?

Sujata: It's an old *Star Trek* joke . . . did I tell you I used to watch *Star Trek* all through graduate school? Well, I made up the word from something to do with *Star Trek*, for the people who've figured it out.

Veenu: Figured what out?

Sujata: You know. That the universe is a sham run by aliens. They know there is no point trying to come up with grand unified theories of the physical universe. Or of human nature. The aliens did a shoddy job of putting together a foundation for the universe, and they take our ideas and improvise with them to do the finishing touches. Take the Higgs boson . . .

Veenu: Never mind the Higgs boson. You already told me how it took so long for the aliens to construct the evidence for it. Tell me about the deadjims.

Sujata: There's this homeless guy who hangs around outside the grocery store, looking for a handout. Big, smelly guy with a salt-and-pepper beard. Used to be a brilliant physicist. All he'll tell me is that it doesn't mean anything to him anymore. There's this look in his eyes, like he's seeing through everything. You know, from the parking lots and the walls to the scripted conversations between people—he sees what's under it, what's real. And it's not a grand unified theory he sees, it's a mess.

Veenu: So he's a deadjim?

Sujata: He's a deadjim.

Veenu: Is there no other choice? Confronted with your hypothesis a person could become a nihilist, an existentialist, even a bodhisattva!

Sujata (annoyed): Not necessarily. There are different reasons why people become nihilists or bodhisattvas. A deadjim is a person who's seen through the façade, the surface illusions . . . oh, I see your point. Damn!

Veenu (consolingly): Still, it's a damned cool idea. The aliens-at-the-controls is nothing new, but the deadjims! Nice touch.

Sujata (growling): Stop mocking me.

Veenu (thoughtfully): Tell me something else, though. If I dream up an idea, something totally crazy, like "the distant stars are made of cheese," does that mean the aliens will have to scramble to make it so?

Sujata: It doesn't work like that! That would be stupid. See, ideas have to have weight. Weight comes from internal consistency, and how much in line the idea is with the bedrock, the foundation the aliens have already laid. Weight also comes from how long the idea has lain around, and how many people believe it.

Veenu: You really believe this, don't you? So why do you keep publishing papers in physics?

Sujata: One, we have to eat. Two, I don't want the aliens to suspect that I'm on to them, do I? Plus it's fun to have a role in the construction of the universe. Hey, don't look at me like that! I don't really believe this shit! I like making things up, in case you haven't figured it out by now!

Over the next few days Sujata went about her life doing what was expected of her, in a blind and oblivious fashion. She had to play the game for now. That's what everyone else did, didn't they? Step around each other in polite little circles, mouthing scripted lines, as though from a play. When the actor realizes it's just a play, what can the actor do but continue to repeat her words? When there are no words she can come up with as a substitute?

In the evenings she wrote furiously on sticky notes until she ran out of room on the white wall. She stuck some around her mother's little altar, so that they formed colorful little haloes around the Buddha, the Nataraja, the garish Lakshmi, and Jesus.

Sujata's Cosmic Censorship Principle: All material objects are surrounded by clouds of ambiguity—which may be virtual particles or prejudices or paradigms. Nothing in the universe is naked.

Sujata's Cosmic Uncertainty Principle: The universe exists as a superposition of unformed possibilities for theorists to speculate about, and experimenters to discover. The alien technicians set things up so that the "discovery" causes a possibility or a combination thereof to become "real."

She submitted her paper on the Higgs boson (the straightforward one) without bothering to review it, and began work on "The Higgs Field Considered as a Metaphor for the Entanglement of Matter in Time."

Just as the Higgs field gives mass to matter through coupling with various particles to different degrees, so does an analogous field tangle us in linear time, like a leaf carried by a river.

De-couple from that field, and you can wander outside of linear time. Aliens do not want you to do this because then you can see what they've been up to.

The thought came to Sujata then that the people she called deadjims must be able to do such a thing, that if she was turning into a deadjim too, she should be able to walk off linear time and see what the aliens were up to, if they were really there.

Sujata had been fourteen when she had first realized there was something strange about the universe. It happened when she began to notice that whenever she drew a graph, within a day or two she would see the shape of it in the real world: a city skyline, the planes of a face, the curving of a stair railing in a tall building. When she drew her first world-line, in her relativity class in high school, the road appeared before her for the first time. It took a few of these ghostly visitations for her to realize that the road was nothing but a world-line, her world-line, her path in life through space and time, made real, or as real as a vision could get. After that first time, the road appeared at random intervals, without warning. She had learned early in life that the universe was more than the notions of theorists and pundits.

As she remembered this, a thought came to her. She had been chewing the end of her pen; she set it down on an untouched plate of fish tacos. She marched up to the white wall and glared at it, and demanded silently that the road appear. This had never worked before. Her head hurt; the sticky notes swam before her eyes. There was a shimmer and a crackle, and the smell of hot plastic and cinnamon. There, before her, was the road.

———

This time she did walk up to the demarcation, the place where the road ended. At first the road seemed to make a half-hearted effort to maintain a distance between Sujata and the clean finish line, but her fury carried her forward until she was at the blank wall where the road stopped. She took a deep breath, tucked a stray tendril of hair behind her right ear, and walked through the wall.

She found herself on the lawn outside her house. The neighborhood was simultaneously familiar and different. She could tell that everything around was a hastily put-together construct. She didn't know how she could tell, because it looked the same. But some inner eye had opened within her. She had wandered backstage at last, and she could see, in a manner of speaking, the supports for the stage-sets, the gantries, the unpainted cardboard backs of the façade that made up reality. She walked around like a child, eyes round with wonder, and saw that her own life was nothing—all her theories and assumptions, her hypotheses about particles or people, were as intangible and meaningless as the cobwebs you brush away from your face when you enter a dark, abandoned room. Even meaning had no meaning. It was all a goddamned sham.

The why of it bothered her, though. Why would the aliens take all this trouble to deceive? What was in it for them?

The kid next door waved to her from his front porch. Bright little seven-year-old with a mop of copper-colored hair—she'd help him with mathematics problems sometimes. She could see him with her inner eye, the atoms and molecules ghost-like, great voids of emptiness between them, the forces and reactions clear in places, fuzzy in others, where the processes had not yet been determined or invented. He was a ghost, a hastily put-together construct, needing and awaiting constant tinkering. She stared at him, at the maple trees, whose branches nodded at her as though in agreement. She saw the door of her own house. How had she gotten outside? Oh yes, she had walked through the wall. That meant she was probably locked out, not that it mattered. The road had ended for her because world-lines were part of the illusion of pattern and order. Once you saw that, no need for the illusion. The world swam before her, unfinished and awkward and imperfect. So that is how the homeless man at the grocery store had seen it. She knew that if she looked into a mirror she would find in her eyes the same look. She was a deadjim, and it was funny and not funny at the same time. Veenu's bizarre behavior had been the thing you could not explain away. Who, or what, was Veenu then?

She caught herself. There she was, constructing another schema. It was an endless obsession. Humans were so desperate for pattern that they had to invent it, construct it, even where it did not exist. Were other animals like that? Other aliens on other worlds? She thought of the gulf of space and time, and the impossibility of two species meeting and understanding each other. Different schemas might simply tear the cosmic fabric apart, shoddily constructed as it was.

She began to wander through the neighborhood. Although everything was as usual—the cars in the driveways, the shuttered windows, the guarded expressions on the faces of the few people she passed, the formulaic greetings, the sun beating down on the parking lot in front of the grocery store—she was suddenly frightened. "A nightmare," she said to herself. "I'm in a nightmare, and I'll wake up and have tea with Veenu and everything will be back to normal." But it wasn't. She passed the place near the store entrance where the homeless man always sat in a dilapidated heap, and as their eyes met, he seemed to solidify, to come into focus. A look of recognition passed between them that terrified her. She turned to go home.

The kid was still there on the front porch of his house. He waved again. Something occurred to her. She went up to him in desperation. Looking at him deliberately made him clearer, more real. She said, "Peter, who else lives in my house?"

Peter's eyes went wide.

"Nobody, just you," he said. He smiled a little tentatively.

"Why am I getting sympathy cards then?"

"Because . . . your mother died." He stared at her.

She rubbed her hand across her face. She stumbled away to her house and sat heavily down on the front steps. She scratched absently at an itch on her left calf, where a mosquito had bitten her. She sensed its fat little body, replete with blood, its hum in her ear as it sailed away. For a moment she could see, through its compound eyes, the crazy, patchwork swaying world.

There was a pad of sticky notes in her pocket. She had no pen. She plucked a blade of grass and began to write in invisible script.

The universe does not need a bunch of control-freak aliens. The aliens are among us. The aliens are us.

The universe is a giant quantum-mechanical relativistic Rube-Goldberg patchwork construct, knit by interactions of its constituents, changed and ever changing through these interactions.

All we ever see are shadows cast on the wall of our limited understanding, and the shadows change depending on how the beast of reality mutates, and which way you shine the light.

She half smiled. She was caught in her net of schemas just as much as before.

She looked up. The bright day was fading. She saw the familiar neighborhoods of middle America, the green lawns of Indrapal University, and the hornbills sailing awkwardly through sunset skies. She saw the tree she'd fallen off as a child. The scar was still there on her knee. She saw the people with whom she'd shared her life, so distant now, separated by space and time and more.

Then she saw Veenu striding through all the jagged pieces of reality, the backpack flung carelessly over one shoulder. She thought of calling out, but then she saw the serenity in Veenu's face, the way her arms swung as though she might take off into the air at any point. In her eyes was the same curious, interested, engaged look that Sujata knew so well. Long after she had gone, Sujata sat on the step, thinking about her choices. Before anything, she had to call her uncle, book a flight to Mumbai. The empty space inside her was filling up slowly with sorrow, like rain. She felt it as surely as she'd felt the mosquito's bite. She would go for the funeral. After that . . . after that, who knew? She'd have to think about it later.

Lifepod

Sometimes the Eavesdropper remembered being a mother. She would stare at the single empty life-sac and think about the man who should have been lying there in cold sleep, the man who had once been the boy she'd held in her arms. At other moments she was convinced that she had done no such thing, that motherhood had never happened to her, that all she had ever been was what she was now: a traveler on an interminable journey between the stars, afloat in the belly of the Lifepod. At these moments, when even the human sleepers seemed to take on a terrifying unfamiliarity, she would feel as though she were at the edge of some calamitous discovery.

But these hanging, empty moments of anticipation were few. Almost immediately she would be distracted by the thought-clouds, the dreams of the men and women in cold sleep. There were two of them in particular who had once meant something to her: a man and a woman. She returned to their thought-worlds whenever she herself was awake, as though the tattered clouds of their remembrances would bring back to her what she had been. It was rather like eating (she still remembered that, at least) and, at the end, still coming away hungry. The life-sacs were filmy, translucent; she couldn't see their faces, only the vague human shape suspended in a watery garden, but she knew them by their thought-signatures, by the worlds of their dreams.

The Man

The man dreamed obsessively of the enemy. Through him she saw the great creatures with their giant, stiff wing (single, like a cloak) folded on their backs, the round, featureless heads swiveling from one side to another, scanning through some invisible means the bleak landscape of his moon-world. The aliens stopped before the broken bodies that littered the battlefield, pausing before human and alien remains, while the young man crouched in the shadow of an outbuilding, trying not to breathe. Through his memories the Eavesdropper saw the long vertical gash on the abdomen of each alien: the lipless mouth open wide into a horrific darkness, the delicacy with which the prehensile edges of the orifice gathered in each body like an embrace and closed around it. She felt the young man's horror, his anger, going through her like a cold knife.

But sometimes he dreamed of a green and primitive place on a distant planet. His childhood: running in a long, green meadow with patches of bare earth and wild tussocks of grass that would make him stumble so that suddenly he would be looking between grass shoots into an ant's world. And the washer with its arms aloft, swift-walking through the grass, back and forth, making the wash billow out in the constant wind . . . The mother was holding a woven-reed tray full of yeri grains, shaking it so the tiny winged grains flew up and caught the currents, streaming out in skeins of spotted gold, up the hill to the tanglewood, where the fine nets of the trees would catch them and they would sprout many months later. She did this just for him, not because she needed to; the seed-blower had done most of the job already, up high. He watched her brown arms, strong and rhythmic, and the seeds rippling out in wide ribbons, and laughed in delight. She smiled at him. Lying with his face against the ground, the boy saw her as a great tree, her bare, callused toes peering from between the folds of the blue sari like roots that would hold them all to the earth, her head up in the clouds, long black hair turning to gray, loosening from the bun at the back of her neck so that the tendrils were fanned by the breeze . . .

But what struck the Eavesdropper about this man, this boy, was the way he felt about his mother: she was the bedrock of his world.

At these times she felt the shock of familiarity: that she had once been the recipient of such an uncomplicated love. But her memories were unreliable; she recalled things that she had apparently experienced or done that seemed distant, unfamiliar, shocking. She knew for instance that she had herself spent a long time with the enemy aliens, but the knowledge of precisely what had happened—the capture, the incarceration of the humans, including herself, their journey through space in the alien ship in cold sleep, the attack or explosion that had blown the little Lifepod away into space on some random trajectory—the details were blurred in her mind, her personal memory contaminated by those of the others. Whatever she remembered came to her in flashes or glimpses: pungent, warren-like passageways, blind gropings in the heat of a room, the press of terrified bodies, the great silhouette of the alien in the doorway, its mind reaching out to her mind, calming it, telling her what to do (what was it she had been told with such urgency?), and she remembered also sweet hunger, and nutrients snaking out into her in thin, aromatic streams, and the mourning and celebrating of a death . . .

The Eavesdropper

The Eavesdropper moved slowly through the darkness of the Lifepod, floating over each womb-like holding unit, tasting the dreams of each dreamer. But what do *I* dream of, then, when I sleep, she thought to herself. She wondered, as she often had, why her own holding sac allowed her to wake and move about, and return to it only when she needed nutrients or rest. Each life-sac was a little eco-system of alien life-forms: bacterial blooms, algal fans that generated currents of nutrients and harvested waste, the whole maintaining a delicate symbiotic relationship with each occupant. But her sac was unique, larger than the rest, its chemistry adjusted to allow her these moments of wakefulness. Why had she been given this privilege? The vision of the alien in the doorway so many years ago came to her mind as the answer: Was that what it had told her so urgently, to see to the safety of her people, the humans? Why? Where were they being taken before the explosion cast them into space? Why hadn't they been killed? What had been her relationship with the alien? Sometimes she thought of it with simple hatred and fear, the unknown, the monster of nightmare moving across the ruined battlefield; then she would realize that she was seeing it through the eyes of one of the dreamers. When she admitted this to herself she felt as though cracks had appeared in her understanding of the universe, little fissures that threatened to open up and swallow her. She had betrayed her people, these people, in some way. Hadn't she? Else why would she have gotten the privilege (or curse) of wakefulness during this long voyage? Why would she remember the alien with half-buried, shameful hunger (what had they done to her? With her?), with—yes, there was no escaping it—longing, as though the alien had satisfied in her some terrible, chemical need?

Sometimes she thought she saw the alien in the Lifepod. She would feel its presence just beyond the edge of her perceptions, as though it was waiting in the shadows beyond that life-sac or this one. Once or twice she thought she saw its face, so unimaginably strange, yet so familiar, hovering ghost-like just beyond the pale radiance from the life-sacs, or half-concealed among the knotted ganglia of the Lifepod itself. When she approached the phantom or mirage it would dissolve into the darkness, so that in her saner moments she knew it was not really there. At other times she wanted to believe it was there, to know that there was someone watching over her, tasting *her* dreams, knowing *her* thoughts.

And then there were her hands.

They were not as she remembered them; in the half-light, the brown skin was mottled, thickened, her nails grown long. She held the hands before her, floating in a shawl of moisture from her life-sac, and wondered if she herself was the alien in the shadows. She would convince herself very quickly that this could not be so, because the memories she had of being human, even the borrowed ones, were so vivid and familiar. These little debates with herself were a comfort; it was such a human thing to do, after all, to argue with your own doubts and fears when awake in the dark.

But she couldn't come to any definite conclusion because of the voices in her mind. Sometimes something spoke to her without words, deep inside her head. She wasn't certain if it was the alien, the Lifepod in which they were adrift, or some lost memory of her own. It could not be the Lifepod, she reasoned; the Lifepod's mind was barely discernible to her, and what she could read of it was child-like and strange. It had been grown quickly from the body of the alien ship to host the captured humans, and when the explosion blew it away from the ship, it had not had time to mature. It knew how to maintain the environment on which they all depended and to protect itself, and to sing out its name on all permitted frequencies, but it did not know that it was going to die. It did not know that after a certain time it would need to find a mother ship, to dock, to hibernate until it renewed itself for further flight. Here, in this uncharted, empty sector of the galaxy, who would hear it sing? Who would tell it what it needed, how to find it? It was hardly more than a child, singing in joyful ignorance in the dark between the stars.

Then who was it who told her things as she floated in her life-sac at the edge of sleep?

Some of the things she heard were memories, she told herself. She had been incarcerated somewhere in the caverns of the mother ship, among alien bodies, overhearing their conversation. Or it was the alien stowaway, if it existed, telling her all this, opening before her mind's eye the strange vistas of other worlds. Sometimes it would chant to her bits of its own lore, meaningless and frightening all at once, repeating the phrases like a child in a dark room, reciting for comfort. But nothing it said made sense.

To eat and be eaten is to become yourself and another. To eat is to give birth, to see with new eyes. Remember, remember this.

And:

We are separate so the whole may know itself. In eating, we edge closer to the Hidden One. Know this!

But she didn't know anything. Only that she might have been a mother once, and the man who was missing—who should have been in the empty life-sac—was perhaps her son. She knew that she, along with the others, had been captured from their colony on a moon-world. And that she had had some dealings with the enemy, things she would rather not admit to herself. So here they were, blasted away from the ship, adrift in the belly of an infant Lifepod, lost in the sea of night.

The Woman

The other sleeper who had once had some connection with the Eavesdropper was a woman who hadn't spoken for years, even before the capture. What had led her into silence was not an emotional or physiological condition, but a philosophical one. The Eavesdropper remembered this woman (whether through her own memories or through those of the other sleepers she could not always say) before the capture as a person who liked to be with the others but did little more than smile or nod. The woman liked the physical labor of the research camp; building and repair work, and tending the greenhouses, and when busy in these things she liked to hum strange little tunes, but spoke no words. The Eavesdropper knew that this woman had come to such a state because she had discovered the inadequacy of words. The woman was a scientist-poet whose reality had once been forged of words and mathematics. "Consider that antique concept, force," she had said once, before the silence, "which makes sense at your scale or mine. The ancients built their theories, their mathematics, around that concept. But the moment you enter the sub-atom, or when you begin to examine the graininess of space-time, you realize that the word 'force' has little meaning. You invent the field, another antique concept, and then that, too, fails. You abandon false analogies, then, you take refuge in strange axioms, in your mathematics. But go far enough and even mathematics fails as a descriptive, a language in which to describe nature. What do you have left, then?"

Somebody had laughed. The woman dreamed of a face, some-times, not yearningly, but with pleasure, and it was the face of the man who should have been lying here in the Lifepod, in the empty sac. "She dreams of my son," the Eavesdropper would say to herself. The man had laughed companionably in the woman's dreams. "When mathematics fails? Then there's only poetry," he had said, smiling—his brown eyes and skin aglow, his black hair so soft and shiny in the light. Only poetry, dreamed the sleeping woman, recalling this, recall-ing him.

This woman had spent a lifetime studying "the graininess of space-time." She had been part of the first team to map the tachyonic signatures that hinted at the existence of another universe underly-ing their own. They were only faint trails, like the tracks of ghost crabs walking on a sandy beach ("Ghost," said the Eavesdropper to herself. "Crab. Beach." And she saw a sweep of yellow sand, a wind-swept blue sky—an old memory, hers or the woman's.). The tachyon trails were regular, their mathematics sublime, their origins mysteri-ous. The woman had lived three hundred and seven Earth-years, trav-eling on slowships from world to inhabited world, cheating time and death so she could study these trails. "They call to me," she had said defensively to that man, the Eavesdropper's son. "They are the shape of something I do not understand. Something large, complex, per-haps self-aware." "How large?" "Of galactic proportions," she'd said seriously, enjoying his surprise. "Why else would you need tachyons? How else can your brain tell your arm to twitch if it is 400 light-years away?" "You have such ideas!" laughed the man, half-admiring, half-mocking. "I thought you said last time that the tachyons were evi-dence of another universe." "I did," she acknowledged, smiling. "It's a matter of words. Whether or not that thing is sentient, it is a universe unto itself."

He was a practical man, an engineer, a pilot, and a poet in three ancient languages, and he kept her sane. "I see a bit here, a bit there," she would tell him, frustrated, after several hours immersed in a holo of her theoretical construct. "But I never see the pattern as a whole, as one complete thing." And he'd looked at her a moment and quoted Kalidasa in the original Sanskrit.

> *I see your gaze in the deer's quick glance*
> *Your slender limbs in the shyama vine*
> *Your luminous beauty in the face of the moon . . .*
> *But, oh misfortune! I see not*
> *All of you in any one thing . . .*

Slowly, trying to put together the mathematics of the tachyon signatures, she had realized that no language existed—verbal or mathematical—that could describe them. "I must invent a meta-language," thought the dreamer, "a language beyond words and equations." She became outwardly silent, although her mind still chattered away in words and equations, but the Eavesdropper sometimes saw great and inexplicable vistas in the dreams of the sleeper: vast abstractions, geometries that defied the imagination, fractal swirls of color that rose and vanished, and she had the impression that the scientist-poet was indeed inventing a new language, iota by iota.

This then is poetry, thought the Eavesdropper to herself, and abruptly the memory of the alien would fill her mind. "Eat," the alien had said to her. "To eat is to become yourself and another." And the great lipless mouth had opened, drawing her in, and she could hear herself screaming. With a great effort she would calm herself, bring herself back to the dark interior of the Lifepod, and the faint, familiar glow of each life-sac. And the alien voice in (or out of) her head recited with childish insistence: "Why do we live? To eat. To be eaten. And so become closer to the Hidden One."

Sometimes the Eavesdropper talked to the Lifepod. It understood only a few pictures she sent to it in her mind, and it seemed to her that the creature resented these interruptions. It would do as she asked, like a sullen child—once it had opened for her a round, translucent eye in the wall of the chamber through which she could see the unmoving starscape—and as soon as she was done, it would return to its play. In the early months (or years) of this uncharted journey, she had wept and railed at it, asking it to find the way back to their world, but, not knowing what she was talking about (which world? She herself didn't know), it had simply shut her out.

So the Eavesdropper floated through the Lifepod, sipping at the dreams of the sleepers, sometimes going to sleep herself. If she could remember her dreams, if she could be aware of them as she was of the dreams of others, she would know who she was. But she couldn't remember. So she waited, sometimes for death, sometimes for that knock on the door that would signal the return of the lost son, the missing sleeper. He would come back. This she knew about him, he was the kind who never gave up, who came back against all odds. As far as she could remember she hadn't seen him captured. He was on his way to find them. He would knock on the door, she would open it and she would know who she was. She waited for that or for death. Sometimes she couldn't tell the difference.

The Eavesdropper

The Eavesdropper was thinking about the moon-world. Her hands—she saw her hands, brown and fragile against the leaves of the greenhouse: they curled to form a round window through which she could see her world. In the foreground was the leaf, heart-shaped, slightly serrated, with fine white hairs on the green surface, and behind it the transparent wall of the greenhouse, with the familiar view of low, barren hills. Half the sky was dominated by the mother planet, the gas giant with its rings, its phantasmagoria of storm clouds, the orange glow diffusing into the little room, turning her hands red-brown. And the other half of the sky was speckled with stars.

This, she thought to herself, not without a certain incredulity, was a memory all her own: not the view (which was in the dreams of the man and the woman, and some of the other humans who lay sleeping in the Lifepod) but the two hands, and how the fingers had curled around in a circle.

"Look through it!" she had said to someone, a boy who might have been her son. He had peered through the window of her fingers—she remembered glossy black hair that fell to his shoulders and was always getting in his eyes. He had long, brown legs; he liked to run, to chase the other children. He looked through the window and laughed, and ran off on those long legs. Did he understand how moving it was to her, to see that particular juxtaposition of those objects? The moon had been in just the right position for Half-Night, when its night side faced the planet instead of the endless field of stars. In that moment, at that time, the window told all: the sap rising in the green stem, the green leaf opening like a hand toward an alien light, against a partial backdrop of stars. She had been moved to tears.

Remembering, she wasn't sure what had brought her to the middle of the chamber. She had thought she had been sleeping in her life-sac, but here she was, floating in the middle of the Lifepod, surrounded by the other sacs with their sleepers. Their dreams lapped around the edges of her consciousness, but some other feeling was rising through her, overcoming the familiar mental background noise: fear, excitement. She realized that the Lifepod was talking to her—to her, after all this time, communicating something urgently. Between the thick, pillar-like sap-vessels of the Lifepod, a portion of the wall contracted, then expanded into a round window, filmed over with a translucent membrane that slowly cleared. She saw through the window a vista of stars, and a bright, spherical, gray object in the foreground. It had locked velocity with the Lifepod. Memory stirred. A human exploration vessel, a small one that may hold one to three people . . .

So this was it, thought the Eavesdropper, suddenly light-headed, her heart thudding: this, the moment she had been waiting for all along. He had come, her son, against all odds, following the song of the Lifepod through space.

"Bring me out!" she commanded the Lifepod, pushing off against a sap-vessel so that she bumped gently against the window. She felt herself encased in a thick film of mucosal secretions; a vast muscular contraction launched her out of the window onto the surface of the Lifepod.

She struggled at first with the thick strands of film around her; she couldn't see because the film was still opaque. A jolt of terror coursed through her and then subsided. The film was slowly hardening and clearing—she could breathe, she was atop the Lifepod, poised over a vertiginous emptiness speckled with stars.

She felt it like a rush to the head, the music of the universe running through her as though she were a stream bed, a cup overflowing. Before, space had been nothing but darkness and stars, something to be crossed so one could get to one's destination. But now she could sense the tachyonic pathways all around her, like fine lacework, like the tangled neural pathways, the guts of some vast beast. The Hidden One, said the alien, exulting, and she looked around for the alien but it wasn't there. Only herself and that strange object motionless above her, round, like an opaque window against the stars.

The rush faded. She saw the small humanoid figure in a spacesuit detach from the side of the craft, attached to it with an umbilicus that reeled out slowly as the figure jetted toward her. The light from the craft spilled over her; she saw the surface of the Lifepod, fissured and full of knobs and warts. She remembered something, a fragment of memory that was not her own: a summer hot and breathless, sandy cliffs, and thousands, perhaps millions of the aliens in their summer sleep, their flightless single wings spread to take in the sunlight, to draw in the fuel they needed for the long winter-to-come. It was an image so strange and yet so familiar that she turned around again to see if the alien had somehow manifested in her little bubble, but it was not there. She pushed the image from her mind, stretched her arms out to the descending figure. "My son," she said to herself, her voice catching. Then a jolt of memory: she was standing barefoot in the grass in a blue sari, setting out the washing. The boy was lying face-down on the ground, watching ants. It was a green and primitive place on a distant planet; he had been born there, some years before the trip to the barren moon of another world . . .

But if that is who I am, she thought in sudden consternation, then the man who lies dreaming in the life-sac below my feet is my son. Then who is this?

Or maybe, she thought desperately, the memory was not hers, just as that other memory—with the aliens stretched out like so many flies on a sand dune—that other memory was not hers. She looked up at the human figure in the spacesuit; he was getting closer and closer, decelerating. She could not see his face. Instead she saw the reflection of the Lifepod in the spacesuit's headgear, all lit up by the spacecraft's beacon, and the clear bubble in which she stood like a fly trapped in amber. And she saw what she was.

A half-alien thing: the shape still human but the face so strange! Ovoid eyes, the bony skull-sheath jutting over her cheekbones. She held her small brown hands before her and saw the tips curving into hard pincers, transforming almost as she stood there, transfixed with horror and wonder. She looked down at herself in the hard, honest light and saw that the reflection was not false. What am I? she wondered, aghast.

And the alien within answered her, not in words but in a swell of understanding that took her breath away. She remembered what it had proposed, what she had agreed to; the terrifying darkness within its body, her screams echoing in her ears as the thin tendrils inside it wrapped around her, penetrated her skin. After that, the chrysalid sleep as the new bridges between the two of them formed and hardened, as alien transforming organelles coursed through her body, as great, chemical swathes of emotion—pleasure and fear, hunger and sweet, nameless desire swept through her. Then she was lifted from the dead shell of the alien into a brief light, and into the life-sac which eased her once more into the sleep of forgetfulness . . .

So the Eavesdropper stood before the stranger who might or might not be her son; she a creature not alien, not human, but a bridge, a thing that was new, the first of its kind. He (or was it she?) stood away from her, bumping gently against the Lifepod, the long umbilicus stretching out into the dark like a luminous, flexible bridge.

The stranger's hands were as yet empty, but the posture was wary, as though poised to activate the spacesuit's weapons systems. She felt some ancient part of her cry out: Do you not know me, son? And something inside her gave way, crumbled like a mud wall before a flood.

I must know, she said to herself. I must know if you are him. She stretched her arms toward him, slowly, saw him tense, then relax. Suddenly she wanted to enclose him in the dark, to exchange blood with blood, to share synapse with synapse, to know him cell by cell, and so become something new. The sharpness of her hunger took her breath away. In that brief moment she saw that the Lifepod itself was her kin, a hybrid of the original alien species and some gravid denizen of a distant ocean-world, and its mind was clear to her for the first time. Why couldn't she know the stranger in the same way? No, she said, feeling or imagining the infant mouth straining to open in her chest. That was the alien within, as it had once been, remembering. There had to be some other way.

She opened her hands to show him that they were empty. She put the palms together in the old Indic gesture of greeting, then moved the fingers to make a circle, a window through which she could see him against the Lifepod and the infinity of stars. Around her, along pathways invisible to human and alien, sang the tachyons, leaving ghost trails in space-time that the sleeping woman in the chamber under her feet could only imagine. Only the Eavesdropper could sense them, could see where they were leading, to the heart of the great galactic beast, the Hidden One. She saw for just a moment that she had been conceived and forged for a great purpose. But for now she was only a bridge in the darkness between ship and ship, being and being. Through the window of her hands she watched the stranger come slowly toward her.

Oblivion: A Journey

Memory is a strange thing.

I haven't changed my sex in eighty-three years. I was born female, in a world of peace and quietude; yet I have an incomplete recollection of my childhood. Perhaps it is partly a failure of the imagination that it is so hard to believe (in this age of ours) that there was once such a place as green and slow as my world-shell, Ramasthal. It was the last of the great world-shells to fall, so any memory of childhood is contaminated with what came after: the deaths of all I loved, the burning of the cities, the slow, cancerous spread of Hirasor's culture-machines that changed my birthplace beyond recognition.

So instead of one seamless continuum of growing and learning to be in this world, my memory of my life is fragmentary. I remember my childhood name: Lilavati. I remember those great cybeasts, the hayathis, swaying down the streets in a procession, and their hot, vegetable-scented breath ruffling my hair. There are glimpses, as through a tattered veil, of steep, vertical gardens, cascading greenery, a familiar face looking out at me from a window hewn in a cliff—and in the background, the song of falling water. Then everything is obscured by smoke. I am in a room surrounded by pillars of fire, and through the haze I see the torn pages of the *Ramayana* floating in the air, burning, their edges crumpling like black lace. I am half-comatose with heat and smoke; my throat is parched and sore, my eyes sting—and then there are strange, metallic faces reaching out to me, the stuff of my nightmares. Behind them is a person all aflame, her arms outstretched, running toward me, but she falls and I am carried away through the smoke and the screaming. I still see the woman in my dreams and wonder if she was my mother.

In my later life as a refugee, first on the world of Barana and after that everywhere and nowhere, there is nothing much worth recalling. Foster homes, poverty, my incarceration in some kind of soulless educational institution—the banality of the daily struggle to survive. But there are moments in my life that are seared into my mind forever: instants that were pivotal, life-changing, each a conspiracy of temporal nexuses, a concatenation of events that made me what I am. That is not an excuse—I could have chosen a different way to be. But I did not know, then, that I had a choice.

This is the first of those moments: the last time I was a woman, some ninety years ago in my personal time frame. I was calling myself Ila, then, and doing some planet-hopping, working the cruisers and blowing the credits at each stop. I found myself on Planet Vilaasa, a rich and decadent world under the sway of the Samarin conglomerate. I was in one of those deep-city bars where it's always night, where sunshine is like a childhood memory, where the air is thick with smoke, incipient violence, and bumblebees. I don't remember who I was with, but the place was crowded with humans, native and off-world, as well as mutants and nakalchis. There was a bee buzzing in my ear, promising me seven kinds of bliss designed especially for my personality and physical type if only I'd agree to let the Samarin Corporate Entity take over half my brain. I swatted it; it fell into my plate and buzzed pathetically, antennae waving, before it became non-functional. Somehow I found this funny; I still remember throwing back my head and laughing.

My fingers, slight and brown, curved around my glass. The drink half-drunk, a glutinous purple drop sliding down the outer surface. Reflected on the glass a confusion of lights and moving shapes, and the gleam, sudden and terrifying, of steel.

There was a scream, and the sound of glass breaking that seemed to go on forever. This was no barroom brawl. The raiders were Harvesters.

I remember getting up to run. I remember the terrified crowd pressing around me, and then I was falling, kicked and stepped upon in the stampede. Somehow I pushed myself to safety under a table next to a stranger, a pale woman with long, black hair and eyes like green fire. She looked at me with her mouth open, saying one word:

"Nothen . . ."

A Harvester got her. It put its metal hands around her throat and put its scissor-like mouth to her chest. As she bled and writhed, it rasped one long word, interspersed with a sequence of numbers.

Her body turned rigid and still, her face twisted with horror. Her green eyes froze in a way that was simultaneously aware and locked in the moment of torment. It was then that I realized that she was a nakalchi, a bio-synthetic being spawned from a mother-machine.

The name of the mother-machine is what pushes a nakalchi into the catatonic state that is *Shunyath*. When they enter Shunyath they re-live the moment when that name was spoken. Since the nakalchis are practically immortal, capable of dying only through accident or violence, Shunyath is their way of going to the next stage. Usually a nakalchi who has wearied of existence will go to one of their priests, who will put the candidate in a meditative state of absolute calm and surrender. Then the priest will utter the name of the mother-machine (such names being known only to the priests and guarded with their lives) so that the nakalchi may then contemplate eternity in peace.

For first-generation nakalchis, Shunyath is not reversible.

That is when I realized that this woman was one of the ancients, one of the nakalchis who had helped humankind find its way to the stars.

So for her, frozen in the state of Shunyath, it would seem as though she was being strangled by the Harvester all the rest of her days. No wonder she had asked me for Nothen, for death. She had known the Harvesters had come for her; she had known what they would do. I remember thinking, in one of those apparently timeless moments that terror brings: somebody should kill the poor woman. She was obviously the target of the raid.

But to my horrified surprise the Harvester turned from her to me, even as I was sliding away from under the table to a safer place. While the Harvester had me pinned to the floor, its long, flexible electrodes crawled all over my skin as it violated my humanness, my woman-ness, with its multiple limbs. Through the tears and blood I saw myriad reflections of myself in those dark, compound eyes, from which looked—not only the primitive consciousness of the Harvester, but the eyes of whoever manipulated it—the person or entity who, not content with finding their target, fed like a starving animal on the terror of a bystander. In those eyes I was a stranger, a non-person, a piece of meat that jerked and gibbered in pain. Then, for a moment, I thought I saw the burning woman from my memories of childhood, standing behind the Harvester. This is death, I said to myself, relieved. But the Harvester left me a few hair-breadths short of death and moved on to its next victim.

I don't know how many they killed or maimed that night. The nakalchi woman they took away. I remember thinking, through the long months of pain and nightmares that followed, that I wish I had died.

But I lived. I took no joy in it. All that gave my mind some respite from its constant seething was a game I invented: I would find the identity of the person responsible for the Harvester raid and I would kill them. Find, and kill. I went through endless permutations of people and ways of killing in my head. Eventually it was no longer a game.

I moved to another planet, changed my sex to one of the Betweens. Over the years I changed my body even further, ruthlessly replacing soft, yielding flesh with coralloid implants that grew me my own armor-plating. Other people shuddered when I walked by. I became an interplanetary investigator of small crime and fraud, solving trivial little cases for the rich and compromised, while biding my time.

It was already suspected that the man responsible for the Harvester attacks that terrorized whole planets during the Samarin era was no other than the governing mind of the Samarin Corporate Entity, Hirasor. The proof took many years and great effort on the part of several people, including myself, but it came at last. Nothing could be done, however, because Hirasor was more powerful than any man alive. His icons were everywhere: dark, shoulder-length hair framing a lean, aristocratic face with hungry eyes; the embroidered silk collar, the rose in his buttonhole. It came out then that he had a private museum of first-generation nakalchis locked in Shunyath in various states of suffering. A connoisseur of pain, was Hirasor.

But to me he was also Hirasor, destroyer of worlds. He had killed me once already by destroying my world-shell, Ramasthal. It was one of the epic world-shells, a chain of island satellites, natural and artificial, that ringed the star Agni. Here we learned, lived, and enacted our lives based on that ancient Indic epic, the *Ramayana*, one of those timeless stories that condense in their poetry the essence of what it means to be human. Then Samarin had infiltrated, attacking and destroying at first, then doing what they called "rebuilding": substituting for the complexity and beauty of the *Ramayana*, an inanely simplified, sugary cultural matrix that drew on all the darkness and pettiness in human nature. Ramasthal broke up, dissolved by the monocultural machine that was Samarin. I suffered less than my fellow citizens—being a child, I could not contribute a brain-share to Samarin. I grew up a refugee, moving restlessly from one inhabited world to the next, trying and failing to find my center. Most of the ordinary citizens of these worlds had never heard of the *Ramayana* epic, or anything else that had been meaningful to me in that lost past life. In my unimaginable solitude my only defense was to act like them, to be what they considered normal. When the Harvesters invaded the bar, I had been living the fashionably disconnected life that Samarin-dominated cultures think is the only way to be.

Hirasor was so powerful that among my people his nickname was Ravan-Ten-Heads, after the demon in the epic *Ramayana*. Near the end of the story, the hero, Ram, tries to kill Ravan by cutting off his heads, one by one, but the heads simply grow back. In a similar manner, if a rival corporation or a society of free citizens managed to destroy one Samarin conglomerate, another would spring up almost immediately in its place. It—and Hirasor—seemed almost mythic in their indestructibility.

What I wanted to do was to find Hirasor's secret vulnerability, as Ram does in the epic. "Shoot an arrow into Ravan's navel," he is told. The navel is the center of Ravan's power. When Ram does so, the great demon dies at last.

But Samarin, and with it Hirasor, declined slowly without my help. An ingeniously designed brain-share virus locked Samarin's client-slaves—several million people—into a synced epileptic state. After that Generosity Corp. (that had likely developed the virus) began its ascent to power while the Samarin Entity gradually disintegrated. Pieces of it were bought by other conglomerates, their data extracted through torture; then they were mind-wiped until the name Samarin only evoked a ghost of a memory, accompanied by a shudder.

But Hirasor lived on. He was still rich enough to evade justice. Rumors of his death appeared frequently in the newsfeeds for a while, and a documentary was made about him, but over time people forgot. There were other things, such as the discovery of the worlds of the Hetorr, and the threats and rumors of war with that unimaginably alien species. "Give it up," said the few people in whom I had confided. "Forget Hirasor and get on with your life." But finding Hirasor was the only thing between me and death by my own hand. Each time I opened my case files on him, each time his image sprang up and I looked into his eyes, I remembered the Harvester. I remembered the burning woman. Despite all the reconstructive work my body had undergone, my old wounds ached. Find, and kill. Only then would I know peace.

I knew more about Hirasor than anyone else did, although it was little enough.

He liked absinthe and roses.

He had a perfect memory.

He was fastidious about his appearance. Every hair in place, fingers elegant and manicured, the signature ear-studs small and precisely placed on each ear lobe. His clothing was made from the silk of sapient-worms.

He had no confidant but for the chief of his guards, a nakalchi female called Suvarna, a walking weapon who was also his lover. He wrote her poetry that was remarkable for its lyrical use of three languages, and equally remarkable for its sadistic imagery.

Later I killed three of his functionaries to learn his unique identity-number. It did me no good, or so I thought, then.

In the years of his decline he lost his Harvester units; his three main hideouts were found and his assets destroyed, his loyal bands of followers dwindled to one, Suvarna—and yet he seemed more slippery and elusive than ever. Although he left trails of blood and shattered lives in his wake, he managed to elude me with trickery and firepower.

He left me messages in blood.

Sometimes it was the name of a planet or a city. I would go there and find, too late, another clue, spelled out in corpses. It was as though we were playing an elaborate game across the inhabited worlds, with him always in the lead. Slowly the universe began to take less and less notice. We were two lone players on a vast stage, and the audience had other, larger-scale horrors to occupy them.

I began to think of myself as a modern-day Ram. In the *Ramayana* epic, Prince Ram's wife, Sita, is abducted by the ten-headed demon, Ravan. Prince Ram, beloved by all, has no difficulty raising an army of animals and people and following Ravan to his kingdom.

I was no prince. But Hirasor had stolen my whole world, as surely as Ravan stole Sita. I could not bring back Ramasthal or my childhood, but I could bring Hirasor down. Unlike Ram, I would have to do it alone.

Alone. Sifting through travel records, bribing petty little mercenaries who may have had dealings with his people, tracking down witnesses at the scene of each orgy of violence, trying to think like him, to stand in his shoes and wonder: What would he do next? I would sleep only when I could no longer stand.

Sleep brought a recurring nightmare: Hirasor standing before me at last. I shoot an arrow into his navel, and as he falls I leap upon him and put my hands around his throat. I am certain he is dying, but then I see his face change, become familiar, become my own face. I feel his hands on my throat.

I would wake up in a sweat and know that in the end it was going to be only one of us who would prevail: him or me. But first I had to find him. So I worked obsessively, following him around from place to place, always one step behind.

Then, quite suddenly, the trail got cold. I searched, sent my agents from planet to planet. Nothing but silence. I paced up and down my room, brooding for days. What was he waiting for? What was he about to do?

Into this empty, waiting time came something I had not expected. A reason to live that had nothing to do with Hirasor. Her name was Dhanu.

She was an urbanologist for whom I had performed a small service. She was a small, fierce, determined woman with long, black hair turning to grey that she tied in a braid. The job I did for her was shoddily done, and she demanded a reason. "I'm preoccupied with something more important," I snapped, wanting her out of my office and my life. "Tell me," she said, sitting down and waiting with her whole body, her eyes mocking and intrigued. So I did.

We became lovers, Dhanu and I. Somehow she found her way past the armor-plating of my mind and body; she found cracks and interstices, living flesh that remembered loving touch, regions of vulnerability that I hadn't cauterized out of myself. Here is a memory fragment:

We lie in bed in my dingy room, with moonlight coming in through the narrow window, and the sounds outside of voices raised in argument, and the sweaty, chemical scent of the dead river that lies like an outstretched arm across this nameless, foul city. She is a shadow, a ghost limned with silver, turned into a stranger by the near-darkness. I find this suddenly disturbing; I turn her over so that the light falls full on her face. I don't know what I look like to her. I don't know what I am. I've been calling myself Vikram for a few years, but that doesn't tell me anything.

"Tell me a secret," she says. "Something about yourself that nobody knows."

I pull myself together, settle down next to her and stare at the ceiling. I don't know what to tell her, but something escapes my lips unbidden.

"I want to die," I say, surprising myself because lately I haven't been thinking about death. But it's true. And also not true, because I want this moment for ever, the light from the broken moon Jagos silvering her hair, and the way she looks at me when I say that: a long, slow, sad, unsurprised look. She begins to say something, but I stop her. "Your turn," I say.

"I'll tell you what I want to know, more than anything," she says after a pause. "I want to know what it is like to be somebody else. I remember, as a very small child, standing with my mother on a balcony, watching the most amazing fireworks display I had ever seen. It made me happy. I looked at my mother to share that joy, and found that she was crying. It was then that I realized that I was a different person from her, that she was in some profound way a stranger. Since then I've sought strangeness. I've wanted to know what it is like to be a tree, a sapient-worm, and most of all, a made-being. Like a nakalchi or a Cognizant-City. Can you imagine what the universe would look like to an entity like that?"

We talk all night. She teaches me what she has learned about nakalchis and Cognizant-Cities, Corporate Entities and mother-machines—in particular, their rituals of death, because that is what interests me. I realize during the conversation that I am no more than a vessel for the death of another, and that is perhaps why I seek my own. Some time during the night she teaches me the song with which nakalchis welcome Nothen, their conception of death. She learned it from a nakalchi priest who was dying, who wanted someone to say the words to him. I cannot pretend to understand the lore and mysticism that the priests have developed around Nothen, which to me is simply irreversible non-functionality, the death that comes to us all. Or the philosophical comparison between Nothen and Shunyath. Dhanu tries to explain:

"If you go into Shunyath, you contemplate what nakalchis call The River, which is inadequately translated as the Cosmic Stream of Being. If you go into Nothen, with the Last Song echoing in your mind, then you *are* the River. You are no longer separate from it—you *become* the River, see?"

No, I don't see. Never mind, she says, laughing at me. She says the words of the Last Song, breathing it out into the moonlit air.

It has a pleasing, sonorous lilt. It is supposed to induce a state of acceptance and peace in a dying nakalchi. I am not sure why, but there are tears in my eyes as I repeat it after her in the gray, hushed light of dawn.

Shantih. Nothen ke aagaman, na dukh na dard . . .

Lying with her, seeing her hair unbound on my pillow like seaweed, I find myself in a still place, as though between breaths. Hirasor does not walk the paths that Dhanu and I tread.

Looking back, I see how the paths branch out of each temporal nexus. For every pivotal event in my life, there was always more than one possible path I could have taken.

This is the path I chose:

I had accompanied Dhanu during one of her urbanology expeditions. We were in the bowels of a dying Cognizant-City on the ruined planet Murra. This was the first time she had had a chance to explore what was probably one of the earliest Cognizant-Cities in the galaxy. She was a few levels below me, attempting to salvage what was left of the City's mind. All its recorded history and culture, its ruminations over the years of its existence, lay spooled in cavernous darkness below. The inhabitants had been evacuated, and even now I could see the last of the ships, a glint or two in a reddening sky over the bleak mountains of Murra's northern continent. I was perched on the highest ramparts, standing by our flyer and looking out for rogue destroyer bots. Every now and then I saw one rise up, a distant speck, and crash into the cityscape in a small fireball. Thin spires of smoke rose all around me, but there was as yet nothing amiss where I was waiting.

Then I lost Dhanu's signal.

I searched the skies, found them clear of bots, and descended quickly into the warren-like passageways that led into the city's heart. Two levels later, my wrist-band beeped. She was in range.

"I'm all right, Vikram," she said to my anxious query. She sounded breathless with excitement. "I had to go down a couple of levels to find the rest of the data-banks. This city is one of the first Cognizant-Cities ever made! They still have direct human-to-City interfaces! I am hooking up to talk to it as I record. Go on up! I'll only be a few minutes, I promise."

When I relive that moment, I think of the things I could have done. I could have insisted on going down to where she was, or persuaded her to leave everything and come. Or I could have been more careful going up, so I wouldn't lose my way.

But I did lose my way. It was only one wrong turn, and I was about to retrace my steps (I had the flyer's reassuring signal on my wrist-band as a guide) but what made me pause was curiosity. Or fate.

I found myself in the doorway of an enormous chamber which smelled faintly of blood and hydrogen peroxide, and was lit by periodic blue flashes, like lightning. I saw the great, monstrous hulk of an old-fashioned mother-machine, her long-abandoned teats spewing an oily broth, her flailing arms beating the air over the shattered remains of her multiple wombs. She was old—it had been a long time since she had brought any nakalchis to life. As I stared at her I realized (from what pictures Dhanu had shown me of ancient made-beings) that she was probably a first-generation mother-machine. A priceless collector's item, salvaged from who-knew-where, abandoned in the evacuation of the City. And now the City's madness was destroying what little functionality she had, taking her to Nothen. Moved by a sudden impulse I went up to her and spoke the words of peace.

Shantih. Nothen ke aagaman, na dukh na dard . . .

Peace. As Nothen comes, there is no sorrow, no pain . . .

I regretted my impulse almost immediately because after I stopped, the mother-machine began to recite the names of her children, the first part of her death-ritual. In her final moments she had mistaken me for a nakalchi priest. I don't know what made me stay—there was something mesmerizing about that old, metallic voice in the darkness, and the proximity of death. Perhaps I was a little annoyed with Dhanu for delaying, for wanting to join with the City in an orgy of mutual understanding. Dhanu's signal flickered with reassuring regularity on my wrist-band.

Then I heard the mother-machine utter the name that to me meant more than life itself: Hirasor.

I will remember that moment until I die: the grating voice of the mother-machine, the dull booms in the distance, the floor shaking below my feet, and that pungent, smoky darkness, pierced by occasional sparks of blue lightning.

In the midst of it, clear as a bell, the name—or rather, Hirasor's unique numerical identifier. Each of us had our identity numbers, given to us at birth, and I was one of the few people who knew Hirasor's. But I had never suspected he was a nakalchi. Partly because of nakalchi lore and history—there never had been any confirmed master criminals who were nakalchi, conceived as they had once been to gently shepherd the human race toward the stars. Meanwhile the great uprising of the nakalchis in times long before Samarin, the consciousness debates that had preceded them, had all ensured that they were treated on par with human beings, so I had no way of knowing from the number alone. You can't tell from appearance or behavior either, because nakalchis claim access to the full range of human emotion (or, if their priests are to be believed, to more than that). By now even we humans are so augmented and enhanced that the functional difference between nakalchi and human is very small—but important. To me the difference meant—at last—the possibility of vengeance.

Hirasor: a first-generation nakalchi!

That is why I had to wait. That is why I couldn't go down to find Dhanu, why I ignored her frantic signals on my wrist-band. I had to wait for the mother-machine to tell me her name.

At last she said it: Ekadri-samayada-janini, intermingled with a sequence of numbers that made up a prime.

I left her then, to die. I left, repeating her name—what would always be, to me, the Word—so I would not forget. The floor was twisting and bucking beneath my feet, and a lone siren was blaring somewhere above me. I staggered against the rusting metal wall of the passage, and remembered Dhanu.

I got up. I went back. I wish I could say that I went into the bowels of the City, braved everything to find her and rescue her. But I didn't. I went down until I was stopped by the rubble of fallen masonry. Her signal still flickered on my wrist-band but she did not answer my query.

There was a seismic shudder far below me, and a long sigh, a wind that blew through the wrecked passageways, running invisible fingers through my hair. I sensed—or imagined—Dhanu's breath flowing with the breath of the dying City, her consciousness entangled inextricably with that of her host. But as I turned away I knew also that my real reason for abandoning her was that I was the only living being who had the means to bring Hirasor down. For that I couldn't risk my life.

The roof of the passageway began to collapse. I was running, now, veering from one side to another to prevent being hit by debris. I burst into open air, my chest aching, and flung myself into the flyer. As I rose up, three destroyer bots honed into the very spot I had vacated. I had no time to activate the flyer's defenses. A great fire-ball blossomed below me. I felt its heat as I piloted the rocking craft upward through the tumultuous air. Up, in the cool heights, I saw that there was blood flowing down my right arm. My shoulder hurt. I looked down and saw the myriad fires blooming, forming and dissolving shapes that my imagination brought to life. Monsters. And lastly, a woman, arms outstretched, burning.

In the *Ramayana,* Ram braves all to recover his consort, Sita, from the demon Ravan. But near the end of the story he loses her through his own foolishness. He turns her away, exiles her as he himself was once exiled, and buries himself in the task of ruling his kingdom.

All that: the war, the heroes killed—for nothing!

One of the most moving scenes in the epic is at the end of the story, when Ram goes down on his knees before Sita in the forest, begging her forgiveness and asking her to come back to him. She accepts his apology but she does not belong to him; she never has. She calls to her mother, the Earth; a great fissure opens in the ground and Sita goes home.

In the *One Thousand Commentaries,* there are different views on the significance of Sita. Some interpret her as signifying that which is lost to us. For a long time I had thought of Sita as my world, my child-hood. I had seen myself as Ram, raising an army to win back—not those irredeemable things, but a chance for survival. Abandoned by my fellow investigators, hunting for Hirasor alone, I had, after a while, given up on analogies. Certainly I had never thought of Dhanu as Sita.

Dhanu was what I had to sacrifice to reach Hirasor, to rescue Sita. Dhanu had never belonged to me anyway, I told myself. She could have come up out of the City at any time; it was her obsession with the made-beings that led to her death. Sometimes I was angry with her, at other times I wept, thinking of the fall of her hair in the moonlight. At odd moments during my renewed pursuit of Hirasor, she would come unbidden into my mind, and I would wonder what her last moments had been like. Had she seen the universe through the eyes of the dying City? Had she had her epiphany?

But I had little time for regret. My life narrowed down to one thing: find Hirasor. I set various agents sifting through mountains of possible leads; I re-established contact with criminal informers, coaxed or threatened information from scores of witnesses. At night I lay sleepless in my lonely bed, thinking of what I would do when I found Hirasor. My mind ran through scenario after scenario. I had to first put him in a hundred kinds of agony. Then I would say the name of the mother-machine and lock him in Shunyath forever.

His silence lasted over two years. Then, at last, one of my agents picked up his trail. This time, curiously, it was not marked with blood. No small, artistically arranged orgy of violence betrayed his presence. All I had was proof from a transit shuttle record that he had been headed for the planet Griddha-kuta two months ago.

I went to Griddha-kuta. Apparently he had headed straight for the Buddhist monastery of Leh, without any attempt at covering his tracks. I went to the monastery, suspecting a trap. There, to my angry surprise, I found him gone.

An elderly monk told me that yes, Hirasor had been here. What had he done during his stay? Apparently nothing but walk around in the hill gardens and read in the library. Where was he now?

"He said to tell you that he had gone to Oblivion," the monk said, watching me. "But why don't you stay here awhile, before you go? There is no hurry. Hirasor is not running anymore. Why don't you walk the gardens and ease your burdens a little?"

They let me search the grounds and the building, but there was no sign of Hirasor. I wondered if he had really gone to Oblivion, a planet about which I knew little, except that it was as close to hell as you could get among the inhabited worlds. It made no sense that he would go to such an uncomfortable place.

While I was wondering what to do, I walked briefly in the gardens with the monk, Chituri. I told him a little about myself and my quest;

in return he confided to me that he had been a world-shell citizen, too, before the fall. His world-shell had been Gilgamesh.

There is no doubt that there was some magic about the place, because I stayed longer than I intended. The gardens in the terraced hills were tranquil, verdant, misty with waterfalls. Amid groves of moss-laden stone trees, pale clusters of flowers hung in the sweet air. Memories of Ramasthal, which had faded with time, returned to me vividly. Meanwhile Chituri tried to persuade me to stay, to give up my quest for justice. As we walked, he would tell me stories from the Indic tradition, even resorting to his knowledge of the *Ramayana.*

"Don't you see," he would tell me, "it is only when Ram forgets the god in him, forgets he is an avatar of Vishnu, that he acts foolishly? What is evil but ignorance of our true nature?"

"You are forgetting that Ravan is the villain of the story, not Ram," I would say coldly. "If you want to talk about evil, talk about him."

"But, Paren," he said, using the name I had given him, "don't your commentaries say that the entire epic is more than a literal telling of an old heroic tale—that the great battle is really the battle within . . ."

He had a peculiar way of sidling up to me, of speaking as though imparting a great confidence, and yet his manner was ingratiating, tentative. He hardly spoke above a whisper. I guessed he had suffered much before his arrival here, but I took a dislike to him after a while.

For me this period was, like the time I had met Dhanu, only an interstice, a time to catch my breath before resuming my quest. I was not interested in academic discourses on morality. Chituri did not understand that. He had seen Hirasor walk these very gardens—Hirasor, who had brought down his world as well as mine—and he had done nothing.

I finished my researches on the planet Oblivion, and made arrangements to go there. It was a difficult place to get to, since there was only one settlement, if one could call it that, and only a small scientific research craft visited at rather long intervals. The day I left, Chituri again tried to persuade me to give up my pursuit of Hirasor. He did this in his usual oblique way of telling me a story.

This time it was an ancient Buddhist tale about a murderer called Ungli-maal. Ungli-maal had been a bandit in the time of the Buddha, a man so depraved that he wore the fingers of his victims as a garland around his neck. The Buddha was the only man he waylaid who was unafraid of death, who faced him empty-handed, with compassion. Eventually Ungli-maal—despite all he had been—became a Buddhist monk and a great teacher.

"If you are trying to persuade me that Hirasor has become a saint," I said between clenched teeth, "you must think me naïve indeed. He is still the man who butchered millions, destroyed countless worlds. He will not escape justice."

"That was not the point of my story," Chituri said, rather sadly. I was glad not to see his face again.

Oblivion, they say, is another word for hell. A bleak world, barely habitable, it was once known as Dilaasha, and was considered a reasonable candidate for terraforming. Those hopes have long since vanished. The "habitable" zones are deserts, subject to violent dust storms, and all indigenous life is primitive—bacterial, algal, and inimical to coexisting with humans.

But all this does not explain why the planet Oblivion is hell. Oblivion earns its name because those who stay there long enough slowly lose their minds.

It begins with forgetting and slips of tongue, peculiar speech disorders, waking terrors, and finally, silence. The rescue teams who first observed the early explorers (consisting of both human and nakalchi) could only speculate as to why the subjects walked around without apparent purpose, neglecting the basic needs of their bodies, muttering in unknown languages, reacting to things that nobody else could see. The second stage was one of great distress—the subjects howled or whimpered and ran about the compound as though to escape a terrible, invisible enemy. They could still, at times, respond to their names; they would look up when called, frowning, as though trying to remember who they had been. Sometimes they would weep in the arms of the staff; a terrible, heart-rending weeping it was. The final stage was silence and withdrawal. In this last stage the sufferers seemed to have completely lost any knowledge of who they were—they did not respond to their names or to instructions; they wandered around with dead eyes, tracing out complicated patterns with their feet.

Only three victims had been taken off-planet. When removed in the second stage they would resist with maniacal strength—both such subjects had met violent death at their own hand. The third had been in the final stage and had simply faded away after removal, although he had been in fine shape physically. However an autopsy had revealed a bizarre restructuring of his brain that no scientist had yet explained.

So now all that is left of the original settlement on Oblivion is a study center where the remaining subjects are incarcerated. Regulations decree that nobody can stay on Oblivion for more than a hundred and ten local days. It's after that that most people seem to start losing their minds, although in some rare cases twenty days is enough.

There are theories—volatile compounds containing nano-organisms that are slowly released by the soil, pervading everything, that act like psychotropic drugs, low-frequency sound waves that boom through the barren hills, disturbing the inner functioning of the body, peculiar surges in radioactive emissions in the environs—but none of these are adequate explanations. Oblivion remains a mystery.

So I came, at last, to Oblivion, to the final confrontation. It was a fitting place for a last stand. The dome-town was mostly uninhabited, the empty buildings testament to the defeated hopes of the original settlers. The insane were housed in a primitive building built around a dusty compound. The skeleton crew that had managed the place for the last shift was irritable and moody, waiting to be taken off-planet in a week, and the few scientists looked depressed and preoccupied. Nobody seemed interested in talking with me, despite the fact that I was apparently a representative of a rich philanthropist considering a major donation. Everyone seemed curiously lacking in vitality or enthusiasm, as though under the influence of some drug. Within a few hours of my stay there, I, too, felt a distinct mental lethargy, punctuated by spikes of nervousness and paranoia. The medic who examined me, a thin, dark, spidery man, was pessimistic.

"You're one of those who will succumb fast," he said, not without some relish. "This is a terrible place, affects some people much more quickly than others. Get out while you can, or you'll be joining them!"

He waved his long fingers toward the observation window behind him. There was something ghoulish about the way he stood watching the crazies, describing for me in painful detail every stage of the terrible sickness. The afflicted—men, women, most of them half naked, wandered aimlessly around the yard, muttering and drawing patterns in the dust with their feet. Some wailed incessantly, beating their chests, while others tore at their clothes. Still others sat very quietly on the ground, looking straight ahead of them with blank eyes. I felt as though their pain and confusion was somehow connected to me, that theirs was a sorrow that was drawing me in slowly. The dust patterns on the ground (the subject of much debate among the scientists) seemed almost to make sense, as though they were the script of a language I had known and forgotten. I shivered and looked away. The medic was right. I couldn't stay here long.

But when I looked back into the compound, there was Hirasor.

He came into the yard through a door in the wall. A tall man, he now walked with a slight shuffle. He sat down on an unoccupied bench and watched the sufferers. I couldn't see his face clearly, but the gait, and the arrogant set of the shoulders, was unmistakable. My heart started hammering.

"That's the other visitor," the medic said, noting the slight start I gave. "Claims to be interested in our subjects, but he seems to have problems of his own."

He didn't explain. Hirasor sat for a while, then moved his hands upward in a gesture that I didn't recognize, and returned through the door, which shut behind him.

I went into my narrow cell of a room to make my plans.

It was hard to think clearly. Blood, revenge, murder—the sufferings of those who had lost to Hirasor—my own long years of trailing him, giving up love and life for this one obsession—these thoughts reverberated in my mind When I closed my eyes I saw Hirasor's face, or the Harvester's toothed mouth. When I opened them, I saw the stark, claustrophobic room, and the view from the skylight of a yellow dust plume over the dome. The air smelled faintly of dust and burning. I knew then that Hirasor had chosen wisely. I didn't know to what extent he, as a nakalchi (and a hardened one at that) would be affected by the place, but he had gambled on it being a disadvantage for me.

The next day there was a message from him, an audio. Giving me the location of his rooms, and telling me that he would let me know when I should come, when Suvarna was not around.

Bring your weapons, he said.

This is the last memory fragment, the one most fresh in my mind.

I had been waiting for days. Hirasor and I would make an appointment, then he would abruptly cancel it because Suvarna had returned unexpectedly to their quarters. He did not want her to be in the way. I could sense that, like me, he wanted our final confrontation to be between us alone. At times I suspected that he was playing with me, that I should be more circumspect, perhaps induce someone to spy on him—but this was not the time to play detective. It was fitting that at the end there should be no tricks and subterfuges, only him and me, face-to-face at last.

There was no doubt that he was wearing me down, however. I lay restlessly in my room, plagued by headaches and nightmares. I started at every sound, and the dust devils visible from my window became fiery-eyed monsters.

Thus Hirasor and I waited, like illicit lovers, for the final assignation.

Then his summons came.

I will remember that last journey to the end of my days:

My armor-plated body, all weapons systems readied; the dull, booming pain in my head keeping time with my footsteps. The walk through the complex, through which the other inhabitants seem to float like ghosts. Everything tinged faintly with red, as though the world itself is rusting. The stairs, dusted with Oblivion's fine grit. The door, a white rectangle, that scans me with a round eye and opens in silence.

Inside is a sparsely furnished receiving room. On a low divan sits a woman. Her hair cascades over her shoulders in black waves; her legs are crossed, her long, tapering, steel-tipped fingers folded over one knee. Her eyes are a metallic dark gray, multi-faceted like the eyes of moths; a quick blink in the direction of the door behind me, and it shuts.

"Greetings, Suvarna," I say, as calmly as I can, after the first heart-stopping moment. "Where's Hirasor?"

"Out," she says. "I intercepted some of his messages to you. It was I who sent you the last one."

I am standing before her, outwardly calm, inwardly berating myself for my foolishness. Her nakalchi eyes track every move I might make, every muscle twitch.

"My business is with Hirasor," I say. I am determined that at the end of it all, she will not stand between Hirasor and I. But she will be hard to kill.

"I don't think you understand," she says, rising. She's an impressive woman, tall, all teeth and muscle, but also beautiful.

"This may be a game for you and him," she says, "but my job is to keep him alive. If it hadn't been for you, he wouldn't have taken to planet-hopping. He wouldn't have found this accursed place. It's time we stopped playing, Vikram, or whatever you are calling yourself now."

I can sense her coming alive, the way a killer weapon comes alive when it finds its target. Through the fog in my brain it occurs to me that Suvarna might be Hirasor's sibling, birthed by the same mother-machine.

I say the Word.

"What?" she says. She laughs. "Are you trying to distract me with nonsense?"

So it means nothing to her. She raises a fingertip.

The next moment my alarm system begins to scream coordinates and trajectories; I leap aside just as a spot on the wall behind me blackens with heat.

I remember that she likes to play.

"If only you'd left us alone," she says, watching me. "Hirasor is old and sated now, Vikram. All he wants—I want—is to be left in peace."

"Don't give me this old-man nonsense," I say breathlessly. "I know Hirasor is a nakalchi. He could live for hundreds of years."

She stares at me, the perfect mouth hanging slack with surprise. I tongue a mouth-dart, but she recovers quickly, catching it in mid-air with a burst of flame. It falls smoking to the floor.

"How did you find out?"

Before I can answer, a door opens behind her. I see real terror on her face, then, as Hirasor walks into the room.

Except for the slight shuffle, he still walks tall, like Ravan-Ten-Heads.

"Get out!" she tells him, covering the ground between them in long strides, watching me all the time. "I'll deal with him!"

He gives her a glance of pure hatred.

"Let me fight my battles, will you?" A look passes between them, and I see in that instant that what they had once shared has turned bitter; that they are locked in their relationship out of habit and necessity rather than passion, hating each other and yet unable to let go.

I study him as they glare at each other (one of her eyes is still tracking me). Now that I see him at close range, I am shocked by his appearance. How he has fallen! All that is left of his affectations is the silk tunic with the embroidered collar. His hair is ragged and unkempt, and his face, lean and aristocratic as a prize hound's, is covered with scars. His burning dark eyes look out as though from a cage. I remember those eyes; I remember him peering down at me from the Harvester's face. Silently I mouth the Word, waiting until he will be in my power.

He has turned toward me. He holds out his hands to show that they are empty.

"I want to die," he says. "Even here, I can't get rid of . . . I can't go on. I have a perfect memory; I remember everything I have ever done, whether awake or in my dreams. All I want now is death . . . at your hands—"

"No, no," Suvarna says to him. "Don't talk like that. I won't let anyone kill you." She holds his arm, trying to pull him away. Her voice rises in a scream. "Don't let him kill you! I'll be all alone!"

"She thinks it will get better with time," he says to me, ignoring her. "But I want to end it more than anything. I have had not a moment—not one moment of peace. Six times I tried to kill myself, and six times she prevented me."

He turns to her: "Foolish Suvarna, we are all 'all alone.' I can't allow you to interfere this time. Now go away and let me die."

He pushes her suddenly and violently, throwing her across the room. She lies against the far wall in a huddle, staring at him with wide, shocked eyes.

"Death is not what I had in mind," I say, coming closer. "Death would be too good for you, Hirasor." I bring my armored hands up to his throat. He stands in front of me, not resisting, waiting. For a moment I think it is the old dream again, him and me at each other's throats at the world's end, but it is all going wrong. His wild eyes beg me for death. He shudders violently. I dig my claws into his neck, feel the pulse of the machine that he is, prepare myself to rip him half to death, to say the Word that will condemn him to perpetual hell, a hair's-breadth short of death. "Please, please, hurry" he begs, half choking, not understanding what it is I am giving him.

I cannot do it. This pathetic being—Hirasor, destroyer of worlds! He is no adversary. He sickens me.

Besides, he is in hell already, without my help.

I let my hands fall.

"Live, then," I say angrily, backing toward the door.

His nostrils flare, his eyes widen. He begins a terrible high-pitched keening, clawing with his hands at his face and hair. Suvarna, who seems to have forgotten about me, has stumbled to her feet and is by his side in an instant. She puts her long arms around him.

"You are safe now," she says, crooning, putting her red lips to his hair. "I'll take care of him later. Nobody will take you away from me."

"Let me go, Suvarna," he weeps. "Leave me here on Oblivion. Leave me alone!"

As he thrashes in her arms, she says it, loudly and clearly.

The Word, which I had let slip in one panicked moment.

He becomes limp in her arms, his horrified gaze locked on hers. She lets him down gently on the divan.

She will not be alone now; she will have the perpetually suffering Hirasor to care for all her life.

I shoot him once, in the chest. She falls in a heap by his side, screaming and cursing. Over the wreck of his body, the slow and certain ebbing of his consciousness, I begin to speak the words of passing.

"*Shantih. Nothen ke aagaman, na dukh na dard . . .*"

And I walk out of the room.

Hirasor got his freedom, but what of me, the man-woman with a hundred aliases, none of which were Ram after all? There I was, boarding the first shuttle out of Oblivion, cheated of true victory at the end, my life's purpose lost. I had been tempted to stay on, to live with the crazies and let my mind descend into chaos, but the people there wouldn't let me. They seemed to think Suvarna had killed Hirasor; nobody cared to connect me directly with the crime, but his violent death was enough for them to send the stranger packing. I don't know what happened to Suvarna; I never saw her again.

At the first opportunity I switched from the shuttle to a passenger ship that made numerous stops on various inhabited worlds, thinking I might go back to my last residence on the planet Manaus. But when it came time to disembark I couldn't manage to do it. I am still on the ship, waiting until the impulse comes (if it ever will) to step out under the skies of a new world and begin another life. What has passed for my life, my personal *Ramayana,* comes back to me in tattered little pieces, pages torn from a book, burning, blowing in the wind. Like patterns drawn in the dust, half-familiar, a language once understood, then forgotten.

Here are some things I have discovered about myself:

I have no pleasure in life. I like nothing, definitely not absinthe or roses.

I want to die. But a curious inertia keeps me from it. The things of the world seem heavy, and time slow.

I still have nightmares about the burning woman. Sometimes I dream that Dhanu has a mantram that will bring me peace, and I am looking for her in the tunnels of a dying city, its walls collapsing around me, but she is nowhere to be found. I never dream of Hirasor except as a presence behind my consciousness like a second pair of eyes, a faint ghost, a memory. There are moments when I wonder what led a first-generation nakalchi to become a monster. The *Ramayana* says that even Ravan was once a good man, before he fell prey to hubris and lost his way. If legend is to be believed, there is a cave on some abandoned planet where copies of the first-generation nakalchis are hidden. Were I to come across it, would I find Hirasor's duplicate in an ice-cold crypt, dreaming, innocent as a child?

Lately I have begun to let myself remember that last climactic moment of my encounter with Hirasor. I shot my Ravan, I tell myself, trying to infuse into my mind a sense of victory despite the loss of the chance for true revenge—but I no longer know what any of those words mean: victory, revenge. Still, there is a solidity about that moment when I shot him, small though it is against the backdrop of all the years I've lived. That moment—it feels as tangible as a key held in the hand. What doors it might open I do not know, although I am certain that Sita does not wait behind any of them. Perhaps it is enough that it tells me there are doors.

Somadeva:
A Sky River Sutra

I am Somadeva.

I was once a man, a poet, a teller of tales, but I am long dead now. I lived in the eleventh century of the Common Era in northern India. Then we could only dream of that fabulous device, the udankhatola, the ship that flies between worlds. Then, the sky-dwelling Vidyadharas were myth, occupying a reality different from our own. And the only wings I had with which to make my journeys were those of my imagination . . .

Who or what am I now, in this age when flying between worlds is commonplace? Who brought me into being, here in this small, cramped space, with its smooth metallic surfaces, and the round window revealing an endless field of stars?

It takes me a moment to recognize Isha. She is lying in her bunk, her hair spread over the pillow, looking at me.

And then I remember the first time I woke up in this room, bewildered. Isha told me she had re-created me. She fell in love with me fifteen centuries after my death, after she read a book I wrote, an eighteen-volume compendium of folktales and legends, called the *Kathasaritsagara: The Ocean of Streams of Story.*

"You do remember that?" she asked me anxiously upon my first awakening.

"Of course I remember," I said, as my memories returned to me in a great rush.

The *Kathasaritsagara* was my life's work. I wandered all over North India, following rumors of the Lost Manuscript, risking death to interview murderers and demons, cajoling stories out of old women and princes, merchants and nursing mothers. I took these stories and organized them into patterns of labyrinthine complexity. In my book there are stories within stories—the chief narrator tells a story and the characters in that story tell other stories and so on. Some of the narrators refer to the stories of previous narrators; thus each is not only a teller of tales but also a participant. The story frames themselves form a complex, multi-referential tapestry. And the story of how the *Kathasaritsagara* came to be is the first story of them all.

I began this quest because of a mystery in my own life, but it became a labor of love, an attempt to save a life. That is why I wove the stories into a web, so I could hold safe the woman I loved. I could not have guessed that fifteen centuries after my death, another very different woman would read my words and fall in love with me.

The first time I met Isha, she told me she had created me to be her companion on her journeys between the stars. She wants to be the Somadeva of this age, collecting stories from planet to planet in the galaxy we call Sky River. What a moment of revelation it was for me, when I first knew that there were other worlds, peopled and habited, rich with stories! Isha told me that she had my spirit trapped in a crystal jewel-box. The jewel-box has long feelers like the antennae of insects, so that I can see and hear and smell, and thereby taste the worlds we visit.

"How did you pull my spirit from death? From history? Was I reborn in this magic box?"

She shook her head.

"It isn't magic, Somadeva. Oh, I can't explain! But tell me, I need to know. Why didn't you write yourself into the *Kathasaritsagara*? Who, really, is this narrator of yours, Gunadhya? I know there is a mystery there . . ."

She asks questions all the time. When she is alone with me, she is often animated like this. My heart reaches out to her, this lost child of a distant age.

Gunadhya is a goblin-like creature who is the narrator of the *Kathasaritsagara*. According to the story I told, Gunadhya was a minion of Shiva himself who was reborn on Earth due to a curse. His mission was to tell the greater story of which the *Kathasaritsagara* is only a page: the *Brhat-katha*. But he was forbidden to speak or write in Sanskrit or any other language of humankind. Wandering through a forest one day, he came upon a company of the flesh-eating Pishach. He hid himself and listened to them, and learned their strange tongue. In time he wrote the great *Brhat-katha* in the Pishachi language in a book made of the bark of trees, in his own blood.

They say that he was forced to burn the manuscript, and that only at the last moment did a student of his pull out one section from the fire. I tracked that surviving fragment for years, but found only a few scattered pages, and the incomplete memories of those who had seen the original, or been told the tales. From these few I reconstructed what I have called the *Kathasaritsagara*. In all this, I have drawn on ancient Indic tradition, in which the author is a compiler, an embellisher, an arranger of stories, some written, some told. He fragments his consciousness into the various fictional narrators in order to be a conduit for their tales.

In most ancient works, the author goes a step further: he walks himself whole into the story, like an actor onto the stage.

This is one way I have broken from tradition. I am not, myself, a participant in the stories of the *Kathasaritsagara*. And Isha wants to know why.

Sometimes I sense my narrator, Gunadhya, as one would a ghost, a presence standing by my side. He is related to me in some way that is not clear to me. All these years he has been coming into my dreams, filling in gaps in my stories, or contradicting what I've already written down. He is a whisper in my ear; sometimes my tongue moves at his command. All the time he is keeping secrets from me, tormenting me with the silence between his words. Perhaps he is waiting until the time is right.

"I don't know," I tell Isha. "I don't know why I didn't put myself in the story. I thought it would be enough, you know, to cast a story web, to trap my queen. To save her from death . . ."

"Tell me about her," Isha says. Isha knows all about Suryavati, but she wants to hear it from me. Over and over.

I remember . . .

A high balcony, open, not latticed. The mountain air, like wine. In the inner courtyard below us, apricots are drying in the sun in great orange piles. Beyond the courtyard walls I can hear men's voices, the clash of steel as soldiers practice their murderous art. The king is preparing to battle his own son, who lusts for the throne and cannot wait for death to take his father. But it is for the queen that I am here. She is standing by the great stone vase on the balcony, watering the holy tulsi plant. She wears a long skirt of a deep, rich red, and a green shawl over the delicately embroidered tunic. Her slender fingers shake; her gaze, when it lifts to me, is full of anguish. Her serving maids hover around her, unable to relieve her of her pain. At last she sits, drawing the edge of her fine silken veil about her face. A slight gesture of the hand. My cue to begin the story that will, for a moment, smooth that troubled brow.

It is for her that I have woven the story web. Every day it gives her a reason to forget despair, to live a day longer. Every day she is trapped in it, enthralled by it a little more. There are days when the weight of her anxiety is too much, when she breaks the spell of story and requires me for another purpose. Then I must, for love of her, take part in an ancient and dangerous rite. But today, the day that I am remembering for Isha, Suryavati simply wants to hear a story.

I think I made a mistake with Suryavati, fifteen centuries ago. If I'd written myself into the *Kathasaritsagara*, perhaps she would have realized how much I needed her to be alive. After all, Vyasa, who penned the immortal *Mahabharata*, was as much a participant in the tale as its chronicler. And the same is true of Valmiki, who wrote the *Ramayana* and was himself a character in it, an agent.

So, for the first time, I will write myself into *this* story. Perhaps that is the secret to affecting events as they unfold. And after all, I, too, have need of meaning. Beside me, Gunadhya's ghost nods silently in agreement.

Isha sits in the ship's chamber, her fingers running through her hair, her gaze troubled. She has always been restless. For all her confidences I can only guess what it is she is seeking through the compilation of the legends and myths of the inhabited worlds. As I wander through the story-labyrinths of my own making, I hope to find, at the end, my Isha, my Suryavati.

Isha is, I know, particularly interested in stories of origin, of ancestry. I think it is because she has no knowledge of her natal family. When she was a young woman, she was the victim of a history raid. The raiders took from her all her memories. Her memories are scattered now in the performances of entertainers, the conversations of strangers, and the false memories of imitation men. The extinction of her identity was so clean that she would not recognize those memories as her own, were she to come across them. What a terrible and wondrous age this is, in which such things are possible!

In her wanderings, Isha hasn't yet been able to find out who her people were. All she has as a clue is an ancient, battered set of books: the eighteen volumes of the *Kathasaritsagara*. They are, to all appearances, her legacy, all that was left of her belongings after the raid. The pages are yellow and brittle, the text powdery, fading. She has spent much of her youth learning the lost art of reading, learning the lost scripts of now-dead languages. Inside the cover of the first volume is a faint inscription, a name: Vandana. There are notes in the same hand in the margins of the text. An ancestor, she thinks.

This is why Isha is particularly interested in stories of origin. She thinks she'll find out something about herself by listening to other people's tales of where they came from.

I discovered this on my very first journey with her. After she brought me into existence, we went to a world called Jesanli, where the few city-states were hostile toward us. None would receive us, until we met the Kiha, a nomadic desert tribe who had a tradition of hospitality. None of the inhabitants of this planet have much by way of arts or machinery, civilization or learning. But the Kiha have stories that are poetic and strange. Here is the first of them.

> Once upon a time our ancestors lived in a hot and crowded space, in near darkness. They were not like us. They were not men, nor women, but had a different form. The ancestors, having poor sight, lived in fear all the time, and when one intruded too close to another, they immediately sprang apart in terror. It was as though each moment of approach brought the possibility of a stranger, an enemy, entering their personal domain. Imagine a lot of people who cannot speak, forced to live in a small, cramped, dark cave, where every blundering collision is a nightmare—for that is what it was like for them. Their fear became part of them, becoming a physical presence like a burden carried on the back.
>
> But every once in a while two or more of them would be pushed close enough together to actually behold each other dimly through their nearly useless eyes. During these moments of recognition they were able to see themselves in the other person, and to reach out, and to draw together. In time they formed tight little family units. Then they had no more need to carry around their burdens of fear, which, when released, turned into light.
>
> Yes, yes. You heard that right. Although they continued to live in their furnace-like world and be cramped

together, what emanated from them—despite everything—was light.

Isha's eyes lit up when she heard this story. She told the Kiha that
the story had hidden meanings, that it contained the secret of how
the stars burn. They listened politely to her explanation and thanked
her for her story. She wanted to know where they had first heard the
tale, but the question made no sense to them. Later she told me that
for all their non-technological way of life, the Kiha must have once
been sky-dwellers.

They had told Isha the story to repay a debt, because she brought
them gifts. So when she explained their story back to them, they had
to tell her another story to even things out. They did this with reluctance, because a story is a gift not easily given to strangers.

Here is the second story.

In the beginning there was just one being, whose name
was That Which Is Nameless. The Nameless One was
vast, undifferentiated, and lay quiescent, waiting. In that
place there was no darkness, for there was no light.

Slowly the Nameless One wearied of its existence. It
said into the nothingness: Who am I? But there was no
answer because there was no other. It said unto itself:
Being alone is a burden. I will carve myself up and make
myself companions.

So the Nameless One gathered itself and spread itself
violently into all directions, thinning out as it did so.
It was the greatest explosion ever known, and from its
shards were born people and animals and stars.

And so when light falls on water, or a man shoots an
arrow at another man, or a mother picks up a child, That
Which Was Once Nameless answers a very small part of
the question: Who Am I?

And yet the Once Nameless still reaches out, beyond
the horizon of what we know and don't know, breaking

itself up into smaller and smaller bits like the froth from a wave that hits a rocky shore. What is it seeking? Where is it going? Nobody can tell.

I could tell that Isha was excited by this story also; she wanted to tell the Kiha that the second story was really about the birth of the universe—but I restrained her. To the Kiha, what is real and what is not real is not a point of importance. To them there are just stories and stories, and the universe has a place for all of them.

Later Isha asked me:

"How is it possible that the Kiha have forgotten they once traversed the stars? Those two stories contain the essence of the sciences, the vigyan-shastras, in disguise. How can memory be so fragile?"

She bit her lip, and I know she was thinking of her own lost past. In my life, too, there are gaps I cannot fill.

The stories in the *Kathasaritsagara* are not like these tales of the Kiha. Queen Suryavati was of a serious mien, spending much time in contemplation of Lord Shiva. To lighten her burdens I collected tales of ordinary, erring mortals and divines: cheating wives, sky-dwelling, shape-shifting Vidyadharas, and the denizens, dangerous and benign, of the great forests. These were first told, so the story goes, by Shiva himself. They are nothing like the stories of the Kiha.

Isha has so much to learn! Like Suryavati, she is a woman of reserve. She conceals her pain as much as she can from the world. Her interaction with the Kiha is impersonal, almost aloof. Now, if it were left to me, I would go into their dwelling places, live with them, listen to gossip. Find out who is in love with whom, what joys and sorrows the seasons bring, whether there is enmity between clans. I have never been much interested in the cosmic dramas of gods and heroes.

However, the third Kiha tale is quite unlike the first two. I don't know what to make of it.

Once, in the darkness, a man wandered onto a beach where he saw a fire. He came upon it and saw that the fire was another man, all made of light, who spun in a circle on the beach as though drunk. The first man, warmed by the glow of the fire-man, wanted to talk to him, but the fire-man didn't take any notice of him. The fire-man kept spinning, round and round, and the first man kept yelling out questions, spinning round and round with the fire-man so he could see his face. And there were three small biting insects who dared not bite the fire-man but wanted to bite the cheeks of the other man, and they kept hovering around the other man, and he kept waving them off, but they would go behind him until he forgot about them, and then they'd circle around and bite him again.

Then?

Then nothing. They are all, all five of them, still on that dark beach, dancing still.

Isha thinks this story is a more recent origin story. She speculates that the ancestral people of the Kiha come from a world which has three moons. A world that floated alone in space until it fell into the embrace of a star. There are worlds like that, I've heard, planets wandering without their shepherd stars. It is not unlikely that one of these was captured by a sun. This story was told to Isha by a child, who ran up to us in secret when we were leaving. She wanted to make us a gift of some sort, but that was all she had.

If Isha is right, then the Kiha told us the stories in the wrong order. Arrange them like this: birth of the universe, birth of their sun, coming into being of their world.

But these old stories have as many meanings as there are stars in the sky. To assign one single interpretation to them is to miss the point. Take the second story. It could be as much a retelling of a certain philosophical idea from the ancient Indic texts called the Upanishads as a disguised theory of cosmological origin. In my other life I was learned in Sanskrit.

But it is also important what *we* make of these stories. What meaning we find in them, as wanderers by the seashore find first one shell, then another, and form them into a chain of their own making.

Here is the start of a story I have made by braiding together the Kiha tales.

> In the beginning, Isha made the world. Wishing to know herself, she broke herself up into parts. One of them is me, Somadeva, poet and wanderer. We circle each other forever, one maker, one made . . .

Sometimes I wonder if I have made her up as much as she has concocted me. If we are fictions of each other, given substance only through our mutual narratives.

Perhaps the Kiha are right: stories make the world.

I wake and find myself on that high stone balcony. The queen is watching me. A small fire in an earthen pail burns between us, an angeethi. Over it, hanging from an iron support, is a black pot containing the brew.

"Did it take you too far, my poet?" she asks, worried. "You told me of far worlds and impossible things. You spoke some words I couldn't understand. An entertaining tale. But I only want a glimpse of what is to come in the next few days, not eons. I want to know . . ."

I am confused. When I first opened my eyes I thought I saw Isha. I thought I was on the ship, telling Isha a story about Suryavati. She likes me to recite the old tales, as she lies back in her bunk, running her fingers slowly over her brow. I wish I could caress that brow myself.

So how is it that I find myself here, breathing in pine-scented Himalayan air? How is it my mouth has a complex aftertaste that I cannot quite identify, which has something to do with the herbal brew steaming in the pot? My tongue is slightly numb, an effect of the poison in the mix.

Or is it that in telling my story to Isha I have immersed myself so deeply in the tale that it has become reality to me?

The queen's eyes are dark, and filled with tears.

"Dare I ask you to try again, my poet? Will you risk your life and sanity one more time, and tell me what you see? Just a step beyond this moment, a few days hence. Who will win this war . . ."

What I cannot tell her is that I've seen what she wants to know. I know what history has recorded of the battle. The prince, her son, took his father's throne and drove him to his death. And the queen . . .

It is past bearing.

What I am trying to do is to tell her a story in which I am a character. If I can have a say in the way things turn out, perhaps I can save her. The king and his son are beyond my reach. But Suryavati? She is susceptible to story. If she recognizes, in the fictional Somadeva's love for Isha, the real Somadeva's unspoken, agonized love, perhaps she'll step back from the brink of history.

My fear is that if events unfurl as history records, I will lose my Suryavati. Will I then be with Isha, wandering the stars in search of stories? Or will I die here on this earth, under the shadow of the palace walls, with the night sky nothing but a dream? Who will survive, the real Somadeva or the fictional one? And which is which?

All I can do is stall Suryavati with my impossible tales—and hope.

"I don't know how far the brew will take me," I tell her. "But for you, my queen, I will drink again."

I take a sip.

I am back on the ship. Isha is asleep, her hair in tangles over her face. Her face in sleep is slack, except for that habitual little frown between her brows. The frown makes her look more like a child, not less. I wonder if her memories come to her in her dreams.

So I begin another story, although I remain a little confused. Who is listening: Isha or Suryavati?

I will tell a story about Inish. It is a place on a far world and one of the most interesting we have visited.

I hesitate to call Inish a city, because it is not really one. It is a collection of buildings and people, animals and plants, and is referred to by the natives as though it has an independent consciousness. But also it has no clear boundary because the mini-settlements at what might have been its edge keep wandering off and returning, apparently randomly.

Identities are also peculiar among the inhabitants of Inish. A person has a name, let us say Mana, but when Mana is with her friend Ayo, they together form an entity named Tukrit. If you meet them together and ask them for their names, they will say "Tukrit," not "Ayo and Mana." Isha once asked them whether Ayo and Mana were parts of Tukrit, and they both laughed. "Tukrit is not bits of this or that," Mana said. "Then who just spoke, Mana or Tukrit?" Isha asked. "Tukrit, of course," they said, giggling in an indulgent manner.

"I am Isha," Isha told them. "But who am I when I'm with you?"

"We are *teso*," they said, looking at each other. Isha knew what that meant. "*Teso*" is, in their language, a word that stands for anything that is unformed, not quite there, a possibility, a potential.

It is hard for outsiders to understand whether the Inish folk have family units or not. Several people may live in one dwelling, but since their dwellings are connected by little corridors and tunnels, it is hard to say where one ends and another begins. The people in one dwelling may be four older females, one young woman, three young men, and five children. Ask them their names and depending on which of them are present at that time, they will say a different collective name. If there are only Baijo, Akar, and Inha around, they'll say, "We are Garho." If Sami, Kinjo, and Vif are also there, then they are collectively an entity known as "Parak." And so on and so forth.

How they keep from getting confused is quite beyond Isha and me.

"Tell me, Isha," I said once. "You and I . . . what are we when we are together?"

She looked at me sadly.

"Isha and Somadeva," she said. But there was a faint query in her tone.

"What do you think, Somadeva?" she said.

"*Teso*," I said.

Here is a story from Inish.

There was Ikla. Then, no Ikla but Bako walking away from what was now Samish. While walking, Bako found herself being part of a becoming, but she could not see who or what she was becoming with. Ah, she thought, it is a *goro* being; one that does not show itself except through a sigh in the mind. She felt the *teso* build up slowly, felt herself turn into a liquid, sky, rain. Then there was no *teso*, no *goro*, no Bako, but a fullness, a ripening, and thus was Chihuli come into happening.

And this Chihuli went shouting down the summer lanes, flinging bits of mud and rock around, saying, There is a storm coming! A storm! And Chihuli went up the hill and sank down before the sacred stones and died there. So there was nothing left but Bako, who looked up with enormous eyes at the sky, and felt inside her the emptiness left by the departure of the *goro* being.

Bako, now, why had the *goro* being chosen her for a happening? Maybe because she had always felt *teso* with storms, and since storms were rare here and people had to be warned, there was a space inside her for the kind of *goro* being that lived for storms and their warning. So that is how the right kind of emptiness had brought Chihuli into being.

Pods kept forming around Bako but she resisted being pulled in. It was because of the coming storm, because she could sense the *teso* with it. Nobody else could. With others it was other beings, wild things and bright eyes in the darkness, sometimes even the slowtrees, but only with Bako was there the emptiness inside shaped like a storm. And so she felt the *teso*, the way she had with the *goro* being.

The air crackled with electricity; dark clouds filled the sky, like a ceiling about to come down. Everywhere you looked, it was gray: gray water, gray beings, looking up with wondering, frightened eyes. Only for Bako, as the *teso* built, was the excitement, the anticipation. Many had felt that before when they found their special pod, their mate-beings. The feeling of ripening, of coming into a fullness. The wild sweetness of it. Now Bako felt something like that many times over.

Samish came sweeping up the hill where she was standing, trying to swoop her back with them, so they could be Ikla again, and the *teso* with the storm would become nothing more. But she resisted, and Samish had to go away. This was a thing stronger than the love-bonds they had known.

Came the storm. A magnificent storm it was, rain and thunder, and the legs of lightning dancing around Bako. Rivers swollen, running wild over land, into homes, sweeping everything away. Hills began to move, and the beings ran from their homes. Only Bako stood in the rain, on the highest hill, and the storm danced for her.

The *teso* became something. We call it T'fan. T'fan played with the world, spread over half the planet, wrapped her wet arms around trees and hills. The storm went on until the beings thought there would be no more sun, no more dry land. Then one day it ceased.

Samish gathered itself up, and went tiredly up the hill to find Bako, or to mourn the death of Ikla.

Bako was not there. What was there was standing just as they had left Bako, arms outstretched to the sky. She looked at them with faraway eyes, and they saw then that although the sky was clearing, the storm was still in her. Tiny sparks of lightning flashed from her fingertips. Her hair was singed.

They saw then that the storm had filled her empty spaces so completely that there would never be Ikla again. They did not even feel *teso*. They walked away from her and prepared for mourning.

T'fan stands there still, her eyes filled with storms, her fingers playing with lightning. Her hair has singed away almost completely. She needs no food or water, and seems, in the way of storms, to be quite content. When storms come to her people they cluster around her and she comes to life, dancing in their midst as though relatives have come again from far away. Then T'fan goes away and is replaced by something larger and more complex than we can name.

"What does that story mean, I wonder," Isha said.

"Sometimes stories are just stories," I told her.

"You've never told me what happened to Suryavati, after you took the next sip, told her the next tale," she told me, turning away from the consequences of my remark. The fact that you can't wrest meaning from everything like fruit from trees—that meaning is a matter not only of story but of what the listener brings to the tale—all that is not something she can face at the moment. She is so impatient, my Isha.

I steeled myself.

"The queen was distraught with grief when her son took the kingdom and destroyed his father," I said. "She threw herself on his funeral pyre. I could not save her."

But in this moment I am also conscious of the queen herself, her eyes dark with grief and yearning. Her hand, with its long fingers—a healed cut on the right index finger, the henna patterns fading—her hand reaches up to wipe a tear. And yet in her gaze leaps a certain vitality, an interest. Her mind ranges far across the universe, carried by my tales. In that small fire in her eyes is all my hope.

Perhaps all I've found is a moment of time that keeps repeating, in which, despite the predations of history, I am caught, with Isha and Suryavati, in a loop of time distanced from the main current. Here my stories never end; I never reach the moment Suryavati awaits, and Isha never finds out who she is. Gunadhya remains a whisper in my mind, his relation to me as yet a secret. Here we range across the skies, Isha and I, Vidyadharas of another age, and Suryavati's gaze follows us. Who is the teller of the tale, and who the listener? We are caught in a web, a wheel of our own making. And if you, the listener from another time and space, upon whose cheek this story falls like spray thrown up by the ocean—you, the eavesdropper hearing a conversation borne by the wind, if you would walk into this story, take it away with you into your world, with its sorrows and small revelations, what would become of you? Would you also enter this circle? Would you tell me your story? Would we sit together, Suryavati, Isha, and I, with you, and feel *teso* within us—and weave meaning from the strands of the tale?

I am Somadeva. I am a poet, a teller of tales.

Are you Sannata3159?

Jhingur was deep in his favorite dreamvid when Langra came scuttling up to him, appearing like a twisted ghost against the great grassland, behind the bison and the thunder in the sky. The ghost gained corporeality; the sweep of land and sky, the smell of dust and sweat, the sweetness of roast meat faded to nothing, and there was Jhingur, wiping saliva and memory on his dirty sleeve, taking off the visor, squinting at Langra.

"Dreaming again, boy? Not that I blame you," Langra said with his sideways smile. He looked out of the hole that was the shop entrance. The shop's metal suspension creaked and shuddered as a sleeker passed on the highway above them. "There's nobody come today to buy dreams or mind-patches, now that the slaughterhouse is opening. All the riff-raff are out gawking! Go on, you go too! I'm going to be expecting something from Upside."

Jhingur knew that Langra was a guptman, that he dealt with secrets and mysteries, including strangers from Upside. You don't ask a guptman questions. Besides, Jhingur had forgotten about the opening day. Grieving was like that. He got up slowly, staring at the view from the hole that was the entrance to the shop. The tall towers of Upside rose like specters over the mean streets, the rope-ladder web-ways of Patal. Rubble-ware huts and wall-holes and swing-shacks suspended from the cables between the great concrete feet of the towers—that was Patal, the greatest of the Undercities, refuge of the world. The canyons were so deep between the sides of the great towers, with the first-tier highways rising four to ten stories overhead, that sunlight couldn't reach all the way down. The sun was a dream. He could see yellow patches of light on the face of a tower far above, and the sky was a sliver of blue between the towers. He looked and sighed, and felt the absence of the woman who had captured his heart like a weight in the chest. Had it really been only a few months ago that she has been there, up there?

"You in love, boy?" Langra said, sneering in his good-natured way. Ordinarily Jhingur spilled everything to Langra, or to his mother and sister. He had never been able to keep a secret. But this was the first time he felt compelled to keep things to himself. He thought he must be growing up, after all, because wasn't that what grown-ups did? Keep secrets, like Langra? But he said to Langra: "I forgot about the opening. My mother and sister will be going to work. They're employed there, you know! At the slaughterhouse!"

That gave him a good feeling, to think about his mother having a real job, earning money, bringing real meat home. He got up and grabbed the rope, ready to be let down to the smoky, sepia-coloured depths below.

"Have fun, boy!" Langra shouted over the squeal of the pulley, leering crookedly at him. "You'll be the best-fed fellow in Patal!"

The slaughterhouse was something to gawk at. It rose from the dust and filth of Patal like a shining metal dream, a long, curved building like the thigh of a beautiful woman. There was a café with tall windows for the employees, and you couldn't see inside, because the windows were opaque one-way and maybe even had illusioneering. There was a lot of jostling and sweating in the crowd in front of the building, and then a cheer went up when the new employees, in their uniforms, lined up to be let in by the guards at the gate. Jhingur's mother saw him and left the line to hug him, because he had remembered to come. His sister gave him a wave of pure happiness, and to him it seemed that the two of them, so strangely confident in their shiny blue uniforms, had become almost like Upside people, not quite real. He was suddenly shy of them, but there was no time to get used to the new feelings. They were out of sight now, in the compound, and the great white metal gate was sliding shut. Jhingur turned and elbowed his way through the crowd, past the long-braided rat-men standing at the edge. He ducked his head, avoiding the gaze of the Cameras that dived down from the heights above. Ordinarily he liked smiling for the Cameras, in the hope that he would see himself on some Net show like *Reality Deep Down*. But today he didn't feel like it.

The streets of Patal seemed strangely empty. In the daytime the light was diffuse and murky. Jhingur preferred the colour of night, with the little fires in the hutments, the aromatic smoke rising above the spires of smoke depots, the anemic streetlamps run by noisy generators. Where Jhingur lived was a peace zone between the territories of two self-styled demon kings, so there were fewer raids and killings here than in other places in Patal. Which is why, maybe, the slaughterhouse had opened here, in an old warehouse filled with hazardous chemware that the slaughterhouse people had to clean out. They had to chase out the rats and the rat-folk who ran, calling in their high voices through the alleyways of Patal with their long braids swinging out behind them and their children on their backs. The other residents of Patal didn't mind this. The rat-people were not well-liked, although they supplied Patal with rat meat and strange, fungal concoctions to cure diseases. The rumor was that rat-folk ate everything, even rubbish and dead people. Right after someone died they'd show up and bargain for the corpse.

Jhingur climbed up to his swing-shack to check on his grandmother, who was asleep, with her toothless mouth hanging open and drool on her chin, which he wiped carefully without waking her. She seemed to be getting more and more insubstantial every day: a bag of bones in sackcloth. He called to his mouse, who came out of a hole in the sacking and chattered at him and accepted some instameal crumbs. The mouse looked at him with beady eyes. "Did you find your love today?" Jhingur asked the mouse. "Did you write her a song?" This had been a joke between them ever since Jhingur read in an old viewbook that male mice compose vocalizations for their mates that might be compared to love songs. The mouse washed its face, twitched its nose at Jhingur, and disappeared into its hole. Jhingur sighed. Why, I'm sighing like Mama, he thought. I'm sighing like a grown-up. He wondered whether the woman who had so briefly shone in his life like a star had wrought this change in him.

She had left him with an unsettled feeling that was new to him. Perhaps that feeling was the source of his discomfort about working at the slaughterhouse. He couldn't explain it to himself, except that he didn't like changes, and the slaughterhouse was a big change. He did like eating meat, though; after the tasteless cubes of insta-meal, the spiced-up-old-leather flavor of the dubious rubbish that street vendors sold, it would be sheer joy to sink his teeth into the savory, juicy chunks of meat swimming in rich broth. Not like the dreamvid with the bison, which left him with a sweet, yearning hunger. No, this would be real.

He had only had meat twice before in his life. As a seven-year-old, he had fallen ill with some debilitating sickness, knowing he was dying, when his mother brought him a stew of something indescribably satisfying. "What is it?" he had asked weakly when he was done, but his mother had turned her face away and not answered. His grandmother had already begun to retreat into her private world then, but an awareness had come into her eyes for a moment: "I wanted to lick the bowl," she said petulantly to her daughter. "You never let me." It was his sister who told him the new food was meat, and whispered fiercely: "Don't ever ask her about it!" He had understood then that it was something for which his mother had paid a price. Perhaps it was that knowledge that had given him the will to survive: that there was a world beyond his knowing, and there were things to live for. Perhaps it was the stories his mother had told him; my dreamer-boy, she called him, because of his insatiable appetite for stories. Growing up, he was still like that: a dreamer, never quite here in this hell-hole, this Patal.

The woman had come into his life without warning. He had been lounging at the door-hole of Langra's shop when he had seen her. A Citizen! Not on a Net show, but for real, in the flesh, up high in one of the tower windows. The windows of Upside were tilted up, turned away from the grime and squalor of Patal, and in any case they were one-way. So in the ordinary course of things Jhingur wouldn't have seen the woman, but for the fact that she had opened the window and was peering down. Until that moment Jhingur had never known that the window could snap open, like an eyelid. He watched the woman stretching her thin body, raising her head in as though in supplication to the sun, and a feeling like an electric shock went through him. There was something in the language of her body—a yearning—that he thought he understood.

He leaned out from the door of the shop to look at her. The shop was suspended from the underside of the Narak fly-over. Above his head the trains hummed and swayed, making a low roar that filled his ears and made his head ache gently. The Narak fly-over was the oldest and lowest-level road-bridge—above it were two roadways that carried sleekers—sometimes you could catch the glint of sunlight on the polished metal as the sleekers swooshed by like beings from another world. Jhingur had been stuck in Langra's shop for more than a day because there was a feud going on in the peace zone in Patal, with lots of fighting and killing, and it wasn't safe to go home. He found himself staring up, above the hell that was his home, imagining a world far removed from his. And there she was.

"Look!" he said to Langra, pointing. Langra looked and shrugged.

"One of the Citizens gone crazy," he said. "Some of them do that. Open windows, I mean. Curiosity, you know. To see what's outside the illusioneering."

"You mean they don't see . . .," Jhingur said to Langra, sweeping his arm across the grimy glory of Patal.

"They do, if they want, from the sleekers," Langra said. "And they know a little from the Net shows, you know, like *Reality Deep Down*. But Patal is not what they want to see when they look out of their windows."

Jhingur regretted showing Langra the woman. There was something unpleasant in the way Langra looked at her, with his tongue hanging out, as she twisted and stretched, pale against the dark mouth of the window. When she appeared again he didn't tell Langra. Anyway Langra liked to be in the back of the shop, communing with the Net, while Jhingur dealt with customers. And now with the fighting there were no customers, so all Jhingur did was to sprawl in the front and look up.

When she came back to the window it occurred to him suddenly to signal to her, to make her aware of his presence. With trembling hands he found a discarded dreamvid cover amid the rubbish in the shop, and a flashlight. He did not know any signaling languages but he tilted up the shiny cover and pointed the flashlight at it.

She paused in her stretching and swaying. She leaned down. He imagined what she would see: the darkness between the great span of the roadways, wisps of smoke, the murky light of fires, perhaps the dark hole of Langra's shop suspended from the lowest bridge, and in that darkness a light, blinking.

It was beyond any hope he had that she would signal back. She disappeared for a moment and returned with something in her hands. Heart in his mouth, Jhingur saw the flash of light. There were regular intervals between flashes, and there were long and short flashes as well so that he understood she was telling him or asking him something. But he had no way of comprehending what it was. He thought of her life up there, as he had glimpsed in Net shows, and found that he couldn't imagine it. With fumbling hands he signaled back, hoping she would understand that he was illiterate in the language of light.

This was his secret for three days. For three days Jhingur did little but to send messages of light across the great gulf between them, and she answered. They had no common tongue. But Jhingur felt he understood her. She was a mythic being from up there, who had looked down and seen him, acknowledged him. She wanted to talk to him. He imagined her asking questions: What is it like, down there? He asked her questions too: How does the sky look? Have you ever seen grass, or trees? He thought she might have been on the grassland, with the bison, experiencing the things he saw only in dreamvids.

She came into his dreams. In his dreams she held his hand. Her hand was smooth and cold. He could not imagine her human. But in his dreams he had looked into her eyes and found an answer to something he could not name.

Then, one morning, Langra called him to the back of the shop for something. When Jhingur returned to the door-hole, the woman was no longer at the window, which lay dark and open, a gaping mouth. He waited, but nothing happened for a very long time. Then he saw other silhouettes, other shapes at the window, after which it shut abruptly. Although he couldn't hear it clang, he jumped.

What had happened? Where had she gone? Had those other people stopped her?

All day he stayed in the shop front, staring up at the shut window, hoping for a sight of her. She didn't return. Dozing, he dreamed she was falling toward him like a star, or a bird.

By the next day he understood she wasn't coming back. He was bewildered with pain and loss, until Langra shook his shoulder and told him it was all right to go home. He remembered then that a feud had been going on all these days below him.

Where Jhingur lived, the no-man's land between the territories of the demon kings Johnny Walker IV and Ghatotkacha, the truce had broken and fighting had escalated out of control. Not the common-as-day quick-killings of fools who ventured out at the wrong time or carried merchandise without care, but knife fights and shoot-outs between thugs, right there in the middle of the littered streets. Blood pooled in dirt-hollows and rival clans dragged away their dead and dying. The usual residents of the peace zone stayed trembling in their hovels. Only the rat-folk came out to scavenge, loitering at the edge of battle, their bone ornaments swinging from their necks and ears.

That night the truce was celebrated on the street near Jhingur's swing-shack, where Johnny Walker IV and Ghatotkacha sat together over a great table groaning with food. The food had been brought by the subjects of both domains, a kind of obeisance or tribute, and even the rat-folk had contributed. The centerpiece was a great hunk of meat, roasted to perfection. Jhingur could smell unfamiliar spices, rich aromas that made him mad with hunger. He didn't want to be hungry; he wanted to be in mourning because he had lost his love, the woman from another realm who had looked down from paradise and seen him. But the noise and the smells of revelry drew him. So he perched up on an old utility pole so he could see above the crowd of onlookers, mostly riff-raff from his own area of Patal. The people below him were licking their lips at the aromas, although a man was saying: I wouldn't eat what the rat-folk bring, you know, even if it is a special gift for the demon-kings. Did you hear that, they brought the main course!

There was loud, raucous music and the rhythmic clash of steel as the army of rag-tag thugs from both sides performed their ritual dance of swords. Up above them the cameras of the popular Net shows, like *Reality Deep Down*, paused in their ceaseless roaming of the cityscape and descended like falling stars, making people roar and wave as they hovered over the revelry. Ghatotkacha and Johnny Walker IV had been on such shows before and loved the attention. They looked up and leered, and Ghatot stood up and pulled his pants down, at which everyone cheered as though there had been no war and no killing. Ghatot smiled and rearranged his clothing, waving to the crowd like a monarch. The two demon kings embraced and sat down to their meal again, grinning self-consciously at the cameras. Every once in a while one or the other would toss a piece of meat into the crowd. The onlookers would fight for the morsel, getting down on hands and knees in the dust and rot as the cameras went wild above them. Jhingur had been wondering if he should get down and join the fray when a piece of meat hit him right in the face. By sheer reflex he caught it with his free hand and stared at it in surprise. The people below him were all hunched over the ground, looking for it. He grinned and put his mouth to the hunk like a lover, chewing as slowly as he dared, hoping nobody would look up. The juices ran down his chin; he licked his lips. The taste! Oh, so this was Citizen meat! It was better than any dreamvid. He almost wept when, after three bites, it was gone.

He still dreamed of the woman of the tower. In the new dreams she was falling from the window, a star against the darkness, falling toward him. His arms were outstretched to catch her, but at the last moment she slipped through his fingers like dust. And there were Ghatot and Johnny Walker IV at the feast, eating, inviting him to join them, leering at him with bloody jaws. Jhingur woke from these dreams sweating and distraught. The first couple of times he had to lean out of the swing shack and vomit onto the street below.

It seemed to Jhingur that his life had been lived in a deep darkness, with occasional moments in the sun. Now, months later, the memory of the woman was a vivid longing, a dream of grass and sunlight.

The slaughterhouse made Jhingur both hungry and uncomfortable, but the good thing about their newfound prosperity was that his mother began to sing again; it had been years since she had sung. Some of the songs he half remembered as lullabies, although she told him they were songs of longing for the Lord. Jhingur wanted to know who this Lord was, and if there were any stories about him, but his mother said that he didn't live in Patal, that all they had here was riff-raff and demons. Where his mother had come from, before the Great Drying, was a place of verdure and beauty, and the Lord had lived there. Her singing voice was lovely and full of longing for that old country; it made Jhingur think of a Net movie he had once seen, and not understood at all—but the images: green fields, a distant river—had stayed in his head all these years. His grandmother didn't seem to care one way or another about the slaughterhouse or the singing; she sat nodding and drooling on her mat all day long, staring through the weave of their swing-shack at the dirt and debris below.

Everything ran like clockwork at the slaughterhouse: all the floors and counters were shiny-clean and hygienic, and the employers took good care of the employees. Apart from the weekly meat portion they got a high-protein drink in the morning and at lunchtime, although they had to bring their own lunch. The drink was fruity and pleasant and gave them all the energy to keep working, and when everybody finished work at five, they went home a cheerful, happy group.

Only Jhingur still refused to work there. He didn't think that people who work at a slaughterhouse should be cheerful or happy. He thought they should be grim and heroic and not talk so much, and flinch when they saw the animals being led to the guillotine. "But you like meat," his sister said. "Yes, I do," Jhingur said. He didn't know how to explain what bothered him about the slaughterhouse, where the animals were both raised and processed into meat. He wanted to explain about the bison and the grasslands, but he couldn't find the words. Being obstinate, he continued to work at Langra's store selling pirated mind-patches and dreamvids, and viewing old view-books, and he ate his portion (a rather large one) of the weekly meat-fry in the community cookhouse.

That is, until the day Langra told him that what he was eating was a piece of his grandmother.

One portion of the meat was different—tough and stringy instead of succulent. Jhingur had a chunk of it in his teeth, and it was so hard to chew that he spat it out on his palm to look at it. Langra was standing next to him, eating with relish. "Yes, some of the meat is tough," he said. "That's because they send the old people to the slaughterhouse, you know! Have you seen your grandmother today?"

Jhingur was indignant. "Of course I have!" he said. He knew Langra could say mean things, things that weren't true. Maybe it came from being a guptman. But the thought was so terrible that he couldn't eat anything anymore. Langra just laughed and punched him on the shoulder, and kept chewing and smacking his lips.

So Jhingur, feeling sick, went and looked at the raw pieces that were waiting to be cooked. What were those things—toes? A human-sized rib? Jhingur began screaming hysterically, making people drop their plates and spill their food. In the confusion he heard his mother saying: "What are you talking about, fool? Your grandmother's alive and fine!"

Jhingur ran out into the night, past the night-fires and demon-smoke depots, around the rat nests, up the web-ways where the swing-shacks hung like great gourds. It seemed to him at first that indeed his grandmother was still there in the darkness of the swing-shack, drooling and nodding. Jhingur said to her: "Shall I bring you some food?" He was upset that nobody had taken food to her. But she didn't say anything, and when he reached out to touch her arm she faded away and disappeared.

There came his mother and sister, climbing up the rope-ladder, entering the round hole of the swing-shack, their muscular arms shiny with sweat. They didn't seem to think anything was wrong. His mother said that the grandmother had been gone for days, hadn't Jhingur noticed? She had been sent to a home for dependents of the employees, where she was being taken care of. In fact, Jhingur's mother said, she had talked to her during the lunch break on the new talkline. And Jhingur was being a disgrace and a fool, not acting like the almost-grown man he was, making all this trouble in the community. This bewildered Jhingur very much, because he was sure he had tucked his grandmother into bed last night. "You've just been playing pretend, like you used to," his sister said, with some scorn. "When will you grow up, Jhingur?"

The next day there was an invitation for Jhingur to come work at the slaughterhouse. "They really could use you," his mother said.

"Won't go!" he said stubbornly. He preferred, he told her, to stay on at Langra's shop.

His mother and sister were annoyed with him, but only mildly. After all these years they had gotten used to Jhingur's perversities. Before she left his mother stroked his hair, saying, "My dreamer-boy!" although she said it sadly.

At Langra's shop there were fewer and fewer customers. Langra said it was because of the slaughterhouse and the new jobs. He said it without rancor, but his gaze went up, up the concrete wall to the towers of Upside.

So Jhingur lay in the shop, viewed dream-vids and ate insta-meal strips. The best dream-vid of all was the one about the bisons. If he had been good at telling stories he would have told this one to his mother and sister. It would explain to them, he thought, why he felt the way he did about the slaughterhouse, even before the disappearance of his grandmother. He didn't have the words to describe what he meant, what he felt. But the story said it all.

Long ago, the story went, there was a tribe of people in another part of the Earth who had once hunted bison, great, god-like animals. These people had lived in the city for a while and forgotten their old ways, so one day they resolved to go back to the wide place under the sky where they had once dwelt. They called upon the old men, the memory-keepers of their tribe, to instruct them in the art of the bison hunt.

So there they went, young men and old, out in the great, unimaginable space where the bison lived. The herd was grazing, their shaggy heads lowered. The plain was as vast as the sky. The sky was low with clouds.

The people stopped before the bison herd and their chief drew his ancestor's hunting knife. The metal gleamed in the air. There was a roll of distant thunder, and a few raindrops pock-marked the ground. There was a moist, heady aroma of sweat and wet ground. The chief waited.

After a while a young bull left the herd and came up to them, and bowed his head.

The tribe's chief thanked the bull and raised his knife in the air. But just then an old bull came raging out of the herd, snorting and pawing at the ground. The tribe members leaped back in alarm, raising their weapons, but the old bull simply pushed the young one out of the way and bowed his head in his place.

The blade flashed in the air, and the old bull met his death for his tribe.

And the humans honored his memory at every meal. They remembered, the vid said, that life is short and precious, and sacrifice is worthy of honor, and animals are our kin.

The story always made Jhingur weep, and he wondered if it had ever been true. He wanted to eat the meat of such an animal, to become like him, to sacrifice himself for his tribe. He wanted his mother and sister to view the story, but they didn't have the time or patience for it.

"You live too much in stories," his mother said. "You want to be a hero. Here in Patal there are no heroes, no gods, not even demons, no matter what they might call themselves. Just a bunch of sorry folk. You dream too much, Jhingur!"

It was true. When Jhingur was a child, just recovering from his illness, she had told him an old story about gods and demons and the battle that raged between them. It was a great story, full of the clash of steel and the rumble of war chariots and the tears of brave warriors. Jhingur had become so immersed in it that when he got better he had pretended for weeks that he was a god, or a demon. He stole a pike from a smoke depot to use as a spear and was chased and thrashed by a minion of the demon-king. His mother thrashed him too, in her anger and fear.

But that day as he lay in Langra's shop, waiting for customers who never came, he caught sight of his sister staggering home in the middle of the afternoon. When he caught up with her he saw she was in tears. He put his arm around her and helped her home.

"My protein shake spilled," she said when they were inside. "At lunch. I was too embarrassed to ask for another one so I went into the afternoon shift without it. And it was horrible, Jhingur! The animals were so terrified. My ears were filled with their screaming. They don't always kill them before they load them on the conveyor belt, you see. And when they hit them or shock them, the animals scream. All this time I couldn't see some of the animals were alive when I cut into them. I didn't know! The animals behind can see what is happening to the ones in front, and they can't move, because they are injured, and they just cry. Or they look at you, with those eyes. I couldn't do it, Jhingur! I couldn't!"

"Don't go back," Jhingur said, horrified.

But then his sister's supervisor came in, all smiles, swarming her way up the rope-ladder like a big spider, entering the round hole of the swing-shack. She wrinkled her nose at the smell but didn't stop smiling. She had a tall bottle of protein shake in her hand, and when Jhingur's sister drank it up she was ready to go to work as though nothing had happened.

In the evening Jhingur tried to remind his sister of what she'd seen, but she was feeling particularly cheerful just then and shrugged him off. "I was just feeling a bit unwell," she said. "I was just babbling nonsense. How silly of you to believe me!"

That night there was the weekly meat-fry. Jhingur couldn't bring himself to go, although the aroma of meat cooking made him faint with longing. He lay in their swing-shack, chewing insta-meal strips and feeding crumbs to his pet mouse, feeling useless and miserable. He didn't know whether his sister had really seen what she had said she'd seen that afternoon. If only he, Jhingur, had the courage to find the truth! He wished he were a hero. But it was much more sensible to accept that his sister had been mistaken.

The next day Langra told Jhingur he was packing up.

"Nobody wants my mind-patches," he said. "Or the dream-vids, or the old books. They are all working at the slaughterhouse and they are content. Nobody needs my fantasies. So I'm off."

"Where will you go?" asked Jhingur.

Langra grinned his lopsided grin. He said: "There's always work for a guptman! I'm going to be working with the *Reality Deep Down* shows, boy! I'll be living one level up, like a star."

Working for a famous Net show! Jhingur couldn't imagine it! He tried to look happy for Langra, but Langra saw through the attempt.

"I'll give you my Net-link number, boy," he said. "Send me a photo some time, or a tip next time the demons have a fight. The show might use it."

Already Langra sounded as though he was a Citizen, even though living the next level up didn't make you one. It seemed like he was going big places, though. He patted Jhingur on the shoulder, gave him a present of his favorite books and dreamvids (not that anyone wanted them anyway) and scuttled off toward the capsule, which had descended for him on a long, metal rope. Jhingur watched the capsule go up at impossible speed into the darkness between two roadways.

So now there was no longer work for Jhingur. His mother and sister were not pleased, and people looked at him in disapproval at the community kitchen. He wondered whether he should leave home, but beyond the neighborhood was unknown territory where the demon-kings unleashed their monsters every day and recruited unwilling young men for their battles—and besides he loved his mother and sister and mouse. And every night his mother would sing her old songs of loss and longing, which, Jhingur realized, he could not do without anymore. He had been born with her singing to him; he wanted to die like that too, to fade away in her arms to the sound of her voice. When she sang, his very soul found sustenance.

But he wasn't happy because of the way the slaughterhouse had changed everything, and because he could no longer eat the meat. Some other old people went away from the neighborhood, but they sent postcards from the old-age facility, and they all seemed content. Then the neighbor's aunt went away.

This made Jhingur quite miserable because although the aunt was crippled her mind was just fine and she used to tell Jhingur stories of the old days. It was a sort of secret between them, because nobody really had the time to listen to the old lady and they didn't know she had anything worth sharing. But she had told Jhingur about the life she had led in a far-away place, driving goats over hillocks, working in paddy fields, throwing handfuls of rice out for the birds. Her stories had made Jhingur happy because it was good to know that the things his books talked about had actually existed somewhere, sometime: grass, trees, wildflowers.

Now she was gone. And the postcards she sent sounded like they were written by someone else, which (he thought) they probably were.

There were other disappearances, even among the rat-folk, and the smoke people with their pipes and dried herbs, and the riff-raff and knife-wielding thieves and troublemakers, but who cared about them? People who worked at the slaughterhouse said that the streets had become easier to traverse, even in the deeper darkness of night.

Only Jhingur wasn't happy. He began to wonder whether his sister had indeed told the truth the first time. I want to be a hero, he thought. I want to find out what really happens to the animals and the old people. Obviously the only way to do this was to join the workers in the slaughterhouse. But he had to be careful not to drink the protein shake, because it addled the brain and made everything seem fine when it was not. So he attached a little spy-eye to his shirt lapel and announced to his mother one morning that he was coming with them.

"It's about time," she said, smiling. "You are young and strong, and we can use you."

The first thing the manager did was to ask him to change his clothes, but while he was doing that (in their presence) he managed to put the camera under his tongue. When they weren't looking he set it on the collar of his new blue shirt.

They gave him a glass of the protein shake.

He muttered and made excuses, and they were polite but firm. He had to drink it.

So he did. Immediately he felt relaxed and cheerful. He could have danced with joy. He went to work with hope in his heart.

The world looked different. The slaughterhouse was still clean and beautiful but people's faces looked strange. He couldn't tell one person from another very clearly. Even the animals on the conveyor belt looked a bit like people. Only the orange flashing lights on the workers' shirts distinguished one from the other. It was as though everybody had become strangers for a spell. All the world took on a soft, mushy quality—boundaries were smudged, details blurred, even sounds were muffled.

But he found that he didn't mind this. It really wasn't so bad. It was like being in a painting, or a dream. The animals were quiet and cooperative. They did not scream or kick; their eyes did not roll in fear. Jhingur busied himself in keeping the floor clean, picking up meat chunks that fell off the conveyor belt. He forgot all about the camera.

While she worked, his mother sang. She was happy too, as was his sister. It was nice to work together, even though their faces were unclear and his mother's voice sounded as though she was at the other end of a tunnel. His sister said:

"Animals really don't feel pain like we do, Jhingur. So don't feel bad."

"I don't," he told her, smiling.

At home he felt content. He was earning for his family and soon they might have enough to go on a holiday, perhaps to some place with air and light. Maybe even grass and wildflowers. He played with his mouse, fed it, and fell asleep dreaming.

The next day was Sunday so everyone stayed home. Jhingur had a bit of a headache so he lay in his sack after breakfast. It was then that he remembered the spy-eye. He had snapped it off the workshirt and put it in his pocket without really thinking about it. Now there it was.

The pictures were not very good but he could make out a few things. A cow, mouth open in terror, on a conveyor belt. A goat, legs hacked off, half-drowning in its own blood, its eyes white and terrified. And a human hand in a bin. Not attached to a body, as far as he could see. And a rack of sheep hanging from a series of hooks, bleeding, their intestines spilling out. Their eyes were full of a terrible awareness.

The world turned sick again for Jhingur.

His mother and sister were drinking their weekend quota of protein shake. They glanced at the pictures and shrugged.

"It's your wild imagination," they said. "You can't tell anything in these pictures. Besides, it's illegal to take pictures in the slaughterhouse. Promise you won't do this again."

Jhingur promised.

But he thought: How can I go back to work now?

He lay there feeling miserable. What could he do? Who could he tell? After some thinking an idea came to him.

He used an empty bottle of protein shake. He filled it with a shake of his own, made from pseudomilk and banana powder. It looked about the same.

The next day he took the spy-eye to work again. In the workers' café he took out the shake and began to drink it. Left over from yesterday, he said to the manager. I forgot to drink my quota on Sunday. The manager frowned at him and told him not to forget again.

This time he couldn't take it. The terror of the animals, the relaxed composure of the workers, his mother's voice singing his favorite songs over the screaming.

He threw up. He found himself falling to the floor. Other workers came running, and Jhingur was sent home.

The pictures were clearer this time. Jhingur climbed shakily out of his shack and wandered the grimy streets in the brown light of afternoon. He found his way to a local nexus, paid all his scrupulously saved earnings to connect to Langra's Net-link number, and sent the pictures off.

At first there was a problem because of the way Langra had scribbled down his Net-link address: was it Sannata3154 or Sannata3159? Jhingur couldn't be sure so he sent his message to both addresses. One of them ought to be the right one. He didn't know how to write, but he told Langra in an audio-message what he had found. "Tell someone who will stop the slaughterhouse people," he said. "Let it run on *Reality Deep Down*. Patal is not just demon-king fights. Tell them how the animals suffer. They feel pain, like we do. And sometimes . . . there is human flesh . . ."

People would see the pictures, know the truth, be horrified. He didn't know what would happen to him in the meantime. But he would be the hero who gives it all up for his tribe.

He could not bear to go to work next morning so he feigned illness. After his mother and sister left there was a knock at the door.

It was his manager, with two guards. "Jhingur, you are under arrest," he said. "Someone saw a spy-eye on your shirt last time. Where is it?"

Jhingur saw that there was no point in denying the truth. He had already sent the pictures to Langra. He handed the manager the empty spy-eye without a word. "There are no pictures on it," he said. "I didn't take any."

"Doesn't matter," the manager said. "You have to come with us."

He went with them through the litter-strewn mean streets, under the web-ways of his home. A dreamvid cover glittered in a trash heap. He took a deep breath and smelled the familiar smells: filth, rotting matter, a pungent smell of demon-smoke.

When would the cameras come? Where was *Reality Deep Down?*

The manager said: "Why do you keep turning around? Looking up?"

Jhingur said, with a touch of defiance: "I've sent the pictures to a Net show. Whatever you do to me, the world will know tomorrow."

"You stupid boy," the manager said. "That fellow, the guptman whom you contacted, was the one who told us. *Reality Deep Down* would never show anything like this. You must have been crazy to think it."

"What are you going to do with me?" Jhingur said. There was a terrible cold feeling in his stomach.

"You'll find out," said the manager.

Jhingur thought he knew. A shudder went through him. His knees began to shake, and one of the men had to push him to get him to move.

Then he remembered that he had sent the pictures to two addresses.

"Sannata3159," he said aloud. "I hope there is a Sannata3159." The manager didn't seem to hear him.

When Jhingur was brought into the slaughterhouse, they didn't make him drink the protein shake but gave him something else that tasted bitter. He couldn't understand what was happening to him. Even if Langra had betrayed him, someone would have gotten his messages, surely? If Langra was Sannata3154, it stood to reason that there must be other Sannatas. Maybe they were around him, in disguise, waiting for the right moment to rescue him and reveal all, like on the Net shows. In his imagination he saw Sannata3159: the shadowy hero, the rescuer who was going to save him. He wanted to tell Sannata3159 that he, Jhingur, was in danger, and the time for rescue was now. He kept asking the people in the manager's office: "Are you Sannata3159?" Nobody answered. They made him go into a small, empty room after his drink was done. Behind a partition he could hear the hum of the conveyor belt.

They stripped him, hit him with something that made his whole body sing with electricity, and threw him onto the conveyor belt. When he came to he realized that he was not dead, although he couldn't move one arm and his legs no longer obeyed him. Suddenly he was in the bright light of the carving hall. On both sides of him were great masses of animals. Their terrified screams drowned his. There was thick, half-clotted blood on the conveyor belt; his back was sticky with it. He tried to lever himself off the belt, but the pain nearly made him pass out. He fell back and lay gasping and crying. How could this be happening? How could there be so much pain?

His mother! His sister!

He called Mama! Into the cavernous ceiling his voice went. Surely she would hear him?

There she was, smiling. She began to sing, her eyes lighting up the way they always did when she sang. It was a song he had always loved. He could hear her clearly now: her voice soared like a bird, singing of freedom. He called again, Mama!

She saw him and didn't see him.

She hacked off the hand he couldn't move away because that arm was useless. She tossed the hand expertly into a bin, without missing a beat, then aimed a blow at the animal behind him, as the conveyor belt moved him forward.

He screamed and screamed. He held the bleeding stump hard against his chest. His blood seemed thick and slow. Maybe there had been something in the drink. Then he saw his sister ahead, wielding her carving knife. He called her name. A look of confusion crossed her face for a moment, and the carving knife stayed up in the air, motionless. The conveyor belt moved on, the knife flashed. Her confusion had spared him being cut up, but the sheep behind him cried out, a long, high sound.

After a very long time he lost sight of his mother and sister; his throat was bleeding and raw; he coughed up blood. He felt so faint he wondered whether he would die before he got to the guillotine. It was really a coarse chopper, dividing up the rest of the meat when the unwanted parts and the choice parts had been cut. The sound of the blades on bone and flesh was terrifying.

In the middle of his nightmare his mind cried out: Sannata3159, if you exist, where are you?

But nobody came.

He paused for breath, and in the same instant the great mountain of beef ahead of him turned at looked at him. The wild, rolling eye, mad with terror, seemed to calm suddenly. The bull looked at him and in his clear gaze Jhingur felt a tenuous link. For a moment he was on the prairie, a bison in the herd, and he was going out to where the humans waited so respectfully, to sacrifice himself for his tribe. And the bison would remember him, and the humans who ate his flesh would salute him.

But then it came back to him, where he was; he saw the guillotine ahead, blades stained with blood. He had never known the prairie, or sunshine, or wildflowers, and neither had the bull. And he knew that his sacrifice was in vain, and that when his flesh was packed neatly in plastic and sent away to the Citizens, or to his own people, those who ate him would not know him or honor him, as they would not know or honor the other animals. Their pain, which was also his pain, meant nothing to them, because they could not see the animals as they were, fellow travelers on the great journey, who sang love songs to their mates, and knew joy and suffering and sacrifice.

Then, without his bidding, he remembered: the woman from the tower who had seen him despite all odds, who had flung a message in light across the canyon that separated them. He had loved her; he understood suddenly his dreams about her flying toward him, crossing that gulf in a great arc. She had fallen to her death, to be scavenged by the rat-folk and turned into a tribute for the demon-kings. He had eaten of her flesh without knowing. In that moment of realization she seemed to sing in his veins, blood of his blood, flesh of his flesh. And he knew there was still something he could do, even in this darkness, this charnel house.

The bull in front of him was nearly at the guillotine now; great pieces had already been carved out of him, and he was beyond pain, his eyes wide with incredulity, longing only for death; Jhingur maneuvered his good arm, gritting his teeth against the pain, reaching out so that his hand rested on the back of the beast, who shuddered once, then looked at him again, in silence and pain, and Jhingur once more felt the link between them, a jolt of love and understanding. At least I can do this, Jhingur thought, although the world was turning black before his eyes.

He had always dreamed he would die in Mama's arms, with her singing to him. So when the guillotine flashed, his last feeling was a flash of joy, because once again she had begun to sing.

Indra's Web

Mahua ran over the familiar, rock-studded pathway under the canopy of acacia trees, her breath coming fast and ragged. She would have to stop soon, she wasn't as young as she used to be, and there was a faint, persistent pain in her right knee—but she loved this physicality: heart thumping, sweat running down her face in rivulets, the forest smelling of sap and animal dung, grit on her lips from the dust. The forest was where she got her best ideas; it was an eternal source of inspiration. It was why her work was getting recognition across the world. But the forest didn't care about fame or fortune—here she was just another animal: breath and flow, a kite on the wing, a deer running.

Running, she liked to have the net chatter going on in the Shell in her ear: Salman monitoring the new grid, Varun and Ali reporting on the fish stocks in the artificial marshland by the river, Doctor Sabharwal's monitor relaying Mahua's grandmother's condition at the hospital: stable, stable, stable, still on life support. Thinking about her grandmother's stroke made Mahua feel like she was about to fall into a pit of despair; she distracted herself with the reminder that she had promised Namita she would try out the myconet music app during this morning's run. "It's just for fun, Mahua-di, but try it, you'll like it." They were so anxious about her, these young people, knowing she was not quite herself these days. Moved and perversely annoyed by their concern, she had spent some hours with them in the Biosystems lab learning the app . . .

There is a fungal network, a myconet, a secret connection between the plants of the forest. They talk to each other, the acacia and the shisham and the gulmohar tree, in a chemical tongue. They communicate about pests, food sources, the weather, all through the flow of biomolecules through the fungal hyphae. Through this network, large trees have even been known to share nutrients with saplings of the same species. Mahua's protégé, Namita, is part of the team that helped decipher (to the extent that humans can) this subtle language. In the forest they have planted sensors in the soil to catch some of the chemical exchanges between plants. The signals are fed back into the interpreter and then analyzed. Some members of the team have made music from the signals: convert the concentration of a certain biochemical transmitter changing in real time into succession of notes where the duration indicates the strength of the transmitter. Add a few other transmitter signals as sounds of a slightly different frequency and you'll get a sometimes musical chatter that is at once soothing and intriguing. Mahua is new to this and she's never tried it out in the forest before. She's always encouraged play in their research—it is not only fun, but important, *she tells them—play leads to new insights, shakes up preconceived notions . . . And now they* need *the relief of play, after having spent the past few months calculating and putting in place Ashapur's first smart-energy grid, the Suryanet, modeled on the myconet itself.*

Mahua turned on the app. As she ran she picked up information from the closest few sensors so that she had a "picture" that changed in time and space. At first she heard nothing but the soothing semi-music of the various tones. Then the surprise came: a peculiar sensation rather like vertigo, a kind of slippage, as though she was leaving her human self behind, dissolving into something infinitely vast. It was like looking up at the Milky Way from the top of a high mountain on a clear night. She had always been quick to discern webs of relationships—it was her particular skill, after all—but this was different. A feeling like an electric shock coursed through her, a long moment of recognition, as though her deepest mind already knew this pattern. The effect was so startling that she stumbled over a tree root. Then the Shell beeped urgently in her ear, and the spell broke.

It was Salman, calling out an alert: Suntower I had failed. There were random fluctuations going on all over the new energy grid that nobody could explain, Salman said, breathless. It seemed likely that the Suryanet, so painstakingly put in place over the past few months, the result of years of effort, on which everyone was depending for the survival of Ashapur and maybe of the biosphere itself—the Suryanet could be a spectacular failure.

One of the things Mahua had learned from her grandmother was that when trouble struck, unless it needed immediate attention, it was good to slow down and meander a little. So she wandered to the top of the ridge, where the height enabled her to see Ashapur in all its glory.

A former slum, it used to lie on the edge of Delhi like a sore. In the last ten years the Ashapur project had transformed it. The hutments of cardboard and tin had been replaced by dwelling houses built mostly by the residents themselves with traditional materials: a hard mixture of mud, straw, rice husk, surfaced with a lime-based plaster. In use for thousands of years, then forgotten, and revived in the 20th century by visionary architects like Laurie Baker, the material had so far survived nearly ten years of baking heat and monsoon rains. The majority of the residents were the original slum inhabitants, climate refugees from the drowned villages of Bangladesh, who had been transformed by the Ashapur project. When Mahua looked at Ashapur from this height she saw mostly an uneven carpet of green and silver—rooftop gardens broken by the gleam of solar panels, and corridors of native trees, neem, khejri, gulmohar, running down the hill from her forest like green arteries through the settlement.

Above this vista rose the suntowers like a surrealist's dream: four functioning, and the fifth under construction, their tops capped by sun-tracking petals of biomimetic material containing tiny, environmentally benign artificial cells, the suryons, that drank up photons. The largest, oldest facility was Suntower I, now mysteriously moribund. Ashapur was nearly self-sufficient in food and energy, and with the new grid, the Suryanet, they should have been able to *donate* power to the Delhi grid, thereby silencing the naysayers and establishing the need for a thousand Ashapurs. Four solar plants making hydrogen from the breakdown of water—sewage-fed biogas plants—enormous energy savings from building construction and layout (none of the buildings needed air conditioning)—numerous rooftops with solar panels—even greater energy savings from the fact that these former villagers were traditionally energy-efficient, living in clusters, throwing away nothing, re-using almost everything. And all the energy sources were now connected on the Suryanet. Yet . . .

She took the long way to Suntower I. She always found it calming to walk through Ashapur. The narrow roads were not built on a rectangular pattern but instead curved, moving obligingly around an ancient peepul tree or dwelling. Her designers had kept the street pattern of the original slum but had improved on it, allowing room for people to congregate in front of this chai-house or in that niche, so that old women could gossip and mind the little ones, and the wandering cows and pariah dogs had room to rest. Here, right at the corner she was passing now, between an internet café and an agricultural research center—here's where a potential foreign funder had stopped her six years ago. "I don't understand," he'd said, "why this town is so untidy. There's no order, no proper grid for the streets. It looks very inefficient. And the roads are too narrow for traffic flow! Where are your cars?"

In response to this sort of thing her grant-writing team had developed a slide show—apparently some of these potential funders could only understand things if they were in a PowerPoint presentation—to show how optimal city function could be best achieved by having connectivity at multiple scales. Large, coarse, fewer pathways for cars, smaller, more dense ones for people. And for other animals as well as people, the green corridors that branched into the city, maintaining biodiversity and the psychological benefits of closeness to nature, while providing Ashapur with cooler summers, seasonal supplies of fruit and nuts, and raw material for a new cottage industry in crafts.

Now she entered Energy Central, the building below Suntower I. It was cool here—the thick mud-based walls ensured that—and the curving stairway with its murals gave no hint of the troubles of Suntower I, rising high above the roof. At the lab door there was the familiar sign that Salman had installed by encouraging a vivid green moss to grow on an earthboard so that it spelled out the motto of the Biomimetic Energy Materials Lab—*To Learn from Nature, not to Exploit Her.* His colleagues had teased Salman about the irony of exploiting a moss to write these noble words, but the moss seemed to have decided things for itself. It spelled "To learm from Natur, not to Explod," which still made her smile.

Inside there was a dim coolness and the glow of multiple terminals. A meeting was in progress, chaotic and impassioned as usual. Arguments and discussions in Hindi, English, and Bangla: Salman, deep in agitated conversation with Namita and Ayush; Hamid, a young trainee who had once begged on the streets as a child, patiently explaining the situation to the boy who had brought the tea. Mahua stayed just inside the door, unnoticed, letting the words flow around her, sensing the web of ideas and feelings raging through the room.

". . . no guarantee that modeling the Suryanet on the myconet was going to work—why risk everything on one crazy idea?"

". . . calculations, have you forgotten we did the entire constructal analysis? Besides, scale-free networks are everywhere . . ."

"Nobody's networked a suryon-based system before or allowed it to self-regulate! There were safer ways of doing this, better ways! But no, you have to go on about minimal control! It's centralized control systems that make everything work!"

"Yaar, stop being a control freak, OK? We're just mimicking the natural control systems that exist in nature. Stop panicking . . . obviously there's a bug in the system somewhere . . ."

". . . oldest suntower, beta version of the suryons, it's bound to fail . . ."

". . . not *this* quickly, idiot . . ."

Chanchal, from one of the terminals:

"Salman, look at what's happening to the other suntowers! Energy collection is now above average by seven percent in 2, 3 and

4! But . . . dekho, boss! These numbers! More inflow than outflow. There's a major bug somewhere!"

"Or energy is no longer conserved," someone said, as there was a mass movement to the terminal.

Mahua found herself curiously detached from the mayhem. A signal sounded repetitively in the lab like the beep of the monitor in her grandmother's hospital room.

She is remembering the first time she sees these young people in various colleges and universities, nearly a decade ago. They are bound for brilliant careers as engineers, managers, CEOs, their upturned faces curious, skeptical, polite. She has nothing to offer them so she gives it all she has.

"I come to you with empty hands," she says. "I can't offer you much money. I can't offer you big houses, two cars, five air-conditioners. Nor the jet-setting lifestyle with its cross-continental board meetings, the wife or husband who will ultimately cheat on you, the children who will drive you crazy. What I can give you is a chance to be part of a revolution. A revolution that might just save our earth from the climate crisis. One that comes up with not just new technologies but new ways to live that are more whole and deep and satisfying than anything you've known. Most of you have enjoyed being in college. You are the best of the lot, the ones who get high on learning, and on the company of like minds. The Ashapur project is like college, except that you have the chance to learn by doing, and to do more good than you ever could with the life now laid out for you. We will take care of your housing and healthcare, and you will get as much salary as I do. Which isn't saying very much. But you'll get up every morning knowing that by the end of the day you would have made a new discovery, a new friend, a new way of looking at the world. You will blow old paradigms out of existence on a near-daily basis. I promise you that. Are you with me?"

Some of the faces look incredulous, even mocking, but there are others who light up. She's struck a chord deep inside them. She lets out a deep breath of relief.

Now she thought: Had she betrayed them after all? Would they forgive her, if this turned out to be the disaster she had always feared?

Finally they noticed her, surrounded her, pulled her before the screens, presented their arguments before her. "Look," she said at last. "You know how to check everything according to the protocols. Do that. Then come up with some wild theories and shake up the possibilities, but don't panic. We can survive a couple of power failures; it isn't as though we haven't grown up with them. The hospital seems to have enough power right now; so do most key-need places. Make sure backup generators are working and just wait."

Mahua was named by her long-dead mother because she was born under a mahua tree on the way to Delhi. The two of them—mother and grandmother—had migrated from their village in Bihar after her father died. She grew up in the slums, where her mother died when Mahua was eleven, only three months before their fortunes changed.

So it's been Mahua and her grandmother, who now lies in a hospital bed after a stroke, kept alive by the machines that surround her. The woman with the temper and the loud laugh, who always had something to say, now looks at Mahua with wide, frightened eyes. She can't speak but she can croak a little. Sometimes she lies peacefully while Mahua holds her hand, but at other times she seems to be trying to tell Mahua something. Mahua, who can discern connections with a skill that frightens her sometimes, cannot tell what her grandmother is trying to say. She tries to reassure her— there are all kinds of new techniques the surgeons want to try. There's hope.

When she was a child Mahua used to follow ants as they moved purposefully across the dirt floor of the room. She wanted to know where they were going in such a hurry, and whether their abrupt pauses and frantically waving antennae had some hidden significance. Later she came to realize that the ants followed invisible trails across the floor—that the world was full of secret communication channels, like the electric wires between poles that rose above the tenements. It was as though some inner sense within her had opened, because following this realization she was suddenly aware of walking through a tangled spider's web of relationships. The gossiping old women who sat around her mother's sewing machine, jabbering about this and that, speaking as much with meaningful glances and shakes of the fist as with their cracked voices—the way people looked at each other, signifying feelings and relations, how people spoke as much with their silences as with words. Even the winds that brought the monsoon rains had some sort of pattern or cycle, a network in both time and space. She was delighted with this discovery, but she didn't understand it then.

The narrow little lanes of the slum are like spiderwebs, intersecting at odd angles, curving around hutments, like a stream of water. Everywhere there are people and smells and here and there an internet café or a soda stand or a chaatwala. In this mess and confusion someone's placed a computer in a niche on a wall and the street kids play with it between school and errands and work. After a long time she's found the courage to go up to the shiny, inviting screen, the keyboard, where the letters are in Hindi—thank goodness she can read—but the screen itself has a number of floating objects, tumbling and combining when they meet. She stares at it, mesmerized, and after a while she tries a hesitant tap on the keyboard. Three days later she's learnt that she can save the game in her own name. She keeps playing. In a strange way it makes sense the way the slum itself makes sense. It's pattern and rhythm, although she will not know those words for a long time. At the end of this period there is a person at her door, and a scholarship to go to a really good school with housing for herself and her grandmother, and guidance from the Slum Children's Education Trust, which is inhabited by kindly aunties.

At thirteen Mahua fell ill. She diagnosed the malady herself as anxiety brought on by acute apophenia. Becoming sensitive to networks and relationships, she saw connections everywhere, even when they weren't actually present. This drove her crazy but she didn't want to take medicines to suppress her ability for pattern recognition. Instead she resolved to train her mind to distinguish between false apparent connections and real ones—the only way to do that was to study the world. With this determination, her new school, with its snooty, unfriendly girls and regimented routine, became a matter of finding the grain in the chaff, the flashes of joy in the misery.

For instance: Mrs. Khosla introducing the concept of energy in her usual monotone. A classroom full of bored children, and only Mahua sitting up, recognizing that she has just been handed the golden key, the central concept, that through which the entire universe interacted, the currency of all communication. Energy! And its conservation law. All real systems were governed by fundamental laws that acted as constraints. That is how you differentiated apparent relationships from real ones!

But as she stands in the hospital room looking at her grandmother (the old woman is made almost alien by the tubes and wires of the life-support system), she feels that she has failed after all. What good is it to be able to sense patterns and relationships when she can't tell what her own grandmother wants to say? Tomorrow they'll try once more to work with the eyelids to see if her grandmother can learn to communicate thus. But the old woman, always contrary, has apparently refused to cooperate. What does she want? Not death, surely, not before exploring all the options. Her grandmother has such a zest for life. She'd opened a small business of her own at the age of seventy-three, making simmerpots. This is a pot that is made of mud and straw rather like the walls of the dwellings but in different proportions—and it is one reason why energy usage is so low in Ashapur. You cook your stew or curry on the stove for two minutes, until it is simmering nicely, and then you take it off the heat and put it inside the simmerpot. The simmerpot is such a good insulator that the food keeps cooking in there for hours afterwards. Not her grandmother's invention—it had been in use in her village for centuries. But here only her grandmother and a handful of trainees know how to make it, and when you walk around Ashapur you see simmerpots everywhere, on kitchen windowsills and in the large community dining rooms. And the woman who made it popular and indispensable, who had such vivacity at eighty-one that she could gossip nonstop with her neighbors until three in the morning, now lies hooked up to machines like a captive, with death in her eyes.

Mahua has finally seen it. Her grandmother wants to die.

That evening Mahua goes walking down the lanes of Ashapur, following a hunch.

There before her is Suntower 5. While physically connected to the grid, it is still under construction; only the skeletal frames of the petals are complete, the tubing through which the suryon-embedded substratum will eventually be pumped up. There is a sleepy boy in the control room, one of the former street urchins assigned to do some after-hours caretaking. Tousling his hair and sending him off for some tea, Mahua sits before the computer. Suntower 5 is the newest design;

the suryon-distribution architecture is so complex and bug-ridden that it will take a while to implement. Since the work began on the grid so many months ago, nobody has been able to attend to Suntower 5.

It doesn't take Mahua long to zoom into an image of a petal atop the tower. At first she sees just the skeleton, but there, between the supports is a new, delicate, lace-like integument. The suryons are distributing themselves, filling in the empty spaces. Somehow the Suryanet has not only decided that Suntower 5 should be functional, but has allocated resources to it, which is why Suntower I—the oldest, and least efficient—has shut itself down. Temporarily, perhaps, but who knows? Does a sufficiently complex network give rise to its own wisdom? She sends a hint to the team at Suntower I. By the morning they will have figured it out. She sips her tea, talks to the sleepy attendant. At last she goes back into the night, thinking about the networks in which she exists, and how tomorrow a major node on which her very life depends will be taken off-line forever. She thinks of the forest on the ridge. The forest lives on because it accepts death—with every twig that falls, with every ant that meets its annihilation, a thousand life forms come into being. Danger walks there and so its denizens learn adaptation; here, too, we must rebuild ourselves, define ourselves anew with each loss, each encounter. She remembers a story her grandmother once told her about Indra's Web, the ultimate cosmic network in which every node mirrors the whole.

In the twilight hush there are sleepy sounds of birds settling in the trees; a family of rhesus monkeys chatters softly in a rooftop garden above her head. A radio is playing an old film song, very softly. It is a warm night; someone has a khas-khas cooler working, the sound of the fan almost drowning out the steady drip of water. If she wants, her Shell unit can pick up energy data from the sensors in each dwelling place. She loves this marriage of the traditional and the new, the forest and the city, this great experiment, this marvel that is Ashapur, City of Hope.

Ruminations
in an Alien Tongue

Birha on the Doorstep

Sitting on the sun-warmed step at the end of her workday, Birha laid her hand on the dog's neck and let her mind drift. Like a gyre-moth finding the center of its desire, her mind inevitably spiraled inward to the defining moment of her life. It must be something to do with growing old, she thought irritably, that all she did was revisit what had happened all those years ago. Yet her irritation subsided before the memory. She could still see it with the shocking clarity of yesterday: the great, closed eyelid set in the enormous alien stronghold, opening in response to her trick. The thick air of the valley, her breath caught in her throat, the orange-and-yellow uniforms of the waiting soldiers. She had gone up the ladder, stepped through the round opening. Darkness, her footsteps echoing in the enormous space, the light she carried casting a small, bobbing pool of illumination. This was the alien stronghold considered invincible by the human conquerors, to which the last denizens of a dying race had crawled in a war she had forgotten when she was young. She had expected to find their broken, decayed bodies, but instead there was a silence like the inside of a temple up in the mountains. Silence, a faint smell of dust, and a picture forever burned into her mind: in the light of her lamp, the missing soldier, thunderstruck before the great mass of machinery in the center.

That was the moment when everything changed. For her, and eventually for humankind. She had been young then.

"Hah!" she said, a short, sharp sound—an old woman laughing at her foolishness. It felt good to sit here on the doorstep, although now it was turning a little cold. On this world, the sun didn't set for seven years as counted on the planet where she had been born. She knew she would not live to see another sunset; her bones told her that, and the faint smell in her urine, and her mind, which was falling backward into a void of its own making.

But the clouds could not be ignored, nor the yellow dog at her knee, who wanted to go inside. There would be rain, and the trees would open their veined, translucent cups to the sky. There would be gyre-moths emerging from holes in the ground, flying in smooth, ever-smaller circles, at the center of which was a cup of perfumed rain—and there would be furred worms slithering up the branches to find the sweet moth-meat. In the rain under the trees, the air would quiver with blood and desire, and the human companion animals— the dogs and cats and ferrets—would run to their homes lest the slee-hawks or a feral arboril catch them for their next meal. Yes, rain was a time of beauty and bloodshed, here at the edge of the great cloud forest, among the ruins of the university that had been her home for most of her life.

She got up, noting with a grim satisfaction that, in *this* universe, old knees creaked. She went in with the dog and shut the door and the windows against the siren-like calls of the foghorn-trees, and put some water on to boil. Rain drummed on the stone walls of her retreat, and she saw through the big window the familiar ruined curve of the university ramparts through a wall of falling water. Sometimes the sight still took her breath away. That high walk with the sheer, misty drop below was where she had first walked with Thirru.

A Very Short Rumination

When I was born my mother named me Birha, which means "separated" or "parted" in an ancient human language. This was because my mother was about to die.

Difficult Loves

Thirru was difficult and strange. He seemed eager to make Birha happy but was like a big, foolish child, unable to do so. A large, plump man, with hair that stood up on end, he liked to clap his hands loudly when he solved a difficult problem, startling everyone. His breath smelled of bitter herbs from the tea he drank all day. Even at their pairing ceremony he couldn't stop talking and clapping his hands, which she had then thought only vaguely annoying and perhaps endearing. Later, her irritation at his strangeness, his genius, his imbecility, provoked her into doing some of her best work. It was almost as though, in the discomfort of his presence, she could be more herself.

One time, when she was annoyed with Thirru, she was tempted by another man. This man worked with her; his fingers were long and shapely over the simulator controls, and he leaned toward her when he spoke, always with a warmth that made her feel as though she were a creature of the sunlight, unfurling in the rays of morning. He made her feel younger than she was. She didn't like him very much; she distrusted people with charm as a matter of principle, but he was more than charm. He was lean, and wore his dark hair long and loose, and every posture of his was insouciant, inviting, relaxed as a predatory animal; when he leaned toward her she felt the yearning, the current pulling her toward him. At these moments she was always stiff and polite with him; in privacy she cursed herself for her weakness. She avoided him, sought him out, avoided him, going on like this for days, until, quite suddenly, she broke through the barrier. She was no longer fascinated by him. It wasn't that his charm had faded; it was only (she congratulated herself) the fact that she had practiced the art of resisting temptation until she had achieved some mastery. You practice and it becomes easier, just like the alien mathematics on which she was working at the time. Just like anything else.

This freedom from desiring this man was heady. It was also relaxing not to feel drawn to him all the time, to be able to joke and laugh with him, to converse without that terrible, adolescent self-conscious-ness. She could even let herself like him after that.

In this manner she carried herself through other temptations suc-cessfully. Even after Thirru's own betrayal she wasn't tempted into another relationship. After the reconciliation they stayed together for an entire cycle, some of which was marked by an easy contentment that she had never known before, a deep wellspring of happiness. When they parted, it was as friends.

But what he left behind was what all old loves left behind: the ghostly imprints of their presence. For her, Thirru came back when-ever she looked up at the high walk where she had first walked with him. Thirru was the feel of damp stone, the vivid green of the moss between the rocks, the wet, verdant aroma of the mist. She didn't have to go there anymore; just looking up at the stone arch against the clouds would bring back the feel of his hands.

After Thirru she had had her share of companions, long and short term, but nobody had inspired her to love. And when the man happened along who came closest, she was unprepared for him. His name was Rudrak, and he was young.

What she loved about him was his earnestness, his delight in beautiful things, like the poeticas she had set up on the long table. He was an engineer, and his passion was experimental craft designed to explore stars. She loved his beautiful, androgynous face, how it was animated by thought and emotion, how quick his eyes were to smile, the way his brow furrowed in concentration. That crisp, black, curling hair, the brown arm flung out as he declaimed, dramatically, a line from a classic play she'd never heard of. When he came, always infrequently, unexpectedly, always on a quest for the woman Ubbiri, it was as though the sun had come out in the sky of her mind. Conver-sation with him could be a battle of wits, or the slow, easy, unhurried exchange of long-time lovers. She never asked him to stay for good (as though it were possible), never told him she loved him.

Now she was pottering about in her kitchen, listening to the rain, wondering if he would come one more time before she died.

The last time he had come was a half-cycle ago (three and a half years on her birth planet, her mind translated out of habit). There was not much more than a half-cycle left to her. Would he come? Pouring her tea, she realized that despite the certainty with which she loved this man, there was something different about this love. She felt no need for him to reciprocate. Sometimes she would look at her arms, their brown, lean strength, the hands showing the signs of age, and remember what it was like to be touched, lovingly, and wonder what it would be like to caress Rudrak's arm, to touch his face, his lips. But it was an abstract sort of wondering. Even if she could make him forget Ubbiri (and there was no reason for her to do that), she did not really want him too close to her. Her life was the way she liked it: the rising into early mornings, the work with the poeticas—which was a meditation in sunlight and sound—then the long trek up the hill to the now-abandoned laboratory. Returning in the early evening before the old bells rang sunset (although the sun wouldn't set for half a cycle yet) into the tranquility of her little stone house, where the village girl entrusted with the task would have left her meal warming on the stove just the way she liked it. The peace of eating and reading by herself, watching the firelings outside her window, in the temporary, watery dark created by the frequent gathering of clouds. In those moments the universe seemed to open to her as much as it seemed shut to her during the long day. She would stare out at the silhouettes of trees and wonder if the answers she was seeking through her theories and equations weren't instead waiting for her out there in the forest, amidst the ululations of the frenet-bird and the complex script of the fireling's dance. In those moments it would seem to her as though all she had to do was to walk out into the verdure and pluck the answer from the air like fruit from trees; that it was in these moments of complete receptivity that the universe would be revealed to her, not in the hours at the simulators in the laboratory. That the equations would be like childish chatter compared to what was out there to know in its fullness.

She took her tea to her favorite chair to drink. On the way she let her fingers brush lightly over the wires of the poeticas that stood on wood frames on the long table. The musical notes sounded above the crash of the rain, speaking aloud her ruminations in the lost alien tongue. Rudrak had left his ghost behind here: the remembrance of his body leaning over the instruments, brushing them as he might, in some other universe, be brushing the hair from her face. Asking how this sequence of notes implied those words. Since she had walked into the alien stronghold so many years ago, since the time that everything had changed, Rudrak had visited her nine times. Each time he remembered nothing of his previous visits, not even who she was. Each time she had to explain to him that Ubbiri was dead, and that he should come in, and wouldn't he like some tea? She went through the repetition as though it were the first time, every time, which in a way it was. A sacred ritual.

Rudrak.

Would he come?

A Rambling Rumination

Simply by virtue of being, we create ripples in the ever-giving cosmic tree, the kalpa-vriksh. Every branch is an entire universe. Even stars, as they are born and die, leave permanent marks in the shadow universe of their memory. Perhaps we are ghosts of our other selves in other universes.

It was not right for Ubbiri to die. There is a lack of symmetry there, a lack even of a proper symmetry breaking. Somewhere, somehow, Ubbiri's meta-world-line and mine should connect in a shape that is pleasing to the mathematical eye. Sometimes I want to be Ubbiri, to know that a part of me did wander into another universe after all, and that separated, the two parts were joined together at last. There is something inelegant about Ubbiri's return and subsequent death. Ubbiri should have shared consciousness with me. Then, when Rudrak asks: "I am looking for Ubbiri. Is she here?" for the umpteenth time, I, Birha, will say yes. She's here.

Instead this is what I say:

"I'm sorry, Ubbiri passed away a long time ago. She told me about you when she died. Won't you come in?"

What is the probability that I am Ubbiri? If so, am I dead or alive, or both?
Ubbiri is dead. I am Birha, and Birha is alone.

The Discovery

When Birha was neither young nor old, when Thirru had already moved off-planet, a young soldier volunteered to test-fly an alien flyer, one of two intact specimens. The flight went well until upon an impulse he decided to swoop by the alien ruins in the valley below the University. During the dive, he lost control of the flyer, which seemed to be heading straight for a round indentation like an eye in the side of an ancient dome. The indentation revealed itself to be a door, by opening and then closing behind the flyer.

When Birha was consulted about the problem, she suspected that the door worked on an acoustical switch. Calculating the frequency of sound emitted by the alien flyer at a certain speed in the close, thick air of the valley took some time. But when a sound wave of the requisite frequency was aimed at the door, it opened almost immediately, with a sigh as though of relief.

She volunteered to go alone into the chamber. They argued, but she had always been stubborn, and at the end they let her. She was the expert on the aliens, after all.

The interior was vast, shrouded in darkness and her footsteps echoed musically. She saw the flyer, in some kind of docking bay, along with a dozen others. There were no decaying alien bodies, only silence. The young man stood in front of the great mass of machinery at the center of the room. In the light from her lamp (which flickered strangely) she saw a complexity of fine, fluted vanes, crystalline pipes as thin as her finger running in and out of lacy metalwork. The whole mass was covered in a translucent dome that gleamed red and blue, yellow and green, in the light from her lamp. There was a door in the side of the dome, which was ringed by pillars.

"My hand . . ." The soldier was staring at his hand. He looked at Birha at last. "My hand just went through that pillar . . ."

Birha felt a loosening of her body, as though her joints and tendons were coming apart, without pain. If she breathed out too hard, she might fling herself all over the cosmos. Her heart was beating in an unfamiliar rhythm. She put her hand in her pocket and took some coins out. Carefully she tossed each one in the air. Thirteen coins came down on the floor, all heads.

"There's nothing wrong with you," she told the aviator. "It's the machine. It's an alien artifact that changes the probabilities of things. We're standing in the leakage field. Look, just come with me. You'll be all right."

She led him into the light. The round door was propped open by a steel rod and there were crowds of people waiting at the foot of the ladder. The young man was still dazed.

"It tickled," he said. "My hand. When it went through the pillar."

A Rumination on the Aliens

What do we know about them? We know now they are not dead. They went through the great probability machine, the actualizer, to another place, a place we'll never find. The old pictures show that they had pale brown, segmented bodies, with a skeletal frame that allowed them to stand upright. They were larger than us but not by much, and they had feelers on their heads and light-sensitive regions beneath the feelers, and several limbs. They knew time and space, and as their culture was centered around sound, so was their mathematics centered around probability. Their ancient cities are filled with ruined acoustical devices, enormous poeticas, windchimes, and Aeolian harps as large as a building. Their music is strange but pleasant to humans, although its frequency range goes beyond what we can hear. When I was just an acolyte at the university, I chose to study what scripts were left after the war. They were acoustical scripts, corresponding to the notes in a row of poeticas on the main streets of their cities. I was drunk with discovery, in love with the aliens, overcome with sorrow that they were, as we thought then, all dead. For the first time since I had come to this planet, I felt at home.

To understand the aliens I became a mathematician and a musician. After that, those three things are one thing in my mind: the aliens, the mathematics, the music.

Rudrak's Story

A bristleship, Rudrak told Birha, is like no other craft. It burrows into the heart of a star, enduring temperatures beyond imagination, and comes out on the other side whole and full of data. The current model was improved by Rudrak in his universe, a branch of the cosmic tree not unlike this one. He did it for his partner, Ubbiri, who was writing a thesis on white-dwarf stars. Ubbiri had loved white-dwarf stars since a cousin taught her a nursery rhyme about them when Ubbiri was small:

> *Why are you a star so dim*
> *In the night beyond the rim*
> *Don't you want someone to love?*
> *In the starry skies above?*

Ubbiri had to write a thesis on white-dwarf stars. As dictated by academic custom in that culture, her thesis had to connect the six points of the Wheel of Knowing: Meta-networking, Undulant Theory, Fine-Jump Mathematics, Time-Bundles, Poetry, and Love. To enable her to achieve deep-knowing and to therefore truly love the star, she took a ride on the new bristleship with Rudrak. They discovered that when the ship went through the starry core, it entered another reality. This was later called the shadow universe of stars, where their existence and life history is recorded in patterns that no human has completely understood. Some poets call this reality the star's memory-space, or its consciousness, but Ubbiri thought that was extending metaphor beyond sense. The data from the bristleship told her that this star, this love, had been a golden star in its youth and middle age, harboring six planets (two of which had hosted life), and much space debris. In the late season of its existence it had soared in largeness, dimming and reddening, swallowing its planetary children. Now it was content to bank its fires until death.

After this discovery, Rudrak said, the two of them lived quiet lives that were rich and full. But one day before he was due to take off for another test flight, Ubbiri noticed there was a crack on the heat-shielded viewscreen of the bristleship. Rudrak tested it and repaired it, but Ubbiri was haunted by the possibility of the tiny crack spreading like a web across the viewscreen, and breaking up just as Rudrak was in the star's heart.

Perhaps that was what she thought when Rudrak disappeared. Rudrak only knew that instead of passing through the shadow universe before coming out, the bristleship took him somewhere else, to a universe so close to his own that he did not know the difference until he had crashlanded on a planet (this planet) and been directed to people who knew the truth. They led him to Birha, who sheltered him for fifteen days, allowed him to mourn and to come slowly to life again. Each time, she sent him back to his universe, as protocol demanded, by way of the alien probability machine, the actualizer. Somehow he was caught in a time-loop that took him back to the day before the ill-fated expedition. He had returned to her in exactly the same way nine times. His return visits were not predictable, being apparently randomly spaced, and her current (and last) calculation was an attempt to predict when he would come next.

Each visit was the same and not the same. Surely he had had less gray hair the last time? And that healed cut on his hand—hadn't that been from his last trip, when he was trying to help her cut fruit and the knife had slipped? And hadn't his accent improved just a little bit since last time? They'd had to teach him the language each visit as though it was new, but perhaps it became just a hair's breadth easier each time?

She tried to make each experience subtly different for him. She was afraid that too drastic a change might upset whatever delicate process was at work in the time-loop. He was like a leaf caught in an eddy—push too hard and the time stream might take him over a precipice. But a little tug here, a tug there, and perhaps he'd land safely on a shore, of this universe or that one.

So far nothing had worked. His bewilderment was the same, each time he appeared on her doorstep, and so was his grief. It was only these small, insignificant things that were different. One time he wore an embroidered collar, another time a plain one. Or the color of his shirt was different.

Birha worked on her calculations, but the kalpa-vriksh gave senseless, contradictory answers.

A Rumination on Timmar's Rock

I remember when I first came to the University, I used to pass a flat-topped boulder on the way to class. There was a depression on the flat surface of the rock in the exact shape of the bottom of a water bowl. When I met Thirru, he told me that the great Timmar Rayan, who had founded the School of Wind and Water, had sat there in daily meditation for three entire cycles, placing his water bowl in the same spot every time. Over the years the depression had developed. I have always marveled that something as unyielding as rock can give way before sheer habit, or regularity, or persistence, whatever you might call it.

Practice, whether in mathematics or in love, changes things.

Sometimes.

Ubbiri's arrival

It was one thing to realize that the alien device in the center of the chamber was some kind of probability-altering machine. That it was the fabled actualizer hinted at in alien manuscripts, which she had always thought of as myth, was quite another thing. This knowledge she owed to Ubbiri, who was discovered lying on the floor of the chamber not three days after Birha had first opened the round door. Ubbiri was immediately incarcerated for questioning and only after several ten-days, when her language had been deciphered and encrypted into a translation device, had Birha been allowed to speak to her. They said the old woman was mad, babbling about shadow universes and tearing at her silver hair, but Birha found her remarkably sane. Ubbiri told her that she had tired of waiting for her partner, who had disappeared during a flight through a certain white-dwarf star, and when he didn't return, she had taken an old-model bristleship and dived into the heart of the star. When the ship passed through the core she defied its protestations and stepped out of it, seeking either him or death in the shadowy depths of the other reality. Instead she found herself lying on the floor of the chamber, aged beyond her years.

Over the course of four ten-days of conversation Birha determined that the constants of nature were a hair's breadth different where Ubbiri came from, so it was very likely another universe entirely. She realized then that the machine at the center of the room did not merely change probabilities. It was an actualizer: a probability-wave interference machine, and the portal inside it led to whatever branch of the kalpa-vriksh you created by changing the parameters. But the portal only opened if you'd satisfied consistency checks and if (as far as the machine could tell) the universe was stable. Somehow the pathways to other universes intersected within the cores of stars, hence Ubbiri's surprising arrival.

Not long after, Ubbiri died. She left a note stating that there were three things she was grateful for: her white-dwarf star, Rudrak, and spending her last days with Birha.

A quarter-cycle after Ubbiri's death, Rudrak came for the first time into Birha's life.

A Rumination on Thirru, or Rudrak

There is a rift valley between us, a boundary that might separate two people or two universes. I've been exploring there, marveling at the tortured geometries of its sheer walls, the pits and chasms on its floor. Through them I've sometimes seen stars. So far I've avoided falling in, but who knows? One day maybe I'll hurtle through the layer between this universe and that, and find myself a meteor, a shooting star falling into the gravity well of a far planet.

What if a meteor changed its mind about falling? Would the universe allow it? Only if the rock fell under the sway of another imperative that lifted it beyond gravity's grasp. But where, in that endless sky, would it find the rift from which it had emerged? It would have to wander, searching, until the journey became an end in itself.

And then, one day when the journey had changed it beyond recognition, it would find the rift and it would stand on the lip of it, wondering: Should I return?

But I am not a rock. I am a person, slowly ripening in the sun of this world, like a pear on a tree. I am not hard, I am not protected by rocky layers.

Still, I cannot soar through your sky without burning.

Theories of Probability

What the actualizer did was change probabilities. So sometimes things that were highly improbable, like walking through a wall, or tossing five thousand coins so that heads came up every time—all those things could become much more likely.

Birha thought that in some sense people had always known about the other branches of the kalpa-vriksh. So many of humankind's fantasies about the magical and the impossible were simply imaginative leaps into different regions of the cosmic tree. But to go to the place of your imagining in the flesh . . . that wasn't possible before the actualizer's discovery. If you adjusted the parameters, the actualizer would tweak the probability amplitudes to make your fairytale universe. Or perhaps it only opened a portal to an already existing one. What's the difference? So much for you, entropy, for heat death, for death. Make it more likely that you live from fatal cancer than an ant bite . . .

But you couldn't always predict how the amplitudes would work for complex systems like universes, and whether programming in coarse features you desired would give too much creative freedom to subsystems, resulting in surprises beyond imagining, and not always pleasant ones. Thus a mythology had already grown around the actualizer, detailing the possible and impossible other universes and their dangers. One made-up story related how they put in the parameters, the universal physical constants and the wavefunction behavior in space and time, and there came to be an instability in the matter of that universe that made people explode like supernovas when they touched each other with love. It was a fanciful lie, but it made a great opera.

In her idle moments, Birha wondered whether there was a curtain through which she could slip to find the place that always stays still amid the shifting cosmi, like the eye of a storm. But the foghorn-trees were calling in the rain, and she was nodding over a bowl of soup, like the old woman she was. She looked at the veins standing out on the backs of her hands and the thick-jointed fingers, and thought of the body, her universe, which was not a closed system at all. Was there any system that was completely closed? Not in this universe, at least, where the most insulated of systems must interact with its environment, if only very slowly. So was our universe completely disconnected from the others, or did they bleed into each other? Exchange something? Not energy in any form we recognized, perhaps, but something more subtle, like dreams. She wanted to know what connected the universes, she wanted to step back from it all and see the kalpa-vriksh in its entirety. But she was caught in it as surely as anyone else. A participant-observer who must deduce the grand structure of the cosmic tree from within it, who must work at it while being caught in it, a worm in a twig, a fly in amber, to feel the knowing, the learning, like a new intimacy, a love.

"All matter is wavelike in some sense," she told the dog. "The actualizer generates waves, and through interference changes the probability amplitudes. The tiny bubble universe so formed then resonates with an existing universe with the same properties, and a doorway opens between them."

The dog sighed, as though this was passé, which in a way it was, and wagged his tail.

A Rumination, Dozing in the Sun

One day I dreamed I was the light falling off the edge of a leaf, nice and straight, but for the lacy diffraction at the edge. At night I flew into the clouds, to the well of stars, and became a piece of the void, a bit of dark velvet stitched on to the sky. In the afternoon I am just an old woman dozing in the sun with a yellow dog sitting beside her, wondering about stars, worried about the universes. If I could be the tap of your shoe, the glance out of the corner of your eye when you see that man or this woman, if I could be the curled lip of the snarling arboril, or a mote in the eye of a dog. What would I be, if I were to be any of this?

I am myself and yet not so. I contain multitudes and am a part of something larger; I am a cell the size of a planet, swimming in the void of the night.

When They Left

After the actualizer's discovery it became a subject of study, a thing to explore, and ultimately an industry dealing in dreams. Streams of adventurers, dreamers, and would-be suicides, people dissatisfied with their lives, went through the actualizer to find the universe that suited them better. The actualizer became a wish-fulfillment machine, opening a path to a universe just like this one, but with your personal parameters adjusted ever so slightly, the complexity matrices shifted just so. (This was actually not possible: manipulating individual meta-world-lines was technically an unsolved problem, but tell that to the dreamers.) Among the last to go were the people who had worked with Birha, her colleagues and students. They claimed not to be deceived by the dream-merchants; their excuse was academic, but they went like so many other people into the void. The exodus left certain towns and regions thinly populated, some planets abandoned. Imagine being dissatisfied enough to want to change not towns, or planets, but entire universes! It was all Birha could do in the early days to stand there and watch the insanity until finally her dear companions were sundered from her by space, time, and whatever boundary kept one universe from another. Some people came back, but they were strangers, probably from other planets in her universe. She had discovered the infinite branches of the cosmic tree, but it was not hers to claim in any way. She was the only one who wouldn't travel its endless ways.

Who knew how long her erstwhile companions would be gone, or in what shape they'd return, *if* they returned? She was too old to travel, and she liked the pleasures of small things, like tinkering with the tuning on the poeticas, designing and constructing new ones, and sipping the pale tea in the morning. She liked watching the yellow dog chase firelings. But also she was a prickly old woman, conservative as they come about universes and parameters, and she liked this one just fine, thank you. She liked the world on which she lived, with the seven-year day-cycle.

No, she wouldn't go. She was too obstinate, and she disapproved of this meddling with the natural unfolding of things. Besides, there was the elegance of death. The neatness of it, the way nothing's wasted after. It seemed as though only in this universe was death real. She liked to sit on the sunny doorstep and talk to the dog about it all. Dogs, she thought, don't need other universes; they are already perfect for the one in which they exist. She wondered if humans were refugees from some lost other branch of the Tree, which is why we were so restless. Always dissatisfied, going from planet to planet, galaxy to galaxy, branch to branch of the Cosmic Tree, and maybe rewriting our own life-histories of what-has-been. But we are not all like that; there have always been people who are like the dog, like Birha, perfectly belonging in the worlds of this universe.

A Rumination on Poeticas

A poetica consists of a series of suspended rods or wires under tension, mounted vertically on a frame. A sounding stick run by an ingenious mechanism of gears and a winding mechanism not unlike an old-fashioned clock brushes over the rods at a varying speed, forward and backward. A series of levers controls which rod or wire is struck. While this instrument can be designed to be played by an adept, it can also be fully automated by the mechanism, which is built to last. The enormous ones on public display recount the histories and great epic poems of the people, and are made of wood and stone and metal. Some kinds are designed to be played by the wind, but in these instruments, the sounds, and therefore the meanings, are always new, and ambiguous.

It took me years to learn the musical language of the aliens, and more years to learn to build miniature poeticas.

To sound these ruminations, I have had to interpolate and invent new syllables, new chords and phrases, in order to tell my story. There are no words in their language for some of what I feel and think, and similarly there are sounds in their tongue I'll never understand.

We call them aliens, but this is their world. We took it from them. We are the strangers, the interlopers, the aliens.

Birha's Loves

So Birha waits, watching the clouds gather over the university ramparts, walking every day to the abandoned laboratory, where her calculations give her both frustration and pleasure. Following the probability distribution of a single meta-world-line is tremendously difficult. Through the skeins and threads of possibility that arc across the simulator's three-dimensional result-space, she can discern several answers that fit the constraints. A problem with a multiplicity of answers as scattered as stars. Rudrak will be back in 0.3, or 0.87, or 4.6 cycles. Or in 0.0011, or 5.8, or 0.54 cycles. She is out of temper with herself and the meta-universe at large.

As she goes down the slope in the cloud-darkness that passes for evening, tripping a little bit because she wants to be in the stone house before the rain starts, it occurs to her that her irritation signifies love. For Thirru, for the man who temporarily attracted her, for the lesser loves of all the years after, for Rudrak, for Ubbiri, for all her long-gone colleagues and students, for the yellow dog who lives with her, for the village girl who brings the evening meal and cleans up in silence. For Timmar's rock, for the aliens and their gift to her, for the cloud forest, for that ever-giving Tree, the cosmic kalpa-vriksh, and especially her branch of it. And for death, who waits for her as she waits for Rudrak.

As she thinks this, her impatience at Rudrak's non-arrival dissipates the way the mist does when the sun comes out. In the stone house, she is out of breath; her chest hurts. There is an aroma of warm food, and the yellow dog looks up from where he is lying and wags his tail lazily. She sits down to eat, dropping bits for the dog, sipping the pale tea. She thinks how it might be good for her to go out, when the time comes, into the deep forest and let her life be taken by a stinging death-vine, as is the custom among some of the natives. The vine brings a swift, painless death, wrapping the body in a shell of silken threads until all the juices are absorbed. The rest is released to become part of the rich humus of the forest floor. She feels like giving herself back to the world that gave her so much, even though she was not born here. It is comforting to think of dying in this way. The yellow dog will be happy enough with the village girl, and the old stone house will eventually be overcome by the forest. The wind will have to learn to play the poeticas, and then it will interpolate its own story with hers.

Only closed systems are lonely. And there is no such thing as a closed system.

Three days later, as the bell for morning tolls, there is a knock on the door. There is a man standing there. A stranger. No—it takes her a moment to recognize Rudrak, with his customary attitude of bewilderment and anxiety. The change is just enough to render him not quite familiar: more silver hairs, a shirt of a different fashion, in blue with an embroidered sash. He's taller, stoops a little, and the face is different too, in a way that she can't quite explain. In that long moment of recognition, the kalpa-vriksh speaks to her. The mistake she had made in her calculations was to assume that through all the changes between universes, through space and through time, Rudrak would be Rudrak, and Birha, Birha, and Ubbiri would always remain Ubbiri. But finally she's seen it: identity is neither invariant nor closed. No wonder the answers had so much scatter in them! The truth, as always, is more subtle and more beautiful. Birha takes a deep breath of gratitude, feels her death only a few ten-days away.

"I'm looking for Ubbiri," says this almost-stranger, this new Rudrak. His accent is almost perfect. She ushers him in, and he looks around, at the pale sunlight falling on the long table with the poeticas, which are sounding softly. His look of anxiety fades for a moment, to be replaced by wonder. "This looks familiar," he says. "Have I been here before?"

Sailing the Antarsa

There are breezes, like the ocean breeze, which can set your pulse racing, dear kin, and your spirit seems to fly ahead of you as your little boat rides each swell. But this breeze! This breeze wafts through you and me, through planets and suns, like we are nothing. How to catch it, know it, befriend it? This sea, the Antarsa, is like no other sea. It washes the whole universe, as far as we can tell, and the ordinary matter such as we are made of is transparent to it. So how is it that I can ride the Antarsa current, as I am doing now, steering my little spacecraft so far from Dhara and its moon?

Ah, there lies a story.

I have gone farther than anyone since my ancestors first came to Dhara four generations ago. As I stare out into the night, I can see the little point that is my sun. It helps to look at it and know that the love of my kin reaches across space and time to me, a bridge of light. I am still weak from my long incarceration in the cryochamber—and filled with wonder that I have survived nearly all the journey to the Ashtan system—but oh! It takes effort even to speak aloud, to record my thoughts and send them homeward.

I am still puzzled as to why the ship woke me up before it was time. During my long, dreamless sleep, we have sustained some mild damage from space debris, but the self-repairing system has done a good enough job, and nothing else seems to be wrong. There were checks against a half-dozen systems that were not of critical importance—I have just finished going through each of them and performing some minor corrections. In the navigation chamber the altmatter sails spread out like the wings of some marvelous insect—still intact. I put my hands into the manipulation gloves, immediately switching the craft to manual control, and checked. The rigging is still at a comfortable tension, and it takes just a small twitch of a finger to lift, rotate, lower, or twist each sail. It is still thrilling to feel the Antarsa current that passes through me undetected, to feel it indirectly by way of the response of the altmatter wings! A relief indeed to know that the sense I had been developing of the reality, the *tangibility*, of the Antarsa sea is not lost. We are on course, whatever that means when one is riding a great current into the unknown, only roughly certain of our destination.

There is a shadowy radar image that I need to understand. The image is not one of space debris, but of a shape wide in the middle and tapered at both ends, shutting out the stars. It is small, and distant, traveling parallel to us at nearly the same speed, but subsequent scans reveal no such thing. My first excited thought was: spaceship! But then, where is it? If it came close enough for my sensors, why did it choose to retreat? If this is why the ship woke me, which seems logical, then why didn't it wake me earlier, when a nearly spherical piece of space rock hit us? When we grazed past a lone planet that had been shot out of some distant, unstable solar system?

The ship's intelligence is based on the old generation-ship AI that brought my ancestors to Dhara. It has a quietness and a quick efficiency that one would expect of an artificial thinking system, but there are aspects of it that remind me of people I know. A steadiness masking a tendency to over-plan for contingencies. That might be why it woke me up—it is a secret worrier, like my superficially calm mother Simara, so far and so long away. I will never see her—or any of them—again. That thought brings tears to my eyes.

Why does one venture out so far from home? Generations ago, our planet, Dhara, took my ancestors in from the cold night and gave them warmth. Its living beings adjusted and made room, and in turn we changed ourselves to accommodate them. So it was shown to us that a planet far from humanity's original home is kin to us, a brother, a sister, a mother. To seek kinship with all is an ancient maxim of my people, and ever since my ancestors came to this planet we have sought to do that with the smallest, tenderest thing that leaps, swoops, or grows on this verdant world. Some of us have looked up at the night sky and wondered about other worlds that might be kin to us, other hearths and homes that might welcome us, through which we would experience a different becoming. Some of us yearn for those connections waiting for us on other shores. We seek to feed within us the god of wonder, to open within ourselves dusty rooms we didn't know existed and let in the air and light of other worlds. And the discovery of the Antarsa, that most subtle of seas, has made it possible to venture far into that night, following the wide, deep current that flows by our planet during its northern winter. The current only flows one way. Away.

So I am here.

I look at the miniature biosphere tethered to my bunk. One of my first acts upon waking was to make sure that it was intact—and it was. Parin's gift to me is a transparent dome of glass within which a tiny landscape grows. There are mosses in shades of green, and clumps of sugarworts, with delicate, brittle leaves colored coral and blue, and a waterbagman, with its translucent stalk and bulbous, water-filled chambers within which tiny worms lead entire lives. Worlds within worlds. She had designed the system to be self-contained so that one species' waste was another species' sustenance. It is a piece of Dhara, and it has helped sustain me during each of the times I have been awake, these years.

It helps to remember who I am. This time when I woke up, I had a long and terrifying moment of panic, because I couldn't remember who I was, or where I was. All I knew was that it was very cold, and a soft, level voice was talking to me (the ship). I cannot begin to describe how horrific a sense of loss this was—that my *self* had somehow slipped its moorings and was adrift on a dark sea, and I couldn't find it. Slowly, as memory and warmth returned, I found myself, anchored myself to the rock of remembrance, of shared love under a kind sun. So as I ponder the situation I'm in, the mystery of why the ship woke me—I will speak my own story, which is also many stories. Like my mothers who first told me of the world, I will tell it aloud, tethering myself through the umbilical cords of kinship, feeding the gods within.

I have been traveling for nearly eight years. Yet I seem to have left only yesterday, my memories of the parting are so clear. I remember when my craft launched from the Lunar Kinship's base, how I slowly shut down conventional fusion power and edged us into the Antarsa current. How it seemed hours before I could maneuver the little craft into the superfast central channel, manipulating the altmatter wings so that my spaceship wouldn't fall apart. But at last we were at a comfortable acceleration, going swifter than any human on my world—and I looked back.

The moon, Roshna, was slipping away beneath me with vertiginous speed. The lights of the Lunar Kinship were blinking in farewell, the radio crackling with familiar voices that already seemed distant, shouting their relief and congratulations. At that moment I was assailed with an unfamiliar feeling, which I recognized after a while as my first experience of loneliness. It was unbearable—a nightmare of childhood from which there is no escape.

Looking at the screen, with my kin's images flickering, hearing their voices, I was severely tempted to turn around. I was close enough to still do this—to arc my trajectory, turn from the Antarsa current into a high moon orbit and then use conventional fusion power to land. But I had pledged I would embark on this journey, had planned for it, dreamed of it—and there had been so much hard work on the part of several Kinships, so much debating in the Council— that I clenched my fists against temptation and let the moment go. I feasted my eyes on the thick forests, the purple scrublands of the moon, and the shining blue-green curve of Dhara below, the planet we had called home for five generations, memorizing the trails of white clouds, the jagged silver edge of the Mahapara continent, the

Tura-Tura archipelago like a trail of tears, as a lover memorizes the body of her beloved.

This was the moment for which my friends from Ship University and I had planned and prepared for nearly ten years, soon after the discovery of the Antarsa. We had placed a proposal before the World Council, which debated for eight years. There were representatives from all the Kinships (except the People of the Ice, of course—they have not attended Council in two generations): the People of the Himdhara Mountains, the People of the Western Sea, the Roshnans from the Lunar Kinship, and of course my own People of the Devtaru, among a number of smaller Kinships. There was endless discussion, much concern, but they let us design and send the first few probes into the Antarsa current. Interpreting the signals from the probes, the University experts determined that the current appeared to run in a more-or-less straight line toward the Ashtan star system five light-years away. The last signal from the last probe had arrived seven years after its launch, when the probe was as yet some distance short of the Ashtan system. There was something ominous about the probe's subsequent silence—what had befallen it?—although the explanation could have been as simple as malfunctioning equipment or a chance hit by a space rock.

Some argued that an expedition was justified, because we hadn't heard from the Ashtan system since my ancestors had arrived on Dhara. Two generation ships had left the old world, one bound for Dhara, the other for Ashta, and they had been one people before that. So our people had always wondered what befell our kin around the brightest star in our sky. Others in the Council argued that this was the very reason we should not venture out, because the silence of the Ashtans—and the probe—pointed to some unknown danger. And what if the current took us somewhere else entirely? What guarantee that we would wash up on a world as kind as our own? To go out into the void was to seek kinship with death before our time. And so on.

But at last the Council gave its reluctant blessing, and here I was, on a ship bound for the stars. I am a woman past my youth, although not yet of middle age, and I have strived always to take responsibility for my actions. So I watched the moon and the great curve of the planet that was my home fall away into the night, and I wept. But I did not turn around.

I float within my ship like a fishling in a swamp. I have swum through the inertial webbing (softer and more coarse at the moment since we are at low acceleration) from chamber to chamber, checking that all is well. No more strange images on the radar. All systems working in concert. The bioskin that lines each chamber, produces the air I breathe, recycles waste, and spins the inertial web looks a healthy gold-green. We are now moving at half the speed of light, absurdly fast. From the porthole, the distant stars are like the eyes of the night. I sip a tangy, familiar tea from a tube (I have a little cold) and breathe slowly, remembering what my friend Raim told me.

Raim taught me to sail on the Western Sea. His people designed the altmatter wings that spread within the navigation chamber (surely the only ship ever built whose sails are on the inside). When I woke from cold sleep there was a message from him. He said: Mayha, far-sister, when you are lonely, make a friend of loneliness.

So I make kinship with the dark. I whisper to it, I tell it stories. Perhaps the dark will have something to say to me in turn.

At first our plan was to make the inside of the ship a biosphere, rich with life, choosing the most appropriate and hardy species, so that I would feel more we than I. But after debating on it the Council decided that unless I wished it very strongly, this would not be right. To subject other life-forms to human whim, to put them in danger without compelling reason, was not our way. Besides, we ran the risk of upsetting the balance of life on other worlds in case our containment protocols failed. When I heard the reasoning, I too fell in with this. We compromised thus: the inner surface of the ship would be a bioskin, but that was all. To save energy and to enable the long years to pass without pathological loneliness, we would install a cryochamber. My apprehensions at the length and solitude of the journey were nothing to that old desire within me since childhood: to soar skyward in search of our kin, new and old.

But as I was leaving, saying my forever good-byes amidst tears and jokes and good wishes, Parin came up to me, indignant. She was worked up about the Council decision to not install a biosphere within the ship. She thrust something at me: a transparent dome of glass within which a tiny landscape grew.

"Mayha, take this!" she said fiercely. "I can't believe they're going to condemn you to such a long journey alone!"

I tried to argue that the Council's position was an attempt to be just to all life-forms, and that I didn't know how her sealed-in, miniature biosphere would adapt to zero gravity—but I've lost most arguments with Parin. And the little biosphere was beautiful. Besides, I did not want our parting to be acrimonious. Parin and I had grown up with the rest of the horde of children under the same kinhouse roof. Through much of my childhood I had been part of her schemes and adventures. I remembered the time we had rescued a nest of firebirds from some imagined danger, and how we'd wept copiously when they died. Most of Parin's schemes had involved guilt and good intentions in about equal measure.

I took the little biosphere, as she'd known I would. She scowled at me, then started to cry. We hugged and wept. Then the others had their turn at good-bye. Good-byes at the kinhouse always take a long time; there are so many of us. And this time, for this historic one-way journey, there were people from nearly all the hundred-and-twenty-three kinhouses of the Kinship of the Devtaru, waiting to see me off on the shuttle that would take me to the moon, where I was to board my craft. There were also representatives from the People of the Western Sea, my friend Raim, tall and gray-skinned, stared at by the children, waving at me with one webbed hand. The Ship University folk had adapted the spacecraft from one of the shuttles aboard the old generation ship and tested it. A knot of them was present, waiting at the edge of the crowd for their turn. Closest to me stood my mothers, each displaying grief and pride consistent with her nature: Kusum yelling about the dangers of the journey and how I should be careful about this or that, as though I were three again, Brihat simply holding my arm and staring into my face, with tears streaming down her broad cheeks, and Simara being sensible and controlled although her smile wavered. My birth-mother Vishwana was behind them, regal as always, our representative to the Council. She nodded and smiled at me. Although I had never known her well, I had always been in awe of her. My kin-sisters and brothers were there, alternately cheering and weeping, and Sarang, grown so tall since I'd last seen her, tossed me a braided ribbon over the heads of the crowd.

My father was not there. I saw him rarely, since he was a traveler and a trader, and when I did we always took pleasure in sharing stories with each other. He had sent me a message by radio wishing me luck, but he was halfway across the world, too far to come in time.

Then near the back with the guests I saw Vik. He had partnered with me for fourteen years, and we had gone our separate ways, in friendship, until my decision to go on this journey became public. He had become a bitter opponent in the Council discussions, and would no longer speak to me. He looked at me from the back of the crowd and looked away again.

I have partnered for long and short periods with both men and women, but Vik was the one with whom I spent the longest time. There were times I thought we would always be together, as some partnerships are, but we sought joy in different things that took us on diverging paths. He was a historian at Ship University, content to stay in one place and let his mind go into the deep past. Like my father, I needed to wander. It was as simple as that.

I wanted very badly to end things well with Vik. I took a pendant off the string around my neck and flung it over the heads of the crowd toward him. It hit him on the cheek—he caught it, looked irritable, put it in his pocket. I smiled at him. He rubbed his cheek, looked at me and away again.

The shuttle finally took off. I scarcely remember my time at Roshna, at the Lunar Kinship, where my spacecraft was waiting. They took care of me, asked me again the ritual question before one goes on a long journey: Is your heart in it, kinswoman? Do you really want to go on this quest? And I said yes, yes, and there were more good-byes. At last I was in the craft, up and away. As I manipulated the sails in the navigation chamber, as I'd done so many times on my way to the moon—except that this time I would be going beyond it—as I felt the familiar tug of the Antarsa current, the old excitement rose in me again. It was too soon to feel lonely, or so I thought, because the love of my people was an almost tangible presence.

As I float by the porthole, I can see them all so clearly. Their faces tender and animated, as I turn from the raised platform into the doorway of the shuttle, turn once more to look for the last time at my people and my world, to breathe the forest-scented air. There is the wide, woven roof of the kinhouse, and the vines running up the brown walls, the gourds ripening green to gold. Here I had played and climbed, looked at the stars, dreamed and wept. There is the gleam of the river, the pier, the boats waiting on the water. Dwarfing them all, the great, shaggy forest, trees like spires, trees like umbrellas, reaching leafy arms into the sky, taller than the tallest kinhouse. I think: when I rise up, I will see again the devtaru, the one closest to us anyhow, greater than any tree that exists or can be dreamed. The devtaru has shared its secret with us, and because of that I will fly beyond the moon. As I rise I will speak my gratitude to it, to all the world for having formed me, made me into myself. And so I did.

The devtaru is not a tree. It is perhaps what a tree would dream of, if a tree could dream.

The first one I ever saw lies two days away from my kinhouse. In my thirteenth year some of us trekked through the forest with Visith, one of my aunts, who has been a sister of the forest most of her life. On the way we learned plant lore, and we practiced the art of offering kinship to the beings of the forest.

"Kinship isn't friendship," my aunt said. "Don't go doing stupid things like putting your hand into a tree-bear's nest, or poking around inside an occupied bee-apple. Learn to sit still in a clear space, and let the creatures observe you, as you observe them."

We did a lot of sitting still. It was difficult at first but I got the idea of it quicker than the others. The forest whispered around me—sunlight dappled the ground. A wind-around approached me, its tendrils a-quiver, looking for something to climb. I nudged it away with my toe—it was kin, but I didn't want it taking advantage of my stillness. I sensed that I was being watched: a moon-eye monkey, which meant we were close to the devtaru. It was up in a tree, the white rings around its eyes giving it an expression of permanent astonishment. My heart thundered with excitement as the little creature peered out from its leafy shelter. But it was only after two days of seeing and being seen that the moon-eye came out into plain sight. A day later it took an apple-rind from me. After that the moon-eyes were everywhere, moving above me over the trees, chattering to each other and glancing at me from time to time. Then I could walk about without them hiding. I had made kinship!

Parin was in trouble for being too impatient, trying to climb up to a moon-eye's nest before it was appropriate to do so. The other two hadn't yet obtained the knack of it and needed to practice stillness without fidgeting or falling asleep. We lingered in that place until their impatience gave way to resignation, and they broke through. We got a congratulatory lecture from Visith.

"A kinship is a relationship that is based on the assumption that each person, human or otherwise, has a right to exist, and a right to agency," she intoned. "This means that to live truly in the world we must constantly adjust to other beings, as they adjust to us. We must minimize and repair any harm that we do. Kinship goes all the way from friendship to enmity—and if a particular being does not desire it, why, we must leave it alone, leave the area. Thus through constant practice throughout our lives we begin to be ready with the final kinship—the one we make with death."

We looked at each other and shivered.

"You are a long way from that," Visith said sardonically, then smiled a rare smile. "But you've taken the first step. Come, let us keep going."

So the journey to the devtaru took several days, and when we were standing at its edge we didn't even know it.

The ground changing should have been our first clue. The forest floor was dotted with undergrowth, but here we found that great roots as thick as a person reared out of the ground and back again, forming a fascinating tangle of steps and crevices that invited climbing. The trees had changed too—the canopy above seemed to be knit together, and trunks dropped down and joined the roots, making a three-dimensional maze.

Visith didn't let us go into the tangle. Instead we made camp and practiced stillness between meals and washing, and took walks along the perimeter of the maze. After two days of this, during which our impatience gave way to resignation, and then, finally, the open, accepting alertness of mind that births the possibility of kinship—Parin pointed at the tangle.

"It's a devtaru! And we didn't even know it!"

It was indeed. The enormous central trunk was deep inside the forest of secondary trunks, likely several hour's journey. The roots went deeper down than any other organism on the planet. To see a devtaru in its entirety, one has to be airborne, or on a far-away hill.

Under the canopy, the moon-eyes led us over the maze of roots and trunks. We found shelter in the crook of a giant root, underneath which flowed a clear stream of water. The bark against which I laid my head was a thin skin that glowed faintly in the darkness, pulsing in response to my presence. To make kinship with a devtaru is extraordinarily difficult—Visith is one of the few who has succeeded, and it took her nearly twenty years.

"Tomorrow we will go to a place I know, where the devtaru was fruiting moon-pods last I came," she told us. "If the devtaru wishes, perhaps we will see a launch!"

I had seen the usual fruiting pods of a devtaru during our journey inside it, but never the legendary moon-pods. This devtaru was too young to make anything but small, empty moon-pods, but it would be a sight worth seeing. My heart was full. I wanted so much to be kin to such a being! Like Moon-woman, whose story Parin began to tell in the soft darkness.

There was a girl once, who sat in stillness seeking kinship with a devtaru for a hundred years. Potter-ants built a dwelling around her, and wind-arounds made a green tangle around that, so no rain or wind could trouble her. Flitters brought her crystals of sap and placed them between her lips so she knew neither hunger or thirst. She saw the devtaru and its beings, and it observed her with its thousand eyes, and at last they made kinship.

She lived within its forest, among its roots and trunks, and learned its moods and sensed its large, slow thoughts. She became familiar with the creatures who lived in its shelter, the moon-eyes and the dream-flitters, and the floating glow-worms, and the angler-birds with their lures of light. Then one day a moon-eye led her to a place within the devtaru forest where she found a large pod attached to the top of a trunk. The pod was just about as tall as she was, and just about as wide in the middle, and it was covered over with a shimmering patina, so that she had to blink to make sure it was actually there. It pointed away from her toward the moon in the sky as though it yearned to break free, and it quivered gently as though caught in a breeze, although no breeze blew. The trunk glowed and patterns formed and dissolved on its surface, and the girl knew she had to climb right up to the pod.

And she did. She found that the pod's lips weren't closed as yet, and inside it was empty of seed. Within it there were little creatures, buzzwings and a grumpworm or two, and some leafy, mossy debris.

She felt a great shudder from the trunk so climbed down hastily, just in time, because the trunk contracted, and the pod shot with a great noise into the sky. As it did, the trunk split and the girl fell down.

She walked for days through the forest and at last found the pod. It lay in a clump of bushes, already half-covered by leaves and branches from a storm. It made her wonder why the devtaru had bothered to send an empty pod into the air at all.

Now I've said she lived with the devtaru for a hundred years. When she was old, and the devtaru even older, something changed. The devtaru's leaves had been falling for a decade or more, and now she could see that its long arc of life was ending. The moon-eyes and the other creatures left the shelter of the devtaru but the girl couldn't bear to do so. The devtaru produced one last enormous moon-pod. The girl, now an old woman, crawled into the pod before its lips closed, and felt around her the creatures who were also stowaways, and felt also the smooth, shiny hard seed, half her size, larger than the seeds in the normal seed-pods. She had decided she could not bear to watch the tree die, and she would let it take her away to her final destination.

The pod grew and grew, and the old woman fell asleep inside it. Then one day the time came. She could sense a tensing in the limbs and sinews of the devtaru, preparing for the launch, but this time there came to her faintly a strange slight smell of burning. The lips of the pod closed completely, and if it hadn't been for the stowaways making air to breathe, she would have suffocated. Off she went into the sky.

Now there was a sister of this old woman who came to see her from time to time, and she was watching from a hilltop not far from the devtaru. She liked to look at the stars through a telescope, so she was known as Sister Three-Eyes. She saw the great pod quiver and align with the now risen moon. Tendrils of smoke emerged from the crevices of the tree. Then the pod launched.

There was a noise like a clap of thunder, and the devtaru shattered. As it did, it began to burn from its deep internal fires, slowly and magnificently. What a death! But Sister Three-Eyes soon turned her attention from the dying devtaru and trained her telescope on the pod, because she wanted to know where it landed.

To her surprise, it didn't land. It went higher and higher, and soon it was a speck she could barely see. Just before she lost sight of it, she saw it move into a low orbit, and then, suddenly, the pod changed its mind and made straight for the moon.

So she found that the devtaru's last and final moon-pod is truly destined for the moon. Which is why the devtaru's children grow on the moon, although they do not make such enormous pods as they do on Dhara. The lunar forest and the purple scrublands and the creatures that live there and make the air to breathe are all gifts of the devtaru, the only being known to spread its seed to another world.

As to what happened to Moon-woman—who knows? When the next generation found a way to get to the moon in shuttles, they looked for her in the forests and the grassy plains. They did not find her. Some say she could not have survived the journey. Others say that she did survive it, and she wandered through the lunar forests content that she had found a place among the children of the devtaru, and died a peaceful death there. These people named the moon Roshna, after her, as it is still called today. Her sister thought she saw a light burning or flashing on the moon some months after Moon-woman left, but who can be sure? There are those that believe that Moon-woman went farther, that she found a way to launch her moon-pod into the space beyond the moon, and that she sails there still along the unknown currents of the seas of space and time.

Parin had always told this story well, but listening to it under the devtaru, in that companionable darkness, made it come alive. I wondered whether Moon-woman was, indeed, sailing the void between the stars at this moment, offering kinship to beings stranger than we could imagine. Looking at a small patch of starry sky visible between the leaves above me, I shivered with longing.

We never got to see a pod launch on that trip. But even now I can remember Parin's young voice, the words held in the air as if by magic, the breathing of the others beside me, the feel of the tree's skin glowing gently like a cooling ember.

The story anticipates the discovery of the Antarsa, of course. That I had a small role to play in it is a source of both pain and pleasure, because it happened when I first realized that Vik and I were growing apart from one another.

I have been torn between excitement of a most profound sort, and a misery of an extremely mundane sort. The excitement first: there have been *several* flickering images on the radar. It is clear now that there are others around me, keeping their distance—spaceships from the Ashtan system? Our long lost cousins? I sent a transmission in Old Irthic to them, but there is no reply. Only silence. Silence can mean so many things, from "I don't see you," to "I don't want to see you." There is a possibility that these are ships from other human-inhabited worlds, but it would be strange that they would not have made contact with us on Dhara.

My other thought is that the occupants of these ships may be aliens who simply cannot understand my message, or know it to be a message. This is even more exciting. It also makes me apprehensive, because I don't know their intent. They appear in and out of range, moving at about the same average speed as my craft. Are they curious? Are they escorting me, studying me, wondering if I am an enemy? All I can do is to practice what I did in the great forest: stillness. Stillness while moving at more than 50% of the speed of light—I wonder what my aunt Visith would say to that! Do nothing, says her no-nonsense voice in my memory. Wait and observe, and let yourself be observed.

That I have been doing.

The misery is that I have a message from Vik. Sent years ago of course, but there it is: he is grateful for the pendant I tossed him when I left, and he has found a new partner, a fellow historian at Ship

University, a woman called Mallow. When I first got his message I just stared at it. A sense of deep abandonment welled up inside me; my loneliness, which I had tried to befriend, loomed larger than mountains. Of course I had expected this—even if I had stayed on Dhara, there would have been no going back to Vik—but I felt resentful of his meticulous observation of correct behavior. Yes, it is a graceful thing to do, to tell a former long-term partner when you have found a new love—but I would never come back, never find a new love, someone to hold—there was no need to let me know. Except it would make Vik feel better, that he had done the right thing. He had not thought about me, and it hurt.

For once Parin's little biosphere did not assuage my pain. I couldn't even go outside and run up a mountain or two. Instead I swam from chamber to chamber through the inertial webbing, if only to feel the web break and re-form as I went through it, my tears floating in the air around me like a misty halo, attaching to the gossamer threads like raindrops. There was nowhere to go. After I had calmed down I tethered myself to the porthole and stared into the night, and thought of what it had been like.

After Vik, I had taken no lovers for a while, until I met Laharis. She was a woman of the Western Sea. I'd been working with Raim on the ocean, learning to sail an ordinary boat before I learned the ways of the Antarsa. We had been out for several days, and had returned with a hold full of fish, and salt in our hair, our skin chapped. Raim and I developed a deep love and camaraderie, but we were not drawn to each other in any other way. It was when I was staying at their kinhouse, watching the rain fall in gray sheets on the ocean, that his sister came up to me. The others were away bringing in the last catch. Laharis and I had talked for long hours and we had both sensed a connection, but the construction of the altmatter wings from the discarded moon-pods of the devtaru had taken up my time. Now she slid a hand up my arm, leaned close to me. Her hair was very fine, a silver cascade, and her smooth gray cheek was warm. Her long, slanted eyes, with the nictitating membranes that still startled me, shone with humor. She breathed in my ear. "Contrary to stereotype," she whispered, "we Sea folk don't taste like salt. Would you care to find out?"

So we learned each other for two beautiful months. During our time together I forgot stars and space and the Antarsa—there was only her slow, unfurling self, body and mind, every part an enchantment. I would have wanted to partner with her, had I stayed on planet. Now that I was far away, I could only remember and weep. She never sent me messages, though her brother did. I think it was hard for her and perhaps she thought it would be hard for me.

Dear darkness, help me keep my equilibrium. Here I am, in a universe so full of marvels and mysteries, and I mourn the loss of my already lost loves as though I were still young and callow. What a fool I am!

I shall keep stillness, and feed no more that envious, treacherous god within, the god of a heart bereft.

Vik has rarely ventured from Ship University. He's one of those people who likes to put down roots and ponder how we got here. The past is his country. Ship University is a good place for him.

It is housed inside the generation ship that brought my people to Dhara so long ago. The ship lies in a hollow made for it in the sandy plains near a lake. It contains the records of my people's history and of the home planet, and the cryochambers are now laboratories. The shuttle bays are experimental stations, and cabins are classrooms. In the forests or the sea, the mountains or the desert, it is hard to believe that we have the technology we do. "Have high tech, live low tech," has been a guiding principle of the Kinships. That is how we have lived so well on our world.

Ship University's sky scholars were the first to study the flight of devtaru pods. Vik's friend Manda, a sky scholar of repute, told me how the mystery deepened as the early scholars tracked the moon-pods with increasingly powerful telescopes. I can see Manda now, slender fingers brushing back her untidy brown hair, her eyes alight. I was visiting Vik after wandering for a month through the Bahagan desert, and it had become clear to me that there was a wall between us. I felt then the first hint of the ending to come. I think Vik sensed it too. He sat next to me, looking restive, while Manda talked. She showed us a holo of a devtaru moon-pod launching from a century ago.

Despite my misery, I found myself fascinated. There was the tiny pod, dwarfed by the curve of Dhara, apparently going into low orbit. The moon wasn't in the picture, which was to scale, but we were informed that the planet, the pod, and the moon formed a more-or-less straight line through their centers. In its orbit around the planet, the pod began to tremble abruptly, like a leaf floating on a stream disturbed by a random eddy. Then it swung loose from its orbit and made straight for the moon. It traveled with such astonishing rapidity that all we could see was a silver streak. Then the scene cut to the moon, and the pod approaching it, swinging past it a few times, slowing gradually until at last it made a rough landing in the southern forest. There was a bloom of light, a brief fire where it hit, then the film stopped.

"This was taken by Kaushai, back about a century ago. All this time there have only been speculations as to how the devtaru pods get to the moon, why they suddenly change course from low orbit to the trajectory you saw. The pods themselves have no means of propulsion. There is nothing in the void of space between the planet Dhara and the moon. The first probes that were sent to duplicate the orbit of the pods suffered no strange perturbations, nor were they drawn toward the moon. The devtaru pods apparently violate fundamental laws of nature: that momentum and energy must be conserved."

I knew something of all this, of course. But I had never seen the holo before. It was quite amazing. I felt Vik stir beside me—he looked just as entranced, and when my gaze met his, as miserable as I.

Yet it was a chance remark I made on that visit that set the sky scholars on the right track. I go back to that time in my imagination. Vik and I are both starting to realize that our paths are too different to allow for us to be together, although it will be quite some time before we have the courage to say so to each other. So the golden afternoon and our togetherness have acquired a deep, sad sweetness. We join Manda and her friends for a walk around the lake. They have been talking all day about the mystery of the devtaru pods, telling us how they spent years camping by a certain devtaru, watching it, getting to know it, asking it to share its secret. Now some of them feel as though the devtaru has communicated with them already, that they already know what the secret is, but it is buried deep inside them and needs some kind of stimulus, or reminder, a magic word or phrase to bring it into consciousness.

After evening sets in we find ourselves tired and hungry—we have walked a long way and the stars are beginning to come out in a pale pink sky. We are at a place where a small river empties into the lake, making an intricate delta of rivulets. We are wishing we had a boat to get to the shore from which we ventured, where the bulk of Ship looms, its many windows lit. The air is full of the trembling cries of glitterwings. I am speechless with emotion, with the thought that the end of our partnership is as close as the other shore. Vik is silent beside me. Just as we are talking about boats, I find the remains of one at the bottom of a rivulet. It is full of holes—in fact, most of it has rotted away, but for the frame. It lies indifferently in place as the water rushes through the holes.

"If this boat were solid," I say, "and the current strong enough, it would move. It would carry us home."

A pointless, inconsequential remark. But Manda stares at me, understanding awakening in her face.

She told me later that my remark was the thing she needed to unwrap the gift the devtaru had already given them. What had been one of the saddest evenings of my life was the moment when she and her colleagues solved the mystery of the devtaru pods. Two days later Manda spoke to a gathering of hundreds.

"Imagine an ocean that washes all of space and time. Like the water ocean, it has currents and turbulences. But its substance is invisible to us, as we are invisible—or transparent—to it.

"This is not so strange an idea. As the neutrinos wash through ordinary matter, through you and me, as though we weren't there, as water washes through the broken boat with the holes in it, so the subtle ocean—the Antarsa, named by our poet Thora—washes through planets and stars, plants and people, as though we did not exist.

"We don't know whether the Antarsa is made up of neutrinos or something else. We suspect it is something as yet unknown, because too much is known about neutrinos, which can be caught by ordinary matter if the net is both deep and dense.

"Now imagine a form of matter that is not ordinary matter. This, too, is not strange, because we know that what we call ordinary matter is rather rare in the universe. There are other forms of matter that make up the bulk of the cosmos. One of these forms, what we are calling the altmatter, is opaque to the Antarsa. So if you place a piece of altmatter in an Antarsa current, it will move.

"The pods, of course, have to be made in part of altmatter. How the devtaru acquires it we don't know; maybe it draws it up from deep underground, mingles or combines it with ordinary matter, and forms the pods that are meant to go into space."

That was so long ago, that moment of revelation. Some years later, experimenters took the discarded moon-pods that are empty of seed, the ones that the devtaru shoots out for practice when they are young, to make the first altmatter probes. And now I am here.

Here I am, working the sails in the navigation chamber. I've done enough waiting. I am steering my craft as close to the edge of the current as I dare, as slowly as it needs to go so that changes in speed won't tear it apart. I want to get closer to my mysterious companions.

The shapes on the radar flicker in and out with increasing frequency now. Some are shaped like fat pods, but some appear like vaguely oblong smudges. I want to see a pod ride by with Moon-woman in it, waving. If that happens, I will extend a grappling hook, gently as I can, and bring the moon-pod close to me so she can crawl into my little craft and share a tube of tea. But no, there is no likelihood of moon-pods being this far away from Dhara. After all, the Ashtan system is a few months away. The star is discernibly a round yellow eye, no longer a point, and the planets around it, including Ashta, appear disk-like as well, although I need my telescope to clearly see them. I can just see Ashta's polar ice caps. It is far from my spaceship at the moment, but when I enter the system it should be at a point in its orbit that brings it close to my trajectory. I have to be careful that the Antarsa current does not pass directly through the planet, because I will simply crash into it, then. I am anticipating some delicate maneuvering, and there is no time like this moment to practice.

After a long while, I discover something.

My companions move unobtrusively away as I approach them, which means, of course, that they can sense my presence. Are they simply making room for me, or is it something else? However, what I've found through this experiment is that the Antarsa current, the central, fastest channel at least, has widened considerably. It took me much longer to find its edges, where there are dangerous eddies and rivulets. The speed of the current has not changed, however. Mystified, I continue on my way.

I send my offer of kinship out, but as yet there is no answer but silence.

Listening to the silence, I am reminded of a story my father, the trader, told me when I was small. Among our people the Kinships are fairly self-sufficient, but we do have need of small shipments at regular intervals: metals from the Himdhara Mountains, cloth from Tura-tura and so on. We send out our herbs and jewelry. There is constant flow of information between the Kinships (except for the People of the Ice, about whom my father told this story) and also with Ship

University. Most things are transported where possible by boat, in a rare while by flyer or shuttle, but there are also wandering caravans that go overland, and my father has traveled with many of these. He is from a kinhouse of my own people farther east of here, deeper in the forest and he met my mother during one of his journeys. Neither was interested in a permanent partnership but they remain cordial when they meet. And always he has tried to come see me, to bring me a shell from the Western Sea, or a particularly pretty pebble from Himdhara.

The People of the Ice stopped speaking to us from the time that the second generation of humans was grown. By that time the Kinships had each chosen their place, depending on where they felt most accepted and would do the least harm to the beings already present. My people of the Devtaru had genetically modified ourselves to digest certain local proteins; the Western sea folk had modified their bodies to be more agile in the water and to hold their breath longer than any other human. The People of the Himdhara could thrive in the thin mountain air. The People who settled in the Northern edge of the great continent, where there is ice even in the summer, adjusted themselves to live in that terrible cold. It was said that they grew hairy pelts like the beasts that dwelt there, but this could have been a joke. All the Kinships tell jokes about each other, and most are reasonably good-natured, but the People of the Ice got the worst of it because they were so remote, in both geography and temperament.

When I was little, my father said, his caravan was asked by the World Council to go into the North to find out what had happened to the People of the Ice. Was it that they did not answer radio calls because something terrible had befallen them, or were they being obstreperous as usual?

Take only a few people, said the Council, so that they don't feel invaded. So my father and three others—a man and two women—went. They wandered for days and weeks through forest and scrubland, desert and plateau, until they came to the land of perpetual snow. Here the trees grew up into tall spires, and the wild creatures all had thick, luminous coats and some knew the use of fire. My father knows this because one night the party followed a flickering light through a snowfall, and found large, hairy creatures huddling before a fire, tossing twigs into it and grunting. As is our custom, the four travelers sat some distance away and waited, speaking softly the offering of kinship, until the creatures waved their paws at them and invited them, through expressive grunts, to join them. My father says these were shaggorns, and fortunately this group was full of meat and therefore amiable. They are very curious and they poked at the travelers with twigs to see what they would do (some of his companions laughed but my father only smiled and gently poked back) and one of them wanted to try on my father's coat—my father let him but had to give him his watch to get his coat back.

It was bitterly cold, but the four survived with the help of the shaggorns, and one late afternoon they found themselves at the edge of an icy plain, over which rose a city.

The city was made of ice. The buildings were constructed with ice blocks, and had slit windows, and the streets were ice. People moved about them on skates, and the travelers could not tell whether they wore hairy pelts or if they had grown their own. The travelers set themselves down outside the city's perimeter but in plain sight, in keeping with the tradition of waiting for an invitation.

But there was none. People skated across the ice, from building to building, and didn't even look at the travelers. One little girl stared at them but was roughly pulled away by an adult. The four travelers sang the offering of kinship, but there was no response. This was a terrible thing to witness, my father said, because they had come so far and endured so much to make sure that their kin were safe. They were cold, hungry, and tired, and the song was acquiring rather angry overtones. So they stopped their song, and set up camp there because the evening was setting in.

In the morning they found some supplies—meat, some cooked roots, all frozen by now, a pelt blanket. The meaning was clear: the People of the Ice did not desire kinship, but they meant no harm. There was no weapon left symbolically at the edge of the camp. They did not want a kinship of enmity—they simply wanted to be left alone.

So the travelers began their return journey, somewhat mollified. The next evening, before they were able to go very far (they were tired, as my father said), they saw a small dwelling in the forest. To their surprise they recognized the home of a farsister. Farsisters and far-brothers are people who wander away from their Kinships for a life of solitude, usually seeking some kind of spiritual solace. Some of them have done terrible things and seek to redress them or have suffered a loss and need to find a reason to live. Others simply wander in search of something they can't identify, and when they find it, usually in a place that calls to them, they settle down there.

The farsister's courtyard was snowy and bare, and furnished with only two low flat-topped rocks that my father assumed were intended to be chairs. This meant that the farsister did not like company, but one person would be tolerated. There was an intricately carved block of ice near the door, which indicated the occupation of the person within. That she was female was indicated by a red plume of feathers that hung from her door.

My father sat outside the courtyard and waited. She made him wait for several hours, by which time it was night and getting very cold. Then she came out and ushered him in. She turned out to be a grim, dour woman who seemed to be made of ice as well. The inside of her little hut was just as cold as the outside and this didn't seem to bother her.

She told him that she was not of the People of the Ice, and that there was not anything to be done about them; they kept to themselves. She gave him a cold tea to drink that made my father feel dizzy. He felt himself falling into deep sleep, and the icy fingers of the farsister easing him down into a cold bed.

When he woke up he found that the hut was empty. Moreover, there was no sign that it had ever been inhabited. The hearth was cold, and filled with ashes, and a wind blew through the open window. My father felt frozen to the marrow. He got himself up slowly and painfully and emerged into a snowy dawn. The courtyard of the hut was bare—no sitting rocks, no ice carvings, no evidence that anyone had ever lived here. His companions were waiting anxiously for him at camp.

It was a long journey home, my father said, and they were glad to come back to the warm lands and make their report to the Council.

When he used to tell us children this story in the sunny garden in front of the kinhouse, with the warm sun at our back, we would shiver in the imagined snowfall. We were trapped in the hut of the ghostly farsister, or lost in the enchanted forest with the People of the Ice in their hairy pelts, wandering around to scare us, to take us away. Later we would come up with games and stories of our own, in which the Ice folk were the principal villains.

When I was older, my birth-mother would take some of us to Council meetings. Council meetings rotated from Kinship to Kinship, and when we were the hosts, my mother would let us come. We would see our sea-kin, with their scale-like skin and their webbed hands, and the tall mountain folk with their elaborate head-dresses, or the cave kin with their sunshades over huge, dark eyes, and our own eyes would go round with wonder. In the evenings various kinfolk would gather round a fire or two and tell jokes. We would joke about the people of the Ice, and why they didn't ever come to Council ("they were afraid they'd melt" or "it would be too hot in their fur coats"). During one of these occasions my father was also present—he pulled some of us older ones aside.

"You all talk a lot of nonsense," he said. "Listen, I never told you one part of my story about the People of the Ice. What I dreamed about while I slept in the hut of the farsister."

We were all eyes and ears.

"Listen. I dreamed that the farsister took me to the city of Ice. Some of the Ice people met me and took me in, saying I could stay the night. I was put in an ice-cold room on a bed of ice, and it was so cold that I couldn't sleep. In the night I heard my hosts talking about me, arguing. Some said I should never have been brought here, and another voice said that maybe I could be made to substitute for some relative, an old man whose time had come. The executioners would

not know the difference if I was wrapped in furs and made unconscious, and that way the old man could live a little longer in secret.
This went on for a long time, until the people moved away. I was so
scared that I fled from there. My captors chased me some of the way
but without much enthusiasm. Then I woke up in my cold bed."

My father paused.

"I may have simply dreamed the whole thing. But the dream was
so vivid that I sometimes wonder if it didn't actually happen. Since
that time I have wondered whether the reason for the silence of our
Ice kin is something more sinister than mere bad manners. What if
their genetic manipulations to adapt to the cold resulted in something they did not expect—something that prevents them from dying
when they are old? Since they cannot die, they must put to death the
old ones. And they are terrified that by mingling with us they will let
loose an epidemic of deathlessness. So in their shame and misfortune
they keep themselves separate from all other humans."

We were appalled. To cheat death, even to wish to live longer than
one's natural span, is to show so much disrespect to all living beings,
including one's own offspring and generations yet to come, that it is
unthinkable. It is natural to fear death, and so it takes courage to make
kinship with death when one's time has come. How terrible to have
death itself refuse kinship! To have to kill one's own kin! It was an
honorable thing to isolate this curse in a city of Ice, rather than let it
loose among the rest of the Kinships. After my father's revelation we
found ourselves unable to joke about the People of the Ice with the
same carelessness.

I am thinking about them today because I wonder about the
silence of the spacecraft around me, and the deeper, longer silence of
the Ashtans. Did they settle on their planet, or did they find it unsuit-
able and move on? Did some misfortune befall them? Or did they
simply turn away from us, for some reason?

I don't know if I'll ever find out.

———

So much has happened that I have not had time to speak my story until now. Dear, kind darkness, dear kin on Dhara, I have made such a discovery! My companions, whose flickering images on the radar screen have so mystified me, have revealed their true nature. It is hard to say whether there are simply more of them—they are so clear on the radar now—or whether I have gained their trust and they have moved closer.

They are not spaceships. They are beings. Creatures of deep space, made of altmatter, riding the Antarsa current like me.

I found this out a few days ago, when the radar screen presented an unusually clear image. A long, sinuous, undulating shape, broadest in the middle and tapered at each end, moved parallel to us. Something waved like a banner from the far end—a tail. It was huge. I held my breath. The visual image showed a barely visible shape, lit only by starlight and the external lights of my ship, but it reminded me just a little of the seagu, that massive, benevolent ocean mammal of the Western Sea.

It was clearly made of altmatter. Its flattened limbs—fins?—moved in resistance to the Antarsa current, which propelled it forward. There was a purposefulness, an ease with which it swam that was delightful to see. Here was a creature in its element, apparently evolved to travel between the stars on the great Antarsa ocean. I closed my eyes, opened them, and the image was still there. My fingers were shaking.

How to describe what it meant to me, the company of another living creature, be it one so removed from myself! I had lived with other living beings all my life before this journey. I had played with chatterlings in the great forest near my home, swum with ocean mammals—walroos and seagus, whales, and schools of silverbellies. Even in the high, bare mountains of Himdhara, where life is hardy, scarce and without extravagance, I had made kinship with a mog-bear, with whom I shared a cave for several days during a storm. Nearly always I had traveled with other humans. This was my first journey into the dark, alone. Parin's biosphere had much to do with maintaining my sanity, but how I had missed the company of other life! I blinked back tears. I took a deep breath and thanked the universe that I had lived to see such a marvel.

It was an exhilarating moment. It reminded me of my time with Raim, learning to use the sails on his boat on the Western Sea. Wind and current carried us far from the shore, and that wind was in my hair, whipping it about my face, and chapping my lips. Raim was beside me, laughing, rejoicing that I was finally moving the boat like an extension of my own body. Just then a school of whales surfaced, and leaped up into the air as though to observe us. Crashing down into the water, raising a spray that drenched us, they traveled with us, sometimes surging ahead, sometimes matching our speed, their eyes glinting with humor.

This creature did not seem to have eyes. It must sense the world around it in a different way. I wondered whether it detected my little craft, and what it thought of it. But close on that thought came a new surprise. A fleet, a school, of smaller shapes tumbled past between my ship and the behemoth. They were like small, flattened wheels, perhaps a meter in diameter as far as I could tell, trailing long cords through the current. They moved not in straight, parallel lines, but much more chaotically, like a crowd of excited children moving about every which way as they went toward a common destination.

As though this spectacle was not wonderful enough, I saw that around me, on either side and above and below, there was life. There were fish shapes, and round shapes, and long, tubular shapes, all moving with some kind of propulsion or undulation. They shimmered the way that altmatter does to the human eye, and some had their own lights, like the fish of the deep sea. These latter ones also had enormous dark spots on their bow end, like eyes. What worlds had birthed these creatures? Had they evolved in a gas cloud, or in the outer atmosphere of some star? They were so fantastic, and yet familiar. Our universe is, we know, mostly made from other kinds of matter than ourselves, but I hadn't imagined that altmatter could be the basis for life. It occurred to me now that altmatter life might be much more common in the universe than our kind. Space is so big, so empty. We have always assumed it hostile to life, but perhaps that is true only of our kind of life, made of ordinary matter.

For the next two days I prepared radar clips and visual clips to send home, and watched the play of life around me. I have seen what seem to be feeding frenzies—the behemoth feasted on those wheeled creatures—and I might have witnessed a birth.

Today I saw a new creature, twice as long as the behemoth I had first set my eyes upon. It had armor-plating with fissures between the plates, and apparent signs of erosion (how?), as though it was very old. It trailed a cloud of smaller creatures behind it, evidently attendant upon it. Its round hole of a mouth was fringed with a starburst of tentacles. I was musing on the problem of the radar-imaging system's resolving capacity, wondering what I was missing in terms of smaller-scale life in the life-rich current—when I saw the leviathan's mouth widen. It was at this point ahead of me and to one side of the ship, so I couldn't see the mouth, but I inferred it from the way the tentacles fringing the orifice spread out. To my astonishment a great, umbrella-shaped net was flung out from the fringes of the mouth, barely visible to my radar. This net then spread out in front of the creature like a parachute; the creature back-finned vigorously, slowing down so abruptly that a number of other swimmers were caught in the web. Had I not swerved violently, my craft and I would have been among them. The acceleration might have flung me across the chamber and broken some bones, had it not been for the inertial net, which thickened astonishingly fast. (That the ship suffered no great damage is a testament to the engineering skills of the great generation-ship builders of old, my craft being a modified version of one of their shuttles).

Now that the Ashtan system is nearly upon us, I have a new worry. I don't know whether the Antarsa current flows through any celestial objects, such as the sun, or a planet, or a moon. If it does, I must manipulate the altmatter sails in time to escape a violent crash. I am afraid something like this might have happened to the altmatter probes that were first launched from Dhara, that stopped sending back radio signals. Or perhaps they were swallowed by some creature.

Strangely, the current appears to be slowing; this would be a relief if it wasn't laced with chaotic microflows. I can sense them through the way they make the sails shiver, something I could not have told a few years ago. Sometimes I feel as though I can see the current with some inner eye, almost as though it has acquired a luminosity, a tangibility. I imagine, sometimes, that I can feel it, very faintly, a feather's touch, a tingling.

I have a sense of something about to happen.

What can I say, now, to the dark? How do I explain what I have experienced to my kin on Dhara? What will you make of it, my sister Parin, my brother Raim? What stories will you now tell your children about Mayha, Moon-woman?

Nothing I once assumed to be true appears to be true.

As we entered the Ashtan system, the Antarsa current became chaotic on a larger scale. At that point I was not far from the second planet, Ashta, with its two lumpy little moons. Navigation became very difficult, as there were eddies and vortices and strong, dangerous little currents. There is a backwash from Ashta itself, I am convinced. This can only be the case if Ashta has a core of altmatter. Otherwise wouldn't the Antarsa wind simply blow through it, without becoming so turbulent?

This is not surprising. On Dhara there must be altmatter within the planet, else how would the devtaru have drawn it up? On Dhara, however, the Antarsa current does not go headlong through the planet, nor is it so wide. There is only a soft breeze through the planet, with the current itself running perhaps two hundred thousand kilometers distant. Here a broad channel of the current rushes through a region occupied by part of Ashta's orbit, and includes the tiny, uninhabitable inner planet and the sun. Depending on how much altmatter there is in these celestial objects, there is likely to be quite a backflow, and therefore much turbulence. A mountain stream studded with rocks would behave the same way.

For a long while, I was caught in the rapids. Caught with me were other creatures, altmatter beings of a fantastic variety, swimming valiantly, changing course with an enviable dexterity as the currents demanded. My hands were sore from manipulating the sails, my mind and soul occupied with the challenge of the moment, but the ship's AI managed to send a message in Old Irthic to Ashta. There was no reply but the now familiar silence.

I now know why. Or at least, I have a hypothesis. Because I have seen things I can hardly yet comprehend. I will not be landing on Ashta. It is impossible, and not just because of the turbulence.

This is what I saw: the day side of Ashta, through my telescope, showed continents floating on a gray ocean. There were dark patches like forests, and deserts, and the wrinkles of mountain ranges. I saw also scars, mostly in the equatorial belt, as though the planet had been pelted with enormous boulders. Most dramatically, the edges of the continents seemed to be on fire. There were plumes of smoke, mouths of fire where volcanoes spoke. In the interior, too, the scarred regions were streaked or lined or edged with a deep, red glow, and there were dark, smooth plains, presumably of lava. I imagined the invisible Antarsa current slamming into altmatter deposits deep within the planet, the impact creating internal heat that liquefied rock, which erupted volcanically onto the surface. There must be earthquakes too, on a regular basis, and were there not forests on fire?

That the forests were there at all spoke of a kinder past. Perhaps the Antarsa current had changed course in recent geological time? Now Ashta was a planet in the process of being destroyed, if the current didn't push it out of orbit first. I had never seen a more terrible sight.

But as we got closer, I saw much more to wonder at. The radar picked up something thousands of kilometers in front of the planet.

It first appeared as a roughly rectangular shadow or smear, very faint, that later resolved into a great array—a fine mesh of some kind, reminiscent of the net of the altmatter creature who nearly ate us. But this was on a massive scale, stretching across much of my view of the planet. Studded within it at regular intervals were lumps that I couldn't quite resolve—knots or nodes of some kind? No, too irregular. The net seemed to be held in place by beings, crafts or devices (I couldn't tell the difference at this distance) at corners and along the perimeter so that the whole thing sailed along with the planet. Its relative indifference to the chaotic Antarsa current indicated it was made of ordinary matter. Getting closer, I found that the lumps were creatures caught in the net, struggling. There was an air of great purpose and deliberation in the movements of smaller objects about the net—these craft, if that is what they were, appeared to buzz about, inspecting a catch here, a catch there, perhaps repairing tears in the net. It might have been my imagination but the creatures became still once the busy little craft went to them.

I went as close to the net as I dared. I had already folded the altmatter wings to decrease the effect of the current, although the eddies were so turbulent that this did not help as much as it should have, and my ship shuddered as a consequence. I switched to fusion power and edged toward the net. I wanted to see if the busy little objects—the fishermen—were spacecraft or creatures, but at the same time I didn't want to be swept into the net. One can't make an offer of kinship unless the two parties begin on a more-or-less equal footing. From what I hoped was a safe distance, I saw a drama unfold.

A behemoth was caught in the net. As it struggled, it tore holes in the material. One of the busy little fishercraft immediately went for it. Arms (or grappling hooks?) emerged from the craft and tried to engage the behemoth, but the creature was too large and too strong. A few lashes of the powerful tail, and it had pulled free, swimming off in the current—but the little craft-like object or creature broke up. From within it came all kinds of debris, some of it clearly made out of ordinary matter because it was impervious to the chaotic churning of the Antarsa and only influenced by gravity. These bits had clean, smooth trajectories. Flailing and struggling in the current, however, were three long, slender creatures with fins and a bifurcated tail. Were these the pilots of the craft, or parasites within the belly of a beast? The inexorable currents drew them to the net. I wanted to linger, to see whether they would be rescued or immobilized—two of the busy craft went immediately toward them—but I was already too close and I did not want to subject my ship to more shuddering. So I powered away in a wide arc.

I made for the night side of the planet. I was hoping for lights, indicating a settlement, perhaps, but the night side was dark, except for the fires of volcanoes and lava beds. Whatever beings had engineered the enormous net had left no trace of their presence on the planet—perhaps, if they had once lived there, they had abandoned it.

My kin were clearly not on this planet. The generation ship must have come here and found that the constant bombardment of the planet by altmatter creatures made it a poor candidate for a home. I hoped that they would have escaped the net, if the net had been there at the time. It was possible, too, that they had come here and settled, and when, as I thought, the Antarsa current shifted and slammed through Ashta, they perished. I felt great sadness, because I had hoped, dreamed, that I would find them here, settled comfortably in the niches and spaces of this world. I had imagined talking to them in the Old Irthic that I had been practicing, until I learned their languages. Instead I had to send a message home that they were not here after all.

Where had they gone? Manda had told me that the old generation ships were programmed for at least three destinations. Wherever they had gone, they had not thought it worthwhile to send us a message. Perhaps something had gone wrong en route. I shivered. None of the options implied anything good for our lost kin.

I decided I would attempt a moon landing. The moons did not seem to be made of altmatter as far as I could tell. The moon over the dark side was in the planet's wake, where there should be fewer eddies and undertows. So I brought my craft (still on fusion power) into orbit around the moon.

That was when it happened—a totally unexpected undertow caught the folded altmatter wings in the navigation chamber at just the right angle. I had at that moment cut speed from the fusion engines, preparatory to making an approach, so the undertow caught me by surprise. Before I knew it we were flung head-on toward the moon.

As I saw the moon's battered surface loom larger and larger, I thought of you, dear kin. I thought my moment had come. You would wonder at Mayha's silence, and hypothesize various endings to her story. I couldn't let that happen to you. Quicker than thought, I powered the fusion engines to brake my craft. I made a crash-landing, bumping along the uneven ground, over and over, until at last we were still. I felt the slight tug of the moon's gravity. The inertial web retracted slowly—I winced as it pulled strands of my hair with it. I was shaking, weak from shock. How slowly the silence impressed upon me as I lay in my craft!

Then the ship's AI began to speak. The fusion engine was intact, but one of the altmatter wings was broken. There was some damage to the outside of the ship, and the AI was already launching a repair swarm that clambered insect-like over the cracked and fissured shell. Anchoring cables had dug in and secured us to the surface of the moon. There was a spare wing stored within the navigation chamber, but it would take a long time to shape and match it to the old one. Then I would have to remove the broken wing and put in the new one, and adjust the rigging to the right tension. Working with altmatter meant that as I turned a wing this way or that, it would pick up a current or two and tumble out of my hand, and blow about the chamber. After a while I decided I needed to restore my mental equilibrium to the extent possible under such circumstances. So I did what I would do at home: after suiting up, I went for a walk.

Walking on the moon was both exhilarating and terrifying. To be outside my little home after years! I could spread my arms, move my legs, go somewhere I hadn't been before. There was the great bulk of the planet ahead of me, dominating my field of vision, dark and mysterious, streaked with fires, limned with light. The moon seemed to be a fragile thing in comparison, and I had to fight the feeling that I would fall away from it and on to the smoking, burning planet. I had to step lightly, gingerly, so that the ground would not push me away too hard. I walked half-way around it and found myself at the edge of a deep crater.

Lowering myself down to it was easy in the low gravity. At the bottom it was very dark. My suit lights picked out an opening—a hollow—a cave! I stepped into it, curious, and found a marvel.

The cave was filled with luminous fish-like creatures, each about as long as my finger. They circled around on tiny, invisible currents, so I guessed they were made of altmatter. As I stared at them in wonder, a few darted up to me, hovering over my visor. I stood very still. To make kinship with a fellow living being, however remote, was a great thing after my long incarceration. I was inspected and found harmless, and thereafter left alone. I stood in the dark of the cave, my ears filled with the sound of my own breathing, and fervently thanked the universe for this small encounter.

As I turned to leave, I had a terrible shock. My suit lights had fallen on somebody—a human, sitting silently on a piece of rock against the wall of the cave, watching me.

No, it was not a person—it was a sculpture. Fashioned in stone of a different kind, a paler shade than the material of the moon, it had clearly been brought here. I went up to it, my heart still thumping. It was the statue of a woman, sitting on a rock cut to resemble the prow of a boat or ship. There was a long pole in her hands, and she looked at me with obsidian eyes, her face showing a kind of ethereal joy. I thought she might be one of the old gods of our ancestors, perhaps a goddess for travelers. I touched the rock with my gloved hand, moved beyond tears. Why had my kin left this symbol here? Perhaps they had tried to make a home on Ashta, and failing, had left the statue as a mark of their presence.

I spent three days on the moon. I repaired the wing, a task more difficult than I can relate here (Raim will find a better description in my technical journal) and went back to the cave many times to renew kinship with the fish-like creatures and to see again the statue of the woman. The last time, I conducted an experiment.

I took with me some pieces of the broken altmatter wing. They confirmed that the inside of the cave was a relatively still place, where the Antarsa currents were small. By waving one piece of wing in front of the statue, and using another piece on the other side as a detector, I determined after a lot of effort that the statue was made of ordinary matter except from the neck upward, where it was altmatter or some kind of composite. This meant that my kin had made this statue after they had been here awhile, after they had discovered altmatter. I stared again at the statue, the woman with the ecstatic face, the upraised eyes. She saw something I could not yet see. I wondered again how she had come to be placed here, in a nameless cave on a battered moon of Ashta.

I am now moving away from Ashta, on a relatively smooth current of the great Antarsa ocean. I am convinced now that I can sense the Antarsa, although it blows through me as though I am nothing. I can tell, for instance, that I am out of the worst of the chaotic turbulence. I can only hope that I've caught the same current I was on before I entered the Ashtan system—it is likely that the current splits into many branches here. I will be completely at its mercy soon, since I do not have much fuel left for the fusion engines. I also must conserve my food supplies, which means that after this message I will enter the cryochamber once more—a thought that does not delight me.

At last I have relinquished control of the altmatter sails to the ship's computer. I woke from several hours of sleep to see, on the radar screen, images of the altmatter creatures sailing with me. Unlike me, they all seem to know where they are going. Here their numbers have dropped, but I notice now a host of smaller replicas of the behemoths, and the wheel-like creatures, and I wonder if the Ashtan system is some kind of cosmic spawning ground. I wish very much to offer kinship to these creatures. I already miss the little fish in their cave on the moon. That has given me hope that although we are made of very different kinds of matter, we can make a bridge of understanding between us. Life, after all, should transcend mere chemistry, or so I hope.

I have sent many messages home. In a few years my dear ones will read them and wonder. The young people I will never see, children of my kin-sisters and kin-brothers, will ask the adults with wide eyes about their aunt Mayha, Moon-woman, who forever travels the skies. But I have one faint hope. Out on the Western sea, Raim once told me that the great ocean currents, the conveyor belts, are all loops. It seems to me that it is likely, if our universe is finite, that the Antarsa currents are also closed loops. If I have chosen the right branch, this current might well loop back toward Dhara. Who knows how long that will take—perhaps my descendants will find only that this little craft is a coffin—but the hope persists, however slight, that I might once again see the blue skies, the great forest of my home, and tell the devtaru of my travels.

One casualty of my crash-landing on the moon is that Parin's biosphere is broken. I am trying to see if some of the mosses and sugarworts can still survive, but the waterbagman broke up, and for a while I found tiny red worms suspended in the air, some dead, others dying. There was one still captured in a sphere of water, which I placed in a container, but it is lonely, I think. I am trying to find out what kind of nutrients it needs to stay alive. This has been a very disturbing thing, to be left without Parin's last gift to me, a living piece of my world.

I stare at my hands, so chapped and callused. I think of the hands of the stone woman. An idea has been forming in my mind, an idea so preposterous that it can't possibly be true. And yet, the universe is preposterous. Think, my kin, about this fact: that ordinary matter is rare in the universe, and that in at least two planets, Dhara and Ashta, there is altmatter deep within. Think about the possibility that altmatter is the dominant form of matter in the universe, and that its properties are such that altmatter life can exist in the apparent emptiness between the stars. Our universe then is not inimical to life, but rich with it. Think about the stone woman in a cave on the irregular little moon that circumnavigates Ashta. Is it possible that there is some symbolism in the fact that she is made of both matter and altmatter? Is it possible that the generation ship of my ancestors did not really leave the system, that instead my kin stayed and adapted more radically than any other group of humans? Imagine the possibility that the fate of all matter is to become altmatter, that as the most primitive and ancient form of substance, ordinary matter evolves naturally and over time to a newer form, adapted to life in the great, subtle ocean that is the Antarsa. Suppose there is a way to accelerate this natural change, and that my kin discovered this process. Confronted with an unstable home world, they adapted themselves to the extent that we cannot even recognize each other. Those slim figures I saw, thrown out of the ruins of the little spacecraft after its epic battle with the behemoth— could they once have been human?

How can anyone know? These are only wild conjectures, and what my kin on Dhara will make of it, I don't know. It depresses me to think that I never found a way to make kinship with the creatures monitoring the vast net. If there had been a circumstance in which I could have met them on a more equal footing than predator and prey, I would have liked to try. If my ideas are correct and they were once human, do they remember that? Do they return to the little moon with its cave-shrine, and stare at the statue? At least I have this much hope: that given my encounter with the tiny fish-like creatures of the cave, there is some chance that life-forms composed of ordinary matter can make kinship with their more numerous kin.

My hands are still my hands. But I fancy I can feel, very subtly, the Antarsa wind blowing through my body. This has happened more frequently of late, so I wonder if it can be attributed solely to my imagination. Is it possible that my years-long immersion in the Antarsa current is beginning to effect a slow change? Perhaps my increased perception of the tangibility of the Antarsa is a measure of my own slow conversion, from ancient, ordinary matter to the new kind. What will remain of me, if that happens? I am only certain of one thing, or as certain as I can be in a universe so infinitely surprising: that the love of my kin, and the forests and seas and mountains of Dhara, will have some heft, some weight, in making me whoever I will be.

Cry of the Kharchal

*S*he was no more than a breath, a tongue of air, tasting, sensing, divining. She swept through the hotel ramparts like the subtlest of breezes. She had done it: had made time stand still. Her people, so scattered now, so weak, had helped her draw the power from the sandstorm, turning its energy against itself so that, for a brief moment, it lassoed time itself. Perhaps the moment would be long enough . . .

Incorporeal though she was, she still thought in physical terms. Thus she thought of the threads of stories that she held in her hands, ready to be woven into something that would change the fabric of reality. She thought of the heavy attire she had worn as queen, and the wings, the yearning for flight over the desert sands, the flight west. All that was gone, but she was still here. Six hundred years against the next few hours— how could mere hours matter against the weight of those years? And yet, if the stories came together . . .

The manager. The foreign poet. The woman. The boy.

It was time.

Avinash, running, crashed into a pillar at the edge of the courtyard. The physical pain brought him to his senses. He leaned against the pillar, panting, and surveyed the scene. Something had happened to the sandstorm. It rose above the hotel ramparts, a tsunami of sand, a hundred-headed cobra, a dark wave against the darkness, absolutely still. A faint susurrus of sand seemed only to amplify the silence. What had happened to the blaring alarm, the roar of the approaching storm? There were only soft sounds, the sigh of sand grains falling against a window, or the dance of a wisp of sand across the floor, borne on a breath of wind. And the bodies. Before him, in the great central courtyard, bodies sat in chairs, or leaned against pillars, or stood frozen in mid-run. Thin skeins of sand still blew about, filling plates and tureens, laps and elaborate hairdos, and the corners of eyes. But none of the eyes even blinked. Were they dead or alive? And why was he alone able to move?

"I am Avinash," he said shakily into the darkness, as though to remind himself that he was real, that he had to live up to his name. He searched for *her* again, that comforting, mysterious presence in his mind, but she was turned away from him. "Queen!" He spoke without words, begging for her attention. She did not respond. Sometimes she got like that. He looked around the courtyard. The hotel had been rebuilt on the ruins of a medieval fort to bring to the 21st century the lost grandeur of that era. The courtyard had been designed on the same grand scale. Usually its vastness reminded him of his insignificance: he was only the tech person for the hotel's computer system, a young man with no past and even less of a future. He had come here empty as a gourd, his small, inadequate soul rattling like a seed in the dried shell of his body, so that the scale of the rebuilt fort walls and the lavish excess of the décor always reminded him that he was nothing. Even the long-dead queen rode his mind as though he were a beast of burden . . . yet what sweet possession! Surely she was the key to his coming glory.

Had time, itself, stopped? Why had he been spared, then?

The queen would know, but she was still turned from him. For months now he had indulged her machinations and schemes, petty though they seemed to him: collecting information, and acting on it to obtain desired results. "If you are to control people's lives, Avinash," the queen had told him, "you must start small, by manipulating the little lives around you. Only then will you be able to touch the power within you." So he had been doing according to her instructions, developing story-lines in real time, with real people, collecting information, informing, manipulating. He had found out that the manager was a closet alcoholic; the aged movie star had a thing for young girls; and that the mad Bolivian poet was in love with an elusive woman . . . Then a word here, an act there, and events could be made to unfold according to plan. But the storm was something else. Surely he wasn't yet powerful enough to conjure up a sandstorm, or to stop time? He asked the queen in the depths of his mind, but she was quiet, preoccupied, as though waiting.

Maybe, he thought, striding into the courtyard as he had never dared to do before—*maybe it is I who have wrought this.* Even if he hadn't bargained for a sandstorm, perhaps it was a consequence of some unintended magic, an unleashing of power. He had finally grown large enough in spirit and sheer boldness to fill out and own his name: Avinash, the indestructible. He was *somebody.* He had power over the guests, frozen as they were—look at that young woman in the white silk, frozen in her chair—he could have his way with her if he wanted.

But quite abruptly a swift, cold, feeling came over him, a wave of aloneness so sudden and icy that he withdrew his hand, trembling. The vastness that he had felt in himself vanished. He was nothing, nothing but a small child abandoned in a large, noisy, frightening railway station. *Come back,* he shouted to *her* in his mind, but there was only silence. The queen was gone right out of his mind. He staggered about, pleading with her, forgetting his moment of triumph, his arrogance, begging her forgiveness, seeing nothing, feeling only the terrible emptiness. After a while the queen sighed back into his mind; everything slipped back into place and he was himself again, shaky but sane. She was playing with him; perhaps she was angry, jealous that he had thought of another woman (if only!). Although he had never seen her face, he had imagined it from the old paintings that remained from the original fort. Those almond-shaped eyes, the stern, sorrowful, remote gaze. She had kept herself remote from him also, refusing to reply to his first hopeless adoration of her, until he accepted that she needed only companionship, a tenantship in the spaces of his mind. He could never think of her as a ghost, although the hotel staff did embellish upon the old tragedy when they entertained the foreigners.

Out of habit, he glanced up at the balcony from which she had fallen to her death six hundred years ago. Now it was a place to be pointed to, and talked about, and the room adjoining it was a small museum commemorating the dead queen. Here some of the old paintings still hung, dreadfully marred by time, and on the shelves were the stone statuettes of the birds she had loved, the ones immortalized then and now in the window latticework, the kharchal of the desert— long-necked, with goose-like bodies and long, swift legs. Their eyes were set with semiprecious stones. The old story didn't mean much to him; not as much as her presence now, with him, a constant companion, someone to talk to, an advisor, guide to his own greatness.

Standing in the courtyard, he heard a sound. Half lost in the sibilant whisper of sand and wind, there was a distant, unmistakable tapping. Someone was using a computer keyboard.

He followed the sound through the hazy dark until he realized he was going to his own room, and what he heard was someone using his own computer. Angry, fearful, he ran down the employees' corridor until he reached his door. It was open; a tiny spiral stairway led down to the floor. From the top of it he could see, firstly, that the haze here was considerably thinner than outside, and secondly, his desk lamp was on, the only electric light in the entire hotel as far as he knew. Before his laptop at the desk sat a familiar figure: the odd-jobs boy and itinerant goatherd, Raju.

The boy turned before Avinash could call out. The round, obstinate face, the guarded gaze, the somewhat mocking adolescent smile. Stick-thin, wearing a second-hand pair of blue jeans, and a faded green T-shirt. What was he doing here? He wasn't supposed to come to Avinash's room without permission. But before Avinash could scold him the boy got up, sighing with relief, gesturing Avinash to the chair he had vacated.

"Boss, you are alive, thank God. I've looked and looked for you. Listen, you have to do something!"

"What are you doing here? How is it you aren't like . . . like the others? Oh never mind, get away!"

Avinash shoved him lightly and sat down before the computer. The boy had opened the secret window to the Queen's Game, the tangle of storylines and manipulations, and had been checking status. All right, so no harm done. The story of the Bolivian poet was important, or so *she* had told him, and he had located the woman whom the poet sought, and he had sent her a message purportedly from a state government minister about funding for a nature preserve. She was on her way. Was she here yet? Hard to tell because she only stopped at the Maharajah, the 4-star hotel restaurant, on her way to Delhi or Jaipur. She'd never checked in as a guest on her earlier visits. He looked at the other stories that were currently in progress. Expose the manager's drinking so as to ultimately humiliate the man into resigning. Arrange it so that the two gay men could get a room together. Find a way for the movie star to fund a sound-and-light show—a little bribe and threat had proved effective. All of these stories showed progress, and one was complete. The manager had departed in disgrace, and his room, the best in the old wing (once a royal storeroom), was in the process of being re-done. Avinash checked his online bank information and saw that the money, from whatever unknown source, had already poured in for the successful outcome of the manager's story.

Nowhere in the tangled web of stories was there any hint of a sandstorm.

He turned to the boy who was his accomplice. Raju had been good at gathering information, and in return Avinash had helped him learn to read and write. The boy claimed to be descended from the old kings, which Avinash had dismissed with a show of hilarity—partly because he suspected it could be true. He'd heard that the descendants of so many of the old rulers now lived in poverty, having lost wealth and prestige. Raju had had neither, only a burning ambition to make something of himself. His dream was to live and work in a big city like Jaipur or Delhi, to have a job with some dignity. He didn't think running errands for hotel staff or herding goats in the off-season were dignified enough. Avinash found his mixture of precocity and innocence sometimes annoying, sometimes touching.

"There's nothing I can do . . . now," he said reluctantly. He didn't like to appear less than competent before this boy, who seemed to believe quite readily that Avinash had something to do with the storm. "There is a reason why the timelines have stopped." Yes, that sounded plausible, even to his own ears. "The timelines of all the stories got in a knot, see. All tangled. We have to wait."

The boy gave him a skeptical look, then grinned.

"You don't know what's happening either. But it will come to you, boss! You always come through."

Avinash had not told him about the queen. The voices, the conversations in his head, the reassuring feeling of companionship, of guidance. But what he said about waiting was true. He had to wait for *her* to start talking to him again. He felt her presence lightly, as though she was preoccupied. Perhaps she, too, was waiting.

The poet peered out of his balcony. Never had he seen anything like it: the great, rearing heads of the sandstorm held immobile so many hundreds of meters up into the sky. He coughed and wrapped his linen handkerchief more closely about his face. The haze was thick here. When the storm's roaring had given way to the sudden silence, he had found his way out to the darkened lounge and had seen with horror the silhouettes of figures frozen in various postures. Why had he been spared? "Pachamama," he whispered, "what have you wrought now?" He hadn't spoken that old name, the name of the earth mother, for years. All he had suspected of the world—that the mundane was only a veneer—he now knew to be true. Some deep power had stirred, and caused everything to stand still, even the storm. He thought about Lalita, and the first time they'd met, and how sure he had been that he would meet her again. The fellow Avinash seemed so certain. But who knew where she was, now, the elusive Lalita? He hoped fervently that she hadn't been at the steps of the hotel when the storm hit, that she wasn't among those so grotesquely frozen. A terror came upon him that if he ventured out he would find her among the others, suspended between life and death.

And then upon its heels came a thought that he dismissed immediately: perhaps *this* was the way his talent would return. His once
prodigious talent, honed in La Paz, blossoming in Spain and Italy,
driven mysteriously from him one night in Madrid some seven years
ago, after which he had been unable to write another word. He could
write letters, instructions, but not poetry. He had tried deceit; he'd
written a shopping list and edged it toward poetry, without success.
He lived off his already famous work for a while, and then he had
taken to the road, journeying as far as Siberia, South Africa, and now
India, hoping his power over words would return. Nothing had happened so far. The only poetic thoughts in his head were those of
other poets, most notably Bolivia's Jaime Saenz, posthumous mentor,
Poet-in-Residence of his mind. Even his meeting with Lalita, when
he'd had a thought as close to poetry as he'd come in years, had not
yielded anything.

He had met her in the Thar desert a year and a half ago. He had
thought that a landscape matching the privation of his soul and his
bank account would work some kind of magic on him, but it hadn't
been that kind of magic. He had been captivated by the stark and
unpretentious beauty of the scrublands and the sand dunes, the small
villages with the sparse, thorny trees, and the people and animals who
made their home in this inhospitable place. So different from the arid
beauty of the altiplano where he'd grown up—yet the vastness of the
sky felt like home.

He was sitting outside a tea stall at a village one afternoon, awaiting his first sandstorm. Most of the people who frequented the tea
stall had already left to prepare their belongings and families for the
storm. The owner of the stall had packed up too, but Felipe Encina
Amaru, child of the Andes, wanted to stay and see the storm approach
so he sat outside on a wooden chair after everyone had fled, sipping
tea in a thick glass with bubbles, watching the western sky darken.
The sandstorm, approaching, was an enormous brown, roaring wave,
dwarfing all that lay before it. There was a stillness in the air, and grit,
and he felt the great, pregnant pause.

She came out of the storm. So it seemed to him. In fact her rented jeep had broken down before she had reached the village and she had been walking for a while. But when he raised his eyes from the glass she was striding toward him, in a long orange shirt over gray pants, her blue scarf blowing behind her in the sudden, swift wind. Her hands fumbled at her neck, adjusting her scarf, but to the poet she was manipulating the reins of the storm, which towered behind her, a beast of impossible proportions. She walked to the tea stall, looked in, seemed disappointed that it was empty. She looked directly at him for the first time.

"Got a car?" Her voice was urgent but unhurried. He felt himself drowning and had to gather himself to nod wordlessly toward the blue Zen.

"*I wish to know what wind carries you,*" Felipe declaimed silently in the words of Saenz as he started the car. A wild hope filled him as they rattled toward Jaipur.

She was an ornithologist studying an endangered bird, the Great Indian Bustard. She described it with her voice and hands. A large bird, friendly, inquisitive eyes, swift runner through the desert scrublands. "Think of it like a little ostrich. Or a large goose. " She laughed easily, but her eyes were sad. She told him she fell in love with the bird at a fair in New Delhi when she was a child. He imagined her face pressed to the glass, the bird coming up to her unafraid, curious. "I actually felt a kind of recognition," she told him, looking at him directly, as though to see whether he understood. She had questions for him about Bolivia's new law granting rights to Mother Earth. "You guys got it right," she said. She wanted to know more about it. He told her he hadn't been back in a long time, and all he knew was that it was hard to implement the law. "Greed," he said.

He found himself talking to her without effort. He had spent his childhood tagging along with his mother, hawking herbs in the Mercado de las Brujas. The streets and alleyways, the women with their charms and amulets and dried animal parts, the light of the sky between the narrow, upwinding lanes—had been his world until his uncle took him in. His uncle worked as a janitor in an office building in the modern part of the city. In the two-room tenement that was his home, there were all kinds of strays—a cousin from a remote village, a runaway child, a street dog or two. Always, there would be someone in need, knocking at the door of his uncle's heart. The uncle would frown and wonder how he would house the next abandoned soul. "Hell, what's another one?" he'd say at last, resignation mingled with relief, nodding to the boy or animal, finding a place in the already crowded rooms for the newcomer. Some weekends Felipe would spend with his mother, south of the city, gathering herbs. From here he could see the city of La Paz reaching up the mountainsides, higher every year; if he turned around, there was the white peak of the Illimani, a wave flung up into the sky. His poet's heart had been forged here, in the thin air of the altiplano, in the market's narrow alleyways, among his uncle's rescued flotsam, under the clear blue sky of winter, in the spring rain.

"I can see why you are a poet," she said, smiling, mesmerized by his descriptions.

"No longer," he sighed.

He told her how his talent with words had vanished on a night in Madrid, seven years ago. Hunched over a drink, listening to an unusually strong sirocco howling outside, he had not known until the morning that the poetry had been taken from him.

"Did you try going home?" she asked him. "Sometimes that works."

He said, quietly, remembering: "Two years later, for my mother's funeral."

"And your poetry didn't come back to you then?"

"No." He had nursed a secret hope that it might, but there was nothing. Only grief, and guilt that he hadn't been back in time, as he gazed upon his mother's emaciated body, her hands like claws, as though she had been in the middle of a transmutation that had been arrested by death. He went to the old market and consulted a healer, but there was nothing anyone could do. He remembered arguing with Pedro in Madrid later on, Pedro the friend, later the suicide. Pedro's memory said to him: "Why do you think the world has magic, then, that things are not just of themselves, but of something ineffable? Why do you persist in believing this childish rubbish?" He shrugged defensively at Pedro's ghost.

So they drove to Jaipur with the storm following on their heels like a wild beast, and they talked, and she told him stories. The Great Indian Bustard was once seriously considered for the national bird of India, but was defeated by the peacock. "Because those fools were afraid it would get misspelled," she said. "Can you imagine, the Great Indian Bastard? What kind of name is Bustard, anyway? I like the Indian names better. Kharchal is one of them. Or Hoom . . . because of the male bird's cry—I've heard it a few times, too few times. There's nothing like it."

She fell silent for a while. When she spoke her voice was thick with tears. "There are fewer than two hundred left in the wild," she said. "They are *this* close to extinction. They used to live around people, near villages without harm, but modern agriculture is their enemy. And modern mega-projects signed on by multinationals. No habitat, no bird. And *nobody cares*."

She looked out of the window. Her passionate rage moved him. He sensed a delicate thread of sympathy between them—a kinship beyond the obvious. He wanted to tell her she mattered to him. He wanted to tell her that she could have walked out of one of Jaime Saenz's poems. The dead poet whispered lines into his mind, as was his wont, but they were not Felipe's lines.

"I had my first poetic thought in years when I saw you," he said at last. He told her about his fancy that she was the harbinger of the storm. Her laughter rang out, startling him.

"That's the most ridiculous thing I've heard!" She said, more seriously, with a long sigh as though of despair, "I'm just a human being, Felipe . . . I hate the human race for what we've done to the world, but human is all I am."

"Nobody is just a human being," he said slowly, keeping his eyes on the road. "We have something else in us, yes, a kind of magic, a connection to the world that can transform us. I am hoping it will transform me."

His words sounded unconvincing even to him. But she looked at him without mockery, with a half smile. Jaipur was approaching with distressing rapidity. He wanted to hear her speak. He asked her if there were any more stories, legends, myths about the Bustard . . . the kharchal.

"Not many," she said. "But people who live close to them have fancies about them. They are very compelling creatures. One old man took care of a small flock of them outside his village. He would guard the eggs they laid, and in return he said they would warn him if a storm was coming. He took to believing that they could call storms. There is one major legend about them, though. Have you heard of the queen of Chattanpur? There's a hotel they've built over her fort. I sometimes stop at the restaurant there on my way to Delhi."

That was the first time he heard about the hotel. It was not called Chattanpur any more: it was the Hotel Vikram Royal.

There was a woman who lived outside a village in Rajasthan many hundreds of years before now. Nobody knew where she had come from, but she was a healer and a tantric practitioner with great powers. People were afraid of her but those in need would come to her and she would cure them for a small price of cloth or food. She was young and beautiful but nobody dared to touch her.

Then the king of the region happened to pass by, and he was taken by her beauty and her quality of self-possession, and he desired her for one of his queens. She, too, was struck by his noble mien and his kindness to her, and agreed to marry him, on one condition.

"I am not an ordinary woman," she said. "As a magician I have duties to the great forces from whom I derive my powers. There are times when I will have to go away from you for several days. If you let me do this without question, I will always come back to you."

The king did not like this but he was much in love, so he agreed, and took her away to his fort on the great hill. His other wives were jealous and took to gossiping about the new queen, and spreading rumors about her. For several nights she stayed with the king, but after that she told him she must leave for some days. She went into her room and closed the door, but he stepped out on a balcony and watched her covertly with the help of a mirror. She threw off her clothes and muttered some words, and a mist surrounded her, and then a bird—a kharchal—flew out of the mist and out of the window. He could hear, far away across the desert, a long, melodious call of such yearning that he, too, was moved by it. The bird flew toward the call and was lost from sight. Then the mist in the room dispersed and there was nothing there but her pile of clothing.

Some days later the bird flew back, again under cover of darkness, and returned to the form of a woman. As the king got to know his new wife, he began to wonder whether she was more bird than woman, but he kept his thoughts to himself, not wanting to tell her that he had spied on her. His other wives were not pleased with the king's continued devotion and spread rumors that the new queen went off secretly to meet a lover. The king began to half believe these lies even though he knew the truth. He became jealous of her time away. After all, what was to stop her from turning into a woman again, somewhere far across the desert, and lying with another man? One day he challenged her with the accusation of infidelity. If she wanted to prove her loyalty to him, she would have to stop these excursions.

"I think the time has come for me to leave you," said the queen, sorrowing. "If you will put bars around me, I cannot stay."

And she ran to her room, but the king was at her heels, so that when she turned into a kharchal and flew out, he managed to pull a long feather from a wing. When he did that, the bird shimmered in mid-air and turned back into a woman. The queen fell to her death from that balcony and the king was left holding the feather in his hand.

After that terrible day, ill luck befell the fort city. There was a plague, followed by a storm, and then a fire. It is believed to this day that the queen cursed the place as she fell. It was abandoned not long after, and fell into ruin. For a long time after that the local villagers heard the kharchal call for days upon end, as though in mourning, and they say the cries had such longing in them as to make the hardest-hearted men weep like children. Now the kharchal don't cry so often, or if they do, it is likely for themselves, for their own coming extinction. But who's to hear their cry?

Lalita slipped out of his car with a wave and good-bye somewhere on Mira Marg in Jaipur, as casually as though she hadn't completely changed his life, burned away all he had been before. "When . . . uh, where will I see you next?" he yelled after her over the cacophony of traffic, terrified he would lose all contact with her. She turned back, her blue scarf loose about her neck, her hair long and loose about her shoulders. "I'll come with the next sandstorm," she told him, mocking him, and then she was gone.

Later he Googled her name, send emails without much hope ("I don't do much email, and Facebook, don't even think about it!"), and went to ornithological meetings when he could, asking about her. She always seemed a step ahead of him—he had just missed her, she had just left. To make ends meet he wrote a book about modern Bolivian poetry and the enduring influence of Saenz. The book was reasonably well received; as soon as he could, Felipe took his earnings and himself to the hotel she had talked about. Here he felt an unreasonable hope, not just because she had told him she sometimes stopped at the restaurant on the way to Delhi, but because reminders of her were everywhere, through the latticework on the balcony windows that showed the kharchal amidst leaves and flowers, and the statuettes of the birds in the queen's room. It was all very romantic and very expensive, and time and money were running out. In desperation he talked to Avinash. The errand boy Raju had recommended him. Avinash had seemed so sure he could bring Lalita here, the poet had come to believe him, despite his distrust of the man. And now there was this impossible storm. But she had said, hadn't she, that she would come with the next storm?

She's a modern young woman, and an ornithologist, his mind told him. And as he was thinking this, leaning on a balcony pillar, staring out into the sand-smudged night, he was startled considerably by footsteps.

"Sar! Sar!" It was the errand boy Raju, a handkerchief around his face. "Sar, Avinash boss calls you, sar!"

Raju's explanation in broken English didn't make sense as Felipe followed him through dark corridors, but this much was clear: some others apart from him had been spared. Felipe found himself being led to an unfamiliar part of the hotel.

"What's this? Where are you taking me?"

"Employee wing, sir! King's royal storeroom in old days. New manager's room is being re-done. Boss is there."

The manager's room was small and square. Work had been going on in it apparently for widening—a layer of the thick stone wall had been taken down on one side, and a pile of broken stone pieces lay in the middle of the floor, with tools arranged neatly in one corner. Avinash was standing in the middle of the room. He held a small flashlight in his hand.

There was someone else there, outside the pool of light cast by the flashlight. The person moved suddenly into the light. Felipe's heart turned over.

"Lalita!"

He saw her smile in the inadequate light. She looked both strange and familiar.

"Hi, Felipe. Long time."

Raju had found her in the restaurant, the only person there who could speak, and move. She had been going from figure to figure, trying to see if there was anything she could do.

"Didn't expect to meet like this!" she said. And then in Hindi: "Avinash, what is all this about? Why won't you tell me?"

He was standing in the middle of the room, listening to the queen.

"Don't disturb him, he's thinking!" Raju said.

Felipe watched them. The young man with the flashlight, head cocked to one side, as though straining to hear something. The woman who had intrigued him so, standing some distance away, alert, practical, and yet, to him, extraordinary. The boy looking at Avinash—faith in his gaze. The pile of stones, the widened part of the room casting unearthly shadows.

Then he saw that even in the poor light and the dust haze, there was an opening—a gap where a stone should have been in the wall. He moved toward it just as Avinash did. He was startled by the smell of alcohol.

"The manager was a drunkard," Avinash said. His voice, sudden and loud in the darkness, startled them. "He kept his stock of booze here, in a secret compartment. Must have been a loose stone in the original wall that opened into this little chamber. He smashed one of the bottles in his hurry when he was packing up. Didn't think to look farther in."

"There's something farther in?" Lalita said. They were all crowding around Avinash now. He trained his flashlight into the small chamber, put his arm in.

"There's something . . . At the back."

He drew it out. It was an ornate box, about a foot long and no more than two inches in depth. The silver had tarnished long ago, but the mother-of-pearl inlay work still glowed. It depicted a kharchal, each feather carved delicately as though with a hair strand, standing in a garden.

"This must have belonged to the queen," Lalita said reverently.

Avinash opened the box.

In it, on a bed of white silk, lay a single large feather.

"This was the king's storeroom," Avinash said. He spoke in a monotone, as though repeating someone else's words. "The king took the feather from the queen as she was in flight, and he kept it in this secret chamber."

He paused, frowned.

"Give it to her? You're sure?"

"Whom are you talking to?" Lalita said. Raju looked at Avinash with wide, scared eyes.

Mechanically Avinash held out the box to Lalita. She took the feather out breathlessly.

"Give me the flashlight for a moment. I want to see . . ."

But something was happening. Lalita looked up in alarm; a mist was coming up around her. Felipe felt the change in the air, moved instinctively toward her, but he could not part the mist. Within it she was getting less and less visible—her arms, her clothes, made great sweeping motions. The alarm in her eyes changed swiftly to surprise. Then he couldn't see her anymore. He couldn't move into the mist to reach her. His body appeared to have become heavy and sluggish, his arm going up and toward her with so much effort that it took his breath away. The next thing he knew: a large, heavy bird, awkwardly flapping its wings, was making its way out of the mist . . . out of the doorway, into the courtyard. The three of them ran after it. Silently it flew, with increasing strength and grace, making its way to the queen's balcony. Felipe was hardly aware of their mad rush up the stairs. He arrived, panting, in the little museum with Avinash and Raju. There was the bird perched on the balcony's stone railing.

It seemed to Felipe that in the jewel-like eye of the kharchal was the same humor, the same sadness he had known in Lalita's eyes. Before he could speak there was a terrible cry from Avinash.

"Don't leave me!"

Avinash looked all around him, like a blind man.

"Where are you? You can't leave me after all this! Come back!"

The bird prepared to launch itself as Avinash's tortured gaze finally settled on it. With a terrible shout he lunged toward the bird. But before his hands could close on the bird, Raju had moved, swift and efficient, and pinned Avinash's arms to his side.

"Boss, boss, let her go!"

Felipe felt it, then, a presence barely tangible, like spider thread brushing across one's face in the dark. A presence in the room,

diminishing swiftly, a wave departing. No, not a departure, a dissipation. There was a feeling of sadness, of completion. The bird flew
free. She flew low over the hotel ramparts, a blurry silhouette against
the dusty old moon, and then she was gone.

"You stupid boy! What have you done?" Avinash thrashed in the
boy's grip. Felipe grabbed a flailing arm.

"Calm down!" Felipe said, holding his grief and wonder at bay
with an enormous effort. "What is the matter with you?"

"She's gone! The queen!" His sobs ceased. He looked around him,
searching, unbelieving. "I thought she would go with the bird, but
she . . . she's dead. The bitch! To die after all this! To leave me empty!
All empty!"

He sobbed out his story. "I am Avinash, and I am nothing, with a
mustard seed for a soul. She said she would unleash the power inside
me, so I could fill up. She left me . . . they left me. Five years old on
the railways station because they wanted to save my brothers and there
wasn't enough food."

Through the sobs and the garbled words, Felipe saw in his mind's
eye the railway station, heard the noise, the terror of strangers, the
vastness, the scale of the world. Saw that this had been the boy's
nightmare through all his life. Not the orphanage, not his education,
nothing had taken away the pain . . . until *she* had come, the queen of
Chattanpur, and filled the echoing emptiness inside him. Now she,
too, was gone, gone to the death she had been awaiting for six hundred years.

With one long cry of agony Avinash flung aside the restraining
arms of the others and leapt toward the balcony. Their rush toward
him, their shouts, were all too late. In a moment he was over the edge,
limbs working wildly, and then he dropped. They heard the impact on
the stone floor of the courtyard far below.

There was nothing to be done for him. When they got to the
body there was blood pooling under his head, and the stillness of
death was on him. Raju muttered something under his breath, and
straightening abruptly, began to run. Felipe followed him through the

dusty passageways, through a door, half falling down an unexpected spiral staircase into a room where a laptop screen glowed upon a table. The screen saver showed falling leaves, and birds flying. Raju looked about him wildly. He loosened one of the mosquito net's support rods and brought it down on the computer. Sparks flew; there was a burning smell in the air. The boy wouldn't stop until Felipe took the rod gently from him. Then Raju began to weep.

"I loved him, the fool!"

Abruptly a great roaring filled their ears: the storm. They were suddenly back in the flow of time. Above them, in the rooms and courtyards, people screamed. The poet and the errand boy looked at each other, ran up the staircase into the open. There was complete confusion: people running, tables turning over. The emergency klaxon was blaring and a booming voice attempting to direct traffic. Some lights went on as the backup generator began to run.

Felipe had never known such a night. The storm broke upon them in a fury. He and Raju worked to bring people to safety, to help close and tape windows, to fill up cracks in doorways. Their hands bled, their eyes stung. At last they huddled in Felipe's room, wrapped in shawls and blankets, handkerchiefs around their faces, to wait it out. Felipe couldn't stop coughing. Tears ran down his cheeks as he sipped water. Between coughs, he thought he heard the cries of the kharchal, the cry of the desert itself. His soul called back, again and again, soundlessly.

In the mid-day the storm subsided. They had lost two more people, and there were several injuries. Raju threw himself into the work, running for medical supplies, helping with the dead. But he would not touch Avinash.

Felipe's throat was so sore by mid-day that he could not speak. He was coughing blood. He packed up and went to the van that was taking the injured to hospital. He whispered good-bye to Raju as the boy stood under the great archway of the entrance. "Be careful, sar," Raju said. "Queen's gone to her death, but Boss . . . that old bastard, he didn't die right. Came to me in a dream, begging for asylum.

Maybe it was just a dream, but maybe when the death's not right you can't go away. Like the queen. In the dream I told him I was having none of it. Told him to get lost." The boy's eyes filled with tears. He said, inconsequentially, "He taught me how to read and write. On the computer." Felipe put his arms around the boy, surprising him, and whispered good-bye. From the van he waved. Raju was dirty, disheveled, scraped and bleeding in half a dozen places, but he stood tall. I will remember you, Felipe thought: Raju, errand boy, goatherd, possible descendant of kings.

It was after a few days of tests that the bad news came. The doctors did not think Felipe would get his voice back. There was too much damage to the larynx. When they told him this, he had been doodling on a prescription pad in the waiting room. He stared at their sympathetic faces. All he could do was whisper. He got up, shouldered his bag, and staggered out. He went into the bright sun, the mad traffic of Jaipur, and began to walk swiftly toward nowhere. For a week or more, he lost himself in the city, in its markets and pink palaces, its gardens and residential areas. The days paraded before him like the faces of strangers.

Then one afternoon he found himself outside the railway station. Horns blaring, bells ringing, shouting voices, auto-rickshaws and taxis and cars everywhere, and a surge of humanity going this way and that. A small boy cannoned into him, looked up at the stranger with the long hair and burning eyes, and burst into tears. "Mamma!" he wailed. A terrible, irrational fear that was not his own gripped Felipe. But here was the mother, barreling through the crowds like a battleship, grabbing the child. She gave Felipe a backward look full of suspicion as the two vanished into the crowd.

The spell broke. Felipe rubbed his eyes.

"You're here, aren't you?" Felipe said into the air. "Avinash?" There was a sigh in his mind, a plea. Felipe didn't respond. He walked around the corner of the road, raising dust with every step, weaving his way through the traffic, until he found himself in a small park with a fountain, where he bought an ice-cream cone from a man with a cart. He stood contemplating the water cascading into the pool of the fountain. Small children were throwing pebbles, watching the ripples.

So it is with our lives, Felipe thought. Each life like a ripple, spreading out, changing as it met other ripples, other lives. Some circles die away quickly, others expand into larger circles. A minor character in one story becomes the lead in another. We are all actors on shifting stages. We contain one another.

I should throw you out, like Raju did—you could have killed Lalita.

So what shall I do with you?

The presence in his mind was barely tangible, as though Avinash had cried himself to sleep. Who knew where he would go, what mischief he would cause, if Felipe rejected him? *There must be a way to release you, to bring you the peace you need,* he said after a while. There was no answer.

I suppose we are all haunted, he thought, with sudden insight. All humans carry with them unacknowledged ghosts. He thought of his mother. His uncle. The poet, Jaime Saenz, whom he had never met. Little Carmelita. Pedro. The crowded two-room tenement where he had grown up. He heard his uncle say: Hell, what's one more?

Felipe sighed in resignation. *Well, stay with me awhile then.*

But you'll have to behave yourself, he added.

There was a long, answering sigh in his mind like a child turning over in sleep.

He pushed his hands into his pockets, ready to leave the park, when he found the prescription pad from the hospital. His doodles were all drawings of kharchal. He thought he heard again that reverberating cry.

At once he knew what he had to do. He began running through the streets toward the bus station. He had to get on the next bus to Jaisalmer, get out there in the open desert, find Lalita. He would be whisperer, interpreter between the kharchal and the human race. She held the key, the secret, the question for which his life was the answer. As for the boy Avinash, his story was as yet incomplete. Perhaps it was only in the largeness, the emptiness of the desert that the abandoned child would find his courage, his peace. Felipe found his way from the ticket line to the bus. "I'm taking you home," he said to Avinash in his mind, not realizing he had whispered aloud. He didn't know why he'd said that, but it felt right. The old man next to him looked at him in surprise. Felipe whispered, "Do you hear it? Do you hear it too? The cry of the kharchal? Cry for the kharchal, my brother." He remembered abruptly the night in Madrid, the sirocco howling outside, the stirring within him, an animal waking from sleep, stretching, telling him he was not merely human. He remembered his fright at that discovery, his pushing it away into oblivion. Might as well put a lid on a sandstorm. Now he felt as though some barrier within him was dissolving, something was freeing itself. Without warning, words began to swirl in his mind. Sitting in the bus he found himself afraid they would disappear if he didn't set them down now. He pulled out the prescription pad, found a pen, and began to write.

Wake-Rider

This is a story from the time before she was famous. In the early days she was known as Leli, or Lelia, a tease-name that had stuck. On her first mission for the revolution, she sat cramped, fists clenched with tension, waiting in the tiny scabship *Tinka*, out of sight in a radar deadzone. The salvage ship *Gathering Moss*, which she was stalking, lay like a giant, rusting silver slug in the docking bay. Everywhere the signs and slogans of the Euphoria Corpocracy flashed, in color and in subliminal space—on the ship itself, on the docking arms, on the walls of the great spaceport behind her, and within the minds of the subject population. *Euphoria is Freedom, Better Life Through Euphoria, Rent-A-Share with Fora-ware, Subliminal is Sublime.* Leli had checked three times that her protection against the nanoplague was current and sufficient, but the utter ubiquity of Euphoria was getting to her. It seemed absurd to even consider overcoming such a power. She pulled herself together, thinking of how much so many had lost, and what was at stake. *My first solo mission,* she told herself fiercely. *I can't fall apart just now.* She wiped a drop of sweat from her brow.

"You need to breathe," said Shul's voice in her ear. Shul had rescued her, trained her, and now he was somewhere on the space-station, monitoring her via a clandestine comm channel, reassuring his youngest trainee. "You've stalked salvagers before, remember? You're one of the best wake-riders I've seen. Only, this time you're alone. Don't think of what's at stake. Just breathe and be still. You'll know when the time is right."

So she listened to the familiar voice, and took deep, slow breaths, and her mind eased into the now-familiar state of relaxed alertness.

Shul's voice faded away, and there was only the salvage ship before her, enormous against the stars.

The ship was getting readied to leave—the repair and maintenance arms were retracting, the hatches on the ship closing one by one, like eyes. She saw the scuttlebots roving over the battered surface, seeking out scabships that might be hiding. Finding none, they rose up into a swarm, forming, for a moment, the word "Euphoria," before they soared away. Before the use of scuttlebots became customary, stalking a salvage ship had been easy—a scabship would simply have attached itself to the hull and ridden along. Now, the only option for the scabships, with their relatively weak engine power, was the far more dangerous maneuver of wake-riding.

The ship thrust away in a glory of terrible ionizing radiation that would have destroyed anything in its wake. Leli moved just out of range of the radiation field, pushing her engines to keep up. *Gathering Moss* was about to move into Metaspace—the acceleration lights flashed from her hull, the radiation field dimmed and disappeared, and Leli's ship, swinging to the rear of the salvager, shuddered as streamers of spacetime ripples formed in the wake.

At first the ripples pushed the little scabship farther back, but Leli knew how to play them. You had to get a sense of the frequency of vibration of the spacetime disturbance, wait for sufficient amplitude, position carefully, and let the disturbance hit you. She eased into the rhythm of it until it was as natural as breathing. Jumping from crest to crest on the shipside of each crest, she found herself following the salvage ship at a good pace. When they both reached the critical cruising speed, she shut off her engines, letting inertia do its job. Her ship's grapplers engaged with the great bulk of the salvager for the few subjective seconds it took to engage the Firaaqui drive. Then she was being pulled through Metaspace.

The two ships emerged together into the Sarria region with an abruptness that no longer surprised her. The *Tinka's* grapplers retracted immediately and she pulled away. Her jinn piped data into Leli's headset: there was only one inhabitable planet in the system, four light-years away, now abandoned. Euphoria had been here two decades ago, infecting eighty-seven percent of the population with the nanoplague that left them docile and welcoming, their minds locked in massively parallel calculations for the shareholders of the corpocracy, while they spent their lives buying and consuming the innumerable Euphoria products. A failed revolution wrought by those who had escaped the plague had earned the Sarrian world a total cleansing, and now there was nothing in this sector but empty space, and the remains of dreams.

Now that they were out in normal space again, Leli had to keep in the radio shadow of the salvage ship. The ship had slowed—she set her controls to match velocity, every sense alert. Whatever they were salvaging must be here, not on the planet itself. A dead ship, then.

There was a derelict, suddenly pricking out from the dense backdrop of stars, lit faintly by hull lights. A generation ship by the looks of it (old model, "class four," her jinn told her), drifting dead in space. Euphoria had no use for such things, so why was the ship here, four light-years away from the planet? Given that it was a generation ship, perhaps there was still someone left alive . . .

There was only one way to know. *Gathering Moss* was vectoring toward the docking port of the derelict. Leli moved swiftly away to the opposite side of the generation ship's vast bulk, looking for an airlock hatch. Cruising over the surface of the great ship, she saw mysterious painted letters and symbols, a forest of vents and turrets, a few instrument hatches, and there, finally, was an entry point. She brought the scabship gently to the surface, engaging magnetic anchors so that it sat atop the great dead ship like a fat tick. She got into her nanoplasteen suit. By the time she was outside, her jinn had cracked the ancient code that would open the airlock. The salvage ship on the other side of the derelict would have completed docking. Afloat, one hand on the great hull, she felt the shudder of contact. She looked around at the stars above and below her, the unending depth and distance in all directions, and took a deep breath. She would never get bored with the view.

Now her suit had completed the nanoplague protection sequence, and her jinn was whispering "go!" in her ear; it was time to get to work. She pulled herself into the short passageway of the airlock closing the outer door behind her. In the illumination from her suit-lights she tackled the inner door. Her heart was thudding in her chest so loudly that it was deafening. She made herself pause, took a few more deep breaths, and slipped into the derelict.

There was clearly multiple system failure here, because it was dark and claustrophobic, although she could sense a dim light ahead, possibly woken by her presence. The artificial-gravity drive was damaged or disengaged. Her jinn told her that the air exceeded normal pressure and was a noxious mixture—too much carbon dioxide and methane. There was very little chance that anyone was alive. No doubt the salvage crew at the other end of the ship was coming to the same conclusion. Leli breathed a sigh of relief, because this meant that there would be no new slaves for the taking. Her job now was to take whatever useful material she could find, perhaps in more than one trip, and get back to her ship. If her luck held, she would not be discovered, and she could wake-ride back with *Gathering Moss.*

But why was the ship here in the first place? The most likely hypothesis, her jinn said, was that it had been appropriated by the Sarrian revolutionaries trying to escape when Euphoria threatened the planet with a cleansing. Class-four generation ships were already outdated when the corpocracy came to power. The revolutionaries, if this was indeed their ship, had clearly met with an unfortunate fate. Cascade ecosystem failure was the most common cause for the death of a class-four ship.

She proceeded down the dark main passage toward the light. Pushing herself gently off the walls, she kick-floated swiftly toward the dim glow.

It was spilling from a large chamber, the door of which had buckled open. She saw then that the light was a bioluminescence, and the chamber a farm, or what had been one. It stretched for quite a distance, but the crops had long turned to dust, and the thing that dominated the room—an enormous fungal growth, with bulbs and branches twice as thick as a person, and several times as long—was glowing faintly. It had gradually taken down the door. Whether it was an opportunistic species that had come into dominance as the ecology failed, or a mutated monster of some kind, there was no way to tell. She saw with horror that pale bones lay agleam in piles on the floor, covered by strands of the fungal growth. So much for the Sarrian rebels, if that's who they were.

She left the desolation behind, wondering how long the fungus would last as its food supply diminished. The other chambers revealed villages surrounded by the jungles of unfamiliar plant life that was slowly dying—in some places there was nothing but floating clusters of thick, acrid dust, their peculiar geometries hinting of the shapes of the once-living. There didn't seem anything worth taking from such a wreck. But the engineering sections might have something useful— energy generators, weapons, shuttle parts, and so on would not be wasted. Historical data records, medical supplies too. Where to find them? Her headset laid out the general plan of a class-four generation ship on the inside of her visor.

She could hear, faintly, now, sounds of voices, and things being moved, bumping against walls. The salvagers could not be too far ahead. Then she heard again the voice of her jinn, loud in her ears. It had been trying to tell her something . . .

Cryochamber, it was saying, and there was an insistent, blinking light on the map. Class-four generation ships were the last models that still had cryochambers. She fought sudden panic. If anyone was alive in cold sleep in this terrible place, what must she do? Would she have to rescue them? Kill them to save them from being enslaved? It occurred to her that the salvage ship must know this, must also be heading toward the cryochamber. She must get there before them.

So she followed the directions, which misled her twice. But at last she found her way to the long, low-roofed cryochamber.

There must have been only a couple of hundred bodies in there, each in its frosted casket. The salvagers hadn't come here yet—no doubt their first charge was to get all materially useful things. The frozen humans weren't going anywhere.

She floated from casket to casket, with only her headlamp providing illumination. The first thing she noticed was that the life-sign indicator lights were all red. They were dead, all of them. Still frozen, but something had clearly gone wrong, most likely the life support. Was it an aspect of general cascade failure, or something else?

Peering closely at the face of one man, she saw that his left temple was unmarked. No Euphoria nanoplague sigil on the bare skin. The man looked middle-aged, his eyes closed as though he were sleeping, his head turned slightly toward the adjoining casket. In the neighboring casket a woman lay—past youth, her mouth half-smiling, head turned toward the man. Her forehead too, was free of the sigil.

Leli swallowed. So they were uninfected. This must indeed be a rebel ship, escaping out of the Sarrian system after the revolution failed.

She looked at each face as she floated over the caskets. Death had caught some in the midst of an emotion—fear or pain, or an intimation of the end, perhaps experienced by way of dream. She saw, to her horror, that there were smaller caskets containing children, clustered between groups of adults. They lay in their terminal sleep, long lashes closed over the plump cheeks of innocence. One had dark, unruly hair falling over his forehead, another lay with a small fist closed over a tasseled rod—some kind of favorite toy. She caught her breath. Memories she had not brought to mind for a decade came flooding back.

The domicile where she had been raised, on an archipelago in the southern seas of the planet Rishab: hordes of small children running down the stairs, collecting companions from every floor—gathering mussels from the rocks, shouting, fighting, laughing. Her dearest friend, Rim, with his hair falling over his forehead, nudging her with his elbow, his arms full of fluorescent seaweed. She heard the sea's breath in her memory, saw the light catch her mother's eyes as she smiled. Come evening, the aunties would call to the children to come in from the shore, their voices like the cries of sea birds. The windows of the domicile would glow gold in the gathering darkness, and music and the aroma of food would spill out, drawing the children in until their reluctance gave way to anticipation. That life had crumbled when the war began, when the corpocracy took over seven inhabited worlds, infecting the populace with nanoplagues. The first disaster in her young life was the disappearance of her mother. Her father, an anxious, kindly, distracted man, died a few years later. The life of the domicile fell apart, and she thought she would always be abandoned, time and time again. At last she went to live with her nanny in a backwater village on a forgotten planet. Her nanny's jealous relatives named her Lelia, she-who-takes-away, because of the love that nanny lavished on her, that they felt was subtracted from them. It was a hard life, knowing a poverty she couldn't have imagined in that earlier, enchanted existence, but she had learned to fight, to sail, and to know, deep inside herself, that nothing would ever stay the way it was.

She had seen death in nearly every form. She had known the warm bath of a dying friend's blood as she struggled for breath in a mass of bodies. She had closed the eyes of countless people, loved ones and strangers. Worse than anything, she had seen people she loved taken by the plague, their personalities transformed by servitude, their minds knowing nothing more compelling than the need to obey Euphoria. They became the manufacturers and consumers of the Euphoria economy. Nobody could free them; there was no cure for the nanoplague. It mutated too fast, so much so that the protections against it had to be updated constantly.

But nothing in her past had prepared her for this. Looking at the children lying in their caskets like child actors in a fairy tale, she wanted them to be alive. Perhaps the life-sign indicator lights were malfunctioning. Perhaps "red" actually meant "alive." Perhaps she was fooling herself . . .

The noises from the salvager crew—bumps and vibrations, strange voices coming through the static on her comm unit—were getting closer. She knew she should be out looking for useful supplies, but she had made it a ritual now, to float over each casket, look into every face, to honor the dreams that had been lost.

Then she found something.

There was a man in a casket, youngish, with thinning hair that was swept back from his brow. The right side of his forehead was branded with the Euphoria sigil, a delicate, fractal pattern that was created by the nanoplague itself. What was a slave doing with the rebels? Her hands shook with the shock of it. What if the ship was infected after all? She began to look more carefully, and found several more, perhaps fifty of the dead with the brand of the corpocracy. Some of them were children. How could they be here? Had they been brought by force? But that would be dangerous—those infected with the nanoplague would fight for their masters, betray all loyalties for Euphoria. And yet they lay here in death, comrade-fashion with the others.

She had to see if they were really infected. Sometimes spies from various resistance movements would paint a fake sigil in order to infiltrate the corpocracy, as Shul had done at the space-station fifteen light-years away. She checked with her jinn—yes, her nanoplague protection was updated. She had to open one of the slave caskets. Her hands were cold inside her nanoplasteen suit, and the release controls would not yield. Finally they gave way and the casket door opened with a sigh. At first she couldn't see for the cloud of vapors that rose from the casket, but she already had her medi-kit scanner detached from her belt. Her jinn ran a commentary on the diagnostics. The man was dead; so much for her hopes. The sigil was real, not faked. Her heart thudded at this and she moved instinctively away, as far as the medi-kit cord attached to her belt would let her. Then her jinn said:

Testing negative for nanoplague categories one through seventeen.

She waited. There must be a category eighteen.

Conclusion: This specimen is not infected with the nanoplague.

There had to be a mistake. She went to another slave casket, a woman this time, and repeated the test. The conclusion was the same.

The voices of the salvagers were loud in her comm unit. She needed to get away from here. But she was transfixed, her mind whirling. How could there be people branded with the mark of slavery, yet free of the plague?

The truth came to her in a jolt. The Sarrian rebels had found an antidote, some kind of cure for the nanoplague. There had been many such attempts by rebels and rivals of Euphoria over the years, but the nanoviruses were adaptable in the extreme, and all cures had been temporary. If these former slaves had been freed long enough that they could embark on such a voyage—her jinn had told her the generation ship had been traveling for close on a decade, subjective time, before she failed—then whatever cure the Sarrians had discovered would last at least that long.

Two things became immediately clear to Leli after the shock of the discovery—she must take back a sample. Immediately on that thought came another—that she wouldn't know if she'd got enough tissue. She wasn't trained as a med, although the jinn could help. The medi-kit was non-med issue, which meant it wouldn't have the right equipment to take a good sample. Which meant—she must take back a body.

And she must not let the salvage ship find the cryochamber, if at all she could help it.

She didn't know how she would prevent the discovery of the bodies, but the first problem was paramount. The caskets were large and bulky. How would she drag one behind her all the way back to the scabship? Even in the absence of gravity, there was inertia, and corners and turns every few meters. And would a casket even go through the airlock?

It came to her immediately that she must find a child, an enslaved child who had been cured of the plague. She heard the noise of the salvage crew much closer now. Floating past the dead faces, searching frantically, at last she found a boy marked with the sigil—he could not have been more than four years old—in a tiny casket. She detached it from the holding frame and pushed off to leave.

It was while she was going down the main passage that somebody must have seen a gleam of light or some other hint that gave away her swift retreat, because she heard a commotion, and a siren sounded, loud and shrill, that seemed to echo endlessly in her skull. To be discovered was always a risk; she thought of the self-destruct unit inside her suit and on the ship—but she had to return to her comrades with the casket, with the knowledge of the cure. Stifling a sob of fright, she kicked off the walls as fast as she dared without damaging herself or the casket, twisting and turning her body as she had practiced so many times with her friends, so that she seemed to swim through the passageways with only a light touch to the walls here, there. Her breath was loud in her ears, her suit's voice, giving directions, almost drowned by it. She could not waste oxygen—slipping into a side passage, she made herself slow down for a moment. The sounds of pursuit were still some way behind her. She kept going, working arms and legs until they ached with effort, pulling the casket beside her, the boy's sleeping, dead face coming into view now and then. All her life had contracted to this moment; it seemed she had known nothing but flight and pursuit. Instinct took over, giving her a clear place in her mind to think.

Even if she got to her ship and took off, they would chase her and find her. Their shuttles were far more powerful than a little scabship. Perhaps even now shuttles were taking off from the salvage vessel to prevent her escape. Then the idea came to her, the only possible option. There she was, at the airlock. With shaking fingers she shut one door behind her and opened the other, making herself slow down so that her momentum wouldn't carry her out to space and away from her ship. She float-crawled awkwardly to the *Tinka* and found room for the boy's casket. Returning to the airlock, she attached a cable and a winch to the closed inner door, placing the other end of the cable between the jaws of her ship's ventral grappler. Then, back in the scabship she maneuvered her ship over the open outer porthole and set the winch going to open the inner one. Thank goodness the safety mechanism that would have prevented this was dead. Her own ship's inner bioskin was readying, the inertial fluid seeping into the chamber, forming great, viscous ropes and blobs. Would it work?

Never had all her senses been so alert to the smallest hint of change in her ship's position, the smallest intimation of what was to come. Timing was everything, if she were to survive. She thought she felt a faint tremor, then she shouted "Now!" and the grappling hook disengaged, and the inner door of the airlock opened. The dead, stinking, noxious air inside the derelict exploded out, ripping an enormous hole in the hull, pushing her little ship away with such force that in the first few moments, with everything shaking so violently around her, she thought the *Tinka* would break up. Her chest hurt so badly with compression that she felt she would never breathe again, but the inertial gel around her took the worst of it. The little scabship tumbled through space, going faster than she could remember. She didn't have breath to scream.

When she was able to breathe again, the ship had stabilized itself and was vectoring away into empty space. It brought up an image for her of what had been left behind. The venting of air from the derelict had not only pushed away the docked salvage ship on the other side, which had been her intent, breaking the docking arms and spinning the salvager away, but the torque had swept the derelict around, so that it had collided with the freed salvager. The explosion was a bright flare against the indifferent stars.

She started to shake violently. What had she done? She hadn't meant to kill all those people aboard the salvage ship. She had killed in direct combat before when she'd had to, but her learning had been oriented toward the intelligent avoidance of unnecessary death. Every death meant a mourning, a penance. She remembered her teachers saying that only Euphoria rejoiced at the death of an enemy. She had failed—she had not calculated for a possible collision. How many people had been on the salvager? Sixty-four, her jinn told her. When she found her way back—if she found her way back, would she be treated as the hero she had seen herself to be, in that moment of discovery in the cryochamber—or would the elders shake their heads and look sorrowful, their joy at the possibility of a cure tempered by their disappointment in her? For the revolutionaries of the movement, ends did not justify the means.

The scabship had picked up speed to avoid the debris field from the explosion. She was far enough away that the ships were out of visual range, but she imagined body parts and chunks of metal and fungal dust blowing toward her. She turned around to look at the casket, which still lay in its net of inertial webbing. Intact. Well, she had done some good. Even if she spent the rest of her life in penance, she had brought something important to the revolution.

But how would she get back? Without sufficient power to get to Metaspace, she could drift here forever, like the derelict, her secret safe for eons, utterly useless. Slowly the life-giving systems would shut down and the bioskin would die, and she would be snuffed out, the scabship a coffin. Already, her chest hurt. She wept then, in her fright and loneliness.

Gradually, as she calmed down and sipped the brew the ship had prepared for her, it came to her that the disappearance of the salvage ship would bring other ships to the area. As long as she stayed in the vicinity of the explosion, there was the chance that she could ride back to known space in the wake of another ship. She set drift coordinates that she hoped would keep her close, but not too close. Someone would come soon.

She patted the casket that floated beside her, where the little boy lay in his final dreaming. His face was so serene, she wanted to touch his cheek. She thought the unfamiliar script on the top of the casket must be his name. Her jinn didn't know the script, but somebody would, when she got back. He would be famous in death, this little boy.

In her little cocoon, surrounded by the cold majesty of the stars, she settled herself for the long wait. She clenched and unclenched her hands and looked into the heart of what she had done. *To suffer thus is good*, she remembered Shul telling the new recruits. *To get used to killing, to become indifferent to it, is a terrible thing. May we never become like the enemy.*

There was nothing for it but to begin the mourning and forgiveness rituals for sixty-four strangers, who, before their enslavement, must have been people like her. She cleared her throat and her voice filled the small chamber, trembling at first but then becoming a thing of its own, rich and strong, singing to the unlistening dead.

Ambiguity Machines:
An Examination

Intrepid explorers venturing into Conceptual Machine-Space, which is the abstract space of all possible machines, will find in the terrain some gaps, holes, and tears. These represent the negative space where impossible machines reside, the ones that cannot exist because they violate known laws of reality. And yet such impossible machines are crucial to the topographical maps of Conceptual Machine-Space, and indeed to its topology. They therefore must be investigated and classified.

It is thus that the Ministry of Abstract Engineering has sent the topographers of Conceptual Machine-Space to various destinations so that they may collect reports, rumors, folktales, and intimations of machines that do not and cannot exist. Of these we excerpt below three accounts of the subcategory of Ambiguity Machines: those that blur or dissolve boundaries.

The candidate taking the exam for the position of Junior Navigator in the uncharted negative seas of Conceptual Machine-Space will read the three accounts below and follow the instructions thereafter.

The First Account

All machines grant wishes, but some grant more than we bargain for. One such device was conceived by a Mongolian engineer who spent the best years of his youth as a prisoner in a stone building in the Altai Mountains. The purpose of this machine was to conjure up the face of his beloved.

His captors were weaponheads of some sort; he didn't know whether they were affiliated with any known political group or simply run by sociopath technophiles with an eye on the weapons market. They would let him out of his cell into a makeshift laboratory every day. Their hope was that he would construct for them a certain weapon, the plans for which had been found on his desk and had led to his arrest. The engineer had a poetic sensibility, and the weapon described in his papers was metaphoric. But how can you explain metaphors to a man with a gun?

When the engineer was a young boy, stillness had fascinated him. He had been used to wandering with his family across the Gobi, and so he had made a study of stillness. In those days everything moved— the family with the ger, the camels and sheep, the milk sloshing in the pail as he helped his mother carry it, the stars in the circle of open sky in the roof above his head, the dust storms, dark shapes in shawls of wind, silhouetted against blue sky. The camels would fold themselves up into shaggy mounds between the bushes, closing their eyes and nostrils, waiting for the storm to pass. His grandfather would pull him into the ger, the door creaking shut, the window in the roof lashed closed, and he would think about the animals and the ger, their shared immobility in the face of the coming storm. Inside it would be dark, the roar of the dust storm muffled, and in the glow of the lamp his older sister's voice would rise in song. Her voice and the circle of safety around him tethered him to this world. Sometimes he would bury his face in a camel's shaggy flank as he combed its side with his fingers, breathing in the rich animal smell, hearing with his whole body the camel's deep rumble of pleasure.

In such moments he would think of his whole life played out against the rugged canvas of the Gobi, an arc as serene as the motion of the stars across the night, and he would feel again that deep contentment. In his childhood he had thought there were only two worlds, the inside of the ger and the outside. But the first time he rode with his father to a town, he saw to his utmost wonder that there was another kind of world, where houses were anchored to the earth and people rode machines instead of animals, but they never went very far. They had gadgets and devices that seemed far more sophisticated than his family's one TV, and they carried with them a subtle and unconscious air of privilege. He had no idea then that years later he would leave the Gobi and his family to live like this himself, an engineering student at a university in Ulaanbaatar, or that the streets of that once-unimaginable city would become as familiar to him as the pathways his family had traversed in the desert. The great coal and copper mines had, by then, transformed the land he thought would never change, and the familiarity was gone, as was his family, three generations scattered or dead.

Being tethered to one place, he discovered, was not the same as the stillness he had once sought and held through all the wanderings of his childhood. In the midst of all this turmoil he had found *her*, daughter of a family his had once traded with, studying to be a teacher. She was as familiar with the old Mongolia as he had been, and was critical and picky about both old and new. She had a temper, liked to laugh, and wanted to run a village school and raise goats. With her, the feeling of having a center in the world came back to him.

So he thought of her in his incarceration, terrified that through this long separation he would forget her face, her voice. As the faces of his captors acquired more reality with each passing week or month or year, his life beforehand seemed to lose its solidity, and his memories of her seemed blurred, as though he was recollecting a dream. If he had been an artist he would have drawn a picture of her, but being an engineer, he turned to the lab. The laboratory was a confusion of discarded electronics: pieces of machinery bought from online auctions, piles of antiquated vacuum tubes, tangles of wires and other variegated junk. With these limited resources the engineer tried his best, always having to improvise and work around the absence of this part and that one. His intent was to make a pseudo-weapon that would fool his captors into releasing him, but he didn't know much about weapons, and he knew that the attempt was doomed to failure. But it would be worth it to re-create his beloved's face again, if only a machine-rendered copy of the real thing.

Thus into his design he put the smoothness of her cheek, and the light-flash of her intelligence, and the fiercely tender gaze of her eyes. He put in the swirl of her hair in the wind, and the way her anger would sometimes dissolve into laughter, and sometimes into tears. He worked at it, refining, improving, delaying as much as he dared.

And one day he could delay no more, for his captors gave him an ultimatum: the machine must be completed by the next day, and demonstrated to their leaders, else he would pay with his life. He had become used to their threats and their roughness, and asked only that he be left alone to put the machine in its final form.

Alone in the laboratory, he began to assemble the machine. But soon he found that there was something essential missing. Rummaging about in the pile of debris that represented laboratory supplies, he found a piece of stone tile, one half of a square, broken along the diagonal. It was inlaid with a pattern of great beauty and delicacy, picked out in black and cream on the gray background. An idea for the complex circuit he had been struggling to configure suddenly came together in his mind. Setting aside the tile, he returned to work. At last the machine was done, and tomorrow he would die.

He turned on the machine.

Looking down into the central chamber, he saw her face. There was the light-flash of her intelligence, the swirl of her hair in the wind. *I had forgotten*, he whispered, *the smoothness of her cheek*, and he remembered that as a child, wandering the high desert with his family, he had once discovered a pond, its surface smooth as a mirror. He had thought it was a piece of the sky, fallen down. Now, as he spoke aloud in longing, he saw that the face was beginning to dissolve, and he could no longer distinguish her countenance from standing water, or her intelligence from a meteor shower, or her swirling hair from the vortex of a tornado. Then he looked up and around him in wonder, and it seemed to him that the stone walls were curtains of falling rain, and that he was no more than a wraithlike construct of atoms, mostly empty space—and as the thought crystallized in his mind, he found himself walking out with the machine in his arms, unnoticed by the double rows of armed guards. So he walked out of his prison, damp but free.

How he found his way to the village near Dalanzadgad, where his beloved then lived, is a story we will not tell here. But he was at last restored to the woman he loved, who had been waiting for him all these years. Her cheek no longer had the smoothness of youth, but the familiar intelligence was in her eyes, and so was the love, the memory of which had kept him alive through his incarceration. They settled down together, growing vegetables in the summers and keeping some goats. The machine he kept hidden at the back of the goat shed.

But within the first year of his happiness the engineer noticed something troubling. Watching his wife, he would sometimes see her cheek acquire the translucency of an oasis under a desert sky. Looking into her eyes, he would feel as though he were traveling through a cosmos bright with stars. These events would occur in bursts, and after a while she would be restored to herself, and she would pass a hand across her forehead and say, *I felt dizzy for a moment.* As time passed, her face seemed to resemble more and more the fuzzy, staccato images on an old-fashioned television set that is just slightly out of tune with the channel. It occurred to him that he had, despite his best intentions, created a weapon after all.

So one cold winter night he crept out of the house to the shed, and uncovered the machine. He tried to take it apart, to break it to pieces, but it had acquired a reality not of this world. At last he spoke to it: *You are a pile of dust! You are a column of stone! You are a floor tile! You are a heap of manure!* But nothing happened. The machine seemed to be immune to its own power.

He stood among the goats, looking out at the winter moon that hung like a circle of frost in the sky. Slowly it came to him that there was nothing he could do except to protect everyone he loved from what he had created. So he returned to the house and in the dim light of a candle beheld once more the face of the woman he loved. There were fine wrinkles around her eyes, and she was no longer slim, nor was her hair as black as it had once been. She lay in the sweetness of sleep and, in thrall to some pleasant dream, smiled in slumber. He was almost undone by this, but he swallowed, gritted his teeth, and kept his resolve. Leaving a letter on the table, and taking a few supplies, he wrapped up the machine and walked out of the sleeping village and into the Gobi, the only other place where he had known stillness.

The next morning his wife found the letter, and his footprints on the frosty ground. She followed them all the way to the edge of the village, where the desert lay white in the pale dawn. Among the ice-covered stones and the frozen tussocks of brush, his footsteps disappeared. At first she shook her fist in the direction he had gone, then she began to weep. Weeping, she went back to the village.

The villagers never saw him again. There are rumors that he came back a few months later, during a dust storm, because a year after his disappearance, his wife gave birth to a baby girl. But after that he never returned.

His wife lived a full life, and when she was ready to die, she said good-bye to her daughter and grandchildren and went into the desert. When all her food and water were finished, she found some shade by a clump of brush at the edge of a hollow, where she lay down. They say that she felt her bones dissolving, and her flesh becoming liquid, and her hair turning into wind. There is a small lake there now, and in its waters on a cold night, you can see meteors flashing in a sky rich with stars.

As for the engineer, there are rumors and folk legends about a shaman who rode storms as though they were horses. They say he ventured as far as Yakutz in Siberia and Siena in Italy; there is gossip about him in the narrow streets of old Istanbul, and in a certain village outside Zhengzhou, among other places. Wherever he stopped, he sought village healers and madmen, philosophers and logicians, confounding them with his talk of a machine that could blur the boundary between the physical realm and the metaphoric. His question was always the same: *How do I destroy what I have created?* Wherever he went, he brought with him a sudden squall of sand and dust that defied the predictions of local meteorologists, and left behind only a thin veil of desert sand flung upon the ground.

Some people believe that the Mongolian engineer is still with us. The nomads speak of him as the kindest of shamans, who protects their gers and their animals by pushing storms away from their path. As he once wandered the great expanse of the Gobi in his boyhood, so he now roams a universe without boundaries, in some dimension orthogonal to the ones we know. When he finds what he is seeking, they say, he will return to that small lake in the desert. He will breathe his last wish to the machine before he destroys it. Then he will lay himself down by the water, brushing away the dust of the journey, letting go of all his burdens, still at last.

The Second Account

At the edge of a certain Italian town there is a small stone church, and beside it an overgrown tiled courtyard, surrounded entirely by an iron railing. The one gate is always kept locked. Tourists going by sometimes want to stop at the church and admire its timeworn façade, but rarely do they notice the fenced courtyard. Yet if anyone were to look carefully between the bars, they would see that the tiles, between the weeds and wildflowers, are of exceptional quality, pale gray stone inlaid with a fine intricacy of black marble and quartz. The patterns are delicate as circuit diagrams, celestial in their beauty. The careful observer will notice that one of the tiles in the far left quadrant is broken in half, and that grass and wildflowers fill the space.

The old priest who attends the church might, if plied with sufficient wine, rub his liver-spotted hands over his rheumy eyes and tell you how that tile came to be broken. When he was young, a bolt from a storm hit the precise center of the tile and killed a man sweeping the church floor not four yards away. Even before the good father's time, the courtyard was forbidden ground, but the lightning didn't know that. The strange thing is not so much that the tile broke almost perfectly across the diagonal, but that one half of it disappeared. When the funeral was over, the priest went cautiously to the part of the railing nearest the lightning strike and noted the absence of that half of the tile. Sighing, he nailed a freshly painted "No Entry" sign on an old tree trunk at the edge of the courtyard and hoped that curious boys and thunderstorms would take note.

It wasn't a boy who ignored the sign and gained entry, however—it was a girl. She came skipping down the narrow street, watching the dappled sunlight play beneath the old trees, tossing a smooth, round pebble from hand to hand. She paused at the iron railing and stared between the bars, as she had done before. There was something mesmerizing about that afternoon, and the way the sunlight fell on the tiles. She hitched up her skirts and clambered over the fence. Inside, she stood on the perimeter and considered a game of hopscotch.

But now that she was there, in the forbidden place, she began to feel nervous and to look around fearfully. The church and the street were silent, drugged with the warm afternoon light, and many people were still at siesta. Then the church clock struck three, loudly and sonorously, and in that moment the girl made her decision. She gathered her courage and jumped onto the first tile, and the second and third, tossing her pebble.

Years later she would describe to her lover the two things she noticed immediately: that the pebble, which was her favorite thing, having a fine vein of rose-colored quartz running across it, had disappeared into thin air during its flight. The next thing she noticed was a disorientation, the kind you feel when transported to a different place very suddenly, as a sleeping child in a car leaving home awakes in a strange place, or, similarly, when one wakes up from an afternoon nap to find that the sun has set and the stars are out. Being a child in a world of adults, she was used to this sort of disorientation, but alone in this courtyard, with only the distant chirping of a bird to disturb the heat-drugged silence, she became frightened enough to step back to the perimeter. When she did so, all seemed to slip back to normality, but for the fact that there was the church clock, striking three again. She thought at the time that perhaps the ghosts in the graveyard behind the church were playing tricks on her, punishing her for having defied the sign on the tree.

But while lying with her lover in tangled white sheets on just such an afternoon many years later, she asked aloud: *What if there is some other explanation?* She traced a pattern on her lover's back with her finger, trying to remember the designs on the tiles. Her lover turned over, brown skin flushed with heat and spent passion, eyes alive with interest. The lover was a Turkish immigrant and a mathematician, a woman of singular appearance and intellect, with fiery eyes and deep, disconcerting silences. She had only recently begun to emerge from grief after the death of her sole remaining relative, her father. Having decided that the world was bent on enforcing solitude upon her, she had embraced loneliness with an angry heart, only to have her plans foiled by the unexpected. She had been unprepared for love in the arms of an Italian woman—an artist, at that—grown up all her life in this provincial little town. But there it was. Now the mathematician brushed black ringlets from her face and kissed her lover. *Take me there,* she said.

So the two women went to the tree-shaded lane where the court-yard lay undisturbed. The tiles were bordered, as before, by grass and wildflowers, and a heaviness hung upon the place, as though of sleep. The church was silent; the only sounds were birdsong and distant traffic noises from the main road. The mathematician began to climb the railing.

Don't, her lover said, but she recognized that nothing could stop the mathematician, so she shrugged and followed suit. They stood on the perimeter, the Italian woman remembering, the Turkish one thinking furiously.

Thus began the mathematician's explorations of the mystery of the courtyard. Her lover would stand on the perimeter with a note-book while the mathematician moved from tile to tile, flickering in and out of focus, like a trout in a fast-moving stream when the sun is high. The trajectory of each path and the result of the experiment would be carefully noted, including discrepancies in time as experienced by the two of them. Which paths resulted in time-shifts, and by how much? Once a certain path led to the disappearance of the mathematician entirely, causing her lover to cry out, but she appeared about three minutes later on another tile. *The largest time-step so far!* exulted the mathematician. Her lover shuddered and begged the mathematician to stop the experiment, or at least to consult with someone, perhaps from the nearest university. But, being an artist, she knew obsession when she saw it. Once she had discovered a windblown orchard with peaches fallen on the grass like hailstones, and had painted night and day for weeks, seeking to capture on the stillness of canvas the ever-changing vista. She sighed in resignation at the memory and went back to making notes.

The realization was dawning upon her slowly that the trajectories leading to the most interesting results had shapes similar to the very patterns on the tiles. Her artist's hands sketched those patterns—doing so, she felt as though she were on flowing water, or among sailing clouds. The patterns spoke of motion but through a country she did not recognize. Looking up at the mathematician's face, seeing the distracted look in the dark eyes, she thought: *There will be a day when she steps just so, and she won't come back.*

And that day did come. The mathematician was testing a trajectory possessed of a pleasing symmetry, with some complex elements added to it. Her lover, standing on the perimeter with the notebook, was thinking how the moves not only resembled the pattern located on tile (three, five), but also might be mistaken for a complicated version of hopscotch, and that any passerby would smile at the thought of two women reliving their girlhood—when it happened. She looked up, and the mathematician disappeared.

She must have stood there for hours, waiting, but finally she had to go home. She waited all day and all night, unable to sleep, tears and spilled wine mingling on the bedsheets. She waited for days and weeks and months. She went to confession for the first time in years, but the substitute priest, a stern and solemn young man, had nothing to offer, except to tell her that God was displeased with her for consorting with a woman. At last she gave up, embracing the solitude that her Turkish lover had shrugged off for her when they had first met. She painted furiously for months on end, making the canvas say what she couldn't articulate in words—wild-eyed women with black hair rose from tiled floors, while mathematical symbols and intricate designs hovered in the warm air above.

Two years later, when she was famous; she took another lover, and she and the new love eventually swore marriage oaths to each other in a ceremony among friends. The marriage was fraught from the start, fueled by stormy arguments and passionate declarations, slammed doors and teary reconciliations. The artist could only remember her Turkish lover's face when she looked at the paintings that had brought her such acclaim.

Then, one day, an old woman came to her door. Leaning on a stick, her face as wrinkled as crushed tissue paper, her mass of white ringlets half falling across her face, the woman looked at her with tears in her black eyes. *Do you remember me?* she whispered.

Just then the artist's wife called from inside the house, inquiring as to who had come. *It's just my great-aunt, come to visit,* the artist said brightly, pulling the old woman in. Her wife was given to jealousy. The old woman played along, and was established in the spare room, where the artist looked after her with tender care. She knew that the mathematician had come here to die.

The story the mathematician told her was extraordinary. When she disappeared she had been transported to a vegetable market in what she later realized was China. Unable to speak the language, she had tried to mime telephones and airports, only to discover that nobody knew what she was talking about. Desperately she began to walk around, hoping to find someone who spoke one of the four languages she knew, noticing with horror the complete absence of the signs and symbols of the modern age—no cars, neon signs, plastic bags. At last her wanderings took her to an Arab merchant, who understood her Arabic, although his accent was strange to her. She was in Quinsai (present-day Hangzhou, as she later discovered), and the Song dynasty was in power. Through the kindness of the merchant's family, who took her in, she gradually pieced together the fact that she had jumped more than 800 years back in time. She made her life there, marrying and raising a family, traveling the sea routes back and forth to the Mediterranean. Her old life seemed like a dream, a mirage, but underneath her immersion in the new, there burned the desire to know the secret of the tiled courtyard.

It shouldn't exist, she told the artist. *I have yearned to find out how it could be. I have developed over lifetimes a mathematics that barely begins to describe it, let alone explain it.*

How did you get back here? the artist asked her former lover.

I realized that if there was one such device, there may be others, she said. *In my old life I was a traveler, a trade negotiator with Arabs. My journeys took me to many places that had strange reputations of unexplained disappearances. One of them was a shrine inside an enormous tree on the island of Borneo. Around the tree the roots created a pattern on the forest floor that reminded me of the patterns on the tiles. Several people had been known to disappear in the vicinity. So I waited until my children were grown, and my husband and lovers taken by war. Then I returned to the shrine. It took several tries and several lifetimes until I got the right sequence. And here I am.*

The only things that the Turkish mathematician had brought with her were her notebooks containing the mathematics of a new theory of space-time. As the artist turned the pages, she saw that the mathematical symbols gradually got more complex, the diagrams stranger and denser, until the thick ropes of equations in dark ink and the empty spaces on the pages began to resemble, more and more, the surfaces of the tiles in the courtyard. *That is my greatest work,* the mathematician whispered. *But what I've left out says as much as what I've written. Keep my notebooks until you find someone who will understand.*

Over the next few months the artist wrote down the old woman's stories from her various lifetimes in different places. By this time her wife had left her for someone else, but the artist's heart didn't break. She took tender care of the old woman, assisting her with her daily ablutions, making for her the most delicate of soups and broths. Sometimes, when they laughed together, it was as though not a minute had passed since that golden afternoon when they had lain in bed discussing, for the first time, the tiled courtyard.

Two weeks after the mathematician's return, there was a sudden dust storm, a sirocco that blew into the city with high winds. During the storm the old woman passed away peacefully in her sleep. The artist found her the next morning, cold and still, covered with a layer of fine sand as though kissed by the wind. The storm had passed, leaving clear skies and a profound emptiness. At first the artist wept, but she pulled herself together as she had always done, and thought of the many lives her lover had lived. It occurred to her in a flash of inspiration that she would spend the rest of her one life painting those lifetimes.

At last, the artist said to her lover's grave, where she came with flowers the day after the interment, *at last the solitude we had both sought is mine.*

The Third Account

Reports of a third impossible machine come from the Western Sahara, although there have been parallel, independent reports from the mountains of Peru and from Northern Ireland. A farmer from the outskirts of Lima, a truck driver in Belfast, and an academic from the University of Bamako in Mali all report devices that, while different in appearance, seem to have the same function. The academic from Mali has perhaps the clearest account.

She was an archeologist who had obtained her PhD from an American university. In America she had experienced a nightmarish separateness, the like of which she had not known existed. Away from family, distanced by the ignorance and prejudices of fellow graduate students, a stranger in a culture made more incomprehensible by proximity, separated from the sparse expatriate community by the intensity of her intellect, she would stand on the beach, gazing at the waters of the Atlantic and imagining the same waters washing the shores of West Africa. In her teens she had spent a summer with a friend in Senegal, her first terrifying journey away from home, and she still remembered how the fright of it had given way to thrill, and the heart-stopping delight of her first sight of the sea. At the time her greatest wish was to go to America for higher education, and it had occurred to her that on the other side of this very ocean lay the still unimagined places of her desire.

Years later, from that other side, she worked on her thesis, taking lonely walks on the beach between long periods of incarceration in the catacombs of the university library. Time slipped from her hands without warning. Her mother passed away, leaving her feeling orphaned, plagued with a horrific guilt because she had not been able to organize funds in time to go home. Aunts and uncles succumbed to death, or to war, or joined the flood of immigrants to other lands. Favorite cousins scattered, following the lure of the good life in France and Germany. It seemed that with her leaving for America, her history, her childhood, her very sense of self had begun to erode. The letters she had exchanged with her elder brother in Bamako had been her sole anchor to sanity. Returning home after her PhD, she had two years to nurse him through his final illness, which, despite the pain and trauma of his suffering, she was to remember as the last truly joyful years of her life. When he died she found herself bewildered by a feeling of utter isolation even though she was home, among her people. It was as though she had brought with her the disease of loneliness that had afflicted her in America.

Following her brother's death, she buried herself in work. Her research eventually took her to the site of the medieval University of Sankore in Timbuktu, where she marveled at its sandcastle beauty as it rose, mirage-like, from the desert. Discovering a manuscript that spoke in passing of a fifteenth century expedition to a region not far from the desert town of Tessalit, she decided to travel there despite the dangers of political conflict in the region. The manuscript hinted of a fantastic device that had been commissioned by the king, and then removed for secret burial. She had come across oblique references to such a device in the songs and stories of griots, and in certain village tales; thus her discovery of the manuscript had given her a shock of recognition rather than revelation.

The archeologist had, by now, somewhat to her own surprise, acquired two graduate students: a man whose brilliance was matched only by his youthful impatience, and a woman of thirty-five whose placid outlook masked a slow, deep, persistent intelligence. Using a few key contacts, bribes, promises, and pleas, the archaeologist succeeded in finding transportation to Tessalit. The route was roundabout and the vehicles changed hands three times, but the ever-varying topography of the desert under the vast canopy of the sky gave her a reassuring feeling of continuity in the presence of change. So different from the environs of her youth—the lush verdure of south Mali, the broad ribbon of the Niger that had spoken to her in watery whispers in sleep and dreams, moderating the constant, crackly static that was the background noise of modern urban life. The desert was sometimes arid scrubland, with fantastic rock formations rearing out of the ground, and groups of short trees clustered like friends sharing secrets. At other times it gave way to a sandy moodiness, miles and miles of rich, undulating gold broken only by the occasional oasis, or the dust cloud of a vehicle passing them by. Rocky, mountainous ridges rose on the horizon as though to reassure travelers that there was an end to all journeys.

In Tessalit the atmosphere was fraught, but a fragile peace prevailed. With the help of a Tuareg guide, an elderly man with sympathetic eyes, the travelers found the site indicated on the manuscript. Because it did not exist on any current map, the archaeologist was surprised to find that the site had a small settlement of some sixty-odd people. Her guide said that the settlement was in fact a kind of asylum as well as a shrine. The people there, he said, were blessed or cursed with an unknown malady. Perhaps fortunately for them, the inhabitants seemed unable to leave the boundary of the brick wall that encircled the settlement. This village of the insane had become a kind of oasis in the midst of the armed uprising, and men brought food and clothing to the people there irrespective of their political or ethnic loyalties, as though it was a site of pilgrimage. Townspeople coming with offerings would leave very quickly, as they would experience disorienting symptoms when they entered the enclosure, including confusion and a dizzying, temporary amnesia.

Thanks to her study of the medieval manuscript, the archaeologist had some idea of what to expect, although it strained credulity. She and her students donned metal caps and veils made from steel mesh before entering the settlement with gifts of fruit and bread. There were perhaps thirty people—men and women, young and old—who poured out of the entrance of the largest building, a rectangular structure the color of sand. They were dressed in ill-fitting, secondhand clothing, loose robes and wraparound garments in white and blue and ochre, T-shirts and tattered jeans—and at first there was no reply to the archaeologist's greeting. There was something odd about the way the villagers looked at their guests—a gaze reveals, after all, something of the nature of the soul within, but their gazes were abstracted, shifting, like the surface of a lake ruffled by the wind. But after a while a group of people came forward and welcomed them, some speaking in chorus, others in fragments, so that the welcome nevertheless sounded complete.

"What manner of beings are you?" they were asked after the greetings were done. "We do not see you, although you are clearly visible."

"We are visitors," the archaeologist said, puzzled. "We come with gifts and the desire to share learning." And with this the newcomers were admitted to the settlement.

Within the central chamber of the main building, as the visitors' eyes adjusted to the dimness, they beheld before them something fantastic. Woven in complex, changing patterns was a vast tapestry so long that it must have wrapped around the inner wall several times. Here, many-hued strips of cloth were woven between white ones to form an abstract design the like of which the newcomers had never seen before. People in small groups worked at various tasks— some tore long lengths of what must have been old clothing, others worked a complex loom that creaked rhythmically. Bright patterns of astonishing complexity emerged from the loom, to be attached along the wall by other sets of hands. Another group was huddled around a cauldron in which some kind of rich stew bubbled. In the very center of the chamber was a meter-high, six-faced column of black stone—or so it seemed—inlaid with fine silver lacework. This must, then, be the device whose use and function had been described in the medieval manuscript—a product of a golden period of Mali culture, marked by great achievements in science and the arts. The fifteenth century expedition had been organized in order to bury the device in the desert, to be guarded by men taking turns, part of a secret cadre of soldiers. Yet here it was, in the center of a village of the insane.

Looking about her, the archaeologist noticed some odd things. A hot drop of stew fell on the arm of a woman tending the cauldron—yet as she cried out, so did the four people surrounding her, all at about the same time. Similarly, as the loom workers manipulated the loom, they seemed to know almost before it happened that a drop of sweat would roll down the forehead of one man—each immediately raised an arm, or pulled down a headcloth to wipe off the drop, even if it wasn't there. She could not tell whether men and women had different roles, because of the way individuals would break off one group and join another, with apparent spontaneity. Just as in speech, their actions had a continuity to them across different individuals, so as one would finish stirring the soup, the other, without a pause, would bring the tasting cup close, as though they had choreographed these movements in advance. As for the working of the loom, it was poetry in motion. Each person seemed to be at the same time independent and yet tightly connected to the others. The archaeologist was already abandoning the hypothesis that this was a community of telepaths, because their interactions did not seem to be as simple as mind reading. They spoke to each other, for one thing, and had names for each individual, complicated by prefixes and suffixes that appeared to change with context. There were a few children running around as well: quick, shy, with eyes as liquid as a gazelle's. One of them showed the travelers a stone he unwrapped from a cloth, a rare, smooth pebble with a vein of rose quartz shot through it, but when the archaeologist asked how he had come by it they all laughed, as though at an absurdity, and ran off.

It was after a few days of living with these people that the archaeologist decided to remove her metal cap and veil. She told her students that they must on no account ever do so—and that if she were
to act strangely they were to forcibly put her cap and veil back on.
They were uncomfortable with this—the young man, in particular,
longed to return home—but they agreed, with reluctance.

When she removed her protective gear, the villagers near her
immediately turned to look at her, as though she had suddenly become
visible to them. She was conscious of a feeling akin to drowning—
a sudden disorientation. She must have cried out because a woman
nearby put her arms around her and held her and crooned to her
as though she were a child, and other people took up the crooning.
Her two students, looking on with their mouths open, seemed to be
delineated in her mind by a clear, sharp boundary, while all the others
appeared to leak into each other, like figures in a child's watercolor
painting. She could sense, vaguely, the itch on a man's arm from an
insect bite, and the fact that the women were menstruating, and the
dull ache of a healing bone in some other individual's ankle—but it
seemed as though she was simultaneously inhabiting the man's arm,
the women's bodies, the broken ankle. After the initial fright a kind
of wonder came upon her, a feeling she knew originated from her, but
which was shared as a secondhand awareness by the villagers.

"I'm all right," she started to say to her students, anxious to reassure them, although the word "I" felt inaccurate. But as she started
to say it, the village woman who had been holding her spoke the next
word, and someone else said the next, in their own dialect, so that the
sentence was complete. She felt like the crest of a wave in the ocean.
The crest might be considered a separate thing from the sequence
of crests and troughs behind it, but what would be the point? The
impact of such a crest hitting a boat, for example, would be felt by
the entire chain. The great loneliness that had afflicted her for so long
began, at last, to dissolve. It was frightening and thrilling all at once.
She laughed out loud, and felt the people around her possess, lightly,
that same complex of fear and joy. Gazing around at the enormous

tapestry, she saw it as though for the first time. There was no concept, no language that could express what it was—it was irreducible, describable only by itself. She looked at it and heard her name, all their names, all names of all things that had ever been, spoken out loud without a sound, reverberating in the silence.

She found, over the next few days, that the conjugal groups among the people of the settlement had the same fluidity as other aspects of their lives. The huts in the rest of the compound were used by various groups as they formed and re-formed. It felt as natural as sand grains in a shallow stream that clump together and break apart, and regroup in some other way, and break apart again. The pattern that underlay these groupings seemed obvious in practice but impossible to express in ordinary language. Those related by blood did not cohabit amongst themselves, nor did children with adults—they were like the canvas upon which the pattern was made, becoming part of it and separate from it with as much ease as breathing. On fine nights the people would gather around a fire, and make poetry, and sing, and this was so extraordinary a thing that the archaeologist was moved to ask her students to remove their caps and veils and experience it for themselves. But by this time the young man was worn out by unfamiliarity and hard living—he was desperate to be back home in Bamako, and was seriously considering a career outside academia. The older, female student was worried about the news from town that violence in the region would shortly escalate. So they would not be persuaded.

After a few days, when the archaeologist showed no sign of rejoining her students for the trip home—for enough time had passed by now, and their Tuareg guide was concerned about the impending conflict—the students decided to act according to their instructions. Without warning they set upon the archaeologist, binding her arms and forcing her to wear the cap and veil. They saw the change ripple across her face, and the people nearby turned around, as before. But this time their faces were grim and sad, and they moved as one toward the three visitors. The archaeologist set up a great wailing, like a child locked in an empty room. Terrified, the students pulled her out of the building, dragging her at a good pace, with the villagers following. If the Tuareg guide had not been waiting at the perimeter the visitors would surely have been overtaken, because he came forward at a run and pulled them beyond the boundary.

Thus the archaeologist was forced to return to Bamako.

Some years later, having recovered from her experience, the archaeologist wrote up her notes, entrusted them to her former student, and disappeared from Bamako. She was traced as far as Tessalit. With the fighting having intensified, nobody was able to investigate for over a year. The woman to whom she had left her notes returned to try to find her, guessing that she had gone to the settlement, but where the settlement had been, there were only ruins. The people had vanished, she was told, in the middle of a sandstorm. There was no sign of their belongings, let alone the great tapestry. The only thing she could find in the empty, arid, rocky wasteland was a small, round pebble, shot with a vein of rose quartz.

In the notes she left behind, the archaeologist had written down her conclusions—that the machine generated a field of a certain range, and that this field had the power to dissolve, or at least blur, the boundary between self and other. She wrote in French, and in Arabic, and in her mother tongue, Bambara, but after a while the regularity of her script began to break up, as a sandcastle loses its sharp edges and recognizable boundaries when the tide comes in. Thereafter her notes turned into intricate, indecipherable symbols reminiscent of the great tapestry that had hung in the main chamber of the settlement. These continued for several pages and finally, on the last page, she had written in French: *I cannot bear it. I must return.*

Thus end the three accounts.

Candidates will observe the requisite moment of contemplation.

The candidate will now consult the *Compendium of Machine Anomalies*, the *Hephaestian Mysteries*, and the *Yantric Oracle*, which will help put these accounts in context. Having completed its perusal, the candidate will make the requisite changes to its own parts in order to generate hypotheses on these questions. Is the negative space of ambiguity machines infinite? Is it continuous? Are the conceptual sub-spaces occupied by each machine connected to each other—by geography, concept, or some other as-yet-undiscovered attribute? What can we make of the relationship between human and machine? If an engineer can dream a machine, can a machine dream an engineer? An artist? A mathematician? An archaeologist? A story? Is the space of ambiguity machines set like a jewel or a braid within the greater expanse of the space of impossible machines? Is it here, in the realm of dream and imagination, that the intelligent machine might at last transcend the ultimate boundary—between machine and non-machine? To take inspiration from human longing, from the organic, syncretic fecundity of nature, the candidate must be willing to consider and enable its own transformation.

Begin.

Requiem

The thought of the letter lying on her desk in the untidy apartment was like a little time bomb ticking in her mind. Varsha told Chester about it, between the steamed mussels and the fish course.

"So I'm going to Alaska for spring break," she ended.

"But—what about Atlanta?"

He had been holding her hand in that ostentatious way he had whenever they were in a restaurant known to be a White Purist hangout. He let go of it, looking hurt.

The seafood place was a hole-in-the-wall with a clientele that clustered around the TV screen and yelled epithets during football games. The AugReal entertainment was of poor quality—floating sea captains and naked ladies, mostly, but the food was fantastic. Chester liked to live on the edge, take her to places like this, challenge the status quo. She pulled down her Augs to look at him in the world: the blue eyes, the little cut on his cheek, the slight pout of his lips, a tendril of graying brown hair sticking damply to his forehead from the steam still rising off the dish of mussels, and thought: *he's really quite a kid, even though he's eleven years older than me.* That was the attractive thing about him, this childlike quality in a brilliant young professor, although at this moment it was annoying.

"Atlanta can wait," she said firmly. "This is my favorite aunt we're talking about."

"You were going to go in the summer."

"Didn't you hear what I said? The place is closing ahead of schedule. I have to get her things."

It hit her again that her aunt Rima was dead, had been dead for more than a year, that there was no relief from the shock of it, no matter how many times she mourned. And Chester was being a jerk right now. *And* she had homework to finish, grad school being what it was. She got up, grabbed her bag, and turned and walked away from him, from his shocked face, his half-suppressed "Varsha!", the catcalls and laughter from the men at the bar. At the door she looked back very briefly—he was rising to his feet, arms reaching out, his face filled with rage and bewilderment. The night outside was cold—she fell into her familiar jogging rhythm, ignoring the glances of strangers, feet pounding on the pavement, bag strap tight across her chest—all the way to the T-station at the corner.

The tragically delayed letter was lying on her desk. *I'm coming, I'm coming,* she said silently to Rima. *Just like you wanted me to a year ago, I'm coming to Alaska for spring break.*

I first heard the songs of the bowhead whale on the internet. Varsha and I and a bunch of neighborhood kids and one of the pariah dogs—I think it was Tinku—were gathered in the front veranda of the Patna house, playing a video game. For some reason that I can't remember now, we looked up whale songs, and there it was, the long, strange call, filling the space. The dog Tinku started howling in tandem and wagging his tail, as though he could understand what the whale was saying. All of us burst out laughing. But there was something about that song that tugged at me. It occurs to me now that my journey to the Arctic started there, on that afternoon, with the honeysuckle bush in full bloom and the smell of the flowers almost making me dizzy. The shisham trees in the front garden whispered in the breeze—a kind of bass note to the whale's song—and all those years later it is the whales I hear, and the shisham trees are a warm and distant memory.

We are out in the boat, Jimmy and I, and we are following a pod of bowhead. There is an AUV—an underwater robot—fitted with a hydrophone that is moving with the whales. We can see its output right here on Jimmy's laptop—the spectral analysis of the conversation below, and the sounds themselves, in their immense complexity. We know each individual in the pod—they were tagged decades ago, but even without the tags, the coloring on their flukes or the injury scars on their flanks tell us who they are. We're seeing more propeller scars since the Arctic was opened to shipping. The killer whales have been moving up, too, hungry terrors that they are, and the bowheads that survive bear some horrifying scars. No wonder the bowheads are pushing farther North, toward the pole, where the waters are still cold, tracking the changing currents in search of krill.

I have learned that bowheads may be the oldest-living animals in the world. They live for over two hundred years! Apart from the new threats, their lives are relatively peaceful: the slow migrations around the North Pole, in the sub-freezing waters, with their kin; when hungry, they just open their enormous, garage-sized mouths and sieve in millions of tiny krill. Living that long, they must think long, deep thoughts. What do they think about? What do they say to each other?

When we are back at North Point, Jimmy will put on the headphones and scroll through the video feed and spectral analysis. Apart from language-recognition software, he says immersive attention is a way to use the best pattern-recognition device we know—the brain. It's what his people have always done, paid attention to their environment in a way that makes the most observant scientists among us seem oblivious, blind, bumbling. No wonder I am having such a hard time with the language—Iñupiaq has to be the most precise language in the world.

I wish I could help you all understand what it is about this place that gets me. It is so cold I don't have the words to describe it. Even with global climate change—even with the warming of the Arctic, the winters here are colder than we tropical flowers can ever imagine. When the wind blows, which it does all the time in gales and gasps, I feel like there is no breath in my lungs. I have to put warm gel packs in my gloves and boots so that I don't get frostbite. For six months of the year there is darkness or near darkness, and—what I miss the most—there are no trees! But still, this place draws me and draws *me and draws me, and it isn't just Jimmy or the work. The tundra in early spring is astounding. The way the low sun hits the snow, the blinding beauty of it takes the breath away. Once, out in the field, we saw two Arctic foxes playing, chasing each other round and round in circles, without a sound. But the tundra is not silent. Did you know, ice can speak? It squeaks and grunts, makes little slithering, sliding noises, and great explosive, cracking sounds too. Once, early in my stay here, we were out on the sea ice, Jimmy and I, along with a few others from North Point. It was dark and cold, but very still. The stars were out in their billions, and we could see the faint, translucent curtains of the Northern lights high in the sky. We were getting ready to set up our instruments, talking quietly, when Jimmy said: "Guys, we've got to get off. Now."*

I looked around but there was no obvious threat. I was going to ask Jimmy what the problem was, but then I saw everyone else acquiesce without argument. They packed up in a big hurry too. Hurry, hurry, Jimmy kept saying. I was thinking maybe there was an emergency with his family that he'd somehow remembered, but the moment we got off the ice there was an ear-splitting crack, and the segment we had been on suddenly broke off. You can't imagine what that was like—a whole great peninsula of floating ice suddenly detached from the rest of the shore ice and floated away, ghost-like in the semi-dark, into the black Arctic Ocean. I was shivering and shaking with shock, but the others were slapping Jimmy on the back and shaking his hand, as we trudged back to the trucks.

I asked him later how he knew. It's paying attention. Something he learned from his father and grandfather when he went hunting with them as a little boy, a kind of sixth sense that is developed through experience, a sensitivity to the slightest change in wind direction, the tiniest syllable spoken by the ice. Imperceptible to others, this ability to communicate with the physical environment is what originally earned the respect of scientists for Native Elders.

In the plane, on the final leg of the journey, Varsha's bravado vanished. It was a really small plane, and there was a crack across the plastic of the seat in front of her, which didn't inspire confidence. She could pull on her Augs and edit that all away, but she wasn't such a V-head. Working in the field, you got to know where to draw the line.

It didn't help that there was sick misery rising in her. There was no avoiding the fact of Rima's death. Rima was supposed to have come down from Alaska to settle her in last August when Varsha had first arrived from Delhi—but she was already seven months dead and gone, taken by the ice during a storm, along with her partner and lover, an Eskimo scientist called James Young. It had been hard enough for Varsha to alight in Boston alone, to find her way to the International Graduate Students office at the University, to walk the bewildering streets of Cambridge in search of her apartment. But this was harder. The man who had forwarded Rima's last letter had written to say that the research facility where her aunt had worked was closing down ahead of schedule, and there were some things of Rima's that the family might like to have. The man's name was Vincent Jones, and he would be glad to help in any way he could.

The plane banked. They were about to land in Utqiagvik. Her aunt had always, in her restless travels, been drawn to remote places, but this was the end of the world, or so it had seemed from the pictures on the internet—a town of mostly Eskimo people at the edge of the Arctic Ocean. She pressed her face against the window. There was a whiteness everywhere—white sky, white land, no horizon but the undifferentiated whiteness. For a moment she thought they must be flying through clouds, but the plane's wing was clearly visible. She fought a feeling of wild panic, and reasoned with herself—the plane wasn't going to crash. There were people talking all around her, tourists and Natives, excitedly, because this was the first real winter in a decade.

"Which hotel? That must be new. They say the Castle of Light has the best views . . ."

"Worst winter they've had in a decade . . ."

"This is a *real* winter. This is what winters used to be like. Back then, before the Great Melt. It will be good, maybe, for the whaling."

"The sea ice came back this winter to nearly 70%—no more multi-year ice—it will be thin and dangerous to walk on . . ."

". . . when you were growing up? Every year like this? Man, that must have been crazy . . ."

In the whiteness below, there appeared a pinprick, then another and another. A line of houses or sheds, all in a row. The plane swooped lower and lower and she held on to the edge of her seat, thinking this is what Rima had seen on her first visit to this place—when was it? Five years ago? Maybe she'd been in this very plane, in the same seat. The misery rose in her like a solid wall.

On the ground there was ice everywhere. The runway was ice, and ice rimed the edges of the small airport. It was a large metal shed with a corrugated roof and an extension clearly under construction— behind it were roads of ice, and buildings in the same utilitarian style. The airport was a single large hall with areas sectioned off for tickets, departures, arrivals and luggage. Native Iñupiaq Eskimos, white tourists, a small knot of men in coast guard uniforms. How strange to be in a place where the whites were so clearly the other, and yet this was still America! *Oh America, I thought I knew you.* She heard English around her, and a language she took to be Iñupiaq, the Native tongue of peoples who had been here for thousands of years before the Europeans came. What would Rima have thought and felt, coming here for the first time? Waiting for her suitcase, she texted the family group. *I'm here in Utqiagvik, all fine. I must only be the second Indian to come to this place. It's really different.* There was her little orange suitcase, between wooden boxes and sacks. She hauled it off the belt and looked around with a feeling of panic. Where was her host? Her Augs beeped and she hastily pulled them on. The scene before her was augmented with scrolling information, and a couple of VReal polar bears wearing toothy welcoming smiles were speaking a welcome. "Welcome to Utqiagvik, Northernmost city in the US," they said. "Take your taxi or van directly from the airport area. Polar bears have been sighted in town." Amidst the strangeness and wonder of this was the little message icon flashing, showing her an outline of where Vincent Jones was waiting for her. Near the exit door. She arranged her backpack on her shoulders and wheeled her suitcase ahead of her to the exit.

He was a large man with a broad, quiet face. His thin hair was streaked with white. He looked like the Tibetan refugees she had known in New Delhi. Smiling, he held out his hand.

"Good, good. You're here. Rima talked so much about you. You look like her."

"Thanks for receiving me," she said. It was so strange to be here, to be here without her aunt Rima, who would have stood here shivering like this in this exact spot. There was a wind blowing, sharp in her face like icicles. She pulled up her hood. Vincent seemed unperturbed by the wind. They climbed into a large, black Land Rover which lumbered slowly into the streets of ice.

"It's a little ways to North Point," Vincent said. "We'll go through Utqiagvik and by the ocean, so you can see the sea ice over the Arctic. It's been some years since we've had a winter like this one. Used to be the norm, once upon a time."

All she knew about Vincent was that he was somebody at North Point Polar Research Station, and he had been Rima's friend, and he had sent the letter. It had been found on the desk in her office. He had been going through her desk because North Point was closing down. Rima must have meant to send it right before the trip out to sea from which she had never returned.

"What was it like last winter, when my aunt died?" she said. *Might as well get it over with.* "We got the reports, but I'd like to understand—"

"It wasn't this cold or icy," he said, "but we did get one great storm. The Arctic has been in a warming trend for decades, but it's not steady, it goes up and down. Last winter the sea ice was so thin you couldn't walk on it. Things are changing so fast weatherwise, it's hard to predict whether a storm is going to fizzle out or turn into a howling blizzard. Rima and Jimmy were out in one of the research boats less than ten miles from shore when the blizzard hit."

Her hands clenched on her lap. It was cold despite the heater—the tips of her fingers felt like ice.

"We didn't used to have much of a coast guard presence when I was growing up," Vincent was saying. "But even with a coast guard station right here, they couldn't do anything with that storm. Had to wait two days before they could risk sending out the helicopters and the search vessels. That was the only bad storm we had that winter. This winter the cold and snow and ice are much more steady—this was normal once."

He cleared his throat.

"Jimmy was my cousin."

"Oh—God, I'm so sorry," she said. She glanced at him. He was looking straight ahead, his face set.

She looked out of the window. There were children out on bicycles—bicycles!—with thick treads in the front of a small grocery store. Their parka hoods were lined with fur. An Eskimo couple went by on a four-wheeled open vehicle, their faces ringed with fur-lined hoods. A man was digging out a car from several feet of snow in front of a house. The buildings had the same utilitarian steel-shed look of the airport, except for an extraordinary structure some six floors high that looked like a wedding cake.

"Castle of Light Hotel," declared the ornate sign.

"Tourist trap," Vincent said, a short, amused laugh. "Good for the economy, or so I hope. Used to be we'd make money off oil leases, before the oilfields gave up the last of the oil."

They turned east, leaving behind the houses. Now they were driving into the tundra—ahead and to their right was an expanse of snowy whiteness, flat and featureless. After a while they passed a large sign on their left with a cut-out image of a larger-than-life snowy owl. "Pagliavsi," declared the sign, standing alone in the snowy emptiness. "Ukpeagvik, site of ancient Eskimo Village," Vincent said. Behind the sign the ground rose gently and then fell away into an enormous plain, its smoothness broken only by untidy chunks of ice, like broken piecrust.

"You should know," Vincent said after a while. "Your aunt. She loved what she did. Like Jimmy—they were a pair. We'll stop in a bit so you can see the sea ice."

"I'm sorry I didn't get to know him," Varsha said. "She talked about him to us." She thought of Rima's full-on zest for life. It was possible to be a fifteen-year-old and feel older and duller than her then-thirty-year-old aunt. Those days, Rima's enthusiasms and adventures had led her from a short stint as an adventure and travel writer to a degree in mechanical engineering and the design and customization of wind generators in the high Himalayas. In the lush back garden of the old house in Patna, under the mango tree as old as her great-grandfather, Varsha had sat on the swing with Rima and heard all about the great expanse of the Tibetan desert, the lakes of meltwater from the vanished glaciers, oases in the arid heights. The wind that blew hard and cold, the measuring instruments that recorded wind speed and direction over an entire year, so that Rima and her team could design the best wind-energy-capture system for that particular locale. She saw the pictures and felt the possibilities of the world open up, a familiar side-effect of being with Rima.

And now there was a lump in her throat, but Vincent was already pulling over by the side of the road and motioning her to get down. Here she was, Varsha of the tropics, on the Alaskan North Shore. There was the endless white expanse before her, with only the shiny ice road winding away before them. The sun had emerged from the clouds, and lay low on the horizon—the light on the snow hurt her eyes. She pulled up her Augs in world mode. *You are 1280 miles from the North Pole,* scrolled the message to the right of her field of view. Vincent led her to the top of the rise on the left. Her boots crunched on the snow. At the top they paused. Before them was the great, white plain broken by small piles of cracked ice. It extended all the way to the horizon, as far as she could tell.

"That's the Arctic Ocean," Vincent said. "Sea ice. Frozen sea water. You can tell there's water under there from the way the currents make the ice break up."

"Can you walk on it?"

"In places. Used to be parts of the sea ice attached to the shore stayed all year round, built up a little every season. As much as three, four meters thick sometimes. We used to camp on the ice when we cut whaling trails in the Spring. Your aunt ever tell you about that?"

"A little," Varsha said. "She said the whaling hadn't been very good for a while."

"You're cold—let's get back in the car. Yes, the bowheads changed their migration patterns after the Big Melt. We, the Iñupiaq—my people—had always lived with the whales, and when they started to change, our old knowledge wasn't as much help. The killer whales started coming up into the warming waters, hunting the bowheads. And the TRexes became active at the time."

In the car the heater was running on high. She put her hands in front of the vents.

"We'll get you proper gear for this place," he said. "Your aunt's stuff. She loved this place but never liked the cold."

She nodded.

"Tell me about the TRexes," she said. There was an Augree Experience involving intelligent monster machines that she'd helped debug when it was still in production. She'd been surprised to learn that TRexes were for real, in the world.

"There are about twenty of them working these waters," he said. "Still got oil and methane down on the sea floor. TRexes found two large deposits last year. But they're having trouble with some of them, I hear. Shut-downs and failures. Keep your eyes peeled, we may see one on the way. There's one operating a few miles from us at North Point."

They didn't see any TRexes but after about an hour the North Point Research facility loomed suddenly out of the landscape—a building capped by four tall steel lattice towers, and three rows of small windows on the visible sides of a cubical structure in between. The windows shone in the sun's low light. The place was larger than she expected. It jutted out into the plain of sea ice on concrete pillars.

"We're down to a handful of people," Vincent said, leading her in past a heavy steel door. "Most of the researchers have left. The rest are packing up, finishing up. You'll meet them at meals. I'm the Native liaison here."

Inside, there were white walls and long corridors, gray-painted metal doors, some with windows.

"Who's bought the station?"

"GaiaCorp's Arctic Energy unit," he said. "They run the TRexes."

The dorms were at the back of the facility. Their footsteps echoed emptily in the silence. Lights came on as they walked. Vincent led her to a small room with a white bed and a desk and chair. "Bathroom's down the hall," he said. "Sorry, we live kind of plain here. Why don't you get settled and I'll ping you when it's time for dinner. The door next to yours—that's the suite Rima and Jimmy had. It has an attached bathroom if you want. Here's their keycard, and here's yours. Thought it would be easier to have you right next door."

After she had washed up and unpacked, she saw that it was only four-thirty. She took a deep breath. *Might as well start now.* She went into the suite her aunt had shared with Jimmy Young. It consisted of a tiny outer room and a bedroom and bathroom. When she turned on the light she was startled at how bare it looked. It had clearly been used very little, mostly for sleeping, she imagined. There was a stereo in the small living room, a carving of a polar bear on the coffee table that looked like it had been made from bone, and a picture of two people on the prow of a boat. She picked up the photograph—it was Rima, her face rimmed by a fur hood, and almost-uncle Jimmy, snow goggles pushed back over his head, his dark hair windswept. They were both grinning as though they were having the time of their lives. She set it down again, congratulating herself for keeping her composure so far. She had a job to do, and she simply had to keep herself together until it was done. Pretend she was on an errand for a strict taskmaster like—her aunt. Yes. Sure. In the bedroom she willed herself to open the closet. Vincent had taken care of Jimmy's things—only her aunt's clothes were here. She could donate some to the local town swap, Vincent had said. She breathed the still air inside the closet. Was there something of Rima left here, still, after all these months? A faint whiff of something indefinable—a lotion—yes, the sandalwood lotion from home that everyone in the family used. There was a long, beaded kurta in green, and a pink chikanwork outfit among the flannel shirts and turtlenecks—she buried her face in the kurta and swallowed a lump in her throat—she would keep those. She began to pull things onto the bed, making two piles.

Once she had begun it was easy enough to continue with the suitcases in the closet—mostly empty—and the shoes at the bottom. Then the side table. This was going fast. If she went through the office stuff as quickly she would be done in a day. Whatever had possessed her to plan a four-day stay?

But when Vincent knocked on the door to call her to dinner, there was still the pile on the bed to be arranged, and the books in the bookshelf—she had let herself become distracted by them—well-thumbed volumes about Iñupiaq culture and history, one on biomimicry, a number of technical-looking books on alternative energy and acoustical engineering. There was a book she had gifted to her aunt when Rima had left for the US: *The Best Travel Writing of the 21ˢᵗ Century*—it had "Love, Varsha" on the inside cover. There were books on economics and history, cetacean biology, and interspecies communication.

She was relieved to go down to the dining hall, where a buffet meal was served—rolls and fried chicken and some kind of vegetable greens she couldn't identify. She sat with Vincent and four other people to whom she was introduced, all white except for Vincent and an African-American called Kenny, who was a sea-ice expert. It was strange to be around people who weren't wearing Augs or any other kind of goggles, who were so much in the world. Usually she liked talking to people but suddenly she was almost too exhausted to eat. Fortunately the others seemed preoccupied with the impending shutting down of the institute. Incomprehensible discussions about local politics and who was going where and what Arctic Energy would do with the facility allowed her to concentrate on her food and sit with her thoughts, until the woman with the salt-and-pepper hair sitting next to her said in a low voice:

"Sorry about your aunt. It must be awful—but you don't want to talk about that. How was your trip?"

She would have liked to talk about Rima. It might have helped her feel grounded, she thought tiredly, but she had noticed how most Americans tended to assume that dead people were off-topic. She tried to smile.

"Long. And cold, at least the drive here. I'm still warming up."

The woman laughed. Her name was—yes, Julie. She had very pale skin, and a fine dusting of freckles.

"I've been here for two years and I'm not really used to being here either. For one thing, the Arctic is going through some really rapid changes. Kind of like being married to whatsyourname here." She elbowed the man next to her, who smiled. "But mostly what gets me is the absence of light for six months of the year. If you'd come in December it would have been darker and colder."

"Boston will feel tropical after this."

"Hey," Vincent said. "This is the best place in the world. Even with climate change. No need to enhance reality when you have— this!" He swept his arm around the room. The Arctic night was dark blue outside the small, square windows.

"It would be hard to edit out the cold, or your ass freezing doing fieldwork on the ice," said one of the young men, whose name she had forgotten already. He nodded pleasantly at her. "Vince said you're in VReality, is that right?"

"Not at the moment," she said. The greens tasted bitter and sad, as though they had never known the sun. Even her Augs couldn't fix that. She explained about her Master's program.

"Bet you can't wait to get out of here," said the young man. "The US of A isn't what it used to be. Unbelievable how quickly things have changed in just a few years."

"It wasn't that great before, Matt," said the black man. Varsha remembered his name was Kenny or something. Yes, Kendrick. He looked in disgust at the pile of chicken bones on his plate, and stabbed at the soggy greens with his fork. "Yes," he said. "Try being black in America in any era. It's worse now, of course. And there's North Point. There was a time we couldn't have imagined oil coming back, after the ban. Now we have GaiaCorp promising to protect us through geoengineering. Project Terra! Why study climate change when we can fix it from space? We can burn fossil fuels again! Get the last of the oil and gas out of the Arctic. Five, six years ago, if you'd told me that there would be TRexes in the ocean and North Point bought out by GaiaCorp, I would have said you were crazy. I'll never say 'It can't happen' again!"

"Started with the Space Act in 2015," said Matt. "You start mining the moon and then suddenly you have the corporate wars, then Earth Corp, and the agreements with nations, and—"

"Spare me the history lesson," said the fourth person, the one next to Julie. He put down his fork and dragged his fingers though long, straggly brown hair. "I agree with you in broad terms but you are connecting the wrong dots, Matt—"

Vincent pushed back his chair.

"Got to go finish up some things. Varsha, you got everything you need? Breakfast is from six to nine a.m. After breakfast, if you want, Julie can show you around. Julie—?"

"Sure," Julie said. Varsha felt guilty. These people were winding down what seemed to be their life's work. She didn't need showing around. She had all the sorting and packing to do—

But she wanted to know Rima the polar scientist. She wanted to know her almost-uncle Jimmy. She nodded.

"Thanks, I'd love that. If it isn't too much trouble."

There *was* a TRex at work far on the horizon. She was looking out of the window of the office her aunt Rima had shared with Jimmy Young. Jimmy's space had been cleared and someone called Terra Longfield now occupied it, her absence bounded by pictures of a smiling blond child and drawings in crayon. But Rima's desk was stacked with boxes of her things—papers, books, knickknacks that had used to be on her desk, including a picture of Varsha, and another picture of the family at the Patna house, the colors faded but the faces still poignant in their familiarity. Varsha was the kid tugging at Rima's arm in the picture, pointing off-camera to something in the garden, and Rima was bent slightly forward, laughing, about to follow her niece's glance. They were the only two not looking at the camera.

It was cold in the empty office. She looked up to the window and saw the skyscape, the morning sun still low in the sky, the impossible immensity of the expanse of snow, the pale gray smudge of the horizon— and against it, a TRex somewhere far ahead where the sea ice gave way to open sea. Its skeletal frame, with the long head turning slowly this way and that, looked so alive and purposeful that she shuddered involuntarily. They were smart machines, she knew, but this one, far away as it was, seemed positively *sentient*. Its long labrum sipped hydrocarbons off the ocean floor, and the proboscis sniffed for methane bubbling up off the ocean floor. When exploring, she had heard, it would become buoyant in the water, its array of airguns firing *boom-boom* into the sea, looking for oil and gas under the sea-floor. It was an amazing piece of engineering. Despite the remoteness of this one it felt more real than the ones she had seen in VR games.

A knock at the door made her jump. Without waiting for her response a man came in. He was wearing a suit, which seemed incongruous after the casual clothing of the others. He was tall, with a pleasant, open face, and wavy dark brown hair. He wore a pair of Augs—state-of-the-art—in world mode—she could see his eyes through them, green. He smiled and held out his hand.

"Rick Walters. So pleased to meet you, though in such sad circumstances. I knew your aunt well."

There was something compelling about him, she noticed, as she returned the pressure of his hand. An air of complete assurance and good nature.

"I just wanted to let you know—if you need help, or want to talk, I'll be in and out," he said.

"Thanks. Are you a scientist here?"

He laughed. "Me? Alas, I haven't the temperament. I'm the Transition Liaison. Making sure the handover goes smoothly. Much as I'd prefer an Augs Enhancement, I have to have results in the world. Sorry to say."

She laughed. "I'm glad you're not a V-head. It gives us a bad name."

"I just got my nephew his first real Augs," Rick said, lightly. "He'll be totally thrilled to know I met someone who works with them." He passed his hand over the edge of her aunt's desk, picked up the family photo, and set it down. "Sorry, I shouldn't be interrupting."

Later, after he'd left, she thought how *normal* he seemed. He was from her world, the world of busy metropolises and high tech. But there was an older world than that, and she missed it now. Standing in the cold room, she pulled on her Augs and brought up her favorite program for when she was homesick. The walls of the room turned a sunlight yellow and the view from the window was of her grandparents' courtyard. There was the old guava tree that she had grown up with. There were potted plants on the bench beside the window and she could hear the faint strains of the tanpura from her music lesson in the next room. The program was creative—it took the boxes of her aunt's stuff on the desk and rendered them into piles of multi-colored knitting wool. Her grandmother was a knitter. Someone came into the room—it was her uncle. She waved to him, smiling. But when he spoke, his voice was distorted. "We apologize for the Cognitive Dissonance . . ." The words scrolled across her field of view. "Initiating patch—"

But she had already pulled the Augs down. It wasn't her uncle speaking Hindi, it was Vincent speaking English. His thin gray hair was disheveled, as though he had just pulled off his hat, coming in from the cold.

"Sorry," she said, but he was asking her something.

"Was Rick Walters just here?"

"Yes, he said he was a friend of my aunt's. He offered to help."

"He's no friend of Rima's." Vince frowned. "Rima hated his guts. He was on the original negotiating team for North Point. She fought hard against the buyout. He's here to make sure everything's accounted for. I came to warn you not to tell him anything. He stops by without warning, acts real friendly."

He nodded at her and left.

In the cold and the silence, Varsha shivered. *I don't know what's what,* she told herself. There was no signal on her phone. The last text she had got from the family was a "Be careful out there" from her grandfather, and similar notes from her parents, her cousin Sanjay and her Augs Friends group. Her mother and father were fighting again, and Biru uncle was in Patna because Nanu was having a medical checkup. Chester had sent about twenty pings already, which she had ignored. She didn't feel like resuming the Augs program or sifting through her aunt's things. She sat down at the desk and put her head in her hands, and remembered.

For the longest time she had shared a room with Rima, her mother's youngest sister, every visit to Patna. They decorated the room with strange structures; there were wires suspended across the room with wheeled carts that ran up and down, a plastic monkey in a bucket that jumped out and woke them up at 7 am every morning. Anyone approaching the room, no matter how quietly, would be anticipated— thanks to an IR sensor that beeped a warning in Swedish.

She and Rima used to invent games for the little ones. The one she was thinking of now was a winter game—they would drag a couple of razais down to the carpet to make a huge multicolored mountain, and they would hide under sections of the thick folds, while the little cousins would screech excitedly and try to find them, their fat, slippery bodies like so many wriggling fish on the satin covers. The razais were thick enough that the mountain stood without help, and they would roll the ping-pong-ball collection down from the summit, one by one, trying to guess at first where, among the folds and channels, valleys and crinkles, the balls would end up. It was sometimes tricky because you'd think the pink ball would slide just so, into the long, straight channel leading all the way to the bottom of the mountain, but a little crinkle here, or a little subtle encouragement there (from an aunt half-concealed within the folds) would send the ball careening to quite another destination. This is where Varsha learned about chance, and how a small and sudden change could lead you to quite another path.

Rima and Varsha co-wrote a novel when Varsha was eleven. In the novel, various people and parts of the house, and trees, and stray dogs were characters. It was comic and dark and sad and hilarious, and in each chapter there was a hidden clue to the problem or mystery. The secret was that each clue was concealed by something similar to itself—a Box of Wonders was hidden in the Cube of Amazing Things, a puppy with magical powers was hidden in its mother, since it had yet to be born, and a wish-granting mango hung with other mangoes on a branch of the mango tree. The story had got out of control, with plots and subplots of labyrinthine complexity, impossible to finish. For years when Rima and Varsha would meet, they would say to each other—how did Amroodji become allergic to guavas? Or—did Mad Puppy find the Lost World inside Mobius, or outside? And they would burst out laughing. One of the other cousins had recently discovered the manuscript (copiously and laboriously illustrated) stuck between two of the eight hundred books in the drawing room, and the grand-parents had been having a hilarious time re-reading it with the younger grandchildren, until after the news came. Now, life was forever divided into Before and After. The manuscript was now in Nanaji's safe, as though fate might snatch away even this.

My friend Skip told me this story when I was in California. There is a former killing ground off the southern coast of California in the Pacific Ocean. Here the American whalers hunted and killed thousands of gray whales in the 1850s. In the 1970s, Skip said, well after the age of whaling was over, a Mexican fisherman had an encounter with a gray whale. The whale came alongside his boat and gazed at him.

Looking into the whale's eye, the fisherman had a life-changing experience. Since then, the whales seem to wait for the humans. Whenever people in boats come to that region during the calving season, mother whales and their young will approach them. People will touch them and they seem to welcome these encounters.

So of course we had to go there. We took a small plane down to a town in Baja California. There's quite a tourist business out there, bringing humans to the whales. Skip and my friend Molly, who studies kelp forests, went out in a small boat with a bunch of tourists. I got to practice my Spanish and we were all laughing and having a great time, with the boat rocking wildly on a choppy sea—and then the guide yelled: whales!

I could see nothing—the spray from the waves was in my eyes, and I was trying to keep my balance. Then as we got closer the waters parted and a leviathan surfaced, slowly, as though it had all the time in the world. I leaned over the rail. The ancient eye looked at me—a sentient, knowing, curiously gentle gaze. In that one glance, that tenuous, temporal bridge between being and being, I knew my life would change. At that moment I existed in a way I hadn't before—in the eye of a Californian gray whale. She could have destroyed us with one flick of her massive tail, but she just hung in the water, looking at us. The kids on the boat were already leaning over and touching her, and I did too. Her skin was riddled with scars and clusters of barnacles. She must have been quite old. Later another whale surfaced close to us and blew a great, long breath. The plume of moisture bloomed like a fountain several meters into the air, soaking us. The sun came out at exactly that moment, and among the suspended water drops I saw, for a fraction of a second, a rainbow.

"Congratulations!" Skip said, hitting me across my shoulder blades as I gasped and choked. "Your first rainblow!"

This astonishing experience made me wonder: knowing their bloody and tragic experience with our species, what moved these whales to seek us out, to be so forgiving? Was it one individual's bright idea to try to befriend the enemy?

Jimmy thinks none of this is surprising. Living such long lives, some of the whales may have acquired what we call wisdom. It's rare enough in our species! And why should humans be the only ones with a sense of agency, a desire to make things better for themselves? We already know that whales have culture—different pods of the same species have different habits and tastes in food.

Here's another story—a dolphin was observed apparently assisting a young sperm whale that had lost its way in a saltwater marsh, somewhere off an island in the Indian Ocean. Scientists who received the video (from a fisherman) said that it was inconclusive. But Jimmy has seen it. He's not one to jump to conclusions, but it supports his hypothesis that whales communicate with other species. After all, they live in an environment rich with biodiversity. Wouldn't they want or need to communicate with other species sometimes?

I tell him about how I grew up, in the old house in Patna with the sunlight-yellow walls. How, first thing in the morning, I'd be woken up by mynahs yelling outside the window, and the parakeets in the neem trees. The pariah dogs would be waiting at the back door, ancestors of the current Bossy Pack. We had a parakeet with a broken wing when I was ten, and he would sit on the windowsill and scold the dogs, and drop roasted chana or bits of toast for them. Ma, you would have already been up before dawn, watering the tulsi in the courtyard, and the radio would be playing in the dining room. Apart from the neighbors' conversations wafting through the open windows, and the bells of the rickshaw-wallahs, there were so many living creatures around us, talking to each other. This is why I could believe the old stories as a child, in which animals are speakers and players.

Jimmy had such a different upbringing, here in the Far North, and yet we understand each other so well. He, too, grew up with stories in which animals talk to humans and each other, across the species gap. Some sympathies bridge the distance between cultures. Perhaps it is the same between species, and we modern humans simply don't notice.

"We're in the lowest level of the station. Sorry it looks like a dungeon here, but the best part is just ahead."

"Did my aunt work here?"

"Her lab's upstairs," Julie said. " You've seen it—one of the big rooms, empty now. But she loved it down here. She and Jimmy spent as much time here as possible, planning and arguing and observing. Just past this door—"

A large steel door opened at the press of a metal knob set in the wall. There was a small space beyond, and another steel door. The first door closed behind them with a slow hiss, and the second one opened.

There was nothing beyond it but an ordinary passageway. Puzzled, Varsha followed Julie. Lights turned on as they walked into the dark corridor. There were no doors on either side, just the tunnel going forward into the dark, into the—

"The sea—this is going seaward?"

Julie turned, grinned.

"Yes—hold your horses, we're almost there."

And suddenly they were in a broad open space filled with diffuse light that came in through transparent walls. The roof was a glass dome. It was literally a bubble at the bottom of the sea.

Varsha caught her breath. There were tiny things moving in the water outside—small, streamlined silhouettes against what seemed to be a dank white ceiling, a few feet above the roof of the dome. It was suffused with a faint blue glow in places.

"We're under the sea ice," Julie said. She flicked a switch and suddenly the outside was lit. The floating ice above them discolored with gray-green smudges on the underside. In some places the ice had thickened, forming extrusions that hung in the water like chandeliers. In the light the ice crystals glittered like so many diamonds. Beyond the circle of light, the water was murky, mysterious with small, moving shadows.

"Wow," Varsha whispered. Julie looked satisfied.

"Never fails to impress visitors," she said triumphantly. "If you're lucky you'll see more than a few fish or krill. We've seen a swimming polar bear. And during the spring migration there's bowheads that always stop here. Since about ten years ago they've been venturing closer to the Beaufort coast. Same with belugas."

Varsha looked around the observation chamber. There were desks and instrumentation around the circular perimeter. In the middle was a table with a microwave, coffee maker, and the attendant supplies.

"Your aunt spent a bunch of time here," Julie said. "She and Jimmy used to joke that it wasn't fair for humans to observe the whales and other creatures. We should give them a chance to understand us. You should have seen the two of them dance around the room for the whales! The whales must think humans are deranged."

She laughed.

"Bowheads are wary creatures. They live over two hundred years. Some of them still remember the days of the Yankee whalers, when they were nearly wiped out. So you can't blame them if keep their distance. But they're intelligent creatures. They're curious. So some of them—it's always the same ones—they come and hang out and look at us, and talk about us."

"You're kidding, right?"

"Only a little. Whales have a sophisticated communication system. Don't you know what your aunt was doing? Jimmy had a mission—to decipher the communication system of the bowhead whale. Humans can now speak a little gibbonese—white-handed gibbons, you know? South Asia? No? Well, more people should know about that! We're finally beginning to decode languages of other species. Whales and dolphins are hard—their languages are likely to be more complex than ours. Jimmy was a marine biologist, your aunt was an engineer—they were perfect for the project."

"I thought she was working on alternative-energy systems!"

"That was ongoing. She worked with a group of students at the college in Utqiagvik—there's a really good tribal college in Utqiagvik—they developed some prototypes of wind generation that can work with gusty winds in a place like this. Town's looking into it. She also—here, let me show you."

The outside lights turned off, except for the ones close to the sea bed. Julie gestured to Varsha to get closer to the walls. On the sea bed was an array of two-foot-high devices that looked like Japanese fans mounted on flexible stems. They were swaying gently with the current.

"Wave-generator prototypes developed by Rima," Julie said. "She worked on boat design too—her unofficial project—propeller-free boats that wouldn't injure marine animals. You should've seen her lab. There was this bathyscaph shaped like a squid that used water propulsion. She used to get all kinds of junk from online auctions, naval junkyards, and such. She got interested in whale communication after she went on her first boat ride with Jimmy. They would sit in this room and draw designs of all kinds of crazy stuff. Boats with flippers and wings."

"Did she actually build any of this?"

"There were so many prototypes being tested and taken apart and tested again that I lost count. After—afterwards I heard they sent most of her stuff to the tribal college. They wouldn't have, if she'd completed the project. If they'd lived—she and Jimmy—there's no telling how much they would have accomplished . . . "

"What was he like? Jimmy?"

"I never felt I really got to know him. I feel like that sometimes with the Natives here. It makes me realize we European descendants are the newbies, that this was their home first, and still is. The Native Resistance has been felt here too, even though it is so far away from the action. Vincent I can relate to, he lived for so long down south. But Jimmy, he just went down to California to study what the science of the whites could teach him, and hotfooted it back here. He was quiet. Thoughtful. Don't get me wrong, he could crack a joke and all, but he was a bit of an introvert. No-small-talk kind of guy. Passionate."

"Did he—did they get to decipher whale talk?"

"They made some headway. He's published quite a bit on it. Their tapes and the papers they worked on are all with Vince. But you should talk to Vince or Matt—I'm just a microbiologist. Matt's focus is how land mammals are affected by climate change—caribou, moose, polar bears, seals, and the impact of moose coming up from the South. The three of them would talk up a storm about species communication."

Julie turned the lights off. In the dim natural light filtered through the sea ice, the observation room seemed a world unto itself.

"I just heard on the radio that bowhead whales have been spotted west of Utqiagvik," Julie said. "It's early for them to be coming here, but apparently they are coming. You might get lucky."

I feel her here, Varsha thought. *She's here, Rima Mausi, in this place.* She took a deep breath.

"I hope I see a whale," Varsha said, as they started back up the tunnel.

As the light grew stronger and the thin shore ice started melting back with a distressing rapidity, there came news that the whales were already on the move from their wintering areas in the Bering strait. Vince and Tom and Irene were in Utqiagvik, where the mood was festive. I joined them later in the day. The sun was out and half the town was on the beach. The whale radio had declared that one of the whaling crews was headed back with whales in tow.

At last we saw the first boat chugging toward us over the ocean, the flag waving. Vince was standing next to me and let up a great shout, and everyone started yelling "hey-hey-hey!" It was Vince's uncle, Tom Jones, who was captain of that boat. Kids were running around shouting, it was like a festival. Then I saw the dark bulk of the whale in tow behind the boat, and the red float bobbing close to it. As it came toward land, the man in the forklift drove closer to the water's edge, and we moved out of the way. I couldn't see anything for the crowd for a while, and then I saw the whale's great carcass slide past me, pulled up by ropes attached to the forklift. It lay like a black mountain. Vince came through the crowds with his grand-nephew, a boy of five, on his shoulders. "It was a good catch," he said to me, smiling. He said something in Iñupiaq. "That's a thank-you to the whale for the gift of its life," he said. "The whale captain says that over the body when it is lashed to the boat. It was a good death—it died quickly."

The whale was already being cut up. Long, black strips lined with pink blubber were being hauled off on ropes. The men worked efficiently with triangular cutters on poles. Blood stained the white snow. There was shouting and singing.

"We will eat well this winter," Marie said. Marie works at the grocery store, and is Irene's aunt. That first whaling season was a bewildering time for an omnivore-turned vegan Indian scientist raised in the sub-tropics and freshly arrived from California. I remember asking Jimmy when I first came to Utqiagvik: "How can you bear to eat such amazing creatures?" He just looked at me in his thoughtful, considering way, and replied: "Because we are not apart, we are a part." It took me some time to figure out what he meant. Since then I've attended many a whale carving and blanket toss, and helped cut and prepare whale to feed the community. In the dead of winter, in a place still mostly only accessible by small aircraft, the sole source of fresh food is meat. And because the whale is sacred, it is never sold, only shared. I had a lot of whale that winter, parboiled and dunked into soy sauce, or cut frozen straight from the ice cellar and into the mouth. I have a lot more respect for the hunter who brings in the wild kill and says his prayers over it, than for those who trap animals into constant, unrelieved suffering in their thousands in factory farms.

Thus I am made of many things—mother's milk, fruit of guava and mango trees, rice of the Indian Gangetic Plain, vegetables of splendid variety, meat of many creatures, and now—bowhead whale!

Next morning Rick showed up. Varsha was in her aunt's room, folding clothes and shoes into cardboard boxes. He smiled at her from the door.

"Hey, want to come for a helicopter ride?"

He *was* charming, even if he couldn't be trusted. She should say no—but what harm was there in a helicopter ride? She was sick of this room, sick of grief. She could handle this man—she had known men like him during three years working in industry, before the MS program, before America. Before.

She was glad not to run into anyone else as they went up to the roof of the building.

"Where are we going?"

"Just over the sea. Quick trip out to the nearest TRex and back. You're here for such a short time, you should see a little of the Arctic."

On the rooftop the cold breeze took her breath away. She stumbled—Rick steadied her, his face unreadable behind the goggles. She climbed into the helicopter, a compact yellow-and-black giant bumble-bee of a machine, with "Arctic Energy" painted on the sides, and the circular insignia of GaiaCorp.

"You know how to fly this thing?" she yelled over the engine's roar. He grinned.

"Want to inspect my license?"

She shook her head.

"Just get me back safe and sound," she yelled as they rose into the air. "In time for lunch!"

"Much as I'd like to spend more time with the most attractive woman in fifty square miles, I fully intend to get us back for lunch," he said, laughing. "Although I could get you a better meal in Utqiagvik."

"Mr. Walters, you're flirting," she said. Below them the ice sheet was a great, white wing, fraying at the edges where it met the liquid sea. North Point station had vanished behind them.

"Sorry," he said. He sounded unrepentant. "Look, we're over the ocean now. Those little white patches are part of the shore ice that separated, floated off."

The ocean was incomprehensibly vast, stretching away to the curve of the horizon. Above their heads the helicopter blades were a blur through the transparent walls of the cockpit.

"Why are we going to see the TRex?"

"We've had some trouble with a couple of them, we don't know why. System failures, mechanical wear, hydrophones non-functional. I like to reconnoiter at least semi-regularly. Despite the Big Melt the Arctic is still a really inhospitable place—well, I don't need to tell you that—"

"What kind of trouble?"

"Hang on, we're here."

The craft fell like a stone. Varsha clutched the edge of her seat, but the helicopter slowed and hovered over the dark sea. The tops of the waves glittered in the low-angled sunlight. She gasped.

Before them, rising out of the water like a creature from a mechanized Jurassic nightmare, stood the TRex. It was the one she had seen from the window of her aunt's office. Its long snout swiveled toward them and its optical sensors glittered with iridescence like the compound eyes of an insect. Rick's fingers flashed over the copter's dashboard, and the TRex abruptly bent its head. Its neck collapsed inward until was several meters shorter.

"It's pulling its legs in—I've put it in search mode, so you can see how it works," Rick said. "Look!"

Floats inflated on either side of the machine. It began to move, through some invisible propeller mechanism, purposefully across the sea. The copter followed it.

There was a deafening series of booms below them. A milky froth appeared in the water around the TRex.

"That's the airgun array—don't worry, I've turned it off now. Sound waves penetrate the seabed and are reflected back. See the buoys around it? Hydrophones, receiving the sound, giving it a picture of the sea floor, hundreds of meters down."

"Pretty impressive," Varsha said. "But damaging to whales, I hear."

"Yes, but the TRex has a 360-degree sensor that detects whale pods," Rick said. "It's not just the Iñupiaq who care about whales, you know. We spend a lot of R&D money making sure we don't damage the environment."

His fingers moved over the dashboard controls again.

"There, it's back to doing sampling. Good, it passed the test, and you got to see it in action."

On the way back she asked him whether he'd looked at TRexes self-diagnostics.

"You're smart," he said. "Like your aunt. The diagnostics don't tell us anything, because the non-functionality comes without warning."

"It could be a kind of cascade failure," she said. "I've worked with some sophisticated Augs programs—complexity can cause all kinds of sudden failures."

He looked at her.

"Maybe I shouldn't tell you this," he said, "but I've seen some internal reports—problems with some of the Geoengineering projects that nobody understands. Warming spikes instead of cooling in the upper atmosphere. Plankton die-offs where you expect a bloom. Winds changing in unexpected ways. We could use people like you."

"I thought you were just the transition liaison," she said, mocking him. "I didn't realize you were the CEO of GaiaCorp!"

He threw his head back and laughed. The sky above them was a deep azure. Below and ahead lay the ice, swathed with the sun's gold light.

"I like you, Varsha," he said, looking at her. "I think we're going to be friends."

Rick stayed for lunch. It was an uncomfortable lunch, since the scientists didn't seem to want to talk very much. Only Carl—Julie's husband—held up the conversation. Vince was very quiet. Varsha thought uncomfortably that perhaps he felt betrayed by her excursion with Rick. She wanted very badly to reassure him. After Rick left, she gave herself time to collect her wits, and went to talk to Vincent.

He was in his office. Packing boxes sat on the floor and on chairs. Vincent had his back to her, looking at a large map on the wall. But when she came into the office, he turned, although she hadn't made any sound.

"About my copter ride with Rick Walters," she said. "I wanted to let you know. He was all charm, but I didn't tell him anything. He showed off his TRex and brought us back, that's all. I wouldn't let Rima down in a million years."

Slowly he smiled.

"It's been very tough," he said. "The last year and a half it's been one thing after another. It's not for me to tell you what to do. But thanks for being smart about Rick Walters."

"What is it that he wants to know, anyway? What are we hiding from him?"

"Rick's an information gatherer," he said. "He collects all kinds of details indiscriminately, in the hope that they will come in useful someday. That's kind of how he swung the deal for North Point. In short, he's nosey." He pointed at the map. "I unrolled it and put it back on the wall after he left. Just to look at again before I pack it away. It's Rima and Jimmy's work. They called it the Map of Anomalies. Rick would love to get his hands on it."

It was a map of the coastline, rich with markings and symbols in a rainbow of colors. Lines traced the migration pathways of the Bowheads—different shades of blue indicating how the paths were shifting every year. Rima and Jimmy would follow the bowheads in a boat, or track them with drones and underwater robots, explained Vince. Little red triangles indicated sites of killer whale attacks—red squares were ship injuries, and red lines were TRex trajectories across the shallow seas.

Event markers were in mysterious purple symbols.

"This one—this was the most recent one, after Rima and Jimmy were lost. I put it in. Just this past October, at the time of the Fall whaling. These are places where Jimmy's drones picked up bowhead whales in formations that have never been seen before, sounding together. Those symbols over there are TRexes that malfunctioned without warning. Rick's not the only one interested in the TRexes."

Another symbol off the shore of Baffin Island in the Canadian Arctic indicated a crossing point, where migration routes of belugas, the small white whales of the North, intersected the new bowhead pathways. There were similar intersections with humpback routes in the North Pacific.

"It's a pattern-recognition exercise," Varsha said, remembering games from childhood. "I wish I could see a little of what they saw."

On her third day at North Point, Varsha made a discovery. She had left the bookshelf for last. She started to make two piles on the bed—books to give to Vincent, if he wanted them, and books she would take back with her. On the bottom shelf she found something she had given to her aunt the summer before last—a fat tome that was not a book: *Adventures in the Real and the Unreal.* With shaking hands she opened it. There was her handwriting on the first page— "with love from Varsha—may you have *musst* adventures!" The first few pages were real—but in the middle of the book was a hollow compartment. Inside was a small book with a red-brown cover—a diary. There were also some thin, parchment-like pieces of paper, carefully folded.

She opened the diary first. Her grandparents had given it to Rima when she had visited them, the summer before her disappearance. The last time I saw her, Varsha thought, and I didn't even know it. She remembered Nanu handing his daughter the book. "I know you are too busy to keep a diary," he had said, "but at least write something in it from time to time. When you think of us, write something for us. No engineering diagrams, but just what you are thinking and doing. Fill it up until your next trip home. Then bring it so we can all read it."

It was less than half full. Rima's small, neat handwriting, interspersed with little cartoons. The first entry:

> "*My greetings to the guava tree, the Bossy Pack, and the Human Horde of Chandragupta Park. No engineering diagrams, only deep thoughts in these pages. As promised! Right now I am on a plane back to Alaska, but I will write more when there is something worth sharing with you all . . .*"

She couldn't read any further. She set the journal down and fell to her knees and wept, with her face against the bed, hard, angry sobs. She grabbed the pillow and held it to her. Her chest hurt. I could die with grief, she thought, and close on that came the thought of her grandparents. They had survived the terrible news—how? She thought of her Nanu's face when they got the news, how it seemed to have shrunk. She thought of what he'd kept repeating, over and over, the first week or so—they didn't find the *body*, they *haven't* found the body— And then the discovery of the black box, the relaying of the last words, and the solidity, the incomprehensibility of grief. Her grandmother, who had seemed so fragile, suddenly appeared stronger, weeping her sorrow with a fierceness that kept them from going under. She had taken up knitting with a vengeance. The shawl she was knitting for Rima, that was half complete—she took it up again. Last Varsha heard, she was still at it—the shawl was the size of a blanket by now, and growing larger, as though it was possible for her grandmother to knit her way across the abyss that had opened in their lives. Even the pariah-dog pack that lived in the neighborhood, the Bossys, had howled for three nights. Her parents, uncles, aunts, cousins, the neighbors with whom the children had grown up, all shared the burden of grief. And someone or other would keep saying—look, Rima wouldn't want us to fall apart, we've got to go on for her—and again—how *could* it be? She was the most *alive* person I knew—

But there's nobody I can share this with, she thought angrily. She was far away from everyone.

At lunch she asked Vincent—

"Is there a gym? A track or someplace I can run?"

"There's a treadmill on the upper floor. I think it's still there. You can use it. The only gym's going to be in Utqiagvik."

"You okay?" Julie, sitting next to her, gave her a quick, worried look.

"I'm fine—well, as fine as I can be anyway. I just need—I have this habit, see, of running every day. They might bring the Boston Marathon back this year, so I've been training. I get a little crazy if I can't run."

Later Vincent said: "You only have a couple more days here. I'm going home tomorrow evening. Come have dinner with my wife and me then."

She felt much better after the exercise. Back in her aunt's room, she read some more pages of the diary. She carefully unfolded the sheets of paper—they were thin but tough, like cloth. They were blueprints of some kind, but hand-drawn. There was a delicate and precise sketch of a boat—but what a strange boat! It had flippers, and some kind of sail. A series of drawings showed the boat closing up from the top, like a convertible. There were other fine pages of notes, in a different handwriting, presumably Jimmy's, because she couldn't understand the words. Iñupiaq? There were sketches of whales of various types, and waveforms of sound waves. There was a list in her aunt's writing—people and research institutions around the world—a Kartik Sahay at Marine Research Labs Chennai, a Skip Johnson at a facility in California, others in places as far away as Finland, Siberia, South Africa. Her aunt had thought all this was important enough to hide from prying eyes. Varsha remembered Rick Walters' offer of help. *Fuck off*, she told him silently. On the other hand, what did she know about Vincent? He was not a scientist; he was the Coordinator for the Native Science Collaboration—they matched Native Elders with scientists. Whatever for? There was so much she didn't understand about this place, these people. She was almost sure Rima had mentioned Vincent during her last trip home. She had talked about Jimmy, showed them pictures, and Vincent had been mentioned, and Julie. That was as close to an endorsement she was going to get, unless the diary provided any clues.

She would probably have to trust someone eventually, but for now she would keep the existence of the diary and the papers a secret.

In the afternoon there was some excitement. Matt reported that bowheads had been seen in the waters off Utqiagvik. The whaling camps were still being set up; it was a little early for the whales to have left their wintering grounds in the Bering Sea. A couple of whales were heading east along the coast now. There was a general rush to the observation bubble on the seabed.

The sun's light percolated dimly through the ice above their heads. The water was dark, washed with blue where the ice was thin enough to let in some light. Matt turned on the external lights, but very dim, so that the golden radiance allowed them to see about ten meters further into the water. Fish swam by on the other side of the wall, their pale bellies agleam in the light.

"There!" Vincent said. "Agviq!"

And a dark, mountainous shape loomed just beyond their field of vision, and swam with cloud-like grace toward them. It came deliberately, straight to them, a huge, thirty-foot bulk with its flipper brushing the wall, its great eye looking in. In all her life Varsha would never forget that moment when she looked into the eye of the whale. Near her the others were talking quietly, exultantly.

"She's looking well—look at that healed propeller scar—"

There was another whale behind this one. The two whales took turns looking into the lighted room. There was a low, long, booming sound, like a distant cello. Varsha could feel the walls vibrate. The whales were calling. They must have circled the observation dome for a good fifteen minutes before moving away into the dark.

"Wow," said Varsha, finding her breath. "I've never—I've never seen anything like this. How do you know one whale from another?"

"Marks on the fluke—the tail," Vincent said.

"Are they all so curious?"

"Whales are individuals," said Matt. "Most of them keep away from here, but these two, and there are three others—they stop and say hello whenever they are passing by."

"We have hydrophones set up all along the coast," Julie said. "Here—I'll play the recording."

She pressed a button on the computer keyboard. A waveform scrolled across the screen, and the sound filled the air. It was the strangest call Varsha had ever heard. It filled the room, filled her being.

"It feels as though I ought to understand it, but I don't," she said, shaking her head.

She thought of her aunt standing here, watching the whales, hearing them sing.

One of my former engineering professors, who looked like the crazy prof in the movie 3 Idiots, had this huge construct in his lab made from odds and ends—a Rube-Goldberg machine on steroids. If you dropped a certain ball onto a ramp, the machine would light up and there would be wheels turning, pulleys spinning, weights flying into the air to hit specific targets and so on. The grand finale was that a dart would fly out and bury itself in a large picture of Isaac Newton on a Styrofoam board. The damn thing made a great racket. Isaac's face was so perforated with dart strikes that his visage had mostly disappeared. We loved the machine, and part of our spare time was always spent tinkering with it. The crazy prof called it "Newton's Engine."

I realized when I was quite young that there were two classes of problems, broadly speaking, simple ones and complex ones. Machines are good at solving simple problems. But throw in enough complexity and all bets are off. I went into biomimicry-based engineering because I wanted to challenge this realization. It's only when I got to the Arctic that I realized my first instinct had been right. You can't solve complex problems with machines, without breeding more problems of increasing intractability. Complexity is the spanner in the works of Newton's Engine. But it goes beyond that. You might think a sufficiently advanced AI would think its way through some of the failures (I happen to know they are not just rumors) that are plaguing Gaia-Corp's Project Terra. GaiaCorp has invested so much in its intelligent geoengineering systems, but I think it is inconceivable for autocrats to realize that their slaves might not march to their orders. AIs are a fundamentally different kind of intelligence than humans. We have more in common with the whales than with our household robots.

I think our main problem may be that we think of the Earth itself like a Newton's Engine, something we can tinker with and fix. Jimmy says that even biologists fall into this trap—of putting living creatures into rigid categories of structure and behavior, motivated by simplistic evolutionary imperatives. To him, to understand the whale would mean not just the kind of work he did for his PhD at San Diego, but also traveling with the whale through its great migrations around the North Pole, being part of its way of being, without any preconceived notions. "You see things differently when you are part of them," he says. "Explain," I say, and he laughs and says he can express these ideas better in Iñupiaq. It is so much more precise a language. Jimmy is not a talker—not in English anyway—I think because he dislikes sloppiness. He likes to say things right. You should hear him chattering with his nieces and nephews whenever there is a big family gathering. As I take the first baby steps learning Iñupiaq, I remember what you always used to say, Papa: that every language is a different way of seeing the world.

It turned out that Vincent's wife, Emma, worked in the town government. Vincent had a room at North Point that he used when the weather was bad, but his home was in Utqiagvik. The clouds had cleared a little. It was still -6° F but that was normal, that was balmy for an early spring.

So it was thus that Varsha found herself in Vincent's Land Rover, being driven along the coast road. The sea ice stretched as far as she could see, but it was breaking up in places farther out from shore. A long, narrow channel of seawater had appeared where there hadn't been one before. The sun lay low in the sky, and the light was murky. But the sky was clear, a dim, hazy, ethereal blue.

"Want to walk on the ice?" At her nod he pulled over and stopped. Her boots crunched on the low rise that separated the land ice from the sea ice.

"Walk where I walk," Vincent said. "The sea ice is all right close to the shore, but it is thinner than it should be."

She followed him out onto the plain. The wind was a cold knife in her face. She felt her toes turn numb. The ice sheet was vast, its immensity broken only by cairns of ice chunks that were carelessly piled up all over the plain. But the sky was clear and she could see the horizon, separating sea from sky.

"You are walking on frozen seawater," Vincent yelled over the wind. He pointed. "There's water under the ice. See, you can tell by the broken up piles of ice chunks. That's the wind and the currents breaking up the ice from below."

It was the worst cold she had ever experienced, and it was incredible. Vincent pointed.

"Over there. Do you see those tracks? That's polar bear."

She saw the broad, regular tracks a short run away from where they were standing. The tracks disappeared toward the sea.

"Probably hunting seal. Not that many seal now, because we haven't had much ice. They pup out on the ice to avoid bear, in little dens under the snow. This winter Kenny said there are a few."

She thought of little seal pups under the snow, and the polar bear sniffing the ground.

In the truck the warm blast of heat was welcome. They met no traffic until they got to the outskirts of Utqiagvik.

Home for Vincent was a small, warm, compact house on stilts, on a street with similar houses. Emma greeted them wreathed in cooking fragrances that were surprisingly familiar.

Emma was small and round, with a mobile, humorous face.

"Vince is a better cook than me," she said, "but when he comes home after a bit I do the cooking. I thought you might like to try whale stew with a bit of curry. There's fish too."

"Whale stew?"

"Goodness, don't tell me you're vegetarian? Vince, did you think to ask?"

"Oh, I eat everything," Varsha said quickly. "I've been cutting down on meat lately, but this smells great!"

"It's the last of the spice powder Rima made for us," Vince said, taking her coat. "She told us what is called curry here in America is garbage. So she sent for some spices from Anchorage and roasted and mixed them. Made us whale curry. It was amazing!"

"This meat is from last year," Emma said. "Come, sit down. Are you warm enough? Vincent's uncle is a whale captain. They were fortunate because it had been a poor harvest the year before. With the waters warming, the whales have changed their routes. We see a lot more killer whales coming up from the Pacific, hunting the bowheads. And now there's more shipping and the new searches for oil and gas."

"Noise disturbs them," said Vincent. "We were blessed this one came to us. We sent whale meat to the other villages that didn't have a good catch."

Among the family pictures on the mantel was one of Rima and Jimmy, along with four young people, sitting on top of a harvested whale.

The wine was good. The table was neatly laid with a flowered table cloth. Vincent brought the dishes to the table. The fragrance rose in the air.

"This is so nice of you," Varsha said, taking a ladle of whale curry. "The smells remind me of home!"

"This is the same whale as the one in the picture," Vincent said, indicating the framed photos on the mantel. "Your aunt's eaten of this whale."

The meat was like nothing she had ever tasted. It was melt-in-the-mouth soft and redolent with cumin and coriander, cinnamon and ginger and nutmeg. Tears came into her eyes.

"It's incredible!" she said. Vincent and Emma looked at each other, then they both smiled at her.

"It means a lot to us, the whale," Vincent said, chewing reverently. "It's part of Eskimo identity, a sacred beast that makes us who we are."

"I have only read a little about it," Varsha said apologetically.

"You have to stay awhile, witness a whale hunt to really understand," Emma said. "Here, have some more. The gravy is really good on the rice. At each harvest we thank the whale for its sacrifice. Its meat is never sold, only shared."

It seemed to Varsha that she had passed some kind of threshold that she couldn't quite comprehend. She had thought she had come to perform the saddest of duties, to collect her aunt's things and hope for some closure for herself and the family back home. *I'm an outsider,* she thought, but Rima had at least partially bridged the gap. *And because of her somehow I have a link here. Like a foot in a door to a place I can't see.*

At dessert—an apple tart—she asked Vincent if he had been on his uncle's whale hunt.

"Yes of course," he said. "Since I was a kid. When it's whaling time we cancel everything. Schools, work. Everyone gets together to help."

"Tell her properly," Emma said. She gave Varsha a humorous look. "He talks like a running tap when he's in the mood, but maybe he hasn't had enough wine. Come on, Vince, tell her about how you grew up. She's not going to hear about life in the great North from a better source."

"You're the running tap, not me! But yes, I grew up in Utqiagvik at the time of the start of the Great Melt. Sometimes it would get to 50 degrees Fahrenheit, in the winter. When it was supposed to be 10 or 20 below. My grandfather wanted me to learn to hunt seal and polar bear and whale according to our traditions, but the seals had gone, and the bowheads were moving away, driven by killer whale swimming up from the Northern Pacific. And the sea ice was so thin, it wasn't safe to walk on. I remember when the last of the multi-year ice disappeared. My uncle wept. He was a hunter, a great whale hunter who had learned the skill from my grandfather. "When the ice goes," he said, "so does the way of our people.""

"People down south don't understand that," said Emma. "They think that if the cold goes, and the ice, we would be glad. Not so for us. We are who we are because of the ice. I remember when the Great Melt started—I grew up in Anchorage but I used to come up here to see my great-aunt. We—my cousins and I—drove off polar bears in the streets when they came starving, looking for rubbish. My cousin still works in the local wildlife department."

"Things changed for everyone," said Vincent. "The polar bears—we heard that some were going south into land, mating with the grizzlies. I thought: if the way of our people is gone, maybe I have to go south with the polar bear. That was the summer that moose started coming up North, where they had never been seen before. Everything was changing, faster than the memories of our ancestors that go back thousands of years. Never had the ice gone so fast every spring, or developed so slowly every fall. Now in the summers the ice pack would melt so much that there would be clear passages right across the North pole. The circumpolar countries were vying with each other over shipping routes and oil and gas drilling, even after the bans and the declarations of protected zones. What it meant for us is that the whales left the shores. The bowheads who make us what we are as a people, who have given us their lives as a gift so we may live—they started to change their migration routes around the Arctic. The whale hunts were less and less successful. Some years there were hardly five or six whales harvested per season.

"So I was well into my teens until the time one year that the winter was strong enough that the ice came back. My grandfather was very old by then but just like all the other whale hunters he was very excited. Bowhead had been spotted off the shore ice, and the ice was thin, but thicker than previous years. So we made camp not far from the shore. I remember that first whale hunt of mine. The whale that gave itself to us was an old male, he had been seen many times by my father when he was a boy. Now here he was, giving himself to us, as though to say—*I give you my life so you may be Iñupiaq a little longer.*

"But when I was grown and my grandparents gone, so much had changed that I felt the old ways would not survive. So I left—I went south to college in Fairbanks, and got a degree in business, and had a bunch of jobs that took me from Alaska to Oregon and down even to Colorado. I tried to become this person who changed with the times."

He laughed. Emma gave him an affectionate look.

"Meanwhile my cousin Jimmy—he's my cousin's son—he was of the new generation that was inspired by the Native revival movements—he studied Iñupiaq, got a degree in comparative linguistics, and then he decided he needed to know what the white man knew about the world. He'd always gone whaling with us when he was a boy, just some ten, twelve years younger than me he was. He'd interned for a while at Wildlife—that's the town's wildlife management department, some of the world's best people on whales and marine life out there. It piqued his interest. He wanted to know what science could teach him about the whales. So he did marine biology at the University of California in San Diego. And then he came back here. Helped set up North Point Research. Then your aunt comes here, wanting to study wind generation in a place where you had gusts and gales without much sustained speed. They got to be friends. She started helping him in his research, and next thing, they're a couple."

There was a soft, remembering silence. From the pictures, Rima and Jimmy looked out at them, smiling. Their absence was like a presence in the room.

"What happened to all their things—their research, I mean—after—afterwards?"

"Rima's renewable-energy prototypes are all at the college. The tribal college—she worked with the kids. The program will continue. There's a machinist in town she worked with, we sent him the scrap bits and pieces. Jimmy's equipment and records are all going to go to the University in Fairbanks. Their work will live on."

The wine had softened her spirits. The whale stew had warmed her through. I never knew, she thought—I never knew the world was so full.

"What brought you back here?"

"Well, after two decades in the south I couldn't take it. Came back here and decided if the young were doing it, I had to return too. Figure out what it meant to be Eskimo, to be Iñupiaq without the ice. I couldn't be a grizzly bear anymore. So I started running the radio station."

Emma took up the story.

"There's a popular program we've had for a long time, when not enough young people knew their language, so our elders would come on the air and talk in Iñupiaq. Vince expanded that. We had the elders telling us stories, explaining what certain words meant—you know, people who belong to the land, to whom land is sacred, have words and concepts that are tied to the land, to the context. You lose the context, you lose half the lexicon. There were words that had lost their meaning, orphaned words and concepts—but the elders brought them alive, situating them in stories so people would know what had once been, even if it was no longer there. Then, when North Point Research was set up, Jimmy asked Vince to run the Native Science liaison over here. So that's what he's been doing for the last seven years or so."

Emma was in the town's scenarios planning team. "When things are changing so fast with the climate, we can't plan effectively for the future. So we prepare scenarios of all possibilities so that we can be better prepared. Did Vince show you the sinkhole on the way to North Point? No? Well, it's south of the coast road. Must be fifty feet deep. The permafrost that used to be always frozen is thawing here and there, so the land sinks. They've had that all over the Arctic Circle."

They were so kind to her. They had known Rima and had been fond of her, and the grief that was like a stone in her chest seemed lighter.

The living-room sofa folded out into a guest bed.

"Here are some extra blankets," Emma said. "Rima used to be cold all of her first year, then she acclimatized."

She sat at the edge of the bed. Vince had gone upstairs and Emma and Varsha finished their hot chocolate in the living room.

"She was a special person, your aunt. All kinds of people come to Utqiagvik, either to study us or the ice or both. And lately we have tourists, come here to see the Northern Lights and all. We've kind of become inured to it, you might say. And a bit sick of it, I have to admit. But Rima, she was different. Never gave up on anything or anyone, stubborn as a mule, a good match for Jimmy. Jimmy was our—we never had a child of our own. Always thought we'd have him with us, see us grow old."

She blinked away tears and got up. "Time to sleep or we'll be up all night," she said, smiling. In the dark a few moments later, Varsha thought—the link between us is the link of a shared grief. And sleep came.

When I was in California I once watched a movie of emperor penguins swimming underwater. It was astonishing—they were flying through the water, flapping their wings with an effortless grace. The same wings that look so pathetic and useless on land are amazing instruments underwater. At the time I was with the biomimicry group. We talked about submersible boats and how inadequate their designs were. I didn't think further about it then, but after hearing Jimmy talk about whales, I've been sketching. I sit in the observation bubble—it's the best place for me to think—and I imagine a vessel that can fly through water like a penguin. A squid-inspired propulsion device that takes in and expels water—I'll have to look into energy usage—and then I think—what about ocean currents? If I put an acoustic Doppler device on this boat, it could find ocean currents and use them—and it occurs to me—a sail! A squid-propulsion amphibious boat with penguin wings and a sail to catch the underwater currents! I was so pleased I showed Jimmy, and he got really excited. I've put some rough sketches here.

Oh Papa, I know you said no engineering diagrams, but this is the most exciting thing I've done. Forgive me! It's such a warm winter we're having here, not even one good storm to give us some excitement. Warm is a relative word—you would shiver here, Ma, even when the sun is at its highest. The sun never gets very high in the sky here. I know you are thinking of the shawl you said you were knitting for me, Ma, and I think of it too, when I am feeling cold.

But it is so important that it stay cold here. You know, Papa, how you always emphasized in us that we see connections between things. Never just be content with what's at the surface. Well, here's a connection for you. If the Arctic melts, we are all cooked. The Arctic keeps the whole Earth cool. Next time there is a severe summer back home—and I can't even imagine one hotter than when I was in Patna this July, when I thought I would faint if I stepped out—next time please remember that it's in part because of what's happening here in the Arctic. We've warmed the Earth so much that the Arctic is melting, and that will only warm the Earth further.

So now I've given you an engineering diagram and a science lesson. I've got to make up for it.

I want to write this especially for Varsha and the other kids, although they aren't kids anymore. It is hard to be in the world—if you live in it fully, it is easy to sink into despair. What, after all, can one or two people do, when the world is dying? Why not submit to the alluring logic of GaiaCorp's promise to save the Earth, to their megamachines seeding the oceans, their satellites seeding the skies, their winged shades reflecting the sun's light away from whichever politically expedient, remote, hard-scrabble country is out of favor? Why not bide the time as gently as possible by surrendering our full, human, curious, questing selves, lulling ourselves into dreams? The deal is that to be fully alive you have to be willing to bear pain. That is what I swore to, when I was in my twenties—that I would be fully alive. But nobody can do it alone. I am so fortunate to have been born as part of the Guava Tree family in Chandragupta Park, and to live on the best possible planet, and to have the friends I have, and to have met Jimmy, whom you will all love, I promise.

I think about all this sometimes because my job is occasionally dangerous, and I know Ma and Papa tend to worry, but you must remember, should anything happen to me, that it is love that moves and motivates me, and love leaps all chasms, and you can't get rid of me so easily. So if ever the unthinkable shall happen, repeat after yourself: that Rima is in her own way always and forever with you. Say it now, just for practice.

The morning she was going to leave, Varsha paced back and forth in her little room. There wasn't much room to pace, but she needed to think. At last she came to a decision.

She found the Station office, where a young Iñupiaq woman called Irene was organizing a filing cabinet.

"Sorry, Irene. I need to talk to the machinist who worked with my aunt. Can you get me his name and number?"

"Sure. He sometimes sent her stuff down to Anchorage, in case you are looking for anything in particular."

After a brief conversation Varsha went back to her room and finished packing. The four boxes that were going back to Boston would be dropped off at the post office. Emma had given her an old suitcase—she was carrying a few of her aunt's things on the flight back.

She went to Vince's office and knocked. To her surprise, Rick Walters was there. He smiled at her.

"Sorry you're leaving so soon. I feel we barely met. Vince, I can take Varsha to the airport. Give us a chance to have a final chat."

She smiled at him.

"It's all right," she said, before Vince could say anything. "Vince and I have some important things to talk about. Family stuff."

"Of course," he said. He shook her hand. "I have friends in Boston. Maybe I can look you up next time I'm there."

He gave her hand a squeeze and went out of the room. When his footsteps had died away, Vince shut the door. His face had a closed, remote look.

"Vince," she said. "Before we go, I have to ask you something."

"Sit," he said. He still looked wary. She had to trust him. Rima had. She took the plunge.

"I need to know what happened to my aunt's prototype of the submersible boat," she said. "The one that could sail on the ocean and fly under water. Julie mentioned she'd seen something being assembled in Rima's lab. I called the machinist in Utqiagvik and asked him what parts he received. I'm no engineer but nothing he described sounded like parts of the amphibious boat she was building."

There was a long silence.

"How do you know about the boat? Julie told you?"

"Only casually. But—I have been meaning to tell you—I found my aunt's diary and some papers. She left them for me in a place she knew I would know to look. She didn't say she had completed the prototype. But I got the impression she had. I need to know—did she and Jimmy take the prototype with them on their last trip?"

"They went on the research boat—you know that—the pieces were found on the seabed— there was no sign of a submersible boat."

"But the research boat was a large enough vessel to hold the prototype, wasn't it? They took it with them, they must have! A book inside a book, a boat inside a boat—Vince, I need to know—my family needs to know—if there's any chance—"

She couldn't speak. She swallowed hard.

"What do you want me to say?" Vince put his head in his hands. He looked at her after a moment. "I don't know. I don't know. I want to believe they're both alive. Jimmy—he would tell me since he was a little kid, going to school, or a whaling trip, or California—he would tell me he'd always come back. Do you think I don't want to believe it? But I can't give you false hope. What would you do—tell Rima's parents she might still be alive? What if she isn't? True, they didn't find the remains of the ambiphian. But the winds and the currents here are strong and unpredictable. It could take years before the rest of the debris showed up."

"They would have radioed you," Varsha said. "If they were alive."

"Maybe it wouldn't be so easy," Vince said. "And if they are really out there, there are reasons why they would not have wanted us to know."

"Not wanted us to know? My grandfather is old. I don't know how he has survived this. My grandmother does nothing but knit all day. My parents are fighting more than ever. This is destroying us. My aunt wouldn't keep it from us if she were alive!"

She had raised her voice. Vince motioned her to speak softly.

"Listen, Varsha, there's a lot more at stake than you think," he said. "I'm going to trust you as you have trusted me. If they wanted to hide the prototype, don't you think they could have just dismantled it and hidden the parts? This is much bigger than you think."

"Please explain," Varsha said. "I deserve this much."

"It's time to go," said Vince. "We have plenty of time to talk in the car. Please—carry Rima's diary and the papers on your person."

"Yes, of course," she said. "In my backpack. I'll show you in the car."

After the good-byes were done, they sat in Vince's Land Rover while the engine heated, looking at Rima's diary and the papers. Vince grabbed a battered camera from the back seat and took some pictures. "For Emma," he said. "And for safety. I think these names here are the people who may know something about what Jimmy and Rima intended. I'll make some inquiries, discreetly."

"Vince," Rima said, "she must have drawn the boat designs on her laptop. Through some kind of engineering software, like Design-Works. You told me earlier her laptop had been lost with her, but she might have saved the design on a klipdrive or something. When you get back—look inside your computer—unscrew the base, and see if there's anything small like that, tucked away."

Vince looked startled, then nodded. He looked at his watch, sighed, and started the Land Rover.

The sun sent long rays over the tundra and the frozen sea. The windows of the station glowed in the yellow light. There was a wind blowing, moaning softly, whipping up skeins of last night's snow from the ground.

"Jimmy was interested in whale communication," Vince said as the Land Rover lurched over the ice road. "But he was also curious about the possibility of interspecies communication. I don't just mean human-to-whale, but whales with other species. Nobody really thinks much of that among the scientists. It's not in the white man's way of thinking, to think that there are other species than him, who might want to talk to each other. In our stories polar bears and whales and all the other creatures talk to each other as well as to people. To the white man that's just kid's stuff, or just mythology.

But Jimmy, he wanted to know if it was possible. He'd noticed some odd things."

They bumped along the coast road. The sun was higher in the sky today. It would edge up over the horizon a little every day, until it vanquished the night for nearly six months of the year.

"What odd things?"

"Unusual behavior among some whales. Bowheads hanging out with humpbacks. Blue whales down in the Atlantic lowering their call notes—they call much more bass than bowheads—so they reached right across an ocean basin. Jimmy thought it was logical that the whales had noticed the conditions of climate change—the warming ocean, the changing currents and chemistry. How could they not? Maybe they had always talked to each other. Modern humans are the only species that keeps apart from the others. Not so the other animals. The white man doesn't see what's not in his scheme of things.

"Don't get me wrong. I like civilization—I'm not blaming it for everything. Among my people there is a lot of division on such issues—how do we find balance between the benefits of the modern way of life and the wisdom of the traditional teachings? But back to Jimmy.

"So Jimmy had this idea that if humans are to understand whales, you've got to do it as much as possible in the whale's environment. Drones, underwater robots, tracking, all that's great, but if you can't follow the whales on their Arctic migrations, if you can't dive deep with them, or swim under the ice, you won't know the context in which they sing their songs. More than anything you won't have a relationship with them of mutuality. All true knowing is mutual, Jimmy used to say."

"I hear that bowheads live very long," Varsha said. "In her diary my aunt wonders what they think about, talk about, for two hundred years."

"Yes, that was the sort of thing that fascinated Jimmy. He wanted to understand how whales talked to each other and to other species, if there was maybe a common language among the sea mammals."

"But why the need for secrecy? Doesn't GaiaCorp already have amphibious boats?"

"Not like this one—energy efficient, small and compact, but with enough room for an extended stay. And Jimmy is—was—a hunter, he could keep them alive—"

He looked out over the great vista rolling past them, and was silent.

"I don't understand why—if they really meant to go out deliberately into the ocean and fake their deaths—why?"

"Jimmy suspected that the bowhead whales were learning from the humpbacks how to disable the TRexes. Humpbacks use sound to stun fish. Sound means everything to whales. When the TRexes use their airgun arrays, it's like having an explosion happen ten times a second. Sometimes for weeks or months. If whales are close enough they would get deafened. A whale uses sound for communication and to find its way in the dark under the ice. A deaf whale is better dead.

"Meanwhile Rima learned from scientists in other places around the world that GaiaCorp's geoengineering is failing. Not just that, but the crop failures in your part of the world, and the toxic algal blooms in the South Atlantic, are a direct result of it. Worse, the geoengineers knew they would fail. It's all about money and power, in the end."

"So they can't afford to let the TRexes be destroyed?"

"We can't afford to let it get out that it's not just other humans but potentially other species who are fighting back. The white man almost wiped out the bowheads in the time of the Yankee whalers. Do you think they would hesitate to do so again?"

"This is crazy. This is just crazy."

"This is the world."

"You've just destroyed everything I took for granted about the world."

"Rima used to say: never take anything for granted."

She looked out over the frozen sea. Somewhere beyond the horizon was open water. It was hard to imagine that somewhere on the open sea, or perhaps inside it, two people in an amphibious boat were sailing with the bowhead whales.

The town came up suddenly around them. Over the sea ice, tiny figures could be seen on snowmobiles, hauling sleds behind them.

"They're cutting the trails," Vincent said. "If you were staying longer you could have gone on a whale hunt."

"I don't know how much—how much more I can take of the world," Varsha said. She cupped her hands over her eyes for a moment. Then, as Vince pulled up at the airport parking, she looked at him.

"What do I tell my parents? My grandparents?"

"That's your call. Just—don't let it get around, what I've told you. You can tell them, if you like, that maybe there's a chance they are alive. But keep the other things to yourself. This is for their sake as well as yours. There are larger forces here at play than you and I."

"I feel like I'm in an Augs adventure story. Except there's nothing like this in the files."

"I enjoy VR games from time to time. But you got to live in the world."

"Thanks for everything, Vince. I am glad we talked, and I'm very glad I got to meet Emma. If— if you hear anything—"

"Of course."

He helped her into the check-in line with her two suitcases. The small airport was filled with people—men in the uniforms of Arctic Energy, a knot of coast guard officials, and Eskimo families hauling supplies in sacks and boxes, laughing and chattering. It no longer felt quite so strange.

"We'll meet again, I have a feeling," Vince said, "so I'll say 'see you later,' not good-bye."

He shook her hand, smiled at her, a sudden, warm smile. Then he was gone. She blinked back tears and set her chin.

In the plane she thought of the diary and the diagrams in her backpack, and the secrets they carried. She thought of Chester waiting hopefully at the airport, and what she would have to say to him, and the life she had mapped out for herself. She thought of the house in Patna, and the aging faces of her grandparents.

The tundra dipped and glittered in the sun as the plane turned upward into the sky. The houses vanished. At this height, she saw the open water at the edge of the shore ice, and the expanse of the Arctic, broken here and there by white patches of floating ice. She thought of the great whales traveling in circles through the cold, dark waters, feeding and calling, dreaming and singing. Perhaps at this very moment her aunt and uncle were flying through the water in their little craft, hoping she would have deciphered what they couldn't openly say, that would bring this shattering clarity to her life, and the faint thread of hope to their families, to the world.

Publication History

"With Fate Conspire," *Solaris Rising 2: The New Solaris Book of Science Fiction*, 2013

"A Handful of Rice," *Steampunk Revolution*, 2012

"Peripateia," *End of the Road*, 2013

"Lifepod," *Foundation*, 2007

"Oblivion: A Journey," *Clockwork Phoenix: Tales of Beauty and Strangeness*, 2008

"Somadeva: A Sky River Sutra," *Strange Horizons*, 2010

"Are you Sannata3159?," *Postscripts: The Company He Keeps*, 2010

"Indra's Web," *TRSF: The Best New Science Fiction*, 2011

"Ruminations in an Alien Tongue," *Clarkesworld*, 2012

"Sailing the Antarsa," *The Other Half of the Sky*, 2013

"Cry of the Kharchal," *Clarkesworld*, 2013

"Wake-Rider," *Lightspeed*, 2014

"Ambiguity Machines: An Examination," Tor.com, 2015

"Requiem" is published here for the first time.

Acknowledgments

It is my great pleasure to acknowledge the generosity of Henry Huntington, whose help and advice made it possible for me to visit Alaska in 2014 for an academic education project on climate change. Henry's comments on my story "Requiem" were invaluable. My heartfelt gratitude also to Santanu Chakraborty for help with the setting of my story "With Fate Conspire." Any errors of interpretation or representation are, of course, entirely my responsibility.

My boundless gratitude, as always, for my vast clan of family and friends scattered across spacetime and species, including but not limited to parents, daughter, siblings and sib-in-laws, aunts, uncles, cousins, nieces and nephews, friends who've become family, and family dogs, without whom I would not be who I am, let alone alive and writing today. I am especially thankful to Ashok, Ramaa, and Ruchika. A so-far habitable planet of unsurpassed gorgeousness has also been crucial to the writing of this book.

About the Author

Vandana Singh was born and raised in India and currently lives near Boston, MA, where she professes physics and writes. Her short stories have appeared in many Best of Year anthologies including the *Best American Science Fiction & Fantasy* and she has received the Carl Brandon Parallax award. Her books include the ALA Notable book *Younguncle Comes to Town* and a collection, *The Woman Who Thought She Was a Planet*. Learn more at vandana-writes.com.